Mr Joseph M Connor
205 Middle Quarters Ln
Centreville, MD 21617-2636

3—

THE
BEST
THERE
EVER
WAS

Also by John Ed Bradley

Tupelo Nights

JOHN ED BRADLEY

THE BEST THERE EVER WAS

THE ATLANTIC MONTHLY PRESS
NEW YORK

♦

Published simultaneously in Canada
Printed in the United States of America
FIRST EDITION

Library of Congress Cataloging-in-Publication Data

Bradley, John Ed.
The best there ever was / John Ed Bradley. — 1st ed.
ISBN 0-87113-384-9
I. Title.
PS3552.R2275B4   1990   813'.54—dc20   90-626

Design by Laura Hough

The Atlantic Monthly Press
19 Union Square West
New York, NY 10003

FIRST PRINTING

FOR
BONN

| **Hardheadharold** |

| 1 |

"When it comes time to run through those goalposts," Harold Gravely said almost thirty years ago, "I want your butthole so wide damn open you'll need a pair of tenpenny nails stuck up it to keep your foul business from spilling out."

There in the home dressing room of Tulane Stadium, moments before his Sugar Bowl meeting with Clemson to decide the national championship, he'd never felt more heroic and alive. Outside, in a bitter winter sun, the band played and the crowd made its marvelous noise. Harold was standing on a spike-scuffed bench looking down on his boys, his lips moist with a smear of yellow rose balm, his eyes busy with light. He laughed because otherwise he would have cried.

When at last he led his team into the tunnel to the field, he was shouting, "In with them, hardheads. In with them."

Everyone knew he was talking about the nails.

The Tenpenny Eleven, as this team came to be known, won by three touchdowns and might have taken it by more had Harold not shown some pity and replaced the starters with the scrubs late in the third quarter. In the weeks after the game he appeared on the covers of several national sporting magazines, riding the shoulders of Pogo Reese and Little Shorty Grieg, heading for the midfield crest to shake the hand of the sorry bastard he'd just trounced. At the movies all the newsreels played the same scene, only they caught him in grainy black and white, and you couldn't really make out Pogo and Little Shorty in amongst the state troopers in their wide, starched-brim hats, elbowing, clubbing and spitting at the riotous fans storming the field.

Harold, then in his fourth year as head coach, was only thirty-three years old. But because he looked no older than most of the boys on his squad, some of the newspaper reporters thought calling him the Old Man was clever, and the name stuck.

"Will it be Old Man on my statue or just Harold?" is only one

3

of the questions that lately has caused him to lose sleep. This morning, when the beeping of the digital alarm clock on the bedside table commences before dawn, it's the first thing he asks his wife, who mumbles something he doesn't understand and pulls the covers over her head.

He demands a reply, but still Rena mutters, "Go to sleep"; then, "Idiot."

This stormy August morning is the first day of Harold's last season, and he has been up all night. At this moment, in this bed, sleep is as remote a possibility as sex, or so he tells himself. What Harold would really like, along with an answer to his question, is a drink powerful enough to blind.

"Old Man is better than Harold," he is saying now, nudging Rena with the heel of his right hand. "To my ears Harold sounds like a name for tractor mechanics and hayseeds. When I was a boy, if somebody said it to me wrong I'd take his damn head off. I'd peel the plum-colored skin off his lips."

His voice is willful, potent. One of his vocal chords was paralyzed some ten or twelve years ago, and now when he speaks there's always a spit and quiver. To compensate, he nearly shouts everything. It's like turning up the volume on a radio to try to overcome the electric sputtering of a crack in the speakers.

"But I *like* Old Man!"

"Dead people," Rena mumbles, "don't go by nicknames."

"So cancer wipes me out, and it wipes out my best moment too? I don't understand that, pie. I won't accept it."

"No nicknames," she says, now stirring.

"I want to be standing, pointing straight ahead as if at the past before me." A tear fills his eye, as often happens when he talks about the figure he hopes to cut as a statue. "I want to be twenty pounds lighter, hard and strong and manly. I don't want this moon face I got. I don't want these age spots on my hands and arms, neither."

Scrambling free of the sheets, Harold bolts from bed to stand as he hopes his graven image will, monstrous and erect, and he points as it will point, at nothing in particular. Rena gets up, blindly shoves her feet into cracked leather slippers and moves slowly toward the kitchen to start the coffee. She is fifteen years younger than Harold, but this morning moves as if she were fifteen years older.

"Nor do you want the ruddy complexion of a drunk," she says with a yawn. "Nor the nose of a circus clown."

"No," he replies, still standing and pointing in his pajamas, "I don't want any of it."

If all goes as planned, the statue the university wants to build for Harold Gravely will stand at the north end of its eighty-thousand-seat football stadium. The Tenpenny remark might've helped make him a star, but it won't make it to the monument.

"It's catchy and all, but it sends the wrong message to young people," the chairman of the university's board of supervisors had told Harold repeatedly over the summer months. "It kind of makes little, innocent children think of all those wonderful athletes using the bathroom and of you instructing them to put things up the wrong place." As legacies went, Champs LaRoux said, it just wasn't appropriate.

Last week the board had requested that Harold come up with another, but he complained that he had always been a man of action and passion, "not no poet." LaRoux gave him no more than seven days and thirty words in which to make sense of his life, then slapped his gavel on a wooden block and dismissed his coach with a stare that could crush rocks.

For nearly a week now, the thought of making up a quotation that will endure for all time has been a torment that keeps him up nights, and come mornings he is nervous, petulant and mean. By noon he generally takes his first glass of bourbon to shake the feeling that he will perish before coming up with a line of consequence and that someone else, perhaps someone who hasn't the faintest notion of what it means to be the best coach there ever was, will desecrate his monument with a quote not worth spit. By late evening he is drunk at home, spouting his peculiar wisdom to a wife who frantically writes down everything he says in a spiral-bound notebook, hoping to capture once and for all what he's after and thus to quiet him forever. Rena clips those lines he rejects and places them under magnets dressed as assorted fruits and vegetables arrayed on the refrigerator door. These remain her favorites: *Run and get me the Pepto, pie. I think I'm gonna puke on my feet. . . . The year after Clemson, I used to screw so many girls my nose would bleed and little wax shavers would clog my ears. . . . If you don't like me and don't care I'm dying, then why don't you go live with the goddamn monkeys?*

His selections, each of which has been rejected by the board, run to: *Show me a youth with pride, and I'll show you somebody with a mind for achievement. . . . The only thing near more important as winning is not losing, but I, for one, would rather win than not lose. . . . Being the most distinguished of men don't make your flesh iron and your heart stone. Should they want a coach in paradise, I hope I'm it. Should they not . . . well, send me back to what I used to know.*

Harold plans to retire his post at the university as he started it: the most talked-about man around, famous to the point of legend. The only serious problem as far as he's concerned—even more serious than the fact that he's terminally ill and probably won't live to see Christmas—is that if he doesn't come up with a winning quote by nine o'clock tomorrow morning, the board will discuss the matter in executive session, invent a line of its own and pitch the idea to the public as if it were his.

"It's not everybody who winds up a statue," he tells Rena as he sits down in the living room for coffee. Still in pajamas, he clutches a bottle of whiskey hard to his chest.

"You, for instance—Rena Gravely won't never wind up a statue. I promise you that."

Having heard this before, she laughs it off. "I hope to God yours isn't like all those ones in Italy where everybody's naked to the world," she says. "You wouldn't want to embarrass me by displaying your smirking manhood—would you, Harold?"

"To build one of you," he says, uncapping the fifth and pouring some of the alcohol into his steaming cup, "you'd need a New York City construction crew, not no artist. They'd need an eighteen-wheel flatbed to haul it and then one of them skyscraper cranes to get it in place."

"There's more to living than ending up bronze," she says, reaching to take the bottle away. He slaps her hand and caresses the bourbon even tighter. "You want to disgrace yourself in front of your last team and everybody else? Come on, Harold, hand it here. This is your big day."

"So you'd deny a dying man his pleasure, would you?" Though

he's shouting, there is no conviction or anger in his voice; just that funny quiver.

"They'll take the statue away, Harold."

"They wouldn't think to dare."

"If I told the newspaper you were sitting here drinking at five o'clock in the morning they most certainly would."

Grasping the neck of the bottle, he swings wildly at the space directly in front of Rena, missing her by inches. Accustomed to his rage, she doesn't even flinch and instead takes a deep, satisfying swallow from her cup of coffee and rubs the reddened corners of her eyes. Some mornings it's a golf club Harold chooses to swing at her, others it's a glass-shelled pharmacy lamp, an aluminum baseball bat, a wooden hall tree covered with baseball caps, dusty woolen shawls and neckties. Thus far she has been injured only by a hand-painted, hard-boiled egg rocketed from an Easter basket she'd given him last spring, and then the damage was minor. For a few weeks, questioned in dizzy, often alarmed tones by her friends, she dismissed the oval bruise at the base of her neck as a love hickey.

"How do you think your skull would hold up against that Dakota rifle of mine?" he's asking. He cackles and licks a dribble of bourbon off his forefinger. "Go ahead, tell."

"I think I will," she says, starting for the telephone. "I'll call all seventeen of the board members this very minute, then I'll call the chancellor." Her voice is light and teasing, but something in it infuriates Harold, who once again swings the bottle in a blind, roundhouse fashion, just missing.

"Do it," he says. "Go ahead. I've been looking for a reason to shoot my gun."

"You're nobody special. You don't deserve a statue."

"I'm Harold Gravely, boss hardhead, the Old Man." It seems he can't identify himself quickly enough. "I coached the Tenpenny Eleven. I won the national championship."

"You used to be the Old Man," she says, "but now you're about as special as chicken brains. And the Tenpenny Eleven—well, they're just a bunch of gray-head grandpas with beer guts who couldn't jog to the stop sign at the end of the street."

Cheeks puffed with air, eyes bulging, she staggers around the room, imitating a fat man's attempt at a run. When she finally stops in front of Harold's overstuffed chair, she is breathless and has to bend over with both hands on her knees. "I'm asking you politely to give it here. The bottle, Harold. I'd feel personally responsible if I let you go out into the world and ruin your big day."

Muttering obscenities under his breath, he drops the whiskey to the floor and runs down the hall to the bathroom. There he stands again as his statue will stand, framed by lavatory lights that make his skin look as red and pliable as diseased tomatoes. His hair is everywhere, a dark storm. Imminent drops of blood hang at the upper corners of his nostrils. He has slept only nine hours in the last seventy-two. Liquor burns like acid in his veins, his lungs can't seem to get their fill, and yet he stands pointing at some unseen place in the wide silver glass as one who has been there before and is determined to go back.

| **2** |

As Harold backs his car down the drive and starts up the street, Rena watches to make sure he reaches the stop sign and turns the corner. Several times in the past he parked in front of the Marshall house about a hundred yards away, then ambled back to spy on her through the windows. Although she knew he was hiding in the shrubbery, she in no way let on. Did he suspect her of wrongdoing, she wondered then, perhaps of entertaining a man? Eventually she came to believe he simply wanted to observe what she did in the house when he wasn't around. Rena's daily routine—her "system," he calls it—has long aggravated Harold. "Are your shoes clean?" he's often mocked her among friends at dinner parties. "If not, leave them at the door. I don't want you tracking up my kitchen." What he saw on those surreptitious visits couldn't have surprised him, for what he saw from one day to the next never varied. She made certain of it.

For about half an hour after he left, or pretended to, she would sit in the quiet house drinking coffee, eating dry toast and leafing through one of her self-improvement magazines; next she'd start a load of clothes washing and rinse out the Mr. Coffee; then she'd make the bed, take a bath and, wearing only towels, sit on the floor and call some of her friends on the telephone. She always resisted the temptation to tap on the glass and invite him in. "Checking for beetles?" she might've asked. "Lose something in the azaleas there, Harold?" She once considered dancing around naked, but decided against that as well; she figured the sight of her hips gyrating lasciviously and her boobs bouncing every which way would drop him dead on the spot. The first time, when at last he left and returned to his car, she walked to the end of the drive and stood waving at the long, empty street.

"System okay?" he asked that night when he got home from work.

"Fine."

"Nothing to report?"

"Nope," she answered. "Not a thing."

In her twenty-nine years of marriage she has had only one regular day job, and it lasted no more than seven months. Harold was the one who got it for her, a clerk's job at Champs LaRoux's clothing store when she was—what, nineteen years old? "Champs's experiment," Harold called her then, and every morning she dressed as if for a night on the town. To measure the feet of rich, idle women, to fret over bras and hosiery, to stock shelves with odd-shaped hatboxes, she wore silk stockings and high-heel shoes, costume jewelry and makeup and expensive French perfume. Her job was to help start a women's department in a store that had, for nearly seventy years, catered exclusively to men. "From haberdasher to shaberdasher," Harold said of LaRoux, "all in the blink of an eye." Rena was one of three girls hired to lure in the wealthy grandes dames of the city. She worked on commission, as did everyone but the LaRouxs, and this was intended to keep her from dawdling. Salaried employees tended to nap or give orders, Champs explained when Harold complained about his wife's slave wages; he pointed to himself as an example.

The new department took out advertisements in the city paper, and in the beginning business was almost triple the men's. Even Harold made several appearances, enlisting the help of his favorite clerk in finding a few things for his wife. Everyone knew the department was doing so well because lady shoppers were thrilled to have something new and different to fill their days; but proud Harold felt that Rena was the main reason, if not the only one.

In those days she was still an attraction of the highest order, for she was not only Harold Gravely's most recent acquisition—"the Old Man's child bride," as the gossip columnists liked to refer to her—but the former girlfriend of Pogo Reese who, little more than twenty-four hours after his heroics in the Tenpenny game, was arrested for murdering a man in the parking lot of a notorious after-hours lounge. And she was pretty.

When the doors to the women's department first opened, it was true that as many people came to see Rena as to check out the merchandise. Dozens crowded the narrow aisles, feigning interest in the clothes hanging on the circular racks. Others stood out on the sidewalk, gawking through the plate glass, faces creased with wild curiosity. A few sought her autograph, and some felt absolutely daffy when Rena acknowledged them with a smile.

"The femme fatale to beat all," Paige LaRoux said one night in her mock British accent. She and Champs were having dinner with Harold and Rena at the City Club, celebrating the store's success. "The poor, precious little heathen," she added. "How I envy her terrible fame."

Champs then turned to Harold. "The last time I saw anyone create such a stir was when Jayne Mansfield came through town and paraded her titties at that car show. Maybe we should charge 'em a fee just to get in the front door."

Rena remained unaffected. She was, after all, the daughter of a welder and a housewife, the middle of five girls and two boys, all of whom, she often told Harold, were either prettier or smarter than she was. Because she and Harold were on a budget, she carried a brown-bag lunch to work each morning and put it in the refrigerator in Champs's office. She was supposed to have an hour off at noon but, what with business, rarely got a break until around two o'clock, when all of downtown seemed to snooze. Then she'd call Harold, and if things weren't busy at the stadium he'd drive over and join her. Sometimes after sandwiches he'd take her into the dark storage room, shove her against the tall cardboard boxes and let her kiss him, or she'd let him kiss her, depending on how they happened to be feeling.

She quit because of Champs. One day, alone in his office, she was enjoying an oyster po-boy, some celery and carrot sticks and a small bottle of Coke when he entered without saying a word and flipped on the radio to Paul Harvey's commentary. For ten minutes, sitting in the swivel chair behind his desk, Champs said nothing, though he did giggle at one of Paul's stories about a bumper sticker some businessman spotted at the Chicago airport. Otherwise Champs just stared at the radio as if he were engaged in a deep and silent conversation, and when Paul signed off Champs removed his heavy black shoes and started rubbing his stockinged feet. Rena was sitting across the room on the sofa, her lunch set on a coffee table pulled close to her knees.

"That Paul Harvey's a genius, isn't he," Champs said. Rena said he sure was, though she considered him more clever than anything. "I'd like to get him in the store some day," he said. "Whaddaya think he'd wear in a suit—'bout a forty long?" Champs walked over and sat next to Rena on the couch.

"Guess so," she replied. "He looks pretty tall." It wasn't as if Harold had never warned her about LaRoux's reputation as a shameless wolf and seducer of young girls, but she never thought he'd try something with her when her own husband was one of his closest friends. As soon as Champs pressed his mouth against her ear she popped up off the couch, kicking the coffee table with a knee and spilling her lunch to the floor. A paper napkin clung to her twill skirt by some miracle of electricity, and it seemed the most important thing in the world for her to get it off. Champs stood up as she swiped at the napkin and kissed her ear again. She fell back down on the couch, wondering if maybe she should scream. He came at her again, rubbing his rough, dumb hands all over her blouse, and finally she got rid of him by punching him smack in the crotch. When she left the office she took what remained of her po-boy and vegetable sticks, and though they were speckled with dirt and hair from the floor she ate them anyway, mostly out of a desire to show herself how strong she was. When Paige asked her why she wasn't lunching in the office, she said only, "Just needed some air is all."

The rest of the day she worked as if nothing had happened, outselling all the other girls on the floor, but when she went home that night she knew she couldn't go back. After a hot bath she curled up in her favorite chair in the green room—with its green carpet, green furniture and two baker's racks crowded with assorted greenery in clay pots—and read a self-improvement magazine, stopping to fold the corners of those pages with coupons she'd like to clip. Harold got home around ten, wearing a different suit of clothes than the one he'd left the house in that morning. They looked new. When he asked about her day, she said she thought she'd had enough of the shaberdashery and would go ahead and quit now. In a year or two or three, she said, she might be ready to start their family and she wanted some time to consider it.

"Fine by me," he said, then went to the kitchen sink and poured himself a couple of fingers of Chivas over ice. "I don't think women should be in that joint with that horny bastard anyway."

She broke down, telling him tearfully what Champs had done, but he seemed to find it funny. "That danged LaRoux," he said, shaking his head. "What kind of brass did they pour for his balls?" She asked if he planned to confront Champs about what happened, but Harold said, "Boys'll be boys." Lately he'd heard some pretty strong rumors that Champs LaRoux had a shot at being named to the university board of supervisors. Having a friend in such a powerful position surely might come in handy somewhere down the road, so why ruin it now?

| 3 |

Rena dials Harold's office number from the phone in the bedroom. He'll know who's calling long before he picks up the receiver, she decides, for who but a madwoman—a wife, for example—would let it ring so many times at six-thirty in the morning?

She pictures him at the entrance to the stadium, at the Players' Gate, one hand fumbling around in his pockets for the right key, the other holding an umbrella against the warm rain. Through clenched teeth he curses the ringing phone.

"Rena," he says. "Damn you, girl."

She sees him now at the desk of his secretary, Nancy Claude, pausing to study the framed photographs of her husband arranged around her telephone and Rolodex. In one picture the man—Rena can't believe she can't remember his name—is kissing the side of Mrs. Claude's face as his arms reach around her.

Harold studies the man's profile, the fine nose, the hard chin, the ears half-covered by straight, dark hair. His skin, right below the hairline, is a shade lighter than his neck, indicating a recent haircut.

Then he eyes his name, printed in raised gold letters, on his office door. HAROLD GRAVELY, it reads, and he says it aloud as if for the first time. "Harold . . . Gravely!"

She is lying in bed, the phone to her ear. Her eyes open wide when he picks up; she blinks waiting for his voice. "Harold?"

"Don't tell me," he says, "Joan and Charlie and some Hungarian chef are making omelets on *Good Morning America*."

"I forgot to tell you something," she says, sitting up against the headboard. She folds her legs beneath her.

"What about this for a sentence?" he says. "When it comes time to run through those goalposts, I want your mouths so wide damn open you'll need a net to keep the mosquitoes from flying in." She can hear the rustle of papers; he's writing it down.

"You left and I forgot to tell you that I don't love you anymore. I'm afraid I've fallen out of love with you, Harold."

"It's real visual," he says, "that quote. And what with the mosquito being the state bird and all—"

"I don't love you," she says again. "I just wanted you to know."

"Would you say the rhythm's a little off? It doesn't flow the way the Tenpenny quote does, and that's important."

"What," she says, laughing, "you think I do still love you?"

"It don't sing, does it? It's not as lyrical-like."

For a moment neither speaks, and she wonders if he ever thinks of all those men and women who used to whisper her name in the aisles at Champs LaRoux's store. Would he enjoy returning, as she imagines every day, to the year when she was nineteen and newly married and live one day, no matter how hectic or uneventful, from start to finish? What would she tell those people who followed her from shoes to lingerie, from hats to belts, hoping to hold her eyes with theirs?

"If only you knew what's going to happen to me," she might tell them. "You think I'm special? Well, I'm not. I'm never going to have a family, children of my own. My husband will become a drunken philanderer, and me an embittered wreck."

"Can I go now?" Harold is saying. "Can I hang up?" His voice seems to come from very far away.

"You can go. I'm not stopping you."

"You didn't call to say you don't love me. You were checking up on me. You wanted to be sure I came straight to work."

"I don't love you," she declares in a voice big and strong enough to surprise even herself.

"Thanks for calling," he says. "I don't love you, either."

It isn't Rena who hangs up without saying good-bye.

| 4 |

Today the two-a-days officially begin. By seven A.M. everyone—coaches, players, athletic department employees, student trainers, managers and a few invited members of the Committee to Recognize Harold Gravely—has gathered in the cafeteria of the athletic dormitory. Harold shakes hands all around, then sits with his assistant coaches and the ancient team physician, John Ford Cage, at a banquet table at the head of the room. One of the cooks has prepared a special low-calorie, low-cholesterol plate for Harold, complete with trail mix, whole wheat toast and a cup of unsalted oatmeal, but he rejects it in favor of the training table spread.

"Your heart'll bust and your veins'll clog long before your lungs ever quit," Cage says, pointing at Harold's tray heaped with bubbling strips of bacon, panfried sausage wheels, scrambled eggs whitened with milk and topped with a splash of picante sauce, Roman Meal toast dripping with apple butter, yellow hominy grits covered with gravy. Harold hitches a defiant shoulder at Cage, forks up a mouthful of the food and reads aloud the headline of the lead story in the city paper: OLD MAN WELCOMES LAST TEAM.

After a moment of reflection, chewing noisily, he reads the tagline trailing it: FINAL HURRAH FOR H. G., LAME DUCK COACH.

"Does this lame duck business mean I'm dying?" he asks after another long moment, dipping a folded triangle of toast into his coffee. "Seems like that's what I'm hearing here."

"Means you're between being out of a job and somebody else being in one," Cage reports. No one else at the table would dare be so forthcoming.

"Same thing, ain't it?" Harold says, tossing the paper on the floor. "They can call me dog any day. I can take dog. But to call a grown man a *duck* . . ."

He is washed crimson with the promise of imminent death, marked for a sudden, violent conclusion. It is coming, his eyes say, just wait. Hard as he sucks and swallows, he can't seem to get enough air. The tip of his nose is a lumpy bulb crowded with broken capillaries that seem to beat like drums. The odor of the booze comes not from his breath but from the pores of his skin. At this moment he would very much like to return to his office and have a drink, after informing Mrs. Nancy Claude that he is feeling poorly and needs some time alone, then stretch out on his Naugahyde couch near the window and nap until well past noon.

"They ain't saying you're a duck, son," Cage says. "They're saying your job ain't permanent. After this year you're gone!"

"They're implying I got fired, that I can't cut it anymore. And why'd they have to put last year's record in there?"

To everyone's surprise, Harold remains composed. He does not curse, shout or throw things.

At last he mutters, "Duck, dog, sack of smelly wet fertilizer, they can call me whatever they want. Long as they remember I'm the Old Man. Long as they don't forget that."

Trent Orlansky is sitting at a nearby table, chewing on a bran muffin. Painfully thin gold chains caress his wrists and neck. A black designer sweat suit of a shiny, nearly iridescent fabric covers his long, thin frame, and hundred-dollar air sneakers, the latest fashion rage among the sporting crowd, support the largest pair of feet to ever prance across the playing field at Tiger Stadium: size eighteens. Along with his job as head football coach, Harold is the university's athletic director, but it is Orlansky, one of three associates, who really manages the department's business affairs.

Orlansky was a reserve wide receiver on the Tenpenny Eleven who, at a spring banquet commemorating the squad, received the

Chancellor's Award for maintaining the highest grade point average on the team. Harold—handed the athletic directorship at that same banquet as a sort of present from the board to double his salary—hired Orlansky immediately after the graduation ceremonies in June.

Since then Harold has worked with him and the athletic department only when necessary, which is to say only when construction and concession contracts required his signature and when the football schedule had to be negotiated. Orlansky's uncanny ability to recall the minutiae of the Tenpenny Eleven era, and to deliver every bit with the flair of a troubadour, earned him the moniker "Mr. Memory."

Lately he has grown to resent the honor, but Orlansky remains the one person Harold turns to when some fragment from the past, no matter how insignificant, eludes him.

"Mr. Memory," Harold is saying now, "nice to see you dressed this morning like someone at a goddamn funeral."

Orlansky drops the muffin to his plate. He is all smiles and fluttering eyelashes. "I beg your pardon, sir." He looks at the others sitting at his table and wonders if perhaps Harold intended his remark for one of them.

Harold breathes deeply. "When was the last time I let one of my hardheads wear black on opening day?"

"Pardon?"

"You're wearing black, Mr. Memory. I won't have it."

"You won't have black?"

"Go home and change, hardhead."

"I'm sorry, Coach. But this is all new—" He tugs a sleeve of the sweat suit and holds up a shoe. "I guess I wasn't thinking."

"You'll remove some of that gold, too," Harold says. "I never did like looking at jewelry on a man."

Orlansky gets up from the table.

"And hurry it up. You got things to remember, notes to take. Suppose I say something?"

Orlansky steps quickly across the cafeteria, deposits his tray on a tractor belt leading to the dishwashers and leaves the room by way of a back door.

"Black means death," Harold tells his coaches. "Today I just happen not to want to be reminded."

Fork in one hand, spoon in the other, Harold shovels down

16

what remains on his plate; then, gathering himself to his full height and brushing the crumbs from his shirt, he announces that from this moment forward his coaches are to invite rather than order the hardheads to do one thing or another. "I mean to install some personal attitude changes while there's still time," he explains. "Invitations are more courteous, first off," he adds, bowing at the waist, "and if I'm being more courteous, then maybe I'll come up with something they can chisel onto that statue of mine."

Harold has hardly completed this directive when Chester Tully, one of his senior coaches, spots a freshman who is talking too loud and invites him to hit the floor and perform twenty push-ups. The boy accepts the invitation without argument, but because his twisted grin reflects a confused or defiant spirit, Chester orders him to drop to the ground again and give him twenty more. "And don't bend your back," he says.

"If I say anything that sounds like it'd look good in the history books," Harold notifies the coaches as Chester returns to his seat, "just write it down on a napkin or something and show it to me later. I only wish somebody had thought to bring a tape recorder."

Once the meal is over and the tables have been cleared, Harold motions a crew of barbers over to the front of the dining hall. The five men carry paper-handled shopping bags full of scissors, electric clippers, bottles of hair tonic, tins of talcum powder and white linen hand towels. And to Harold's delight, each possesses the assassin's cool economy of motion. The men stand behind wooden barstools arranged along the front of the sizzling grill and plug their instruments into wall sockets. The musical buzzing of the clippers brings an obligatory storm of hisses and boos and foot stamping from the boys. This, everybody knows, is one of the Old Man's traditions: mandatory head shaves at the beginning of the new season.

"I invite you to enjoy your little haircut," Harold says. "Forget about your girl back home and how she liked running her fingers through your precious goldilocks. She won't be inside your helmet when game time comes. You belong to me now. And I like a naked bucket of brains on my property—smooth as a baby's behind, pink as a pussy."

Harold looks to see if any of his staff is making notes for future use, but none is. Before he can ask why not, Chester whispers that the Committee to Recognize Harold Gravely would surely reject any reference to a woman's genitalia.

"You knew I was trying to catch you," Harold tells him.

Although both John Ford Cage and the head trainer complain that the troops haven't had sufficient time to digest their food, Harold directs the boys to the stadium immediately after the last head has been shaved clean. Under flickering lights and water pipes that hiss, clank and steam, they change into workout gear and prepare for "gassers"—the name Harold has given his famous method of getting his teams into shape. And the first session begins, at nine o'clock sharp, in a room with a blue cork floor. They perform belly flops until their legs betray them and their lungs feel like they've been torched. Deep in the bowels of the old stadium, this room has been designed for pain. Already the day, choked with rain, promises to be brutally hot, yet manufactured heat blows from the overhead vents, a heavy tortured air that smells of sour milk. The temperature, as prescribed by Harold, is near one hundred and ten. Urine-stained mattresses hang along the walls, cushions to protect the recruits from the brick and cinder.

When a coach—it is Larry McDuff this time—invites the boys to slam their forearms into the padded walls, most seem confused. Larry begins to sing a song from childhood, then bursts into a fit of rage and charges the wall, hitting and kicking in a white-hot fury as dust and specks of foam are torn loose. The boys, nearly a hundred of them, scramble to the other side of the room and huddle, gasping for breath. Larry remains at war with the brown cloud of piss staining the center of the bedding until Harold blows his whistle and says, "Lot better'n these hardheads' patty cake," thus ending the session.

"Life is a funny thing," Harold suddenly thinks to say, not knowing exactly what the inspiration was. "I'm the Old Man, I been to the mountaintop, I should know."

Proud that his coaches are writing and comparing notes for accuracy, Harold figures he's let himself down again. He may have seen a few, but never in his life has he climbed a mountain. "Y'all erase that shit," he says, then invites the boys to start another round of belly flops.

Only Harold and his staff possess the right of free speech. When the boys say something without invitation, they are routinely slapped, fisted and sucker-punched for asserting their individuality at the team's expense.

"This is no chatterbox café," Harold warns. "It don't matter what any of you have to say about anything."

Instead they sound like cattle being led to slaughter, making whatever collective racket they can. In the group is one who barks so well, and who so convincingly mimics the cries of a rabid dog, that Harold reaches over and pats him gently on the back of the head.

"If I threw a bone across the room," Harold says, "would you up and fetch it? Would you be a good dog?"

The boy whispers yes, and Harold slaps him with a knuckled hand. "Who the damn hell invited you to talk?"

If only temporarily, Harold has forgotten about his statue and is doing what comes most naturally to him, which, he likes to believe, is inspiring a group of young men to work harder and perform better than they ever thought possible. He's getting their bodies in condition while teaching them discipline as well. He's molding and shaping his last team into champions.

Michael Theodore, a sophomore defensive lineman, is the first to collapse. On the blue cork floor he lies on his back, hands covering his face. "Look here, you coward," Chester Tully screams. "You look here when I talk to you." The flesh around Theodore's lips is blue, the corners pebbled with scabs from shaving cuts.

Presently trainers arrive and check to make sure he hasn't swallowed his tongue. They speak to him softly, in whispers as conspiratorial as those of a priest in the confessional. Still Theodore won't move, won't utter a sound or blink his eyes open. When one of the trainers cracks a capsule of ammonia under his nose, he kicks his meaty legs and gags and spits. At this moment he is thinking his life is over, he will never again be who he was only a few hours ago, when he dreamed of the greatness that surely would be his.

"Back home in Krotz Springs," Harold says, "this quitter's got a twin brother who eats Kotex sandwiches for lunch."

Theodore's bald scalp is slick with sweat, and as the trainers drag him out by the heels his head leaves a trail like a wet mop.

"His daddy's got a menstrual cycle like a girl," Harold says. "And his mommy's got an Adam's apple and a whole bunch of hair growing on her chest."

Harold could use a drink. He spits blood-tinged gobs of phlegm into a paper cup and keeps pounding a fist against the coins in his pants pocket. Hot as it is, he feels a shiver. To his flesh he is standing in a walk-in freezer cold as sleep.

"Some of you will make it, some of you won't," he is saying now above the pained sobs and groans, aware once again that his every word is being transcribed. "Some of you will make hundreds of thousands of dollars when you leave this fine institution of higher learning. We'll watch you Sunday afternoons on the TV and cheer and pretend we knew you better than we did. Others of you will be home in a week picking at the pig's feet in your mama's pot, wondering, Am I good enough? And the truth is, you ain't."

| **5** |

When the tropical storm moves in at sixty miles an hour, Harold, his coaches and the boys are out on the levee of the Mississippi River, completing the morning's gassers. Meanwhile, in the city, nervous homeowners are nailing sheets of plywood over plate-glass patio doors and windows, children are scrubbing soot from the chimneys of kerosene lanterns. People are buying extra milk and meat, canned goods and bottled water. They are leading their frightened pets to shelter.

"Gassers," Chester shouts, "is good for you. It builds sperm, then it builds character." In this recipe, "spoym" is how he pronounces the first result, the way the Old Man says it; character is "cake-ta."

"Whoever heard of no weather pattern getting in the way of the game of football," Harold is saying. "No little rain cloud ever dictated the day and the night of the boss hardhead."

The boys are hopping up the steep embankment using only their right legs and down it using only their left. Near the barbed-wire fence at the foot of the grassy hill, a huddle of Herefords graze, and higher up by the dirt road at its crest, Brahmans stand big as train cars. The boys smell the cow pies as they run and top the levee, breathing for a minute before heading back down. They cough trying to expel the green, fecund odor, but it does no good; they drown in it. The rude air is like a blister on their lungs. Their loins quiver. Their testicles are small, hard knots that pull and work against them.

"Right now," Larry McDuff is saying, "I see some pricks, I see some twats, I see some in-betweens. I don't see no ballplayers, though."

Opposite River Road lies the spread of turtleback practice fields—the Ponderosa, Harold likes to call it. To the west, on the muddy water, tugs and barges belch and move slowly, almost imperceptively. From the crest the boys see the orange flares of the oil refineries downriver and the beehive port along the farther bank. They cannot bear to meet one another's weird, obscene eyes, which seem to implore: Who're you looking at? You looking for something?

They are children. They all wear purple shorts, white sweat tops and turf shoes and yellow-gold helmets with a strip of tape across the forehead. The tape bears the word HARDHEAD followed closely by their last names, all written in a clumsy hand equal parts Old English script and circus print: HARDHEADROE, HARDHEADFIELDS, HARDHEADLEOPARD, HARDHEADC.MAYES, HARDHEADB.MAYES, HARDHEADANDERSON.

"Your hat," Larry says. "You take it off, you wear my foot up your butt."

"You look at me wrong," Chester adds, "I take your eyeballs out, I suck them dry like candy jawbreakers."

They are, these two, competing with each other, and always at the expense of the four other assistants whose place on staff Harold considers entirely negligible. Along with Little Shorty Grieg and Pogo Reese, Chester Tully and Larry McDuff were the most celebrated of the Tenpenny Eleven. They now pretend to carry the memory like luggage packed with someone else's clothes, but they fool no one. Larry was the quarterback, Chester the receiver. Harold turned them into all-Americans, these boys from down the bayou, from places they never return to. In public they speak of their famous days as if some strangers had lived them, as if they had themselves merely watched from seats high in the stands, but this is the champion's lie. They work for Harold in order to remember what heroes they once were, and both are certain he keeps them around for a similar reason: if not as reminders of the Tenpenny year, then as living proof that a coach with guts and talent transformed dumb river rats into perfectly extraordinary young men.

Larry and Chester tell everybody they're best friends, inseparable, yet they despise each other. And they also tell everybody that Harold Gravely is the greatest college football coach of all time.

| 6 |

The rain begins to fall in hard white sheets as Hamilton Darby, a freshman linebacker from Plaquemine, faints and rolls to the bottom of the levee, through ant mounds, over patches of briar, into pockets of cow manure the size of manhole covers. Near the fence Harold nudges him with a toe, as if checking for life in a bag of trash.

"Look at this turd," Harold says, folding a new stick of Juicy Fruit into his mouth, then tossing the foil and paper wrappers at the motionless body. "This turd's got cow all over his face, cow all over his blubbery white legs, cow cow everywhere."

Harold laughs and heads running up the levee. "I'm an old man supposedly dying and I climb this goddamn mound faster than you. How you think the Alabamas and the Georgias and the Ole Misses climb their mounds? I bet them hardheads tear butt up their mounds. You clowns ain't running."

His voice is damp with blood and mucus. Bent way over, his hands resting on his knees, he struggles for breath. The wheezing seems to come from his armpits. When some of the players step up to help him, he pushes them away. "Don't touch me, you slime. Hear what I'm saying? Don't you dare touch me!"

Trainers in plastic ponchos and camouflage hunting caps arrive and lift Hamilton Darby off the wet ground, shove him into the back of a pickup truck and roar off to the infirmary.

"Two down," Larry says, "ninety-some-odd to go."

"Let that be a lesson to you," Chester says. "Don't die. If you die you ain't no use to this university. This university can't win with all y'all dead."

Harold lifts his raw, blistered face to the sky and staggers over to a golf cart parked in the middle of the road. This was a recent gift from the booster club, and in the early summer evenings Harold often took it out on the Ponderosa and cut donuts, leaving elliptical tire tracks in the sod. He liked to go at dusk, when few people were around to see him. Just last week Harold flipped the cart and was momentarily trapped beneath it, unable to move. "Please," he shouted, "don't let me die here. I got too much left to do."

After several minutes Camille Jones, his friend and the head groundskeeper, drove up and righted the cart. Without the seat belt and roll bar Harold would've been crushed. "If you're looking to find some way to kill yourself before the cancer does," Camille told him, "I'd appreciate it if you didn't go do your searching in front of me."

"I knew what I was doing," Harold said, spitting dirt.

"The hell you did," Camille said. "Next we'll see you on a Harley going up some ramp to see how many VWs you can jump."

Parked now on the shoulder of River Road, about fifty yards from Harold's golf cart, a red car idles, its exhaust blowing bullets of smoke the color of cooked bone. The windshield wipers are on, slapping loudly, but because of the distance Harold can't make out who, if anyone, is sitting behind the wheel. He can't even make out the model or year of the car, though by the size of it he knows it's domestic, what some of his hardheads might call a real clunker. It appears to be a convertible with a rag roof, though what he's seeing could well be paint peeling in strips off the hardtop. Shouting above the rain, Harold orders his second assistants to take over the gassers and Chester and Larry to hustle over to the car and make a note of the license plate.

"We're not even in pads or running the offense yet," he yells as loud as he can, "and some spy's out in the rain trying to steal our game plan!"

Chester and Larry stare suspiciously at the vehicle, then walk down from the levee and join Harold in the road.

"You really think he's a spy?" Larry says. "Looks to me like some old fellow waiting till the weather breaks. Driving always was tricky in a storm, Coach."

"I know a spy when I see one," Harold replies.

"Maybe he's a fan come to watch," Chester says. "You know how they like to visit at the beginning of each new season."

"For some reason," Harold grumbles, "a spy likes the color red. It's his favorite." He spits in the space between the men. "This one's got courage, though. You got to give him that much. Look at the sonofabitch sitting right under our eyeballs in a pile of rusty junk that couldn't outrun this electric damn golfing cart."

Afraid to upset him, neither Chester nor Larry reminds him of the spy who showed up for the first day of spring practice a few years ago. He came by plane, an antique prop job that navigated the same route twenty-some times. On each trip he whizzed over the south end of the Ponderosa, looped back and flew dangerously close to a churned-up stretch of ground, then rose a short piece before turning back around and heading toward the Ponderosa again. Harold figured the pilot was taking pictures of their offensive and defensive formations for some rival school. Each time the plane reappeared, he waved a fist at it—"Bastard," he called to the clouds—and noted the numbers on its wings. Doc Cage, who'd been on the sidelines observing the workout, tried to get Harold to see that he was irrational and overly concerned about nothing, but Harold, nearly frantic, pushed him away. Finally the old doctor got into his car, drove less than a mile up the road and saw, as he'd suspected, the alleged spy plane spraying a field with pesticide.

Immediately after the practice, Cage drove Harold to witness the crop dusting for himself, but Harold insisted espionage came in many disguises and Doc Hardhead was naive as a coonass recruit. Together they marched across the wide, sloppy field, breathing in the noxious fumes of the bug spray. Harold checked the cockpit for a camera but found only a pair of sponge earplugs, a greasy bandana, smudged goggles and an unopened pack of cheese crackers. To his credit, the pilot was patient and understanding when Doc explained Harold's suspicions. The man stood sucking his teeth, hardly making a sound. In all his days dusting, he'd never been visited on a job site by two old men with mud up to their knees, nor young ones for that matter.

Over the next few weeks Harold couldn't stop chattering about all the spies out to get him. He even ordered the stadium grounds crew, captained by Camille Jones, to hang green tarpaulins over the mile of hurricane fence that surrounded the Ponderosa, and he called

Champs LaRoux to see if the board of supervisors might consider scratching up funds to build a dome over the fields. At first LaRoux seemed to seriously consider the proposal, but once Harold told him about the spy plane, he suggested Harold bring a bow and some arrows to practice and start shooting back.

"You two hardheads gonna stand in the rain and wait till the spy escapes?" Harold says now, pointing at the car. "Or you gonna go interrogate him?"

Reluctantly they start walking down the road, Larry approaching from the driver's side, Chester from the passenger's. They get within ten yards of it when suddenly the driver, who is still obscured by the rain and fog on the windshield, reverses in a precise U-turn and heads in the opposite direction, skidding on the slick road. Larry and Chester give chase, and Harold follows in his cart, but in seconds the car disappears around the bend of the river, moving in the direction of the city's business district.

"If that wasn't a spy," Harold says, once he's caught up to his assistants, "then I ain't got bronchogenic carcinoma." He spits again in the narrow space between them.

"A spy would drive a nicer car than some beat-to-hell convertible," Chester says.

"Probably drive a Jaguar or Porsche or something," Larry says. "At worst one of them Japanese Preludes."

The hot August rain continues to fall on the winding blacktop. Harold guffaws and checks the swell of his crotch with his big right hand. "Congratulations," he says. "You let the sonofabitch get away." He offers an imaginary toast with an imaginary glass of champagne. Then: "I hold you two eternally responsible."

Chester and Larry stare off toward downtown, saying nothing. They're not as ashamed as they are anxious to get out of the weather, clean up, put on some dry clothes and report to the cafeteria in the athletic dormitory for lunch. Whenever they're pressured by Harold to perform, what they tell each other is, "Let's eat." Food is their passion, their solace, their sex; it gratifies. Both their bellies hang over their belts, and their underchins are flabby buckets of flesh. Unless Harold's paranoia is cured overnight, tomorrow there will be another spy parked on the roadside watching practice, or flying his plane overhead, or walking the ribbon of railroad tracks that bounds the east side of the Ponderosa, and then they'll be able to note the plates and interrogate him.

"Can we go eat?" Larry says.

"Let's scarf," remarks Chester.

"You're dismissed," Harold says, snapping his fingers. He turns back to the levee and signals for the other assistants to lead the members of his last team back to the stadium, about a mile away. Chester and Larry jog over and join the others. Everyone is running now down the short, unnamed road that leads to campus, heading in a swarm away from the river.

"It's rain that makes the grass grow," Harold says, driving past the line of boys and coaches, the tires of his cart whizzing as he picks up speed. "And it's rain that makes the fish smile." He must shout to be heard above the liquid footfalls, the storm of rubber shoes digging for traction on the wet pavement.

"Rain makes the sparrows fly. And rain makes the dirt crud. What else does rain make?"

Chester and Larry jockey for the lead, water streaming down their faces, salt, the consistency of mud, heavy on their tongues.

"Now say it for me," Harold commands, speeding far ahead of the pack, setting the pace. "Tell me what rain makes."

"Rain makes the dirt crud," Chester Tully shouts.

"Rain makes the dirt crud!" everybody repeats as one.

"Louder! Rain makes the fish smile." It's Larry this time, neck and neck with Chester. "Say it. Louder now!"

"Rain makes the fish smile!"

"Rain makes a frog hard," Harold hollers.

"Rain makes a frog hard!"

Chester is waving them on, demanding they pick up speed. His and Larry's strides are even. Their fat rolls.

"Don't puke on me, girls," Harold says, glaring back at the two men. "Don't you dare puke on me." Then: "Rain makes my mama sad."

"Rain makes my mama sad!" everybody shouts.

"Hey,
everybody,
look
how
big
I am!"

| 7 |

Early last season, after three straight losses, Harold and Rena started getting calls saying they were dogs that didn't deserve to live. Harold, rattled at first, had a mind to discontinue the phone service to their house, but Rena argued that this was an impractical, foolish idea. If they got rid of the phone, she said, wouldn't that be the same as giving in to the callers? Was he a quitter as well as a dog?

"Don't overstate what's happening here," he admonished her. "These idiots aren't stuffing bombs under the hood of my car."

"Without a phone," she said, "how will I get in touch with my friends in the morning and Mother on the weekends? And what if there's a fire or a rapist in the house?"

"Fire," Harold said with a snarl, "is always a possibility. But a man interested in . . ." He didn't finish the thought.

She was in favor of getting an unlisted telephone number and releasing it only to family and friends. No person of Harold's public standing should be listed in the white pages anyway, she said, and Harold reminded her that their number was in the book only because he wanted his hardheads to know they could call him any time, day or night, and he'd be available to help them. "Just like some father of the year kind of deal," he told her.

"Two things," Rena said, holding up two fingers. "If you don't have time for your boys at the stadium, why would they think you'd have time for them here at home?"

Harold nodded. "Good point. But that's only one thing. You said there were two."

"Believe me, you don't want to know the other."

"But I do," he insisted.

"You are not—" She stopped herself. "Don't make me say it."

"I'm a big boy. I can take it."

"You are not," she started again, "nor have you ever been—"

"Here it comes." He popped to his feet and started to run from the room, but her words caught up to him.

"You're the one who wanted me to say it!"

"I'm not a father," he said, staggering down the hall. "How many times do you have to remind me I'm not a father?"

In the dark bedroom he sat in a recliner and pondered his infertility as if it were a puzzle that could be readily solved but only by intense concentration. Outside the street lamps were on, and there was so much light shining from the moon and stars that the trees and shrubbery on the side lawn cast long blue shadows. To his and Rena's problem Doc Cage had offered a solution. "Adopt," he'd said, "if it means that much to you." But ten years had gone by and neither Harold nor Rena had ever discussed the possibility.

Now she was forty-seven, old enough to be a grandmother, and he was afraid to consider what he was old enough to be. Harold flipped on the pharmacy lamp next to the chair, aware that with the curtains open the people who lived next door could look in and see him. Of course it would have required a look of about fifty yards, through some live oak branches and ligustrum hedges at that, but with a neighbor like Xavier Monroe, Harold figured anything was possible. After all, Rena once saw the man pushing a lawnmower over his side yard while wearing nothing but a pair of black Keds and a floppy straw hat.

In the yellow lamplight Harold's belly seemed more fleshy than he'd ever thought, and he saw blemishes and tiny purple stretch marks that he hadn't known were there. After removing a wisp of lint from his navel, he leaned his shoulders back against the top of the chair and lifted his butt off the seat, then he pulled his pants down to his knees and had a good long look at himself. Like most men his age Harold wasn't circumcised, but as far as he knew that hadn't a thing to do with his sperm count. He turned his head to the side and coughed, which drew his nuts up a little, just as they were supposed to. Then he kicked his rooter around with his finger and it responded by perking up heroically, though not as heroically as he would've liked. It was true that everything about this part of his person sagged more than it did when he was a younger fellow, and also true that now it seemed to be frowning when before he could always count on a happy, smiling face. But no use snuffling, he told himself.

In all his years coaching, he'd seen, well, he thought he'd make a rough estimate. If each class consisted of about forty boys, and he'd coached thirty-three years, that came to a total of thirteen hundred and twenty hardheads. He'd worked as an assistant for six years and played for four more, increasing the count by four hundred. Harold had looked upon more than seventeen hundred rooters in his time at this university, though not because he particularly wanted to. He'd never coached a boy who showered with his clothes on, not sober anyway. And that accounted for the numbers.

Looking at it now, there was nothing about Harold's rooter that distinguished it from the hundreds he'd seen. In the old days it filled a jockstrap with a weight and confidence that gave Harold immense pride. It worked, too, if you wanted to call getting excited on command working. If your definition of working was more strict, though, it didn't work at all. "Imagine a fishbowl," Doc Cage had told him about ten years ago, trying to cheer him up. "You have the colored pebbles all over the bottom. You have the toy scuba diver clinging to the side of the tank. You have the wondrous rock formations and the bubbly oxidizer. You might even have a snail or two. All you're missing, son, is the fish."

His pants were still down to his knees when the telephone rang. Most of the calls from his detractors came at this time of night, or as he was dressing for work in the morning. And although he often claimed to be deeply troubled by them, this wasn't so. In truth he found them more interesting than sitting in the green room with Rena and discussing the stories she'd read in her self-improvement magazines. "You could bore the embalming fluid out of a dead man," he often told her, and he meant it.

He also liked the phone calls because they gave him a perfectly good reason to raise his voice and use whatever profane language he pleased right there in the house.

"Who plans to bury my rooter in the dirt?" he was shouting at the caller. "Come on—answer me."

"You don't start winning for a change," threatened the voice on the other end, which sounded all of thirteen, "then I'll have no choice but to do it myself."

"You ain't got a shovel deep enough," Harold shot back.

The caller said nothing for a long moment, and Harold feared he had lost interest. "You mean a hole deep enough," the voice finally said. "I got a shovel. I got a shed full of shovels."

"For me you'd need one of them big crane jobs with a scoop." Harold cupped himself and yanked. "Ever been to Chiner, son?"

"Nope," the boy replied.

"Then you'd get lost and what would your mummy say?"

Rena yelled from the other side of the door. "Are you saying nasty things on the phone again, Harold?"

"That your big fat wife?" the caller said.

"What if it is?"

"I seen her picture in the paper once. How's she feel watching her husband's butt get whipped every weekend?"

When Harold didn't respond, the boy continued. "Maybe it's because she ain't putting out enough to make you happy y'all ain't won yet. Maybe it's *her* fault."

After the caller hung up Harold waited another thirty minutes in the room. "Come on," he muttered to the phone. "Speak to me, son." But it didn't ring again.

Finally Harold pulled his pants back up and walked into the kitchen, pretending to be interested in finding something in the refrigerator. "Got any cherry Kool-Aid?" he said.

Rena was wiping the counter. "We haven't had Kool-Aid in this house in, I don't know, twenty years."

She poured out some apple juice. "Drink this," she said, returning to her work at the counter.

Harold took a sip and put the glass in the sink. "Tastes too healthy," he said. "Where's all the good stuff when you need it?"

"By the way," she said as he padded back to the bedroom, "I took the phone off the hook in the green room. I figured you could do without all the commotion."

His mind was muddled, but not too muddled to envision death by asphyxiation. The telephone cord was strong enough to strangle the seeds out of a watermelon, so how long could it possibly take to do the same to a woman?

| 8 |

Harold and the team snapped their losing streak at five, beating the Rice Owls by a field goal, then upset Mississippi State during a sleet storm in Jackson, and the calls stopped.

Each night and morning for an entire week, readying for bed or the job, Harold waited for the phone to ring, but it never did. He missed the calls so much he ached inside. It was almost as if someone close to him had died. He tried making a few himself, dialing numbers at random, but he always seemed to get people who cut him off before he could say anything. Once he got a woman with a flat Cajun accent and asked for her opinion of Harold Gravely.

"Never heard of the man," she said.

Harold could hear her eating something crunchy, probably a cracker. "You're pulling my leg, right?"

"No," she said. "I never heard of him. What has he done to make himself so special?"

"He's the football coach out at the university."

"Who knows a coach? Not everybody in the world cares the first thing about football."

"Everybody in my world does," Harold said. "It's the most important thing to the people in my world."

"Then you must not know Jesus," the lady said, her voice suddenly bright and spirited. "Let Miss Comeaux introduce you to Him."

"Somebody's always stealing my thunder," Harold told the woman. "If it ain't some other coach then it's some poor, sad bastard who's been dead and buried for two thousand years."

The lady started to speak, but Harold ended the conversation by yanking the line out of the wall jack, walking across the room, raising the window and throwing the phone outside. It crashed through a camellia bush before plopping on the leafy ground.

In the kitchen preparing dinner, Rena heard the excitement and came running into the room.

"I dropped the phone," Harold said, extending his hands out in front of him as if to prove his innocence. "Now, pie, it wasn't my fault. It was an accident, I swear."

"You're just lucky I wasn't in the room to see your accident." She waved a finger at him and planted her other hand, fisted, against her swollen hip.

"If I was lucky I wouldn't be getting these terrible phone calls at all hours of the day and night," he said.

"Funny, I don't remember hearing the phone ring. I think you're stretching the truth again, Harold. I think you're lying. You made up that phone call. And I think you need help. I think you need some serious psychiatric attention."

"What I need," Harold said, as she turned and started toward the kitchen, "is a team that'll play for me and win."

After Mississippi State Harold lost the next four straight, all conference games. By season's end, his office was inundated with letters and Mailgrams from alumni urging him to "do the right thing" and resign. Few pieces of mail were supportive, though some, written by friends and relatives, were considerate enough to wonder about the health of Miss Rena and the weather these days down in his intemperate part of the country. Some letters were copies of ones written to members of the board of supervisors, and these were hardest for Harold to accept. The Old Man's best days in the game were behind him, they said, and they listed reasons why: he hadn't won the conference title in seven years, hadn't beaten Alabama in six, Ole Miss in four, Tulane in three. On top of that, he hadn't appeared in a postseason bowl game in five, and the last one, the Florida Citrus in Orlando, saw his team lose by a field goal to a lowly also-ran in a rival conference. They also pointed to this year's dismal record.

Gravely was an embarrassment, they said, a dinosaur. He really was an old man—far too old and unimaginative to compete with all the exciting young coaches who were changing today's game. His methods of reaching the boys were not only archaic but cruel and often sadistic, and it was a wonder he hadn't killed anybody. Some called him a closet drunk, and another also included the Pogo Reese story:

Sunday night after the Tenpenny game, Harold Gravely, Pogo Reese and several others were drinking at a bar across the river—at Tuesday's All-Nighter. Mr. Gravely bought drinks for Pogo and Pogo's girlfriend, Rena Cummins. He encouraged them to chase glasses of beer with shots of vodka, and they, lost in the spirit of the evening, obliged him. Later in the parking lot Pogo killed a man for "keying" his car. By "keying" I mean the man scraped a key along the side of Pogo's Cadillac Biarritz, etching a line in the paint job. In a rage, Pogo threw punches into the man's face and body. The man fell and hit his head on Pogo's hubcap, then on the pavement.

He hemorrhaged to death at the scene.

Pogo, I contend, never would have flushed his young life down the toilet and been sentenced to the state pen had the said coach not contributed to his delinquency.

Justice wasn't done thirty years ago. Here's your chance to do it now—SHITCAN HAROLD GRAVELY!!

This unsigned letter so upset Harold that he couldn't even finish reading it. He called his secretary into his office and directed her to assume the chore, but she read with so much expression, nearly shouting out the capitalized words and exclamation points and chirping whenever she encountered a smart word, that Harold had to take some antacids and stretch out on the couch.

Mrs. Claude, who pronounced her last name "cloud," sat beside him and started rubbing his temples.

"Mr. Gravely?" she said.

"Yes, daughter."

"Are you okay?"

"No, daughter."

Her pleasant Pekingese eyes flashed brilliantly. She daubed her freckled nose with a wad of pink tissue. Her long dark hair tumbled into his face and tickled his cheeks, and Harold, squinching, swatted at it.

"Did my having fun with that stupid old letter make me look common?" she said.

"Somewhat, daughter."

She grabbed his hand and placed it against her breast, and immediately he started to explore the region as if in search of something. "Because I hate looking common."

"I know you do, daughter."

When her blouse was off and Harold had started to breathe heavily, she said, "Were you really there that night—at Tuesday's, I mean?"

He raised his head, long enough to let her observe his disappointment, then plunged his face deep into her bosom. "I was there," he said after a moment, "but I had to leave early. I'd took sick with a sore throat, you see."

She moaned with pleasure. "Don't you hate a sore throat?"

"Yes, I do," he answered. "But a sore throat . . . a sore throat has always liked me."

From the stack at the foot of the couch she selected a letter written by an alumna who used to dress as the school mascot for all the home games. The stationery, covered from edge to edge with a florid script, was the weight and texture of parchment. She read, less excitedly this time:

Coach Gravely took me into his office after the Navy game and asked me to remove my Tiger outfit. He shut the door and said he wanted to see what kind of a person would do such a thing as play like a jungle animal in front of thousands of people. When I refused to undress, he bashed my papier-mâché head with a walking cane. It wasn't until he saw I was a woman (my rich baritone and stature must have thrown him) that he quit assaulting me. Then he invited me to sit down and have a drink with him. I was shaking and scared, so I had some in a coffee cup. It brought tears to my eyes and he thought I was crying and would tell the authorities. He pleaded with me to keep this "under wraps." And those were the very words he used—"under wraps," like it was a murder mystery and he the private eye. After three straight glasses, he drove me back to the sorority house and dropped me off for all the girls to see. The smell of gum on his breath, mingled with the liquor, has never left me.

By now I was near hysterics and hugging what remained of the Tiger head. One of the girls said I was so emotional because I was having a torrid love affair with the said coach, and, because of this charge, I was blackballed from the sorority with a sullied reputation I was never to redeem.

Is this, I ask, the man we want to influence our impressionable young people? Is he, I ask, representative of all the noble sons of university football to come before him?

I, Helen Dumars, say NO, NO, NO and support the drive to have his tenure terminated.

In self-defense, Harold paid visits to the board members. And except with Norman Pepper, who refused to discuss the situation, he argued that he was guilty of nothing other than being a good, tough coach with the school's best interests in mind. As everybody knew, he said, the business about him getting Pogo Reese drunk the night after the championship game was an unfortunate part of the Tenpenny myth, something that had stalked him all these years but was discounted by Pogo himself when he took the stand during his own trial. And the anecdote about the sorority girl in the Tiger suit, he contested, was greatly exaggerated. But even if it was entirely accurate, wouldn't the university want to protect one of its most valued staff members from such a youthful indiscretion?

After a game "nearly a million years ago," he explained, he was looking out of his office window and saw the team mascot stumbling around drunkenly. By the time he got outside to try to help, it'd passed out against a bicycle rack and appeared to be unconscious. He carried it inside. The papier-mâché head of the suit had been damaged in the fall, shutting off the nose and mouth vents and preventing it from getting any air. He did hit the head with a walking stick, but only because he thought the person inside would suffocate. He truly was shocked to discover that a young lady filled the suit. He gave her some spirits in a cup to help revive her—half a lifetime ago, he said, this was a common medical practice. Filled with pity, he drove her home, a sorority house near one of the campus lakes. If he was at fault at all it was for not reporting her indecent behavior to the dean of students the next day and pressing for some disciplinary action.

"It's true that I've indulged on occasion," Harold told the board chairman over lunch at the City Club restaurant, "but never have I in the company of young people. In the first place, I was never so crazy about their company, and in the second, if I was to drink and make a spectacle of myself, it wouldn't of been with no spastic ingenue dressed like a beast."

Champs LaRoux's face was aflame with indignation, and the salty taste of anchovies clung to his tongue. In the past he had defended Harold against his detractors, but now he was leaning forward in his chair, gazing at the giant chef's salad he'd only picked at since the waiter served it. Champs was a dignified-looking man only a few years older than Harold, and for years they had enjoyed a friendship that allowed them to be perfectly candid and forthcoming with each other. Champs picked at his lettuce with his fork, pushing it from one side of the plate to the other, then he finally spoke. "I'm sorry, Old Man." And nothing more.

His voice was so low, and the tone so dismal, that Harold asked him to please repeat himself. "But what for, hardhead?" Harold said. "You yourself been out and drunk with me more than once. And you yourself was the one always bragging about carrying on with some of the clerks at your store. You even tried something on my wife! Who the hell are you to sell me downriver? I got more shit on you, boy . . ."

Harold never tired of defending himself in private meetings with board members. A few of them remarked that the more he lied to save himself, the more it seemed he himself was part of the conspiracy to drive him from the job. It never occurred to Harold that he'd come to resemble a desperate politician stumping the state at the last possible moment for votes he had no chance of winning. Although his campaign appeared to be doomed, Harold could not abide his place in a world that forgot its heroes.

When board member Mary Elaine Watts, finishing up her City Club lunch with Harold, said only he and Pogo knew the truth of what happened that night thirty years ago, suggesting there might have been some evidence against him that wasn't disclosed during the trial, Harold remained quiet. But then she giggled and told him his account of the Helen Dumars incident was as fragile as blown glass, but still wonderfully creative.

"Get a grip, bitch," Harold murmured, then he abruptly pushed away from the table and walked out.

| **9** |

Rena had her own share of Harold Gravely stories.

A few days after the Sugar Bowl and Pogo's dark hour at Tuesday's, one began, Harold goes to a movie and takes a seat in the middle of the theater. It's a William Holden picture, and the house is full. When the newsreel featuring the Tenpenny Eleven plays before the start of the film, the crowd cheers and pounds the wooden backs of the chairs. Hoping to discourage the clamor, Harold stands and raises his hands above his head, but this only raises the din. A chant of "Ha-rold! Ha-rold!" echoes across the room. When his ride to the midfield crest lights up the screen, the crowd suddenly, and quite dramatically, falls silent, as if dumbstruck by their proximity to one whose image now fills the wall before them. Harold, no less impressed, climbs onto the arms of his chair, points straight ahead and says, "Hey, everybody, look how big I am!"

Rena often recalled this story because it almost made them mortal enemies a few short weeks after their marriage. In a dubious but courageous attempt to mask her ignorance of her new husband, Rena had detailed the newsreel anecdote to a newspaperman who had pressed her to "define this amazing, this extraordinary man who is Harold Gravely." The writer, a syndicated columnist with a flamboyant, Runyonesque style that attracted a wide, somewhat fanatical readership, had been working on what he called an "offbeat retrospective think piece" about the Tenpenny year, and Harold had granted her permission to be interviewed and say whatever she pleased. As it turned out, Rena's secondhand report on Harold's day at the movies was the only thing the man chose to write about, and he did so under a headline that declared: AT TENPENNY OPERA HOUSE, OLD MAN'S EGO RUNS AMOK.

Harold had repudiated the story to anyone who would listen, including several who hadn't even heard of it. At home he'd insisted that Rena, his flustered bride, the woman whom he had only recently vowed to love, honor and cherish, name the source of her information; when she couldn't, he wondered aloud if perhaps her sudden memory lapse—"your blank slate," he called it—was one of convenience.

Maybe she'd picked it up at the Frostop Diner or someplace, she answered, and why did it matter so much who told it to her anyway? It was too late now, the story was already in the papers.

If ever there was a time when she thought he might hit her, it was then. His eyes bulged and so much blood pooled at the tip of his nose that it seemed to double in size.

"Long as they spell my name right!" he had screamed. "Hear me, girl?"

So what if he'd gotten excited seeing himself on the silver screen and babbled something stupid? Who wouldn't have? In time she came to consider his violent reaction as a better definition of him than the newsreel anecdote itself, and one afternoon in a moment of weakness and confusion she had called the columnist to see if he might consider writing a follow-up piece.

The man regretted to say he couldn't do it, for "as a bit of a snoop" he appreciated the controversial nature of the information. This was a domestic squabble that would resolve itself shortly, he said, and being "of the bedroom," it certainly didn't belong in a family newspaper. But if ever Harold said anything to match his Tenpenny speech, or if ever he confessed feeling at all responsible for what Pogo Reese did, the man invited her to call again. "You're a teenager yet," he said. "One day you'll thank me for this."

Rena called him a "shameless homer" and accused him of irresponsible journalism. His laughter, booming above the clatter of typewriters, was the last thing she heard before hanging up.

But that was a long time ago, back when Harold was still a star and she was dumb enough to believe he would be forever. Now, a few weeks after his 2–9 season, he was pleading with her to attend his press conference to officially close the previous campaign and announce plans for the next. It was early in the morning and she hadn't had her first cup of coffee yet. She stood looking out the bedroom window, wondering if he meant to use her as a shield against the hard questions he no doubt would be made to answer.

"I don't want to look like a fool," she told him. "You remember last time."

After their weeks of bickering over the newsreel anecdote, she had agreed never again to speak to any reporter unless Harold was present, an arrangement she had honored ever since.

"I know it's been nearly thirty years," she said, clipping on a blue glass earring, "but I've always wondered if you did what everybody said you did at that show . . . and if you got after me for nothing."

"I may of yelled something at the screen about being big," he replied, "but I can tell you I never stood on no chair."

"Did you point straight ahead?"

He shrugged. "You know I've always liked to point."

Her presumption, Harold said then, that the press would go easier on him if she was around, was tantamount to calling him a "ninny baby." This made her feel as if he really did want her along, for support and wifely encouragement, until he directed her to the bedroom vanity and instructed her to "go extra heavy on the perfume, pie—make it seem like you're drowning in the warm, scintillating fumes."

"What if somebody asks me something," she asked later, as they were driving to the campus to confront his critics. She was studying her face in the small lighted mirror at the center of the sun visor. "Do I answer him or turn it over to you?"

"I got veto power over all questions," he said. "Plus no one's seen or heard from you since God knows when," he added, carefully avoiding specific mention of the newsreel.

The postseason press conference, a tradition at the university, was begun some fifty years ago by Bernard Toefield, who preceded Harold as coach. Tired of answering reporters' questions about the next season, Coach Toe figured that if he could gather everyone together at once he could be done with their interviews at least until August, when two-a-day practices began. Then, in the afternoons when he wanted to run his bird dogs, he wouldn't be stuck in his office day after day "squawking," as he put it, "because some boy's got a new notebook he wants to fill up."

Coach Toe's first news conference attracted two radio and three newspaper reporters: they shared a platter of finger sandwiches, a pitcher of root beer made from concentrate and talked about everything, it seemed, but football. This year, however, Trent Orlansky, whose office coordinated the meeting, told Harold to expect "in the general vicinity of one hundred persons, including representatives of several national news organizations, all of whom will be trying to bait you into announcing your resignation."

Orlansky was sitting on a bench near the Players' Gate when Harold and Rena parked in front of the stadium. A briefcase lay open on the marble seat beside him; he was leafing through a stack of papers as thick as the city telephone book.

"Your leader approaches," Harold said, steps ahead of Rena. "Stand and be counted."

Orlansky shook Harold's hand, then put his arms around Rena and kissed her cheek. "What a pleasant surprise," he said. "Coach Gravely didn't tell me you were coming."

"Didn't tell me, either," she said, "until about an hour ago."

Orlansky put the documents back in the briefcase. "I was reading over the report by the accountants on how to get the football program out of the red."

"We win is how," Harold remarked.

"This year season ticket sales were down twelve percent, and for the first time in forty-four years we failed to sell out a single home game. And projections for next year, according to the accountants, aren't worth tooting any horns about."

"Heroes fill Tiger Stadium," Harold declared, "not eraser heads." He drew in a deep breath and pulled tight the knot in his purple and gold necktie. "You might remind them of that."

Orlansky snapped his briefcase shut and guided Harold and Rena across the street toward the student assembly center, where in a basement lyceum the newspeople awaited them. On the path Rena misstepped, lost her balance and stumbled. It was Orlansky, reacting with the ease and dexterity of the kind of athlete he had never been, who threw his arms around her waist and kept her from falling.

"She's a fine woman," Harold said, "just a little goofy." He marched forward as if nothing had happened.

"I hope this year you've got more than promises to give them," Orlansky called ahead to him. Determined not to embarrass Rena more than she already was, he picked his briefcase off the ground and rubbed the scuffed leather with the sleeve of his suit coat.

"Trent wants you to be honest," Rena said. "Ask for their sympathy. Who knows, show some humility and you might get it."

Harold clenched his jaw and quickened his pace.

"I made sure to have a wet bar," Orlansky said as an afterthought. "We've got Bloody Marys and screwdrivers. And the caterer said he'd spike the punch if I didn't tell anybody. I thought if they were drinking they might not be so damn difficult."

Harold spun around and threw his hands into the air. "Sober they only want a piece of your ass," he said, now walking backward. "Drunk they aim for the groin." He pointed at Orlansky. "Mr. Memory, you should of known better."

The reporters were standing in clusters along the side walls, chattering noisily over various colorful libations in clear plastic glasses as Harold and his attendants strode into the lecture hall and down the middle aisle to the dais. They continued to cluster and chatter until Trent Orlansky patted the head of a microphone and called the conference to order.

Harold, displaying a mannerly side few had seen in years, directed Rena to sit in a chair between the ones designated for Orlansky and himself. He even brushed off the seat with his linen handkerchief. Because the group was slow in assembling, Orlansky once again asked everyone to have a seat.

"Harold Gravely," he said into an ancient pineapple microphone, "is accompanied by his wife Rena. . . . Rena Gravely, ladies and gentlemen!"

Orlansky stepped back and began to clap, and a smattering of unenthusiastic applause and flirtatious whistles lifted from the crowd. Rena, hoping to respond appropriately, moved to stand and bow but Harold, waving the handkerchief, signaled for her to remain seated. "Should of seen her thirty years ago," he blurted into the microphone, which boomed, whined and fizzled at the sudden introduction of his voice. Everyone laughed and some shrieked like delinquent schoolboys.

"But you should of seen me too," he added, and the reporters, all of them, fell silent. "God, you should of seen me too."

With a coy tug Trent Orlansky reclaimed the mike. "Rena Gravely, ladies and gentlemen!" he said. "Rena Gravely!"

When he swept an arm in her direction the applause came again, though more polite than the first round.

Rena wondered why she'd agreed to come along. As Orlansky read from a prepared text—"We thank you for your continued patronage, and we hope it continues in the future. . . ."—she studied the audience as it, in turn, studied her. The faces of the reporters were visible all the way to the shadows in the back of the room. If she was able to read them correctly, each seemed to be trying to make a leap of the imagination and accept her as the person with whom Harold Gravely shared his dreams and bed and board. To live with such a man, they seemed to be wondering, was there something wrong with her or was she just kind of, well, dumb?

But they seemed an average lot, hardly the hacks and monsters Harold had railed against all these years. She found it odd that she knew none of them—not a single one in the whole crowd. For too many years she had listened to her husband, had been conditioned by his yellow rage and blather: One was no different from the next and none had a name or face worth remembering. If some had distinguished themselves as journalists she couldn't say; she rarely read the papers.

"I want to talk about something that's been keeping me up nights," Harold said after Orlansky had finished with his introduction and was seated in his chair. "It won't take but a minute and then you can ask as many questions as you like."

He removed a folded piece of paper from his coat pocket and opened it with the precious attention one might show a rare treasury note, then looked only once at his audience before beginning. "What you, my derogators, are partaking in is a conspiracy," he read, the microphone pressed against his lips. "You've forgotten just like the board of supervisors and everyone else has forgotten—I'm talking about that night in New Orleans when I rode bareback on the shoulders of Pogo Reese and Little Shorty Grieg."

Rena saw the eyes of the reporters fall, look away, return to their blank notebooks. Several of the photographers took pictures and a few of the TV cameramen occupied themselves videotaping his words, but no one save Mr. Memory was doing anything with his pen but chewing the plastic tip.

"And you've forgotten that since the Tenpenny season I have, out of loyalty to this university, refused to consider several offers from search committee chairmen inquiring whether I might be interested in moving to their schools. I've been loyal to this university, and what I keep wondering is why can't you be as right and loyal to me?" He stuck the microphone under his arm, producing gusts and whispers of electric feedback, then with painful deliberation he balled up his speech and crammed it in his coat pocket. By the time he put the mike back to his lips nearly everyone was hearing ghostly ticks of thunder drifting in the newly restored silence. "Any questions?" he said.

An ordinary-looking young man wearing wire-frame spectacles stood and shouted louder than seemed necessary. "I wasn't born yet when all that tenny-penny stuff happened," he said. "Tell us, what about next year? Are we to expect another loser."

Harold returned to his chair, placed the mike on the table and covered it with his handkerchief. He leaned into Rena until their faces nearly touched, and Orlansky did the same, but neither man said anything. Harold's lips moved and then Orlansky's followed, but not a word was spoken.

They were pretending, with Rena as their witness, to be sharing something of great, to-die-for importance, information to which the press would not be privy.

"Peaches and peas?" Harold said at last, cupping his hands over the mike. And Orlansky answered, "Peas and peaches."

What with their spontaneous knee-slapping convulsions, neither seemed willing to concede the slightest deficiency of ardor in their little game, though for her part Rena could produce hardly a chirp.

"Peaches and peas," Harold said again, driving home the joke with a fist to the table. "Peas and peaches," replied Orlansky, adding an equally contentious hand to the wood.

Meanwhile, the reporters had ignited in a resounding storm of inquisition, and many more ordinary-looking young men were shouting questions about resignation, the disastrous season, the board and contract renewal. Few, now, were sitting. They had gathered at the foot of the dais, close enough to send vibrations up Rena's legs and raise the fine untutored down at the top of her thighs.

"When you don't know what to say," Harold said, the view of his mouth shielded from the audience by both his and Orlansky's flattened hands, "say peaches and peas . . . peas and peaches."

Finally Rena picked up the microphone. "Are there any questions?" she said.

The reporters shouted furiously and waved their skinny brown notebooks.

"Control yourselves or we leave," Harold announced, seizing the mike.

Rena turned to Trent Orlansky but he was still occupied with his own memobook. "I want to leave," she said. Orlansky nodded but didn't move. "Trent," she said, "I want to leave. Do you hear what I'm saying?" She touched his sleeve. "Will you walk with me outside?"

"I'll take your questions one at a time," Harold was saying as he paced from one end of the dais to the other. His eyes were on his wife. "Who's got a good juicy one for me?"

Orlansky clipped his pen to the tail of his sporty yellow necktie. "Sure you don't want to stay?" he whispered. "Maybe they'll settle down once the bar's closed."

It was Harold, she knew, not the drinks, that had generated the reporters' contempt, and chaos would rule as long as he teased them. Rena stood and walked stage right, to the platform of stairs leading to the seats. "Rena Gravely!" Harold announced, watching her go. "Rena Gravely, ladies and gentlemen!"

This time there were no whistles and applause. The mood of the gathering seemed to darken as she descended from the dais, then brighten when she left the room. If with her onstage the reporters had seemed merely uncollected, now they were frenzied.

In the hall, as she hurried for the exits, she heard Harold declaring the departure of Trent Orlansky.

"There he goes, ladies and gentlemen, the man who sometimes seems to know me better than I know myself! Mr. Memory, ladies and gentlemen! Mr. Memory!"

Orlansky followed her out into the sunlight. They walked the broad plains of cement around the assembly center without speaking, and until they settled themselves on a stone bench under a huddle of pine trees they might have passed for hurried strangers who'd chanced upon the same path.

"Time to regroup," Orlansky said, reaching for the pack of cigarettes in his shirt pocket.

Rena noticed his shoes. At another time in her life she might have paid a quarter to see them in a congested, airless carnival tent. Today, she told herself, had not been for naught after all.

"Must be hard to find anything to fit," she said.

"I beg your pardon." He was looking at something in the sky.

"Your shoes."

"Oh, yes. Pretty silly, aren't they." He knew better than to offer her a smoke. "I guess everybody's got something they're not very proud of," he said, draping one leg over the other and slapping the side of his shiny black wingtip. "This is it for me—longest shoe ever to trot across the field at Tiger Stadium. I guess I belong in the hall of shame."

She gripped the edge of the bench and rocked forward. "It's not like you asked for it," she said, afraid that she'd offended him. "My hands aren't so pretty either. Harold likes to tell me they look like leaves of wilted lettuce." She held them up as proof, but he wasn't interested. He squinted, dragging on the cigarette, and patted his shoe again. "I mean," she added, "your feet and my hands weren't something we freely elected, were they? Not like our marriages, anyway."

"Freely elected?" he said, slightly baffled.

She was making him nervous, she could tell by the way he sucked on the cigarette, pulling in so much smoke that, when he exhaled, a tiny yet audible noise emanated from his nostrils.

"I was wondering if you ever hear from Pogo," she said.

Now he was running his fingers over his shoelaces. "Haven't in twenty"—he paused to make an accurate count—"I don't know, Rena, maybe twenty-five, twenty-six years. It was back when his father died. I sent him a letter of condolence and he wrote back." Suddenly he stood, dropped his cigarette and stamped it into the ground. He was looking at the sky again. "Would you like me to have somebody drive you home," he asked. "I can get somebody from the office. I just remembered I forgot my briefcase in there." He pointed in the direction of the assembly center.

"Don't worry about it," she said.

"Any other time I'd drive you myself."

"Please, Trent." She raised a hand. "I'd walk back with you but I honestly thought I'd suffocate in there. It wasn't all the reporters, either. It was Harold, you know. He was . . . I dunno, it was like he was everywhere."

"I think he likes handling those people more than he lets on. Once I heard him call them a bunch of fish without teeth."

"Up on the stage I kept thinking of Pogo—of how it was after what happened at Tuesday's." She rocked forward again, then back. "I was remembering how all the attention used to make me feel very tired and very old—'almost fifty,' I used to tell my mother. 'I feel almost fifty.' And now that I really am almost fifty . . . well, having to look down the barrels of their cameras again doesn't make me feel any younger, I can tell you."

He put another cigarette between his lips but didn't light it. For a moment he fiddled with his handsome silver-plated lighter as if trying to decide whether to surrender the five or six minutes he would need to enjoy the smoke or save it and return directly to the press conference. He chose the latter with a start. "If you walk to the student union," he said, slipping the cigarette back into the pack, "there's always a cab or two lined up along the curb out in front."

"Thank you for today," she said, standing up. "I'll get along fine, believe me." She brushed the front of her skirt.

"It really was good seeing you again, Rena." He put his hand on her shoulder, leaned forward and kissed her. "I'm sorry we couldn't have talked longer."

As Trent Orlansky started toward the assembly center, carrying rather than stepping with each ridiculous foot, she saw Harold ambling at a brisk, nearly frantic pace on a path that cut the wide lawn. In front and on either side of him, cameramen shot his picture and TV reporters shouted questions from behind microphones adorned with enormous crayon-bright heads made of sponge. At one point Harold slowed his gait and waved, and when Rena looked for the recipient of his gentle greeting she saw that no one was there. On meeting Mr. Memory he embraced him with no less affection than one might show his oldest but most neglected friend, and together, smiling and whispering—about peas and peaches no doubt—they started for Rena, who was now tempted to turn her back and run. "Rena Gravely!" Harold was saying as he approached. "That's right . . . Rena Gravely, ladies and gentlemen!"

Swept up by the circus, Rena suddenly found herself flanked by her husband and his authorized biographer. With the crowd of reporters surrounding them, she thought of the strange, seemingly undirected travels of tree beetles, who in their determination to survive travel across acres of bark the way geese arc through the skies, going as one or not going at all. She only wished she had an owlish pair of sunglasses to hide her eyes, a flowing chapel veil or wimple to cover her scarlet face and neck.

She watched as Harold waved at another fictitious friend on the street, giving him no less than two thumbs up. "Hello there," he called, now cupping an ear. "Thank you . . . thank you, friend. I thank you for your support."

Upon reaching the Cadillac, still swarmed by the media, Harold threw his arms around Orlansky and offered both cheeks for the kissing. Orlansky complied with a rumpled mouth and then opened the door for Harold, forgetting that Rena, stranded beneath a nest of electronic equipment on the other side of the car, was the woman and deserved the favor.

"Now that wasn't so bad, was it?" Harold said as he maneuvered the car through a cluster of newsmen blocking the street. With his right hand he reached over to pat her on the back of the head, but she grabbed his wrist and pushed him away. They were stopped at the corner now; the hacks and photographers were far behind them. "Huh, Rena? You enjoyed that, did you?" When he tried to touch her again she grabbed his thumb and wrenched it until the joints popped. He screeched and she bit into his knuckle as if it were a chicken leg.

"I liked it just fine," she said, straightening her skirt. "It was goddamn wonderful, Harold."

| **10** |

The worst season of Harold's career was now officially over, and banners were beginning to appear on the great houses along fraternity row: GRAVELY TO HIS GRAVE! OLD MEN CAN'T COACH! TO HELL WITH HAROLD! The words were painted clumsily on white bedsheets and tacked to the facades of the wide, unscreened porches. Harold had a notion to burn the houses down just to get rid of the signs. Instead, he dictated a memo to Mrs. Nancy Claude warning that if any football player was a member of or in any way associated with a fraternity he would be dismissed from the team. To no surprise of Harold's, it delighted his hardheads and inspired them to create signs of their own. The sheet hanging over the entrance to the athletic dormitory—FUCK THE FRATS, it said—had to come down, but all the others stayed, including Harold's favorite. GOD SAVE THE OLD MAN, it read in purple and gold paint, AND GOD DAMN THE GREEKS.

This was the first memo he'd dictated since hiring Mrs. Claude some seven years ago, and Harold told her they ought to try it again real soon, what with the results. Only one person complained, though not because he owed any allegiance to a fraternity. McAllen Friend, a starting offensive lineman, was a political science major who knew when his inalienable rights were being violated. Harold sat the boy down on his couch and berated him so violently that Mrs. Claude, working at her desk in the outer office, closed her eyes and hummed a hymn from church. The season had gone so poorly that Harold's starters were now of little more value to him than his scrubs, so to tell McAllen Friend to clean out his locker wasn't a difficult decision. But then the boy threatened to file an official complaint with the student government association.

"Go ahead," Harold said. "Commence your litigation. I hope you don't mind a scandal."

McAllen Friend's expression changed to where Harold thought he looked like somebody else. "What are you talking about?" he stammered, raising himself in his seat.

"Frankly, son, I think you know. I can name someone right now who saw you try something in my dressing room."

"Try something?"

Harold nodded and rolled a rubber band between his fingers. "Let's not pretend. Please."

"I'm not pretending," McAllen Friend said, his voice a mere whisper. He was hunched over, sitting on his hands. In Harold's gaze he recognized something heinous, almost unmentionable. "You think I'm gay, don't you?" he said at last.

Harold winked and kissed the air; suddenly McAllen Friend's face changed again. Harold thought he looked as if he'd transformed into yet a third person.

"You're saying I'm a homosexual, aren't you?"

Harold had known his share of homosexuals, a couple of whom made postseason all-America teams. As he often told his assistants, a person could desire sex with pumpkin squash and that would be fine as long as he knew how to win.

"I'll tell everybody what information I've got in Mrs. Claude's filing cabinet," Harold replied, inspecting his chipped and yellowed

50

nails. "And my telling it all over town is equal to your being it. I'm still boss hardhead around here."

"I know who you are."

"And you're the only boy on my team who wears tie-dyed T-shirts and a goat beard." Harold slammed the flat of his hand on his desk top. "Sunday mornings you don't go to church. People complain you run phonographic records too loud in your room. You burn incense like they do in a whorehouse. You wear a jockstrap under everyday clothes instead of regular step-ins. You don't always shower after practice." Harold's eyes returned to his nails. "You want me to go on? Or shall I stop there?"

"You keep files?" McAllen Friend was about to cry. "You expect me to believe you've kept a file on me?"

Harold laughed and juggled his shoulders. "A person gets a lump of shit on his finger," he said, holding up a manila envelope stuffed with papers, "he's the one got to wipe it off."

| 11 |

That night McAllen Friend visited Harold at home and asked if he could meet him next morning at his office. Dressed in her nightgown, Rena watched from the living-room couch, saying nothing. When McAllen apologized for coming at such an inconvenient hour, Harold turned to her and said, "The hardhead drives all the way to my house at eleven o'clock at night to ask if he can come to my office in the morning. Does that make any sense?"

Harold didn't invite him in. After a few minutes Rena returned to the bedroom, and Harold and the boy stood on the front steps, their faces inches from each other. Harold let McAllen get that close because he wanted to smell for liquor on his breath. There was a tragic, end-of-the-world manner in which McAllen pleaded to meet with Harold in the morning and straighten things out. At one point McAllen reached to grab the collar of Harold's pajamas, but then he thought the better of it.

"The moment you left my team," Harold said, "you left my life. But I'll grant you a couple of minutes. Be there early and show me you're worth the trouble."

Wearing a long-sleeve dress shirt and a striped necktie with a gold-plated clip, McAllen was waiting outside the stadium when Harold reported to work in the morning. He smelled of a sharp cologne fueled by apples and cinnamon. Though still a little long, his hair was neatly parted and glistening with tonic. The whiskers were gone, and the skin around his mouth was a shade lighter than the rest of his face.

"I'm sorry I made an issue of the memo," he told Harold. "Please don't make me walk out of here."

Harold gave him a look full of fire and meaning. "I'll forgive you, hardhead," he said. Then he lowered his voice and added, "But only if you'll forgive me first."

"For saying what was in my file?"

Harold's mischievous smile, lifting the fleshy corners of his mouth, made his face appear even more round and moony. "I never really said you was one," he said.

"I'm not, you know."

"It was a character test," Harold said, squeezing a couple of pieces of Juicy Fruit into a ball and stuffing them into his mouth. "I was trying to see what you're made of. I knew all along you were odd only in the sense that all young hotheads are odd."

The boy seemed to believe him. His deportment had changed so many times in the last twenty-four hours that Harold had to wonder about his health. "I don't want a front-row seat in your doghouse," McAllen said. "I grew up hearing about the Tenpenny Eleven. Playing for Harold Gravely and wearing the purple and gold was my childhood dream. I would have done anything for it. Tell me how to smooth things out between us."

Harold asked him if he remembered what had brought him to his office in the first place.

"The memo," the boy answered in a hurry, figuring he'd finally got something right.

"The banners on the frat houses. I don't like what they're saying. It's as much about you as it is about me."

"You'd like them taken down?"

"Yes," Harold said, offering the boy a stick of gum. "Of course I'd like them taken down."

Within a week McAllen Friend fixed it so that Harold didn't have to read the derogatory comments on the bedsheets when he drove to work in the morning. He noticed that where they'd hung there now were flaky black combs of charred wood, and he figured the boy must have torched them. It wasn't the kind of incident to make the newspapers, because if a fraternity wasn't drunk and disorderly and egging another's living quarters, it was drunk and disorderly and trying to burn it down.

"You and me," Harold told McAllen the next day at the athletic dormitory, "we come from the same people, don't we, hardhead?"

| 12 |

On Christmas Eve, while he and Rena slept, somebody wrapped toilet paper around the century-old oaks and magnolias on their front lawn, beat in their garbage cans and aluminum mailbox with a baseball bat and scrawled HAROLD DON'T WIN SHIT in purple and gold spray paint on the side of the house. Under the words they painted some Greek letters that dripped and ran together illegibly. On the cement driveway was the slogan REVENGE OF THE RULING CLASS and a crude rendering of a hand shooting the bird.

Next morning at dawn, Harold walked around with his hands in the pockets of his flannel bathrobe, inspecting the damage. He tried to keep calm: it was Christmas and he'd hoped to enjoy it. He and Rena had planned to drive to her mother Lottie's for a turkey dinner, but now that would have to be canceled.

"I'm really sorry," he told her. "I know you wanted to see your old mama. Maybe we can go next week."

"Next week isn't Christmas."

"Then we can go later tonight."

"The turkey'll be dry tonight."

Harold said he didn't want people driving up and down the

street to read that he didn't win shit when once he had never lost. He would have to clean it up, he said, starting with the toilet paper in the trees.

"For some reason I suspect your hand in this," Rena said. "Are you responsible, Harold?"

"You think I'd wreck my own house to get out of seeing your mother?" He laughed and kicked a bag of trash. "I always got along with Lottie. It's you I don't like."

On the driveway Rena bent down and ran her hands over the graffiti to see if the paint would rub off. None did. "Who is the ruling class, anyway?" she said. "And why would they want revenge—for what?"

"The rich and powerful rule," he answered. "Most people learn that before they pass from the diddie."

As he went to pick up the flattened mailbox, Harold stopped short feeling something red and unutterably hot wash through him. It started at his feet, moved up his legs, through his intestines and came to a stop at his lungs. There it seemed to turn up its color and temperature before moving into his neck and head, where it finally escaped through his ears. Whatever it was—some quick little virus or, as he would later describe it to Rena, "a germ of premonition of things to come"—it dropped him to his knees.

The sod was cold and wet, and it rolled under Harold's weight. When he was sure Rena was looking, he pulled his hands out of his pockets and raised them high. "My God, my God," he bellowed. "Why have you forsaken me?"

Rena was standing across the yard in a faded yellow nightgown through which he could see the knobby points of her breasts and a bushy black patch in the middle of her legs.

"You don't win enough is why," she said. "God ignores us losers."

| **13** |

It was less than a week later that Chester Tully, so excited he could hardly operate his tongue, told Harold about the petitions. Chester'd been out one night with his wife and kids at a popular $1.98-steak place off the interstate, and there it was at the checkout counter, a list of names "that absolutely, positively refused to quit." He asked the woman at the register if the manager was around, and upon learning he'd already left for the evening, Chester tore up the stack of papers and threw it in the air like so much confetti.

"Good for you, hardhead," Harold told Chester, who swelled with pride. They embraced for the first time since Chester took the job when he was twenty-two years old. He was now fifty-one.

"Don't let them trash your old coach," Harold said wisely. " 'Cause when they do that they trash everything you stand for."

Other copies of the petition were floating around town, and like the one at the steakhouse they demanded that the board force Harold to step down. The smear campaign was well organized and funded by wealthy alumni, Harold and his coaches decided, because for an entire week a full-page advertisement ran in the city paper: "Dear Football Fans Who're Tired of Losing . . ." After disparaging Harold and his record, it included some of the signatures of people who'd signed the petition and their malicious comments.

The name that surprised and hurt Harold the most was Little Shorty Grieg's, his former Heisman Trophy winner. Little Shorty had signed his name triple the size of everyone except ex–university chancellor Burl Mandeville, whose own was so conspicuous it resembled a child's crayon drawing of a buffalo herd.

Larry McDuff and Little Shorty Grieg lived in the same neighborhood, out near an oil refinery on the edge of the city, and with Harold's urging, Larry agreed to stop by Little Shorty's after work and find out why he'd signed the petition. "And remind him he owes me half that trophy," Harold said. "Damn thing should be on my shelf right now."

The next day, after he'd finished the job with Little Shorty, Larry walked straight up to Harold and embraced him just as Chester had some days before. It'd been twenty-nine years for him, too, and he made it count. Some of the coffee Harold was holding spilled onto the sleeve of his expensive dress shirt, and he lit into the coach. "Forget about wanting to love me up, boy," he yelled, "and tell me what that muscle-bound redneck had to say."

Larry showed caution, hoping not to upset Harold any more than he already was, but he overdid the part describing what had become of Little Shorty. Larry said he walked up and knocked on the door in the carport, and through the screen he could see into the kitchen where Little Shorty and a woman were hunched over a cookie sheet crowded with baked sweet potatoes. Little Shorty had a cigarette in his mouth, making him squint, the smoke curling up to a bare bulb hanging by a cord from the ceiling; the woman had a web of bobby pins in her hair and a mask of cold cream over her face. She was wearing only a brassiere and panties, and her figure was as extraordinary as her face was unattractive—nature's way of balancing things out, Larry ventured. It wasn't Little Shorty's wife, though, because Larry knew Betty Anne: a woman with more self-respect than to dress like a walking lingerie advertisement while cooking sweet potatoes.

Larry knocked again, confident they hadn't heard him the first time, and immediately Little Shorty lunged for a butter knife lying on the table. He was even littler and shorter than Larry remembered him and still had more hair on his neck and forearms than most men have on their head and chest. Little Shorty's eyes, once particularly appealing to women, were now like those of a poisonous snake killed dead in the road. But despite his hard physical bearing, Little Shorty had a beautiful mouth. His lips were full and red like strips of salmon flesh or some other exotic fish you find, in this part of the country, only in colorful tin cans on the shelves at fancy food stores.

"Don't stab nobody, hardhead," Larry called through the door. "It's only your old teammate McDuffy come to say hello."

There was a Chrysler parked in the carport, and he and Little Shorty sat on the hood and talked in whispers so the woman couldn't hear them through the screen. Betty Anne was off for a few days visiting her mother at a nursing home in some town to the north, Little Shorty said, and this was a neighbor friend of theirs, a divorcée by the name of Frances who made extra money selling candied sweet potato pies around the neighborhood. Her stove was gas, and she wasn't able to get the pilot light going, so she'd come over to Little Shorty's to use his.

"Ain't she dressed odd?" Larry said.

"Well, yes, she is," Little Shorty answered, thinking hard on the question. It took him a minute to come up with something: "Under-things makes it cooler in the kitchen, what with the stove set to bake. She don't intend no fashion statement by it."

Little Shorty wouldn't admit he was involved with the woman any more than he'd admitted, back in the Tenpenny days, breaking curfew. He was either sleepwalking or he'd been temporarily kid-napped by gamblers who'd warned him to throw the next game or else, but he hadn't broken curfew.

"You want to tell me why you signed that petition on Harold?" Larry said. "Everybody at the stadium's been wondering."

"I really didn't read it to know it was about the Old Man," Little Shorty said, his eyes on Frances at the screen. "Some lawyer who said he knew me came over and you know how a lawyer can get you to sign things. I'm glad it wasn't no lawyer stopped by looking to sell magazines. Betty Anne and me already got plenty of 'em." He pointed to stacks of *Sports Afield* and *Modern Romances* leaning against the wall of the house.

"All the Old Man helped you with," Larry said, "and you let them use you to try and get rid of him." The way it sounded, he might have been scolding a child, and it brought Frances closer to the door. Larry saw how the steam from the potatoes had made her Noxzema run in crooked rivulets down her neck, over her pale chunky breasts and into her brassiere.

"If not for the Old Man, Little Shorty, you never would've won the Heisman. Nobody would know your name."

Larry could tell Little Shorty didn't know how to interpret this charge, whether to laugh because it was a joke or ask him to leave because it wasn't. He settled on something in between. "But if not for the Old Man," Little Shorty said, "Pogo wouldn't of gone off and killed that man."

As best he could, Larry argued the point. He reminded Little

Shorty of what Pogo had said at his trial about Harold being nowhere in sight at the time of the killing. But Little Shorty chuckled and said, "Pogo was too fine a person to pull Harold Gravely into the stew with him."

Larry could tell Little Shorty was telling the truth because he couldn't look him in the eye: lying, he could have, but never when he was being honest. "You're only defending Pogo because he defended you way back when. He was the one making the holes and letting you run and not getting his picture in the paper."

"True," Little Shorty said, "but there's other reasons, too. I should've known what really happened that night, because I was there myself—or at least I was in the bar sitting with the two of them and Rena, right before it happened."

"Yet you'd be perfectly happy to have everyone believe you were an eyewitness." Larry shook his head in disgust. "While you were guzzling cocktails your best friend in the world was out in the parking lot killing someone over getting his car keyed."

Little Shorty turned away from Larry and rested his chin on his chest. "You'd have to laugh if it wasn't so sad," he said.

Larry laughed. "If what wasn't so sad?"

"How it all turned out."

Larry threw up his arms. "How it all turned out? How all of what turned out?"

"I think you know."

From the door Frances said, "I've noticed McDuffy here sounds more like a preacher of the Bible than a football coach. All he needs is a collection basket to pass and his own television ministry. But if I had to guess, I'd say he looks more like a blue-ribbon hog than anything. My god, he's fat."

"Pogo Reese may have seemed all right on the outside," Larry continued, ignoring the woman, "but his innards were corrupt. I ask you, is the Old Man to blame for that? And should he have to answer to something that happened thirty years ago and that somebody else is guilty of? Why punish him now?"

"Don't pretend with me," Little Shorty said, chuckling. "Pogo Reese ain't the reason Harold Gravely is being fired. Harold Gravely forgot how to win is why."

"A mere technicality," Larry said. "There's always next year. And if not then, there's the year after that."

"We been hearing you say that going on seven years now. And every new year is worse than the one before it."

"Next season will be different. I promise."

Now it was Little Shorty's turn to laugh, and though he was powerful enough to shake the whole neighborhood with it, he didn't. He gazed with sad eyes at the woman in the door and said, "Why does it hurt to remember how it was when we was little children playing games? This is what I keep asking myself."

"You got a doozy of a question there," Larry said, "but I think you're asking the wrong person. That woman couldn't tell you the color of milk if she was drinking it."

Little Shorty crossed his arms and inhaled deeply. "The first year Pogo was in the pen," he said, still looking at Frances, "I visited him. He said he was happy and well fed. But he was worried about my leg being tore up at Oakland and what I'd do without football. We didn't talk about what'd happened to him. I told him we was counting the days, but he said not to. Next time I went he wouldn't see me. He just stayed in his cell. And the next time, too. Finally I quit going. Can you believe how long ago that was?" He closed his eyes and seemed to count the days. "He's been out now more years than he was in. I never hear a word from him. The phone rings but it ain't him."

When Little Shorty tried to say something else, the words seemed to stick in the cracks of his teeth. He pounded the car with clenched fists, producing a sound like thunder.

"You never did graduate, did you," Larry asked once Little Shorty had gotten control of himself. "You're the only one in the class didn't get your diploma and move on to a professional career."

Little Shorty took the insult better than Larry had expected; it was Frances who became incensed. "Selling auto parts ain't a professional career?" she said.

"You asking or telling me?" Larry wondered aloud.

"Books always gave me trouble," Little Shorty said. "But that didn't make me unequal. I was in school to play football, which I understood and liked. What's odd is I never really been interested in the game since what happened to Pogo. People thought I'd turned bitter because of the knee and missing out on being a pro, but that wasn't it. I quit going because I knew that when I looked out on the field, I'd see him leading the student body sweep, taking out some big old bastard and giving me room to roam. Pogo did more to get me that trophy than the Old Man. And for all he did, he never asked for no credit. Harold was the one tried to cut a deal with me that the trophy stayed at his house half the year. He said I owed him that much."

They talked until it got dark and the sky turned orange from the flares of the refinery. Little Shorty reminded Larry that Harold had also run off and married Pogo Reese's girlfriend not long after he was packed off to prison, but Larry interrupted. "I won't discuss Miss Rena with you, hardhead," he said, looking at Frances through the screen. "Especially not after what I've witnessed here today. You two ought to be ashamed."

The woman returned his stare, with eyes as hard as Little Shorty's when he was telling a lie.

"She's here baking pies," Little Shorty said as Larry, jingling the change and keys in his pockets, walked to his car parked on the street. "We ain't done nothing that normal neighbors don't do," he added.

Larry lifted an arm and waved without looking back.

"But if we'd done something," Frances called behind him, "it wouldn't of been when I was wearing my teeth. You ever been sucked on by a gal who wasn't wearing no teeth?"

| **14** |

It took Larry about an hour to tell the story, mainly because Harold kept getting up from his chair, walking into the outer office and screaming as if he were in pain. "Why'd I ever give you the ball, Little Shorty!" And, "Wait till I talk to Betty Anne, you worthless sonofabitch!" Each time he returned to the room he unwrapped a fresh stick of Juicy Fruit and stuck it in his mouth, then slurped on a pint of whiskey. The flavor of the gum mellowed the booze, he explained, offering both the gum and the bottle to his coaches.

Larry and Chester were sharing a family-size bag of potato

chips, a tin of French onion dip and a liter of Coke. The other assistants, sitting in the shadows near the chalk- and inkboards, were doing their best not to move and draw attention to themselves.

After each swallow, Harold coughed from deep within his chest and spit into a paper cup, cocking his head back and more or less rocket-firing a wad of hock from his mouth. There was a strange, alarming color to what came up, more bloody than whiskey streaked. Harold seemed to enjoy showing it off to everybody. As soon as they saw it, the coaches coughed and needed to spit themselves.

"What would turn a person pink like that?" Harold said.

If anyone knew, he kept it to himself. Once the meeting was adjourned and everybody left, Harold sat at his desk and spit and spit until he thought he'd dehydrate. Mrs. Claude entered the office and asked if there was anything she could do to help make him feel better. "Maybe we could warm the cushions," she said.

Harold studied the contents of his cup. "Tell me what would turn a person pink like that," he said, holding it up to her.

"Maybe it's the Lord's way of telling you you need to floss more often," she said without bothering to look. "I know sometimes when I don't floss my gums bleed and when I rinse everything's red as roses."

More than two weeks passed before Harold complained to Doc Cage that his chest felt like a furnace and there was something funny coming up with his spit. Lately in the mornings, he said, he blew gobs of mucus into Kleenex tissues, and he went days without an appetite, even for gum and booze. On the telephone with high school recruits, he coughed so much they hung up and wouldn't answer when he called back. He was starting to sound like a zombie and was tired of spooking people.

"You think the stress of the job finally got to me," Harold asked. "Nowadays in this country you get a hangnail on your toe it's stress-related, ain't that right, Doc?"

John Ford Cage was Harold's oldest friend, a general practitioner who'd been with him since the Tenpenny days. Cage said it could very well have something to do with job tension but that more likely it was related to his lungs. He recommended a visit to a local surgeon the next day for tests.

"What kind of tests?" Harold wanted to know.

"They'll probably get you to give them some sputum to check for any abnormalities," Cage said.

"But supposing I don't want to give them no sputum?"

"You'll just cough up some spit in a cup."

"Spitting's one thing, Doc, but I don't know about no sputum. Last time I gave sputum was to check my sperm count, and that didn't make me look so good."

The doctor's face brightened, but he made sure not to laugh. He ran his fingers over his scruffy white beard, which reached all the way down to his shirt collar, then through his wild uncombed hair, which bristled with static. "Sputum is the stuff you been coughing up, son. It has nothing to do with your peter. You're thinking of jizzum."

"Well," Harold said, "I got plenty of sputum, if it's sputum they're after. I can give them all the sputum they want, probably more'n they've ever seen come out of any one man."

"They might also want to do a bronchoscopy," Cage said, "which sounds worse than it really is. There'll be an instrument the doctor'll be able to see your lungs with. He can take a tissue sample with it and see what it is that's been giving you all the trouble. Then they might want to run a lung scan, which is like an X ray. It won't be bad, I promise."

"Why so soon, then?" Harold said. "That's what I don't like about all this—you making me go so damn soon."

Cage said it would make Harold feel better knowing there was nothing to worry about, but Harold protested.

"I feel fine," he said, "for somebody who's always felt like fried meat, that is."

He was nervous and for some reason was clawing at Cage's hand, meaning to shake it, but touching Cage made him feel sentimental and cowardly and he pulled his hand away. "They won't have to put me to sleep, will they, Doc?"

"Nah," Cage answered. "You can eyeball the whole show."

| 15 |

Exactly three days later, a surgeon whose last name Harold couldn't pronounce was telling him his options: surgery to remove part of the diseased right lung, radiation treatments to reduce the size and retard the growth of the cancer, or nothing.

Harold remained expressionless when Dr. Hiburotot of the city hospital and wellness center told him the news. Hiburotot's droning voice was strong and encouraging and fearless and reminded Harold of Doc Hardhead's delivery on the day he'd informed him he was about as fertile as a stone. Instead of looking in Harold's eyes, the surgeon gazed at Cage and gesticulated elaborately with the most remarkable-looking pair of hands Harold had ever seen. They were tiny, fat and pink. It occurred to Harold that if you crossed a baby pig with a pink bird this was what you'd get: Hiburotot's hands.

The surgeon asked if Harold had any questions.

"Well," he said, clearing his throat, which was still raw and sore from all the probing, "of course I do."

Cage waited with patient eyes. "Tell me, son," he said.

"You think . . . ," Harold began, turning away from Hiburotot and addressing his friend. "How serious is it?"

Cage nodded. "Pretty serious."

"Then how long I got?"

"You quite possibly could live to see a hundred and ten, Mr. Gravely," the surgeon replied, leaning back in his big leather chair. "That, however, is only if we act now. Left untreated, this is a terminal illness. But we have every intention of acting immediately and doing what we can to try to avoid—"

"Enough from you," Harold snapped without glancing back at the doctor. "I'm talking to John Ford Cage here. A man hears he's dying and you won't even let him talk to his pal."

"At this point, sir," Hiburotot murmured, "you're no closer to death than I am. Moreover, you should—"

"You think," Harold said to Cage, shutting his eyes and shaking his head, "you think the school might consider keeping the old hardhead around if they knew he didn't have too long? Another season. Two, maybe?"

Tears filled Cage's eyes, and an incredulous smile parted his lips. His chest started to heave and stutter and then he laughed, which made Harold laugh too. "You're kidding me, right, son? You're trying to be brave."

"Bastards wanting to run me out of my own house," Harold whispered. "You know the ones I mean, Doc."

Cage slapped at Harold's knee. "Yes," he said, "I know them. But they're not to die for. They're not that important."

Hiburotot's face soured at Harold's reaction and he topped his bald pate with crossed hands. Harold's blood-streaked sputum had shown abnormal cells, and the bronchoscopy had revealed a small malignant tumor on the lower lobe of his right lung. If the cancer did not metastasize, Harold could easily be saved. "But we've had countless patients here with a far worse prognosis than yours, Mr. Gravely, who opted for the lobectomy, recovered and are now enjoying full, perfectly satisfying lives."

"Is that right?" Harold said, finally turning in his chair to confront him.

As Hiburotot began to answer in the affirmative, Harold suddenly barked like a dog, just as for years he had instructed his hardheads to bark. He snarled and yelped; he yipped and he yapped. His ears flattened against the sides of his head, and his spine rolled. He felt his fingernails grip the arms of the Naugahyde wing chair, his toes peel under and lock.

"Relax now, son," Cage said.

But not until the surgeon left the room did Harold stop the noise and wipe the spit from his jowls.

| 16 |

Outside the hospital Harold half-jogged to the car. Every ten feet or so he leaped and shouted something unintelligible for all his joy. To keep up Cage had to walk so fast the joints in his knees and hips burned and his heart beat loudly in his ears. He was barely through the door of the Cadillac when Harold squealed off through the parking lot, leaving curved streaks of rubber at every turn and sending pedestrians scattering for safety.

"You'd think you'd just won the lottery," Cage muttered, "not that you were damn near dead."

Harold smiled broadly and started drumming the steering wheel with his thumbs. "You should be happy I'm not crying and complaining," he said. "Most people would, you know."

Cage groaned and scratched his whiskers. "You've got some mighty big decisions to make," he said, "and not the kind a normal person wouldn't feel like crying and complaining over." He reached over and stopped Harold's drumming. "I keep telling myself you're putting on, making light of things to prove how brave you are."

Harold was quiet, weighing the effect this news would have on everyone. What he wouldn't do to see the faces of board members who'd turned against him when he asked for help, and of that woman Helen Dumars whose papier-mâché head he'd bashed with a walking cane so many years ago. With joy he thought of Little Shorty, who he was convinced was as responsible as anyone for the drive to have him fired, and of the delinquent on the telephone who'd threatened to bury his rooter in the dirt. How would they feel about themselves when they learned the boss hardhead wouldn't be around for much more of their ugly business? Harold has cancer? they would say. The Old Man's gonna die? What would they make of someone who accepted the fate issued him with the pluck and valor of a champion?

"They'll be on their hands and knees trying to make it up to me," Harold told Cage, who plainly was confused. "They'll be lined up from here to Tioga."

Cage glared at the passing scenery, his head resting against the window. "Nice town, Tioga."

"They'll bake cakes and pies and casseroles and bring them by the house. They'll want to see the pillow where I used to rest my head." He barked a little and pounded the wheel. "And all because I slept there."

Cage didn't want to hear any more of it. "Yes," he said, "and they'll see courage where before there was only arrogance."

They drove on, neither saying a word for several blocks, but both feeling the tension building between them. At last Cage said, "I recommend you get some rest, son. Take it easy for a week or two and stay out of the office. And soon as possible, when you're of sound mind, talk this over with Rena."

"Without the surgery or any radiation or anything," Harold said, ignoring the advice, "will I make the bowl season?"

"As your physician," Cage answered, speaking in a voice that wasn't his but Hiburotot's, "I must advise you to undergo the surgery. Without it you are playing with a loaded gun."

"But as Doc Hardhead," Harold said, "and my best friend in the world, how much time would I get?"

Cage's Adam's apple bobbed in his skinny neck. The rims of his eyes reddened. But he wasn't long getting it out: "It depends on the cancer. If it spreads . . . if it spreads through the rest of the lung, then up into the lymphatic system and then, say, to the brain—oh, God, come on now, son."

"But if it doesn't. If it stays local there in the lung, would I make the bowl season? Would I see Christmas?"

"That's not a yes or no question. I can't answer you."

Harold checked his coat and pants pockets for Juicy Fruit but didn't find any. All of a sudden his appetite had returned, his thirst with it. He rifled through the glove compartment looking for the pewter flask he usually kept there but pulled out only maps, grocery-store receipts and the vehicle registration, all of which fell into the doctor's lap. They passed an oyster bar and when Harold asked Cage to join him for a drink and some supper, he wasn't interested. With a wave of his hand the doctor indicated he'd prefer to get on back. "It's only two o'clock in the afternoon," Cage said, which for some reason inspired Harold to whoop and holler like a man facing midnight after hours on a drinking binge. "Well, not quite two," Cage said, checking his watch. "It's closer to three."

Harold barked again. Cage was slumped against the passenger's door, looking the way Harold figured most people looked after learning someone they knew had cancer. Cage looked sick himself, sicker than Harold.

"Cheer up, Doc," he said, gripping Cage's shoulder and giving it a squeeze. "It's a relief. Really."

"You don't know what you're saying, son."

"The last time I had this kind of timing was thirty years ago when I stood up on that bench in the dressing room at old Tulane Stadium. I knew then something good was coming, and I know it now. I can feel it, down to the bone."

"You don't know squat, son," Cage said.

"God looked down from his cloudy throne, saw what I needed most in this life, then placed his hand on my shoulder. He did it once a long time ago, and he did it again today." Harold's Cadillac had a sunroof, and though it was cold out he cracked it open a couple of inches and spoke up through it: "God bless Harold Gravely. I'm talking to you, hardhead."

Cage was not a temperamental man, but what he said next thundered from his lips. "Ever wonder about what kind of man you might have become if you'd lost that damn Tenpenny game? Not to mention what kind of coach."

Harold sneered, but he didn't speak.

"I think your priorities are all wrong, son," Cage told him. "You spend too much time looking back on something that happened when football was leather helmets and no TV, and you forget there's a forward way to go, too, not just a back."

"We might not of had TV," Harold said, "but we had radio. And right now I'm gonna call you a senile old fool for stating we wore leather hats when you and I both know we didn't."

"You're missing my point, son. I don't see those Tenpenny days as being the most important, though I enjoyed them and wouldn't ever trade them off. There was my wedding day, for example, and the birth of my children and my grandchildren. These are things I count as more satisfying. They endure for me in detail that only sharpens with time. And then there was seeing my wife enroll at the university. That had a meaning that I enjoy to this day."

Harold had heard enough. If it were anyone else seated next to him he might have pulled over and told him to get out. "Seeing your wife walking around campus with a stack of schoolbooks tucked under her arm used to shame me for knowing her. I'd see her gray hair fit in a ponytail, and the ribbons she wore and them stone-washed jeans—"

"Priorities, son," Cage said, cutting him off. The memory Harold described seemed to please him immensely. "In that woman going back to school I saw the birth of something new. She was looking ahead, not back. What can I do today to improve myself? How can I get better? These are the questions she was asking herself, and I found it invigorating, even romantic." He tapped Harold on the shoulder and winked at him. "The past, when I stare at it too hard—it either bores or blinds me, son."

Near the campus gates Harold stopped for some liquor and gum at a package store and was drinking and chewing, mixing the two, before he'd settled back into his seat.

Cage rejected Harold's offer of a swallow of bourbon, but he did accept a stick of gum. Harold was delighted that Cage seemed to enjoy it, and told him so.

"It's nice as gum goes," Cage said. "But unless I'm mistaken it wasn't you who cooked it up."

Harold folded another stick and put it in his mouth. "Used to be this place off the interstate—a K mart or something—where you could buy three plenty packs for a dollar."

"I don't remember it," Cage said, looking worried.

"It went out of business. But the last day it was open I sent Rena for all the gum she could buy. They were on sale at a dime apiece, cheapest I ever heard of, so she loaded up the buggy. She came home with probably a hundred packs, which comes to exactly five hundred pieces of gum. I can say that's one of the nicest things my wife ever done for me."

Cage shook his head. "You'd think a man who only minutes before learned he had cancer would be distraught, shedding an ocean of tears, on the verge of a nervous breakdown. Yet here you sit talking about a deal you once got on Juicy Fruit."

"It was Rena who got it, Doc, not me. And as I tell anybody

who doesn't understand my mortal craving for gum and whiskey, Elvis Presley was stuck on peanut butter and banana sandwiches dripping with mayonnaise. He'd get up in the middle of the night, eat until he couldn't breathe, take a handful of sleeping pills and go back to bed."

"Did he have a snort of whiskey every time he ate one of these sandwiches?" Cage said, tightening his brow.

"He'd of been married to Rena Cummins Gravely he surely would have. I promise you that, hardhead."

I Recognize Harold Gravely! Do You?

17

Rena has decided to let the hair under her arms grow out. This morning, after running her bath, she carries a hand mirror with her into the tub and eyes the progress of the invidious fuzz. She personally knows no women who wear underarm hair, and the few times she encountered some in public, she found herself staring. The recent sight of one at Boone Sweeney's grocery, for instance, prompted her to gawk. "Wanna autograph," the woman asked, hurriedly pushing her shopping cart past Rena.

Those who didn't shave were dirty and best kept at a distance, she believed, and of a type: rebel or slouch. The rebels found it sexy; an article in the health and hygiene section of one of her magazines referred to armpit hair as "devilish and French." The slouches were too slovenly or ill-bred to care. She herself can settle comfortably in neither category, though her behavior of late has demonstrated a definite lean toward the seditious.

The hair under her arms is of its own mind, growing neither straight and soft like the hair on her head nor coarse and curly like her pubic hair. It is nice and silky but sprouting every which way, rather, she has noted, like the teeth of a garden rake that has been used too long.

If Harold were to learn of her little project, she is certain he would refuse to sleep in the same bed with her. He might even leave her. Momentarily she despises herself for thinking that perhaps this is what she's after: a final act of tyranny that would allow her to avoid his slow, proud death as much as she has sought to avoid the last ten years of their life together. He hasn't touched her in more than six months; she hasn't let him. But even if they had managed time together he probably still wouldn't have noticed the hair. In the dark with her arms pressed to her side, he couldn't have seen much anyway. In the light with her arms over her head, her hands clutching the headboard—then, too, the image of Nancy Claude would have competed with her own.

With Harold as with no one else Rena's ever known it is possible to look at one thing and see another.

Only her oldest sister Bonita knows of the hair, and she lives twelve hundred miles away in a northeastern city where such cosmetic modifications are socially accepted. "I figure," Rena told her on the phone, "that it wouldn't grow there if not for a purpose." Bonita acted as if Rena had confided the lurid details of an ongoing infidelity and hung up in tears.

The hair has been growing only a few weeks now—half an inch long and not thick enough to appear all of a piece. She has found that it makes her sweat more than when she shaved, and the odor, though faint, is not unlike that which surrounds a man and a woman after they've made love. This she tolerates, however grudgingly: neither deodorants nor baking powder has proven strong enough to stamp it out entirely. In the tub now she combs the hair downward then upward with a boar-bristle brush she has reserved for this activity alone. Combing herself this way makes her sleepy, and she rests the back of her neck on the edge of the tub and leans back in the steaming hot water.

Having already called Harold to tell him she doesn't love him anymore, she decides a leisurely drive through town and a movie might be an appropriate celebration. Nothing playing at the nearest multiplex cinema looks very interesting, but she decides to go anyway, if only for the chance to sit in a dark, cavernous room and eat chocolate-covered raisins. Rena is a regular moviegoer, favoring space-adventure and horror films. In particular she avoids love stories or anything that suggests the scantest possibility of romance. These films, she has discovered, leave her lonely and blue, wishing for things that will never be hers. Sometimes the picture of two handsome young people holding hands is all it takes to break her heart into a million pieces.

Now in the garage she takes care to warm up her Ford Falcon before leaving for the afternoon. The little white car was a gift from Harold on their tenth wedding anniversary; used primarily for trips to Sweeney's, the mall and the movies, it has less than fifty thousand miles on it and until only the last year or two was in perfect working order. The brake pads need to be changed, the radiator periodically acts up and overheats the engine and the exhaust has rusted out, but all these imperfections add up to what she calls a "real adventure in driving." Empty soda cans and grocery receipts crowd both the front and back floors, and dust lies thick on the dash, making it difficult to read the panel.

About ten years ago, nearing the twenty-year mark in their marriage, Harold suggested they buy her a new car, but she wasn't interested. "An automobile," she told him, "is to get me from point A to point B. At my age I don't much care what it looks like. And you shouldn't either." This was a far cry from what she likes to call "the old days," when she was a college freshman and willing to date almost any good-looking guy as long as he drove a nice, hot car. In fact, she might have never met Pogo Reese if not for his Cadillac.

Parked in the shade of a vast sycamore tree near the dormitory where she lived, it was the finest thing she'd ever seen. Pogo, whom she knew only by reputation, was covering its tail fins with perfect circles of polish. He wore white tennis shorts that brought out the deep color of his heavily muscled thighs and a gray sleeveless sweatshirt with PROPERTY OF UNIV. ATHLETIC DEPT. stenciled across the chest. To this day it surprises her to think that she approached him first. "Weatherman says a storm front's moving in," she said. "No use in washing it now." He told her he'd mind his own business if she'd agree to do the same; then he stiffened his shoulders. "This," he said, "is an Eldorado Biarritz, by the way, one of only eight hundred and fifteen produced by Cadillac this year." This declaration brought a handsome blush to his cheeks. "And I'm not washing it," he added, holding up a can of polish. "This is wax."

"Washing, waxing," she said. "Same thing."

He was too superior to correct her. With precision he began to move a raggedy white cloth over the taillights; instead of turning the hose on the hood he spat when he needed a little water. He was no more interested in learning her name than he was in the banks of dark clouds filling the sky. Who but a jock, she wondered, would be so bold as to wear tennis shorts in late October, even if it was fifty-five degrees out?

"Who do you think you are?" she asked him. "Just because your daddy bought you a big car—"

"This is a Biarritz," he said. "How many times am I going to have to tell you that?"

"One of only eight hundred and fifteen produced by Cadillac, right?" she said. Then she pointed to the tin of polish he was holding. "And that's wax."

They didn't speak for what seemed like hours. She sat at the foot of the tree and watched him work; periodically he turned and stared at her, his eyes so blue and deep. When he was done he said, "I was wondering if you might like to go for a little spin."

She was quiet, standing now with her hands behind her back, peeling the mottled gray bark away in strips.

He lowered the windows and converted the roof to a ceiling of open air. "It's kinda cold out this afternoon," he said impatiently, "but are we going for a ride or not?"

He would skip class to work on his car, and what intrigued her was that it was so beautifully engineered that a periodic oil change was the only real attention it required. He simply wanted to be near it, to rub a cloth over the tail fins, to smell the warm engine, to clean smashed bugs from the grille. Every slip of paper in the glove compartment was in its place, and the trunk, she joked, was as "roomy as an apartment somebody might want to rent."

On the road he was careful to stay clear of traffic, and he often complained about the "herd mentality." Although it almost always took longer, he traveled back streets that promised acres of room and no threat of collision. Out in the open, he was never afraid of driving fast, of testing the engine by pushing it at speeds double and sometimes triple the legal limit.

During the weeks of his murder trial, she often couldn't sleep nights for the loud memory of his car, and this had left her pale with guilt. How could she think about an automobile, she wondered, when the man she loved would soon be picking cotton in a field adjacent to the state pen, sleeping on a straw mattress, sharing table scraps with convicted felons? "If you get over him," her best friend Polly said, "you'll get over his car. You've been double whammied and it'll just take some time." Her mother was less understanding. Her feelings for Pogo Reese were nothing more than a schoolgirl crush, she said; Rena hadn't known him long enough to love him. "Until this," Lottie said, meaning the murder, "he was too perfect for you."

If Rena didn't argue, it was because she knew this to be true. Pogo's winter tan really had been too perfect, and so had his tall, shiny hat of hair. He was rich and she was poor; he was porcelain and she was brass.

With Harold, everyone seemed to agree, she got what she deserved. Every other year he came home with a new Cadillac, compliments of the athletic department. But unlike Pogo's, Harold's Cadillac was always one of tens of thousands made, and an identical model was liable to pull up and stop right across the street from him and Rena at any time of the day or night. Same model, same color. Electric windows that cried like hamsters when wet. Blackwall tires. Spoked hubcaps that seemed to think collecting mud was the reason they'd been invented. And if she got a good peek through the glass, she generally saw people who looked just like Harold and herself: a man and a woman of ordinary appearance gazing back in the common heat of recognition.

The threats of general flooding and power failure had closed both public and private schools less than half an hour ago, at noon, and now on Florida Boulevard Rena is stuck behind a crowded yellow bus creeping along at under twenty miles an hour. The rear windows have clouded with fog, and the children have fingered drawings on them. One is of a boy with what looks like snakes and wieners on top of his head, and below it the caption KELLY DELAUNEY HAS COOTIES. Through holes in the dark windows, the faces of a dozen small boys gaze out, as white and gorgeous as moons. "You were a child once," Rena says aloud, talking to herself. "Ha!"

Even though it has the green light, the bus stops at an intersection. The front and side doors fold open, and instead of children stepping out, four adults in orange slickers board it. One of the women carries a placard that says I RECOGNIZE HAROLD GRAVELY! DO YOU? Through the unshaded portions of the glass Rena sees them walking up and down the aisle, soliciting money for their lidded cups. Few of the children at the rear of the bus give, and those who do offer only change. Behind her several cars have stopped, and now they blow horns that sound musical in the rain. She, too, blows her horn, inciting one of the boys on the backseat. He turns and shoots her the bird, a lascivious smile lifting his dark red lips.

"Oh, no, you weren't," Rena tells herself. "You were never a child." Defiantly she returns the gesture and pumps the horn again. "You were born full grown." In moments dozens of small hands reciprocate, and one of them writes the word BITCH across the top of the back pane.

"I beg your pardon!" she says, addressing the children. She's starting to get out when the bus drives off, blowing black darts of exhaust at her. Before she can get behind the wheel again the light flashes yellow then fixes on red, initiating more musical horns behind her. "Okay, okay!" she mutters, rattled now, nerves sending electric spurts through her fingers. "I'm trying, I'm trying!"

One of the people who boarded the bus approaches the Falcon. Rena's window is up, and she reaches and locks the door. When he taps on the glass she looks down at the trash on the floor on the passenger's side, then pretends to be trying to find something in the glove compartment. Other collectors dressed in plastic ponchos and raincoats try the cars behind her, but from what Rena can see in the rearview mirror no one is offering anything besides angry complaints for being held so long at the traffic light.

Again the man at the door taps the glass, and Rena is shocked to hear him speak her name. "We're here for the statue," he says. "For your husband, Mrs. Gravely."

Rena turns and stares into the man's face, which isn't one she recalls ever having seen before. It's the color of putty, with skin as lined with age as a crumpled paper bag. His eyes move mechanically in their sockets, from side to side, settling on no particular spot on her face. Because of his eyes, she can't bear to look at him but for a moment. "Do you know me?" she says, allowing a crack in the window. "How do you know me?"

"I'm not an idiot," the man says. "You're his wife."

"But how do you know me?" she says. "Tell me why you think I'm who you say I am."

Rainwater drips under his plastic hood and down the man's face, and he licks his upper lip to frustrate a desire to smile. "We met once about—" He stands upright now and shouts at one of the others. "Hey, honey. Joni! How long ago was it we met Harold's wife?"

While he waits for an answer Rena digs into her coat pocket for some money, but all she finds is a slip of newspaper listing the starting times of the movies at the multiplex. From her purse she extracts the first bill she can grab.

"About twenty-eight years ago," the man is saying, resting his elbows on the side of the car and speaking into the inch-wide crack in the window. "You sold my wife an Easter bonnet when you were working at Champs LaRoux's." His haughty laugh is to let her know that what he's about to say isn't to be taken seriously. "Don't you remember?" he says. "Think hard now."

"I don't remember," she replies, expressionless. "I don't remember you at all. And I don't recall ever meeting anyone named Joni, either."

"It's not all our station in life to be recognized," he says. "At one of our committee meetings your husband reminded us of that. Not everybody can score the touchdowns, he said. Somebody's got to handle the water bucket, somebody's got to bore the holes in the line, somebody's got to bring up the cheers."

Through the narrow slit in the window she offers the man a bill. "And somebody's got to go," she says smartly, startled to see that she's just handed him fifty dollars.

He holds it with trembling hands. "This is more than I've made all day," he says, studying its face. "I really didn't mean it serious, you know—tapping your window for money. I saw who you were and hoped to say hello."

Rena rolls down the window. "Then give it back."

"Give it back?"

"You heard me. Give it back."

Rena crunches the money into a ball and throws it on the trashy floor. The man stares at his empty hands. Then with tires squealing on the wet pavement she drives through the red light, nearly sideswiping a pickup. In the middle of the road the man with the mechanical eyes is too startled to move, and he takes the force of the water from Rena's advance dead in the chest.

| **18** |

At around twelve noon, back in the stadium, Harold brushes by his
secretary as if she were a bad odor. In his locked office he drains a
glass of bourbon, then pulls off his wet sweats and sneakers. With a
dirty bath towel he dries off, remarking as he pads his lower belly
that his penis, which he scientifically refers to as a penis, does not
deserve much attention today.

Harold can no longer think too hard or long about the statue
without his arm popping up automatically, his index finger sticking
straight out and his heart beating at a quickened pace. Get him on
the subject, and up goes the arm. Years ago, thinking about young
women had the same effect on his penis. Put the picture of a well-
formed female in his mind, and there it went, pointing out of control.
Now, in the mirror, this same member looks as worthless as it feels.

"In with them, hardheads," he mumbles. "In with them."

He changes into a crisp white dress shirt and silk boxers, socks
so long they nearly cover his kneecaps, an olive windowpane-plaid
suit he bought from Champs LaRoux years ago, a crimson and
brown paisley necktie, an eelskin belt and a pair of fine Italian
loafers. Harold is tired; he is more than tired. He remembers
something his father, sick with consumption, told him not long
before he died: "It gets so my head spins with a violence that could
nauseate a sack of cement."

Through his closed door, speaking with a voice full of coffee
and cigarettes, Mrs. Nancy Claude asks if he's checked his pile of
messages yet. When he doesn't answer, she jiggles the knob. "Mr.
Gravely, are you okay?" She taps the wood lightly.

"What messages?" There are at least four stacks of them scat-
tered around his office, some from yesterday and the day before,
some from last week. "Which ones do you mean?"

"On your desk. There near the telephone."

"I don't feel like reading them now, Mrs. Claude. Maybe later. Thank you."

"Sorry to have disturbed you."

In a moment he hears her typing. "Oh, Mrs. Claude?"

The typing stops.

"Never mind," he says. Slurping down one last good-bye drink, he turns off the overhead lights and for a few minutes sits on the couch watching the weather beat against the window.

Mrs. Claude knocks on the door again. "Harold," she whispers. "Harold, are you sure you're okay?" She tries the knob. "Let me in. Please."

Moving to open the door, he feels his head swim. "I'm fine," he says. "What's the big worry?"

She whisks by him and pivots sharply at the center of the room, confronting him with crossed arms. Nancy Claude is half his age, the wife of an oil field roustabout who works offshore two weeks a month. This week her husband is on a rig—Harold can tell by the sunny glibness of her perfume, her black ribbed stockings, the bounce and shimmer of her long dark hair. "Your name sounds so much older than your looks," he told her one afternoon about six years ago, the first time they made love in his office. Her husband was away then, too.

Now she pouts, lets her chunky lower lip hang. "You didn't check your messages, did you, Mr. Gravely? All my time on the telephone this morning, and you didn't even look at them."

He shuts the door. "No, daughter, I didn't."

"Shall I read them to you?"

"When I get back," he says. "Maybe I'll let you if I feel up to it. I got an important appointment now."

She sits on the couch, her knees touching, her hands resting upon them. "It's warm," she says, feeling the cushion beneath her. "Were you taking a nap?"

"No, daughter," he replies. "I was watching the rain." He points to the window, the white miniblinds locked in place more than halfway up. "It's daytime and the street lamps are on," he adds. "It's wet and dreary, but it's perfectly wet and dreary, which somehow makes it nice."

"You were taking a nap."

He opens the door to leave. "Good-bye, Mrs. Claude." He knows better than to look back at her, to meet her stare. "I'll only be gone a few hours."

"Don't lie to me, Harold," she says as he strides down the hall. "You were taking a nap again without me."

| **19** |

Both hands gripping the top of the steering wheel, Harold drives his rose-colored Cadillac Seville into the downtown business district. Here the rain is falling through a spinning red mist that hangs above the rooftops. Harold weaves and lurches but manages to keep the car in his lane, watching the people on the sidewalks struggling to hold their umbrellas against the lashing wind. Others with the sense of cows seek shelter under the awnings of storefronts or huddle against high glass facades that bloom wet dripping clouds. Up and down the street, lamps burn pale yellow heads that appear sinister in the haze. Harold, searching for a free meter, completes two turns around the block before parking in front of a department store.

Near exhaustion for all his worry over the statue quote, he has come to join Bobby Peel and his wife, Claire, in soliciting donations for the monument. The Peels are longtime members of the booster club and now chair the Committee to Recognize Harold Gravely. Although in the beginning it was not their way to thump a car window with a knuckled fist, these days they beg with an intensity of purpose that surely would shame the most destitute and aggressive of street urchins. Only last week Bobby, generally a reserved, even-tempered sort, drove his elbow into the roof of someone's car, leaving a dent the size of a softball. When the driver stormed out cursing and screaming, Bobby drove his other elbow into the man's rib cage and dropped him to his knees. It was an unfortunate incident, and though the man at first threatened to sue, the Peels won him over to their side with various and exaggerated hard-luck tales about their attempts to rightly serve Harold Gravely, whom they referred to as the best but least appreciated college football coach of all time. Luckily, the man drove a clunker and was operating with an expired license, because otherwise the Peels would have been, as Bobby later told Harold, "in some serious legal soup."

"However you can get it," Harold coached the Peels, "get it. Show no shame. Know no pride. When I'm dead and gone you'll only remember the glory. How you made fools of yourselves in the process will be long forgotten."

At this point, the Committee to Recognize Harold Gravely is several thousand dollars behind its goal, a situation that distresses Harold no end and makes him wonder at the greed and selfishness of people, including some of those on the committee. Why weren't they putting in more hours? He wanted to know if they'd hit the shopping malls, and the giant multiplex cinema. What about the nursing homes?

Harold has pointed an accusatory finger all around, but he has yet to consider that as an object of charity he is no more attractive than endangered whales or seals or brown pelicans, all of whose recent campaigns failed miserably in these parts.

It was finances the Peels blamed when they were forced a few months ago to renege on a deal the committee had made with a celebrated New York artist and assign the project instead to a local artist of dubious credentials.

Oni Welby-White is a sculptor who lives in a small farming community some two hours west of the city; as it turns out, he's also a distant cousin of Claire's who agreed to work cheap. The extent of his art training was a correspondence course in drafting through a small liberal arts college, but what Bobby and Claire pitched to Harold and the university board as a "wealth of real and practical experience" came when he worked as a stonecutter building figures for cemeteries, public parks and libraries. Oni's statues of religious heroes—a crucified Jesus Christ and a weeping Blessed Virgin Mary are his specialties—have earned him numerous citations in both the local arts newsletters and the diocesan Catholic newspapers as a naive artist of enormous talent and runaway ambition.

To the surprise of no one, Harold had a few unkind words about the choice. "I've been dealing with naive, college-age boys all my life," he complained. "Why would you want to go and let one build my statue?" Claire explained that, in art terms, naive simply meant primitive, and that primitive meant self-taught. "Then why couldn't you find one of them terms that meant famous and schooled and highly sophisticated?" Harold replied. No one answered, but he really hadn't expected them to.

Earlier this week Bobby had suggested that the committee might generate more money if the Old Man himself showed up one lunch hour and stood out in the street with the rest of the volunteers rattling their coffee cans, glass jars and paper cups. Harold initially objected to the idea, but Bobby argued that if he was standing there in the flesh, reciting the Tenpenny speech to those most reluctant to surrender their pocket change, he might be surprised by how generous and charitable most folks really are. Harold accepted the invitation but only on the condition that he be allowed to "save some face," as he put it, and not recite from the famous speech. "I appreciate what you're getting at," Harold told him, "but I ain't got time to waste saying sentences I already know."

In the car Harold has neither a slicker nor an umbrella to address the weather, and neither has he the courage. He pines for a drink and a warm, dry bed to flop on. A few hundred yards away, Bobby and Claire are tapping the sealed lids of their give cups against the closed windows of cars stopped at the red light. For weeks now they have dressed identically in high-top Reeboks, starched painter's pants and purple T-shirts emblazoned with the slogan I RECOGNIZE HAROLD! DO YOU? Pinned to their chests were shiny red, white and blue buttons that proclaimed: BE A SPORT, GIVE TO THE OLD MAN! But today Harold can't see what they're wearing under the heavy corn-yellow raincoats that reach down to their calves and whip violently in the wind.

Bobby's floppy golf hat is Day-Glo orange, and to get the attention of the drivers, most of whom ignore him, he removes it and uses it as a give cup, dancing under the traffic light like an organ grinder's monkey.

Bobby Peel was a popular lineman on the Tenpenny Eleven. In the sepia-toned images of the day, he stands to the immediate right of Little Shorty Grieg, on whose shoulder Harold has set his right buttock, and appears to be saying something to Pogo Reese, who ably supports Harold's left. It has always perplexed Harold how someone who went head to head with Clemson in the Sugar Bowl, and who has been assured a place in history, could so humble himself by participating in a spirit group. No other member of his championship team—nor of any other team, for that matter—participates in the cakewalks and spirit drives and wiener roasts sponsored by the ubiquitous boosters. Although he is aware that without fans there could be no heroes, and without heroes no statues, Harold has concluded that, for the most part, these are men and women who live the vicarious life of the leech, sucking the juice out of others in order to feel juiced themselves. They drive to ballgames in recreational vehicles the size of blimps and pay fifty dollars to park within walking distance of the stadium. They spend the best of their autumn Saturday nights dodging mosquitoes, replaying other people's accomplishments and picking over tailgate spreads of Cajun fried chicken, cold egg macaroni, celery sticks laced with Velveeta cheese, potato chips and processed onion and garlic dips that smell as rank as dog food and taste about the same.

In becoming a fan Bobby Peel has forgotten what made him different from everyone else. He has become like all the other cheerleaders with their bullhorns and pompoms and loud false chatter. He has let die the memory of the moment when he was the most extraordinary of men, and the most unique. For this Harold has a mind to drive right over him and Claire and their empty coffers. The front license plate of his Cadillac says 10PENNY, the last thing they would see in this life.

"Once a player," Harold says quite loudly, testing his wrecked vocal chords, "always a player."

Harold steps out into the rain and immediately feels as if somebody has wrapped a rusty strand of barbed wire around his chest and is pulling at both ends. In seconds the weight of his clothes seems to double. Once the liquor begins to riot, he learned long ago, practically the only way to keep your balance is to kick invisible cans, and so he kicks and kicks. On the faces of the people standing under shelter are expressions of horror; Harold smiles politely and waves. His name is like a fleck of breakfast on their lips: there only for the moment, soon to be lost on the wet wind. By his manner Harold could well be the crowned king of a small town parade, so utterly happy he seems to see everyone. "It's me," he shouts to the people. "It's the Old Man come to beg. Harold Gravely—soon to be a statue!"

Splashing through puddles, Bobby Peel hurries over with Claire close behind and throws his arms around Harold, who trembles and lets his body go limp. He groans because Bobby, a huge man, seems determined to force a wedge of internal organs right out of his mouth. "What are you trying to pinch out of me, hardhead? You'll do in my lungs before the goddamn cancer."

Even after Bobby lets go, Harold still has to snort and cough and spit a couple of times before the blood washes out of his face and he can breathe again. "I ain't been held that hard since my wedding night," he says. "And even then it didn't last as long."

Bobby sheds his hat and scratches his princely shock of yellow-gray hair. His head is about a half size too large for his body, but he wears it well, generally under colored duffs like this one. He isn't much better to look at now, at fifty, than he was at twenty, but Harold remembers a good and quiet boy who never sassed back, never cursed, drank, smoked or caroused after curfew, and who read the Bible in the locker room before every game. Bobby Peel was reading from the Book of Revelation before they took on Clemson, and for a moment, delivering his now-famous speech, Harold considered replacing the tenpenny nails with Bobby's Bible, so disturbed was he that one of his boys thought reading about the end of the world could help their cause, which Harold knew was sealed in their favor long before they ever took to the field at Tulane Stadium.

"You remember my wife, Coach?" Bobby says, reaching to take the two Harold Gravely give cups Claire has been holding.

Harold offers Claire a hand to shake, but she too wants to embrace him. Unlike Bobby, who was good about it, Claire makes a face at Harold's liquor smell. Chin resting on his shoulder, she pinches her nose and rolls her eyes.

Bobby wags a finger at her.

"Thank you, daughter," Harold says once they pull apart, and he means it. His heart soars. Claire is every bit as lovely and finely built as Bobby is odd looking, and she smells not of sweat and Brylcreem, as Bobby does, but of soap and shampoo. Her embrace, instead of torture, is delicious. This time he only has to snort and cough and spit once to force the blood out of his face.

"Have all my volunteers gotten lost this morning?" Harold says. "Where in God's name are they?"

"Just me and Claire today," Bobby says. "Been that way for hours now, but we're hoping it'll pick up later in the day."

Harold shakes his head and feels his Adam's apple involuntarily tighten and glide up and down his throat.

"Don't let it get you down," Claire says. "Look at how rotten the weather is. Most of the volunteers have to work during the day anyway. Nine to five has hemmed everybody in."

"There's something I need to talk to you about, Coach," Bobby says, looking away. When he and Claire suddenly decide to hold hands, it tells Harold that what's to follow is of an uncommonly somber nature, and he braces for it.

"The door to my office is always open," he remarks.

"Late yesterday afternoon, at about five o'clock," Bobby begins, trying his best to hold Harold's eyes with his, "some fellow was out here collecting. Claire said she'd seen him before, and he did look familiar, but I didn't get close enough to get a good look at him. The weather was nice the way it is before a storm, you know, and I was busy taking care of some of the other volunteers. Well, he was working a corner up the block and doing fairly well, far as I could tell from such a distance." Bobby points to the place where the man had been standing. "Claire watched him closely for a while, from about twenty or thirty feet away, and said he had a magical way about him. Though he was somewhat disheveled, he was kind of attractive and—"

"Saintly," Claire says. "That's the word I used. The man was saintly. He had this amazing smile and his eyes were so blue I thought of swimming pools."

"He was really raking it in," Bobby continues, "but I kept wondering what kind of money somebody who looked the way he did could get, him being so poorly in appearance. When I took my break I went to introduce myself and see how much he had, but by then he'd disappeared with the give cup Claire had loaned him and all the money he'd collected. We looked everywhere but he was gone, so finally Claire called the police."

Harold clenches his teeth. Suddenly his lungs feel as if they've been dipped in boiling oil.

"Turns out," Bobby says, "he only looks like somebody Claire thought she'd seen before, and this man is miles from being a saint. Cops finally find him at some dive off Airline Highway. He's with a friend drinking liquor with the money he collected. His friend, they tell me, has a face like somebody forgot to turn off the meat grinder and he tripped in. When the cops walk them out to the squad car, the first one starts screaming that it's you who owes him an apology. Finally they stuff something in his mouth and drive him to the lockup downtown."

Harold would like to strangle somebody—Bobby, Claire, any one of the people up the street standing in the rain—but somehow manages to control himself. On his tongue he can taste the warm, acrid dust pushing up from his lungs. He takes a moment to collect a mouthful, then spits it out.

"I went to the police station and gave them my written statement," Claire says. "I would've pressed charges—both Bobby and I would've—but they said it was your money that was stolen, not ours." Beneath the yellow hood of her raincoat Claire's eyelashes hold shimmering beads of water; one curly strand of hair clings to her cheek. "We really think you should do it," she adds. "It'll only take a few minutes."

"Do what?"

"File charges against the man," Claire says. She releases Bobby's hand and reaches to hold one of Harold's, but he buries his deep in the pockets of his suit coat.

"Why should I be the one?" Harold says, turning to Bobby. "Why don't you do it? You're head of the committee."

"Cochairman," Bobby reminds him. "I told the shift commander down at the station that you'd be here today, and he asked if you wouldn't mind calling him after you finished collecting." Bobby has adjusted his tone to sound as obsequious as possible. "Or maybe you could run by there later if you've got the time. I told him it was a big day for you, what with gassers starting and all. He says he can keep the man penned up for disorderly conduct and public drunkenness, but not for long."

Harold doesn't respond. He's too occupied inventing punishments for the man who stole his statue money.

"If you don't do something," Claire says, "he'll be back on the street in a matter of days and who can guess what terrible mischief he'll be up to."

The rain has slackened to a mist, with an occasional spurt of pellets. Bobby hands Claire one of the give cups, and Harold notices it barely tinkles; there's hardly enough tinkle in it to wake a fitful sleeper. Harold turns up the lapel of his suit coat and digs into his pants pockets for some Juicy Fruit. Finding none, his face drops a notch.

"They're calling it Gabriel," Bobby is saying now.

"Calling what what?" asks Harold.

"This storm we're standing in. The weatherman on the radio this morning was calling it Gabriel, after the archangel—employed by God for only the most distinguished services."

Claire recites from memory: "And the angel said unto him, 'I am Gabriel that stand in the presence of God; and am sent to speak to thee and to show thee these glad tidings.' "

"Luke," Bobby explains. "Chapter one, verse nineteen."

Harold spits between them. "The wife once had a poodle name of Gabriel," he says. "Treated it like a human being. He had a bladder problem, though, used to wet the carpets. We had to hold our breath for the smell. Finally the vet says we have a choice to put him to sleep before he turns two years old or spend several hundred dollars getting him fixed." Harold pauses to consider the options, then continues. "He's out now in the backyard under the trees. It was Rena who supervised the burial—stuck a cross at the head of the grave and everything." A smile lifts his swollen lips. "Poor thing mopes some every time she rides over him on the Snapper."

Bobby and Claire look at each other with drawn faces.

"Did you bring a pencil and some paper just in case I thought of something to say," Harold asks, more ebullient now. "Because all of a sudden I feel some words coming on."

Claire extracts a ballpoint pen from her raincoat, and Bobby fingers a reporter's notebook in the side pocket of his. But he doesn't take it out. "Maybe we can memorize what you say and run somewhere for cover and write it down," he says. "This rain'll wreck the notebook and smear your words."

"But I don't think I can hold it another second." Harold's face appears to be flushed with pain, although neither Bobby nor Claire can figure what could hurt about wanting to say a sentence. "Somebody'd better look like writing or I go home."

Claire rips into Bobby's yellow coat and comes up with a scrap of paper, which she covers as best she can with Bobby's golf hat.

"There are two kinds of people in this world," Harold announces: "them that play the game and them that don't."

Even before Harold's finished it's plain that Bobby doesn't like the quote. He scratches his yellow-gray hair as if trying to solve one of the world's profound mysteries. Claire stops trying to keep the rain from wetting the paper. She lets the hat drop to the sidewalk, then ceremoniously puts it back on Bobby's head. In seconds the paper puffs up with rainwater and nearly disintegrates in her hands, Harold's statue quote with it. Claire takes the page with the writing on it, balls it up and offers it to Harold, but he merely stares at it.

"There are them that play," Bobby says, rubbing his prehistoric chin, "and there're them that don't."

Another sentence is taking shape in Harold's mind. Detecting the dramatic change in his face, Claire digs around in Bobby's raincoat and finally comes up with the notebook.

Harold stands as monstrous and erect as his body will allow and points straight ahead as his statue will point.

"There are two kinds of people who play the game," he declares: "them that win and them that lose." The whiskey impels him to add, almost against his will, "And then, of course, there's always them lazy bastards that don't show up."

Claire stops writing and returns the ballpoint to her coat pocket. "You said two kinds, Coach Gravely, but that's three."

"Them that win," Harold says reflectively, "them that lose, and them that don't show up."

"Yes, sir," Bobby says. "Maybe if you left out the 'them that don't show up,' you'd have what you're after. If they don't even play, why include them?"

"You always had a good head on your shoulders," Harold says, starting toward the nearest traffic light. As before, he kicks invisible cans. Bobby and Claire walk on either side of him.

"My lungs could use some mouth-to-mouth," Harold says. "The mouth of a bottle pressed directly to this parched mouth of mine. I feel dead as a doorknob, maybe worse."

"It's doornail," Claire says. Once again she pinches her nose at the whiskey odor and rolls her eyes for Bobby's sake.

"That, too," Harold says. "Knobs, nails . . . whatever."

The three of them take a seat on a bench near the bus stop. At the street corner the Peels have staked a large I RECOGNIZE HAROLD! poster board, but the rain has run the lettering, making it difficult to read.

Claire, tightening her jaw, doesn't say anything when Harold reaches to straighten the curly wisp of hair on her cheek.

"Maybe just one word," Bobby says. "One that says as much as a whole paragraph."

"*Pride* is a nice word," Claire ventures. "It's a word that reminds me of you."

"I am a prideful so and so," Harold allows.

"*Courage*, too, that's nice." This is Claire again. "Probably better than *pride*. What about *courage*, Coach Gravely?"

Bobby slaps his hands together. "You've got something, honey. You really, really do."

"Maybe just that on my statue," Harold says. "The word *courage* in bold letters right under my name and dates of birth and death." His arm starts to twitch and he feels an urge to point, so he does.

"Way to go, Claire," Bobby says.

Give cups in hand, the Peels run back into the street and begin soliciting the long line of traffic backed up at the light. From car to car they move, tapping their cups on the windows, asking for change. A newfound enthusiasm marks their efforts and gives them both a chill.

"*Courage*," Harold calls, standing tall on the bench. The word rolls off his tongue as he points at the coin laundry across the street. "Bobby, Claire—*courage*, friends. *Courage*, everybody. You all got *courage* now."

Last week, after learning at the board meeting that he had to come up with something right away, Harold thought about going to the library and plucking a line with immortality in it from an old book standing back in the stacks, one that hadn't been checked out in years, but then later at home he came across a collection of familiar quotations among Rena's things and read through it while watching television. None of the lines was familiar to him or explained how he felt about the life he'd lived or things in general, and none was by a football coach, professional or college, so he tossed it aside. He wonders now how history would have judged him had he said something different before the Tenpenny game, if he'd stuck Bobby Peel's Bible up their buttholes instead. Would his hardheads have played as hard for him? Would they have won?

Would he now be standing on a city bench in the rain, pointing like a statue?

"Courage, everybody," he shouts as loud as he can. "Claire, Bobby! *Courage.* Let's all have courage."

He waves Bobby over, delighted to hear a heartier tinkling of coins in his give cup. "You remember, hardhead," he says, "what it was like in the dressing room before the Sugar Bowl?"

"Not every bit of it," Bobby admits, "but some."

"Tell me what you remember, hardhead," Harold requests. "All the details. I'm coming to you with this because of Mr. Memory this morning. The sonofabitch was dressed in black on my big day."

"What now?"

"Trent Orlansky," Harold says. "He wore black like it was a damn funeral! I'm not ready for no funeral, hardhead. I just want you to help me remember something."

"I'll do my best." Bobby plants his feet and inhales deeply.

Harold cues him with a pointed finger.

"The dressing room itself," Bobby Peel begins, "I remember how crowded it was. We had to double up in those short wood lockers. There was a heater blowing from the ceiling and it got so hot everybody was a little woozy. I was with Flaubert Rich, who had intestinal flu so bad Doc Cage wanted to put him in one of those nursing home diapers. We all had those purple blazers, white shirts and gold-and-white striped neckties, but I don't remember the pants."

"White with purple stitching," Harold tells him.

"There were two toilets. And because of Flaubert there was a line to the second one."

"What else?"

"Trainers passing around souvenir programs and sticks of gum, two slices apiece. Red Johnson threw up and then whoever looked at it threw up. You know how that works, just like dominoes. Doc Cage thought all those who'd gotten sick would be weak for kickoff, but it turned out they felt okay, or said so. I remember Pogo leading the prayer and getting all choked up toward the end. For a person with a kind of wildness in him, Pogo gave the best prayers of anybody I ever knew, and I've heard a lot of prayers. Then it was quiet except every now and then somebody would curse because the pressure was too much. You'd hear one dirty word and that was it.

Some, me included, read the Bible. I couldn't go into the game without reading something from it. Nowadays I can't sleep without reading something from it."

"I don't want to know about now. I want to know about then."

"Seniors crying like babies when it came to them this was their last game in the purple and gold. I was one of a few juniors who cried, even though I had another year left."

"What else?" Harold smiles, anticipating what comes next.

"I know it's famous now, Coach, but I don't really remember the speech about the nails. I know others who do—Trent Orlansky, for one. They all recite it word for word and their eyes well up. But I don't. Sometimes it seems maybe I heard it but I don't know if I've just claimed it the way memory does or if I really did. I know I didn't know what a tenpenny nail was until I looked it up in the dictionary."

"You know what this is?" Harold says. With both hands he cups his crotch, leaning into Bobby Peel.

"I think it's time you get on down from there," Bobby says.

Claire has come up behind him, a tormented look in her eyes. "Get on down," she says, waving him off the bench, "and we'll take you home and get you warm, let Miss Rena look after you. Time to get out of those wet clothes. I know you're tired."

Harold gestures with his crotch again. "Come on, hardhead. You know what this is?" To Claire he says, "Courage is too small a word for a man my size." Then he starts pointing again.

Bobby reaches to grab Harold's pants leg but gets kicked for his trouble. "Leave him alone now, baby," Claire says, leading her husband back to the cars stopped at the light. Before going back to work, she turns toward Harold. "Think of all the people who are watching, Coach Gravely—the people who love you! And the children! Don't let them remember you this way!"

In response, Harold offers a fair impression of a tongueless man trying to communicate. Trying to speak, he can only bellow and groan. Both arms extended, he opens and closes his hands, clutching empty, whitened fists of mist and air. "My statue," he finally mutters, losing his balance with the effort and dropping to the pavement.

From the ground the sky is gray, rolling with thunderheads and free of birds. He tastes the odor of the street, gritty and fetid, and crawls to a stop sign and pulls himself to his feet.

As he turns and faces the traffic speeding toward him, he spots the red convertible that was parked near the levee earlier in the day. It is in the near lane, moving much faster than the other vehicles, hugging the curb and sending a brilliant arc of rainwater over the sidewalk. The plume of water sparkles with yellow lamplight and sends pedestrians rushing to avoid it. Even those with their backs against the storefronts get showered. Harold has extended both of his arms, signaling the car to stop. It is a heroic pose, and it seems to work.

The car draws to within thirty feet of him, having slowed to allow the rest of the traffic to pass by. As before on River Road, Harold can't see the driver for the rain and fog on the windshield, but as the car approaches he does see a shadowy form move to the middle of the seat, an arm reach to unlock and open the door on the passenger's side.

"Spy!" Harold shouts.

Finally the car comes to a complete stop ten feet away, and the door opens. Harold regards this as an invitation to walk over and meet the driver, who now has shoved over and is sitting behind the wheel again. Harold staggers forward, kicking invisible cans, but when the car accelerates he has no choice but to lurch out of the way, barely avoiding being hit by the open door.

The car roars up the street, blasting through the traffic light under which Bobby and Claire Peel are standing. To keep from hitting them it swerves into the oncoming lane, nearly forcing several cars to climb the sidewalk. The driver reaches the next light before bothering to pull the door shut, then speeds away.

Harold's breath has been knocked out of him, but he has not been rendered speechless. "Spy," he mumbles painfully.

Someone's eyes—Harold can't make out whose—suddenly appear as a pair of enormous suns. "Help me up now," he commands, trying to see beyond the stubborn dark that has overcome him. "Help me get my business straight."

This is the last thing Harold says before passing out in the arms of Bobby Peel.

| 20 |

When he awakens about an hour later, the rain is still falling. Across his cluttered office, palm fronds and bamboo shoots scratch against the window. Harold hears the trickle and tick of water in the overhead pipes, cars splashing along the campus streets. From the illuminated face of a clock hanging between the chalk- and inkboards he knows he has a couple of hours to burn before the second round of gassers begins. He laughs at this good fortune, stopping the moment someone switches on the desk lamp.

"What's so funny? You were drunk again and passed out." It is Mrs. Claude. "Larry and Chester had to carry you in—one had arms, the other legs. The way those two fat bodies fought over you I thought they'd break you apart like a wishbone."

Her gold bracelets jangle as she saunters across the room, her stockinged feet quiet on the floor, and comes to stand before him. Harold, aware of her perfume, wonders at the spots on her body where she sprayed it.

"You broke poor Bobby Peel's heart," Mrs. Claude is saying, pooching her lips. "He and Claire asked me to tell you they've quit the drive. They abhor your unseemly behavior."

She, or somebody, has changed his clothes. The beautiful olive suit is in a pile on the floor, his expensive loafers on top like a sodden paperweight. He wears fresh chinos, a starched button-down shirt with sleeves rolled to the elbow and dark polyester socks that make his toes itch. Harold feels his pockets for a stick of gum, but there is none. With regret he eyes the heap.

"Their empty give cups are in my filing cabinet," Mrs. Claude says. "And, oh, they wanted me to tell you that they'll be praying for you."

Harold mumbles something about Juicy Fruit, but Mrs. Claude is not listening. She's too busy getting out of her own clothes, starting a pile on the seat of Harold's desk chair. He cranes his neck and watches her skirt drop. He used to like to remove her panty hose himself, but he's too exhausted to move. She wriggles out of them, then drops them on his face. There were times when he threatened to make a meal of her stockings, so overcome was he by the delicious smell of her sex on them, but now he swats and slaps at the silky ribbed things as if at a swarm of determined insects. She doesn't wear panties, and she shaves her pubic hair down to a thin strip. Her brassiere, dressed with either starbursts or flowers, comes off with a snap. It is a sound no greater than a pea of gravel falling on cement, but he hears it above the weather at the window. She has the kind of breasts, he told her once, pinching her extraordinarily small nipples, that belong on the refrigerated fruit displays at Sweeney's Grocery; they would bring a nice price, at least a couple bucks a pound. When she demanded he apologize for saying such a thing, he sulked. He'd meant it as a compliment. He was a man of action and passion, Harold reminded her, not no poet.

Back in her newlywed days, Mrs. Claude's husband, Jake, then a student at the city vocational school, often confessed to fantasizing about having relations with her beneath a thick cover of bushes near one of his classroom buildings. She met him beneath the tall hedges a few times and let him have her there, and he got to liking it so much he didn't care to do it anywhere else. For this he cursed and blamed her. She was relieved when he finally graduated and found work on the rigs offshore, far away from the bushes and the broad, dry leaves crackling on the loam beneath her.

"Ready for me to read those messages now?" she asks, straddling him as he tries to unbutton his pants. He shudders as a cynical, depraved look fills her face.

"Better drop the blinds all the way down first." He nods in the direction of the window. "Wouldn't want to scare nobody."

"I like it the way it is. It's naughtier, since you never know who'll look through all that bamboo and see."

Through the slit in his boxers he introduces his penis. While she fumbles with it, the image of a lightning-struck tree limb surfaces in Harold's mind but is quickly dismissed. If only she'd release the blinds, he thinks, and dim the goddamn desk lamp. "Students and teachers on their way to class," he groans, "they'll see us, daughter. My coaches. My wife."

"Yes," she says and moves to meet his lips.

"My god, you're brave."

| **21** |

Rena was vacuuming the carpet in the green room when Harold returned from his afternoon with Doc Cage.

Through the wall of windows she saw his car speed down the drive and brake just inches short of the garage wall, a riot of leaves and dust swirling behind him. The blackbirds that had been feeding on the lawn flew over to Xavier Monroe's property, landed for a few seconds and picked at the ground under the trees, then flew on to the empty lot next to the Marshall house. Rena lamented their going. She had spent the better part of the afternoon trying to figure why they traveled in such a large group, and what it was they ate. It was her theory that the colorful, sporting birds such as the cardinal and the blue jay liked to get around on their own, while the more common birds went in clusters. Why this was so, though, she couldn't even imagine. She was also at a loss to figure out what hundreds of them could find to eat on anything as bald as the patch of ground under Xavier Monroe's trees.

"Guess who's home," Harold called from across the house. When she didn't answer, he shouted "Wrong" and made a sound like a buzzer going off.

Rena took special care when vacuuming: she liked her floors to look as if they'd been swept with a garden rake. Today she'd spent almost an hour in this room alone, trying to get it right. During the day when Harold wasn't in the house to see her, she liked to move from one spot in the room to another by walking on the furniture. Her favorite chaise and magazine rack were in a far corner, and to get there without leaving prints on the carpet she had to traverse the back of a sofa and leap a few feet. She had made a rule: those times she fell short and muffed up the floor, she couldn't sit and enjoy a self-improvement magazine until she had vacuumed the spill.

Seeing Harold walk across her raked floors, as he was doing now, carved a deep pain in her gut, but she didn't say anything. He entered the room imitating the swooshing sound of the vacuum cleaner and, she noted, smelling of liquor. "Knock, knock," he said, tapping a row of knuckles against the coffee table.

Her face red with anger, Rena kept quiet.

"Who's there?" he said.

"Harold," he replied.

"Harold who?"

"Harold Gravely."

"Not Old Man Harold Gravely?"

"That's right," he said. "The one and only."

Now he tapped a fist on her back. "Rena," he said, leaning over to make sure she saw him.

"What?" she shouted above the sound of the vacuum.

"It's me, your husband Harold. I'm home."

She turned off the machine and with a bent wrist wiped the sweat from her brow. "How can I help you?"

"I could eat."

She pointed at the floor. "What have I always told you about walking on my carpet? Look what you did."

Harold stared down. "Sorry," he said, "but when I bought this house twenty-some years ago I was under the impression that that's what these floors were for."

She blew a damp wisp of hair from her face.

"If you'd like," he was saying, "maybe we could hang some vines or ropes from the ceiling and swing like Tarzan and Jane to wherever we need to go."

Against her will she found herself laughing. And she let him kiss her on the lips, even gave a little something back.

"Have to be a monkey to get around," he said, scratching his ribs. He bounced up and down and hooted like an ape.

"I've got chicken tarragon." She started for the kitchen. "I'll make a sandwich."

"Make two," he said.

"I've already eaten."

"I meant for me. Make two for me."

Halfway there she changed her mind. "You make them," she said, heading back to the Kirby.

He was shaking his head. "There was something I wanted to tell you—something really important that you'll want to know."

"Right," she said, chortling. "Next time."

After he disappeared into the back of the house, she stood for a minute staring at his tracks, then, in a defiant turn, decided to add some of her own. She would do this by dancing, slowly at first, with an imaginary partner. Her feet padded across the floor, pressing into the deep teal-colored pile. She held one hand flat against her lower belly, the other, the right, high at her side and folded in on itself. She could hear a dear, mournful melody playing for her alone. There were violins. She lifted her heels to the music, dropped them; her hips followed her knees, her knees her ankles, her ankles her feet.

With Pogo she had liked to dance—he had taught her how to step and breathe and why, once on the floor, you never looked at anyone but your partner—and with Harold, too, but with him it was more rough and tumble. Under the bleached ballroom lights he was both rude and clumsy, driving her into other couples, spinning without direction, showing off. His heavy breathing drowned out the music; his shoes clopped a pathetic tattoo against the dusty wood.

"This ain't gassers at the Ponderosa," someone told Harold once—it was a man he knew, a friend. "So stop busting into everybody." People actually drew back, encircled them and stared. "They're watching us," he would say, shouting in her ear. Then: "Jealous . . . every last one of them is jealous." She knew they were staring for other reasons, and had she not feared embarrassing him she might have compiled a list: "They're watching us because a few days ago my boyfriend got sent to the state pen and here I am with you." Or, "They're watching us because they're tired of getting run over." Or, "We're a pair of imbeciles, so why not watch?"

Pogo had been able to dance to anything: classical orchestrations, jazzy things, a train with a thousand clattering cars, cicadas croaking in the trees, the tireless beat of a metronome, neglected poets reading their words. He could also dance to nothing, as she was doing now.

One night after a game they had parked near a campus lake and stood in front of his Biarritz, both headlights washing over them and falling across the choppy water like twin pale moons. No music played but still they had danced, a slow one, swirling to the same imagined air. On the street an occasional car sped by, rock 'n' roll spilling from its open windows, but otherwise the night was quiet.

"Will you sleep with me?" he said, his face cool on her cheek. They swayed in the wet grass, their feet scratching the sandy ground; his hand trembled. She asked if he meant make love. "I never have," he said and laughed. "I'm still a virgin." He wasn't ashamed; in fact he almost seemed proud. "Dancing close like this . . . I dunno, it's starting to make me crazy." She asked if he wanted to do it here, in the backseat of the car like certain tramps were known to do. "I didn't mean it that way," he said, alarm dimming his expression. "We'll get a room at the Prince." Had he taken the time to consider the consequences, she wanted to know; there were many and not all of them good. "Sure," he said, then squinched his lips and dropped his eyes. "You mean you don't want to get pregnant, is that it?" The headlights on her face made her feel as if the whole world could see them and hear what they were talking about. Had he thought, she wondered aloud, that maybe leaving on the lights of his Cadillac might drain the battery, or did he intend to get stuck out here? "My gosh, no," he said, then hurried to turn them off. "I guess I forgot . . . I sort of stop thinking when I'm with you, Rena." He leaned into the car and everything turned dark. Iridescent dots floated across her field of vision.

Later she decided that a room in the Prince Seurat—sometime after the season, when they knew each other well enough—sounded reasonable. Certainly it wasn't rushing things. By then the consequences would be plain to him, and if anything happened he would do what was right. Besides, she was ready. When they were together she used words like "trust" and "honor" and "commitment." She could belch in front of him and that was okay. She could tell him when she was having her period. "I've got cramps," she told him one night, "and it's not from the dinner."

Another night they visited her best friend from high school, Polly Andrus, who was married and starting her family. Polly and Tommy lived in a little rented house and rarely went out because of the baby. Pogo and Tommy sat on the front seat of the Cadillac and drank a six-pack of beer. The top was down, and their hair shone in the winter sun. They stared straight ahead through the windshield as if they were driving down the road, heading someplace, when all along they were planted under a maple tree that had recently shed its leaves. Rena and Polly could see them from the kitchen window.

Weren't those two gorgeous together? And wasn't it neat how they were becoming friends just as the two of them were?

On the ride home Rena said she was willing to bet that married couples could dance naked in front of each other and think nothing of it. Pogo threw his arm around her and said he was ready for a little of that—all this from a guy who would later beat someone to death in front of a honky-tonk.

Now, as Rena danced from couch to chair, from baker's rack to hope chest, Harold staggered into the green room. "Why if it ain't Ginger Rogers," he said, a toothpick bobbing at the corner of his mouth. "I'd pull the curtains if I were you. Xavier Monroe might be looking in." He pointed to the long bank of windows. "I saw him charcoaling some wieners out on his patio a little while ago. He kept peeping over here like he wanted to drop by and visit."

Suddenly the music died in her ears. She said nothing.

"Chicken tarragon was good, pie. How'd you make that?" He didn't wait for an answer. He bent at the waist to peer through one of the windows, in the direction of the neighbor's house. "I'm going to the bedroom to lie down for a while. I've got some very important thinking to do. Maybe later we can discuss it."

She danced around him and swept to the other side of the room, pirouetted, bowed and started spinning around again.

"Fred Astaire," he said, "had a head shaped funny, and his legs were too short. Frankly I never understood the appeal." He moved the toothpick to the other side of his mouth. "And as far as Miss Ginger is concerned, her hair may of been gold but she had some roots that were pretty damn black."

When he left, dragging his feet to make as much a mess of her floors as possible, the violins began again and she felt lighter on her feet, though heavier of heart.

"By the time I get out of the pen," Pogo had told her the last time she ever saw him, "no telling what kind of new steps they'll be using." He was trying to be funny and wanted her to believe he wasn't scared to death. "Don't think I'm trying to convince you to wait around or anything, so we can go to the Prince and find out . . ." Here he choked on his words and looked past her toward the crush of photographers and newspeople trying to break through the courtroom guards. He nodded good-bye and lifted a finger instead of kissing her, which, as she still liked to believe, probably would have been impossible with all the hurry and confusion. The bailiff cupped the tops of his shoulders and led him to a side door. "I hope you'll accept my apology," Pogo called above the racket. "I never once meant it like it all turned out—not to hurt you, Rena!"

It was amazing what she could remember when she wanted to.

In the early years of their marriage, she and Harold used to vacation each summer at a beach resort in Florida, and one morning while he slept she went to a novelty shop and found a postcard that made her think of Pogo. A young man and woman were standing on the ocean shore in formal evening attire, and they held each other as practiced dancers do. The man's pants legs were rolled up to his knees; the woman's sequined gown was hiked up and pinned just above the calf. He was leading her into the surf, into the vast, blue sea. Beautiful smiles filled their faces. If they continued into the water, she thought to herself, surely they would drown—they would drown dancing. But that, she decided after some reflection, was the whole point of the card. Real romance was dancing until you died; it was going down together.

In the bathroom of their little stucco cottage, as Harold lay in bed watching a fishing show on television, she had written to Pogo for the first time since his incarceration some five years earlier. "Well," she began on the back of the card, as neatly as her shaking hand allowed, "I guess you heard I married Harold Gravely. Have you wondered why? I sure have." She was sitting on the filthy tiled floor, a phone book on her knees as a kind of lap desk. Water dripped in the tub, staining the porcelain a chocolate brown. "Maybe it was because I was afraid. He seemed so normal, you know—the pillar of the community kind of thing. He also was full of promises, and not the boy kind. These were man promises: an old house full of kids and pretty smells, summer trips in a station wagon, church membership and regular attendance, barbecues on the lawn." She paused before writing the next sentence: "Did you think you might be killing more than one person that night at Tuesday's?"

She had only begun to say what was on her mind and already was out of space. That afternoon she returned to the novelty shop and bought five more cards, identical to the first. "I really loved you," she continued, sitting on a towel on the beach while Harold was paddling through the surf on a plastic raft. "Sometimes when you looked at me I thought I'd melt and drip right onto the pavement. Ever wish we hadn't waited that night by the lake? Everything would be different. You would not be where you are now, for one. It would be you bouncing on the waves on a plastic float you inflated yourself. Will you call me when you get out? I'm not hard to find."

The next evening Harold had taken her to a lounge near the water. Tiki lamps burned all along the back gallery, splashing blue and yellow light over the carved busts of Polynesian warriors and dropping shadows on the walls. They had danced so long that blisters formed on her toes and the backs of her heels. By midnight she could hardly walk. When the whiskey had begun to talk Harold cradled her in his arms, carried her outside and set her on the hood of his car. He took off her shoes and rubbed and kissed her feet, then performed what he called a magic spell. In the morning she wouldn't even feel them, he said. The blisters might still be there, but the pain would be gone. He climbed past her, up to the vinyl roof, and beat his chest with clenched fists. He roared and groaned and called her name as if she were his queen, and this, by God, was worship.

She never mailed the cards to Pogo. Back on the beach the following afternoon, she tore the cards into pieces and dropped them into a wire trashcan.

| 22 |

Weary of her solitary dance, Rena returned to the Kirby and vacuumed the tracks in the carpet. It took less than five minutes, and then, quite miraculously, everything looked as if neither she nor Harold had ever been there.

She was winding the electrical cord around the side of the cleaner when someone knocked at one of the windows behind her. It was an eager, insistent knock that rattled the panes. At first she tried to pretend she couldn't see for the glare, but there, smiling with the wicked, undeserved confidence of one who only moments before

learned that his neighbor danced alone, was Xavier Monroe, straddling the privet.

Instinct guided her hands to her face, where for a moment she
hid behind a fan of fingers, staring through the cracks. He was
holding a golf club and presently stepped back from the dense tangle
of shrubbery and took a mighty practice swing. As a swatch of sod
chased his stroke, he stared in the purple distance, following the path
of the make-believe ball.

"I'm working," she said, clutching the handle of the Kirby and
lifting it. "Come back some other time."

He stuffed a finger in his ear and shrugged, then with the club
motioned for her to come outside. He mouthed the words, "It's
important."

On the back porch she busied herself with the plants along the
railing and refused to look at him directly. He stood on the back
lawn, a large, misshapen man swinging a nine-iron in the shade of a
waxy blue magnolia.

"Is something wrong?" she said, anxiety deepening her voice.
"Shall I run and get Harold?"

"Nothing's wrong," he replied casually. "Something's important, though." He set his spiked shoes, reared back and executed a
fine, unhurried swing. "I've got a proposition to make, and I thought
you might like it."

When she didn't reply, he swung the iron again. "Bet you can't
tell me the last time you were propositioned by a beautiful white
man name of Xavier." He laughed obscenely as if to suggest his
comment was designed merely for titillation, but she knew he was
being completely serious.

"Get to the point," she snapped. "I'm busy."

"I saw you dancing. And I was wondering if Harold wasn't
around, maybe you might like a partner."

"It wasn't me you saw dancing."

"Okay," he said. "Fine. But even if it wasn't, will you dance
with me sometime?" He pointed the club in the direction of his
house. "I've got a pretty good radio in the Florida room. We could
push back the furniture and throw some sawdust on the floor."

"Where's Beth?"

"Don't know," he answered. "Don't care, either."

"Please leave, Xavier."

"We were cooking some wienies on the grill. That's when I saw you." He mimicked Rena's dance, caressing the club in his arms and churning his hips. "I guess she got tired of watching me burn link after link—I just couldn't stop looking at you. The hair on my arms was standing up like I'd stuck something in a wall socket. Last thing I heard was the door slam and some tires burning up the carport."

"Do us both a favor," she said. "Go home."

"It's the Monroe blood that made me look," he explained. "We're a darned lecherous bunch—can't help it. Our blood happens to burn a few degrees hotter than everybody else's, on account of our thermostats." He looked down at his crotch and winked. "Know what I mean by a thermostat, doll?"

"You're a sick man, Mr. Monroe."

This time his stroke left a divot in the ground. "Fore!" he shouted, then he shielded his eyes with the flat of his hand and looked toward the east. "Why, if it ain't a hole in one," he said. "Did you see how pretty I hit that shot?"

For as long as she knew him, Rena thought his name was a poor fit for his looks. *Xavier* belonged to a more cerebral lot. This being deep winter, he looked more pale today than usual, and for Rena to keep from saying so was no easy task. His obsession with keeping tanned had wrecked his skin long before he and his wife moved next door about five years ago. "See how brown I am?" he liked to say, admiring an extended arm. "Like a nut." A retired military man, he once spent an entire spring afternoon driving plastic golf balls from his patio onto her back lawn. For this occasion he wore skimpy bathing trunks, sponge flip-flops and a sun visor with REAL DIG BONG hand painted across the crown. Each shot landed near a flowering ligustrum hedge, upsetting the bees that had made their home there. "Harold works a lot," he had told her then, "and Beth shops. Whaddaya say we get together and act neighborly toward each other." Later she had crouched behind a chair in the green room and watched him sunbathe in the nude. While his Smokey Joe barbecue pit slow cooked a giant pork roast and several pork links, he lay on a latticed chaise longue and rubbed tanning butter over every part of his body.

"Harold got home early today," she told him now. "If Beth isn't around to shorten your leash, I'm sure he can."

Beneath the magnolia he had found a bed of mushrooms to

replace his invisible ball, and presently he took several whacks at it, sending feathery brown dust into the afternoon. "Does Harold play golf?" he said.

Rena struggled to keep from smiling. "Why don't we ask him?" she replied, and as he started to protest she bellowed her husband's name with the force and urgency of an old-fashioned supper call.

Xavier looked disappointed. "You really think that was necessary?" He rubbed the head of the club against the side of his foot. "Am I all that threatening?"

"You're ill-mannered," she said, "and uncouth. You bug me."

"I think what it is—" he joined the tips of his forefinger and thumb, forming a hole, then slowly pumped the graphite shaft of the club through it—"is that I pique your many suppressed desires."

"All you make me want to do is throw up," she said. Then she nearly screamed: "Come out here, Harold! Come out here now!"

Harold staggered through the sliding glass doors and over to where Rena was doodling with her plants. Upon spotting Xavier on the lawn he softened his visage from murderous to curious, but he failed to temper the heat in his voice. "I thought I told you I had some very important thinking to do," he said, dropping to his haunches. "Whaddaya want?"

"Miss Rena's a real genius when it comes to green things," Xavier said, pointing at her with the club. "Here it is winter and she's got all these marvelous plants outside. And they're looking darn healthy, too." He chuckled and shook his head. "Who'd ever guess they could survive the weather this time of year?"

"I just brought 'em out for some sun," she said. "It's only when it gets down near freezing that they're endangered, anyway."

"Tell me if I'm hearing this right," Harold said, his face contorted. "You called me out here—out of my important thoughts—to talk about plants?"

"No," she replied, meeting Xavier's eyes. "I wanted to tell you that this man propositioned me."

Harold was agonizingly slow in standing up. He bent his head at a peculiar angle and scratched his brow, and although it took some doing, he allowed a smile to find his lips. "That's hard to believe," he said after a moment. Then, turning to Xavier: "I always thought you were smarter than that."

"Smarter because I'm not interesting," she said, "not pretty enough? Or smarter because you plan to punch him out right here and now?"

"I always liked Xavier," he answered, scratching the tip of his nose. "Why would I want to go and hit him?"

She might have struck Harold herself had Xavier not stepped up closer to the porch. "Actually, my proposition had to do with a business matter," he said, holding up his golf club. "I've been thinking about opening a miniature course here in town, and I'm looking for investors."

"Nobody putts with a nine-iron," Rena told him.

"On our course they will," Xavier said. "Only things we won't allow are wooden clubs and carts."

"Few years back," Harold said, "there was a miniature golf up Florida Boulevard, but it went under."

"Then maybe the city's finally ready for one," Xavier said brightly.

"I might consider it," Harold announced. "But I like a cart. I'd want to be able to drive one wherever I damn well pleased." He laughed and tapped Rena on the shoulder. "Nothing more fun than cutting donuts in a cart."

"Of course we'll make an exception for you, Coach Gravely," Xavier said. "I'll make a mental note of it." He touched his forehead with a finger.

"He wanted to dance with me," Rena said. "That was his proposition, not miniature golf."

Both Harold and Xavier looked at her with expressions of pity and sorrow, nodding as if to say they understood.

Once Harold retreated inside, Rena stopped pretending to be interested in the plants. She told herself to be strong, and in seconds the pep talk made her feel less cheated and violated. Words came to her all of a sudden and seemed to explain not only this incident with Xavier but her whole married life. "Are we finished yet?" she said to her neighbor, sounding not at all like someone who only minutes before had been humiliated. "Because if we are, I'd appreciate it if you left and never set foot on my property again."

"I really didn't mean to lie like that," Xavier said, "but Harold's more volatile than I am—didn't want to set him off or anything. He's got that Dakota rifle, remember?"

She placed her elbows on the railing and leaned forward, taking the weight off her legs. "I hate men," she said. "I hate every last one of them."

| **23** |

Later that night, after supper, Harold sat out on the porch swing drinking highballs, chewing gum and watching the wintry heavens roll. He wasn't in the mood for company until he remembered that he'd come down with the kind of illness that could kill a person.

He pushed open the sliding glass doors. "Pie," he called, "I got something important to tell you. Get out here, please."

She was in the kitchen, putting thick wedges of a three-day-old hummingbird cake into large freezer bags, and she didn't move when he called.

Because she'd snapped at him this afternoon when he asked for a couple of sandwiches, he'd waited until evening to tell her about the cancer. "Come outside for a minute," he said irritably. "It's important. I promise you'll want to hear it."

"Not till nine," she said, checking the clock on the microwave. It now was a little after eight o'clock. "You know I don't broom till then."

"You mean sweep."

She licked the orange icing off her thumb. "Yes. You're right, Harold. That's what I mean. I don't sweep till nine."

He pulled the doors shut and returned to the swing, plopped down on his favorite side and started rocking. The swing was made of wicker and hung by rusty chains: a gift from members of the Tenpenny Eleven on the silver anniversary of their national championship. Pogo Reese, the team captain, hadn't responded to the RSVP invitation—not knowing where to reach him, they'd mailed the card to the state pen at Angola with "please forward" written on the envelope—so Bobby Peel, who arranged the affair, presented the swing on a collapsible stage in the ballroom of the Prince Seurat Inn. "This is for your retirement, Coach," he said. "Whenever it may come, we hope you'll relax and enjoy it." Centered on the back of the swing was a small gold plate that read:

THE BEST THERE EVER WAS

When it comes time to run
Through those goalposts,
I want your butthole so wide damn open,
You'll need a pair of tenpenny nails
Stuck up it
To keep your foul business
From spilling out.
H.G.

The swing was starting to rot, and birds throughout the neighborhood had discovered that the white-painted twigs were valuable in the construction of their nests. Long strips had been torn off the arms and seat, and recently Rena had complained that the bird droppings were ruining her porch. It was time to get rid of "that smelly thing," she said, and replace it with one of the durable Scandinavian teakwood sets she'd seen at a department store in the mall, but Harold had refused. Hardheads, he told her, generally gave engraved, gold-plated whistles or plaques as gifts. That certain members of the Tenpenny Eleven had picked out a swing showed some smarts and ingenuity, a willingness to do things differently. It made him proud and suggested that perhaps he'd taught them a few things more than how to run, block and tackle. Rena had laughed and said it was the wives of the players who'd picked out the swing, and not to go patting himself on the back. Although he slunk away listing a variety of ways he'd like to see her killed, this revelation had not changed his feelings one bit. Almost every evening he still sat and rocked himself, slowly at first, then as high as he dared. When Rena came out at nine to sweep, and to ask what all the racket was about, he'd say he was getting some exercise. Then he would lean back in his seat and raise his feet, allowing her to pass the broom beneath them. Not until she was finished and had gone back into the house did he return to his gum and his booze and the memory of the season when he and a bunch of boys proved that they were better at a certain something than anyone else in the whole country.

When Rena stepped out on the porch tonight and started sweeping, the last of her household chores, Harold made a point of shoving over to make room and patting her place on the seat. As he'd expected, she kept up the chore, saying nothing, not even humming a show tune as she often liked to do. His eyes were fixed on a

111

particular spot in the night sky, as if he alone could see something more than a dark cloud bank, and he hoped she'd look up from her toil and notice his tragic look. Familiar with Harold's corny theatrics, Rena ignored him. After nearly twenty-nine years of marriage, she easily recognized the forlorn look of a hustler when she saw it. All she had to clean by was the muted light from the curtained windows and glass doors, but she did it expertly. Watching her make busy, it again struck Harold that his wife knew the face of the boards better than she knew his own. Once he'd told her as much, and she'd said he was probably right. His face bored her, while there was always something new to learn about the porch: it had accumulated so many leaves from the trees in the yard, a lizard had died in the corner pot of zinnias, a blue jay had lost a feather. With Harold she always knew what to expect, and sadly, she always got it.

"There is something I want to tell you," he said directly. "And what I got to say has to do with my future and your future. I think you ought to sit and look at me when I say it." He patted her spot on the seat again.

Rena continued at her work, but because she hadn't said anything or returned to the house he figured he had her attention. "Last few days I been going to the doctor. Today he politely informs me I got a tumor on my lung the size of a grapefruit."

"A grapefruit?" she said, disbelief lifting her voice.

"Okay," he conceded. "A marble, more like. But that's why I been spitting everywhere and there's blood in it. And that's why I been keeping you up nights coughing."

Her broom scratched against the boards; she didn't break rhythm. "They can get to it, though," he said. "Only I've known too many people who let them do the surgery then turn up dead on the table. Or they come out thinking everything's fine and get dosed with radiation and lose their hair, and next thing you know some sorry bastard's wheeling them in a chair down the aisle at Christ the King, taking them up for last communion."

She rubbed the tip of her nose with her knuckle and sneezed into her apron, but all this meant was that she'd inhaled some dust.

"My heart ain't up for what treatments they can do," he said, twirling the ice in his glass with his finger. "My heart, from the moment Hiburotot told me what it was, has been urging me to take this like a man, to be strong." He laughed, but it was only for show, part of the pitiful facade he'd erected. "A person's got to listen to his own heart, right?"

"The heart is a lonely hunter," she said.

Although he could hear the words clearly, he hadn't seen her lips move. "What's that?" he said.

She repeated the remark, louder now, but again her lips didn't move. "You say the heart's a what?" He sat up tall in the swing. "I'm going to die, and you say the heart is a what?"

She was standing with her eyes on the sky, a look similar to his though considerably less fraudulent, the broom handle leaning against her ribs. Tonight she looked like the girl he married, he thought, and later he might try again to have a go with her, to see if her skin was still as soft and warm as it was the last time they held each other, which was so long ago now it seemed like years and might well have been. He hoped the news of his cancer would loosen her up some, restore her loyalties and serve as a reminder of her wifely duties.

"It's just one more book I never read," she said at last, moving toward the door. "*The Heart Is a Lonely Hunter.* Don't go getting so upset."

She stood the broom against the porch railing and shoved open the sliding glass doors. As they closed behind her, he caught the scent of her perfumed hair; it was rosemary mint, his favorite.

"You'll be sorry," he said after her. "One day you'll regret how you talked to me when I told you I was going to die."

| 24 |

Harold had a rule about not calling anyone after eleven o'clock at night, his and Rena's bedtime, but he broke it tonight and phoned Champs LaRoux. When no one answered, he remembered it was January, an odd month of the year: time for Champs either to snow ski in New Mexico or fish off the Florida coast. LaRoux devoted the odd-numbered months of the year to vacationing and denting his bank accounts, the even-numbered to his clothing store and university business. His was a rich and largely irresponsible life perpetuated by his devoted wife, Paige, who loved him dearly despite his many infidelities. So urgent was Harold's desire to tell someone the news about his health that he considered driving over to their antebellum mansion off River Road to make sure Champs really wasn't in and sleeping. But as soon as he shoved the keys into the ignition of the Cadillac and got a glimpse of his swollen, bloodshot eyes in the rearview mirror, Harold decided it wasn't such a brilliant idea after all and returned to his study.

Norman Pepper was another Harold thought about calling, but Harold hadn't spoken to him in twenty years and he suspected Norman of being the anonymous board member whose quotes in the city paper trumpeted a new day soon to be born in the football program. He knew Norman was the lone member to reject a luncheon invitation to hear Harold defend himself against derogators spreading damaging stories about him and demeaning his days as coach. Now that Harold had cancer, Champs LaRoux would be an easy score. But if he could win Norman, an enemy, over to his side, Harold surely could generate enough support among the rest of the board to extend his contract indefinitely.

It would not be easy, and Harold had only himself to blame. Some ten years after the Tenpenny game, Norman had held a dinner party at his home honoring a prized high school tandem from a tiny hamlet to the west, both of whom were seriously considering going elsewhere. These were boys who spoke in clipped sentences full of axle grease and mama's fried chicken, who showed not a sign of knowing what they intended to study next year, much less make of their lives, but who, as athletes, were so magnificently gifted that Harold saw in them a one-way ticket to another national championship. Their three-day visit featured adjoining suites in the Prince Seurat Inn, complete with wet bars generously stocked with colorful libations in miniature glass bottles and a view of the swimming pool, which, Harold made sure, was also generously stocked with beautiful, darkly tanned coeds clad in the most provocative bathing suits of the day; tickets to a Sinatra concert, the first and last he would perform in the city; enough meal money to support a middle-class family for a month; and the constant companionship of a pair of libidinous sisters who made a modest but thoroughly convincing career of telling everyone they were members of the university's dance troupe but who were, in fact, expensive young ladies of the night selected and hired by Harold himself.

Champs LaRoux had planned to entertain the recruits at his country hideaway, but on the evening before the party Paige was stricken with a killer head cold and Harold, encouraged by LaRoux, turned to Norman Pepper for help. Harold had long considered Pepper just another fatuous, loudmouthed booster who probably would have devoted his Wednesday nights to something like team bowling or ballroom dancing had someone not steered him to the Touchdown Club meetings. Now, though, his request for assistance with the celebrated quarterback–wide receiver combination was so warmly received that Harold quickly reassessed his views. "Norman," Harold said on the telephone, "if we get these two stud hosses and win it all again, I promise your name'll tag along right next to mine in all the history books."

Trembling with excitement, Norman informed Harold that he would prepare the meal himself, for he was a "bit of a gourmet," having once studied under a famous New Orleans chef.

"In that case," Harold told him, "count on about thirty or forty of us. If you're that good it only makes sense to bring the wife and some of the hardheads from the office."

"Bring as many as you like," Norman said. "I'll begin cooking now. We'll eat until everybody drops."

Although the evening started grandly, with the handsome golden-haired sisters, dressed identically in sailor suits, performing somersaults across the living-room floor, and Trent Orlansky regaling everyone with stories about the Tenpenny Eleven, it soured as soon as the party sat down to dinner. Knowing that smothered liver and grits, his favorite, was out of the question, Harold had hoped for a meal featuring barbecue ribs or hamburgers to heap on the recruits, but Norman, wearing an apron with his name, Chef Pepper, scripted across the left breast and a billowy stovepipe chef's hat, served baked apples in cream, oyster soup à la Brennan and crabmeat au gratin. "This food's good for the tuxedo crowd," Harold whispered to Rena, "but these two boys still got pig shit riding between their toes." Instead of beer and soft drinks to refresh them, there was milk rum punch and expensive wines the recruits had to sniff and taste before Norman would fill their glasses. For dessert he situated everyone in the living room and, before their very eyes, created something called bananas Foster, which, at one point, was covered with blue dancing flames that almost reached the ceiling. "A spoon or two of chocolate pudding would of been fine by me," Harold told Rena.

The boys ate greedily, hunkered over their bowls as if to defend them, taking seconds and thirds and thrilling everyone with their enormous appetites. After some Irish coffee Harold moved the boys into Norman's study to discuss business, and it was here they both doubled over, clutching their sides and complaining of stomach cramps and nausea. Their young faces blanched and a cold sweat dampened their shirt collars; both reached for the wastepaper basket, just in case. Harold continued with his harangue, insisting they could help issue in a season as glorious as the one he'd enjoyed ten years before, prodding them to commit verbally to the university.

By now, however, Harold too was beginning to feel a need to go to the toilet, and the only thought his mind could hold was that Norman Pepper had failed him.

"Food here sure is rich," the quarterback said, groaning. "All that cream, I guess."

"I couldn't believe it when that bozo burned the dessert," said the wide receiver, fanning himself with a magazine. "That alone was worth the trip."

The boys spent the latter part of the evening locked in bathrooms on either end of the house. When Rena knocked on the doors and asked if they needed some "tummy medicine or anything," both thanked her and said they hurt too much to come out yet.

Norman pulled Harold into the master bedroom and apologized for making everyone sick. Had his chances of signing the boys been more promising, Harold might have laughed at how silly Norman looked in his extravagant kitchen attire, but now he struggled to see the humor. Norman, recognizing Harold's despair, asked Harold if he'd ever noticed that he wore a toupee, then proceeded to remove the chef's hat and peel an oval chunk of curly brown hair off the top of his head. Thrusting the wig at Harold, Norman asked him to "please see how real my prosthesis feels," but Harold refused and demanded to know why, all of a sudden, Norman felt compelled to show him his balding scalp. Norman rested an arm on Harold's shoulder and explained that only his closest and most trusted friends got to see him as he really was. Harold bristled at the intimacy. "You're just trying to make it up to me for ruining my damn future," he said. "We'll never get them boys now, you know that."

Harold had a fleshy pink scar, a keloid, on his hip, and his right testicle hung far lower than his left, but he would never deliberately show these physical imperfections to anyone, least of all a virtual stranger. In Norman's eyes Harold saw grave disappointment. But hurting the man now, he thought, was better than leading him on and pretending they had a cushy future together as pals. When Norman said it was fine for Harold to go ahead and touch the spots on his head where tape and spirit gum held the polyurethane cap in place, Harold snickered and drove his hands deep into his pants pockets. In those days Harold was still one of the winningest coaches in the country, and he could pick and choose his friends, or so he liked to think.

A few minutes later in the Peppers' living room, the recruits asked Harold if he wouldn't mind taking them back to the hotel now; they wanted to scratch tomorrow's plans to visit the zoo and meet the governor, and after being up all night with "them two horny yellow-headed girls," they figured they really didn't want to play football here after all. They were Christians, they said, and life in a place like this surely would lead them to hell. As Harold begged the boys to change their minds, Norman entered the room carrying a silver tray loaded with bacon-wrapped wiener chips, fried chicken livers and cream-cheese wontons.

"Okay, everybody," he said. "Let's try again and see if Chef Pepper got anything right this time."

In what looked like one fluid motion, Harold slammed a forearm into the platter, sending food all over the room, ripped Norman's toupee off his head and tossed it at the two girls, who, leaping onto the arms of their chairs, squealed as if a mouse had nipped their ankles. Rena fumbled around trying to return the hair to Norman's head, adding to his humiliation. Only a handful of the guests, drunk on milk rum punch, thought it funny and patted Harold on the back, their reward for the utter audacity he displayed in breaking the oppressive formality of the party. Norman retired to his bedroom and wasn't heard from the rest of the evening. Harold shadowboxed around the living room and wondered aloud why no one could take a joke. Rena stormed off angrily with the recruits in tow, and Harold had to hitch a ride home with Trent Orlansky and his wife who, as a matter of principle, would not speak to him. As they whispered infrequently in the front seat, Harold lounged in the back of their station wagon and drew pictures of footballs sailing through goal-posts on the windows clouded with condensation.

Early the next morning, Harold called and tried to smooth things over with Norman; he claimed a wicked mixture of wine and sinus medicine had rendered him temporarily insane. But Norman refused to accept this apology, and then Rena tried. "Your cooking was fine," Harold heard her say. "Everyone was nervous and all, and the cream, you know . . . well, I guess it was a little much for their stomachs."

When, a few years later, the governor appointed Norman to the university board, Harold sent him a note of congratulations on purple-and-gold stationery. In a postscript he apologized again for the toupee incident and penned "Ha! Ha! Ha!" and a crude smiling face, dressed with a full head of hair, in the margin. Neither Harold nor Rena was surprised when the letter was returned unopened.

| 25 |

Harold had the shakes calling Norman at his home in Spanish Town, the historic residential district near the state capitol. Norman picked up quickly.

"This is the Old Man," Harold mumbled. "Can you come by the house tonight? I got something I want to share with you."

"For heaven's sake, I'm in my pajamas," Norman said.

"You been mad at me going on twenty years," Harold said. "That's a long time to hold a grudge. While there's still time I want to clear things up with you."

The man paused, then said, "What are you talking about, 'while there's still time'?"

"Come on over. You know where I live." To be sure, Harold gave him the address and spelled the name of his street.

"Try me at my office tomorrow," Norman said. "That way you won't have to see me again without my prosthesis."

"I've apologized for that enough times now, Norman. And while there's still time, you should forgive me."

Harold waited, listening to the irregular pulse of static on the line, but Norman said nothing.

"You there, hardhead? Norman? Norman! Talk to me, hardhead."

"I'm here, all right," he finally said. "But my hairwear's on a Styrofoam dummy in the bathroom. And I don't feel like combing it out and putting it on."

"Will you forget about your hat a minute and listen to me?"

Once again Norman fell silent.

"This prosthesis business," Harold said. "Norman, how come you keep living in the past? You keep seeing me as part of your ancient history. What I've got to say has to do with my future. And I think you ought to sit down where you're comfortable and look at me when I say it."

"We don't meet on your contract for another two weeks."

"It ain't about that."

"Then why do I have to come over? Why can't you come over?"

"You inviting me back into your house? You mean you ain't afraid to let me loose in your living room again?"

"Is it you've finally decided to resign?" Norman said. "Because if it is, there's no point in coming over. I figure you probably already know we've got the votes to end your reign of terror and bring in a new man."

"Nobody can make me quit."

Norman laughed. "If we vote you out, you're out, Harold. This has nothing to do with quitting. So don't go challenging me in my pajamas at eleven-thirty at night when my wife is waiting for me sound asleep under the covers."

"I'll come over. Give me ten minutes."

"Five," he said. "Or stay where you are."

| **26** |

As Harold was parking on the short gravel drive leading to Norman's townhouse, canary-yellow lights on either side of the front door popped on, assuring Harold he'd come to the right place. Harold thought this was a positive sign until Norman appeared wearing pajamas and his toupee, shouting with both hands cupped around his mouth for Harold to move his Cadillac back on the street or risk being towed.

Harold cracked his window. "Nobody's gonna get me at midnight," he said. "Everyone's gone to bed."

Pepper pointed to the spot where he wanted Harold to park. "You don't move it, Old Man, I'll call the wrecker service myself."

Harold complied but not without wishing a variety of vile, bloody deaths upon Norman, who by now was sitting on the narrow wrought-iron steps leading up to the door, his hands draped over the rails on either side of him, looking down to where Harold stood on the neatly trimmed lawn. Norman's face was shining with artificial light, but only vaguely familiar nonetheless.

"I learned today I'm dying with lung cancer," Harold announced. "If you don't believe me, ask John Ford Cage. He was with me when Dr. Harbold-something give me the news." He coughed and spit a bloody gob on the flagstones in front of Norman's bare feet. "What I come for," he continued slowly, staring at the hock, "is to tell you for the last time I'm sorry for wrecking your party twenty years ago and to try to get you to see I deserve to stay on as coach."

Norman stood up, a medium-tall man shaped like a pear set on its blossom end, a swatch of perfectly combed hair at his northernmost extremity. "Come in," he said, holding the door open and letting Harold walk in first. "Watch your step, please. It can be tricky." His voice was so choked with emotion it sounded as if he were talking through chipped glass and rocks: a voice entirely different from the one Harold had heard on the phone. "The air inside is better," Norman was saying. "We have a lady who cleans—" here he almost fell himself, crossing the threshold—"and she hates dust."

Except for a thick Belgian carpet covering the parquet floor and several pieces of red leather furniture still new enough to smell, the room was as unexceptional as Harold remembered it. Shelves crowded with leather-bound books lined the walls, and a tambour clock ticked loudly on the fireplace mantel. Harold could almost picture the hired girls performing their dance routines, the shaggy-haired recruits wolfing down bowl after bowl of toasted banana spears and French-vanilla ice cream. Although Norman didn't invite Harold to sit down, it wasn't because he hadn't warmed to him. In the soft wash of lamplight Norman looked at Harold with eyes like those of a young boy overcome by some unmentionable sorrow. As he had so many years before, he placed an arm on Harold's shoulders, this time less playfully than the last. Eyes moist with tears, he stared at Harold hard for a minute, then pushed him away as if he couldn't bear to know that such a tragedy had befallen him.

Then he said something: "Aaarrgh," or "raargh," a word that at once meant everything and nothing. Harold nodded his head as if he understood—as if, yes, they now spoke the same language. He tried to make the same sound and let his eyes moisten with tears.

Harold had only hoped his visit would begin this well, and now, clumsily, he struggled to soothe Norman, who'd retreated to the bar at the other side of the room and was pouring whiskey over ice in a converted jelly jar.

"You've got to be strong," Harold said. "You have no choice but to be strong. Chin up, now, hardhead."

This was the advice he figured Rena should've given him earlier in the evening. It implied there was some well of fortitude left in him, that everything hadn't been wasted.

"You shame me with your courage," Norman said.

"No need for flattery, hardhead. That's not why I'm here."

Norman thrust his arms out defensively. "Please," he said. "Hear me out on this." He was careful choosing his words and strained to speak each one. "For years I dodge you, I refuse to sit in the stadium and watch the purple and gold play, I defame your name. All for what, Old Man?" He paused momentarily, waiting for Harold to respond, then continued: "I suppose for vanity, that's what. Because one night many years ago you struck at the core of my sensitivity, challenging me to be who I am, to stop lying to myself and the world."

"Don't be so down on yourself," Harold said. "The crabmeat was good. Those kids just ate too many bananas."

Norman wagged his head. "Not the food part of the night. I mean the hair part: you grabbed my hair and threw it at those young women, remember?"

"Okay." Harold smiled. "I understand now." But he really didn't. Harold knew he'd wanted more than a cheap laugh when he pulled off Norman's wig, but all this time he'd thought it had something to do with letting the man know how badly he'd failed him and how much he resented his attempt to buddy up to him without invitation. Now he was delighted to learn how complicated his intentions actually were.

"Let's let it go," Harold was saying. "What happened to us then is dead and rotten in the grave. Look at me, Norman. For nearly thirty years I been trying to get back what I thought would always be mine. If you and the board don't run me off, I'll be eternally grateful for one more shot at the title."

Their eyes met, but Norman's started to blink nervously and he turned them away. As he raised the drink to his lips, Norman's hand was trembling and unsteady.

"Hope I'm not being forward," Harold said. "But would you mind . . ." With a nod he indicated the bottle.

Norman mumbled an apology and hurriedly poured some of the whiskey into a glass identical to his own. It was Crown Royal, dressed in a blue velvet sack trimmed in gold, and Harold was happy Norman had left out the ice.

"God, I'm sorry for you, Old Man. I'm so damn sorry."

"Thank you," Harold said.

"One more?" Norman was holding up the bottle.

"Yes, please."

Harold drained the second glass and got to wondering what would've happened if, years ago, he had come up with a story about being terminally ill and pitched it to Norman and the rest of his derogators. For one it would've distanced himself from the dinner party at Norman's and spared him that enduring torment; Norman's reaction tonight was proof of that. But then, later, seeing that he wasn't sick and dying, how would everyone have treated him, particularly his enemies?

Had he been successful and turned the program around, they would've had no choice but to want to keep him. He was sure of that. And no doubt he could've talked Doc Cage into standing before the usual gathering of news hacks and declaring him a medical miracle, beating whatever disease he'd invented for himself. If he'd been able to win, Harold believed, they would've accepted the tale of his recovery as fact and considered him among the singularly blessed. There he stood a survivor while they themselves, faced with identical odds, probably would've surrendered and perished. They might have given him a hunting lease in the marsh as a bonus. A free lifetime membership to the City Club. But if he'd lost—God, if he'd lost!—living all along in perfectly good health and showing no signs of physical decay and imminent death, they would've called him a lying, losing bastard and sent him packing. And watching him go, they would've tied that one dim moment to his entire career and convinced themselves that the Tenpenny game had been fabricated in a similar fashion, that everything he'd ever done was a lie.

"And how is Miss Rena taking all this?" Norman was saying from where he stood behind the bar.

Harold shrugged and looked away. "Fine," he said, "if you don't consider she wants to be dead herself."

"If ever she needs time away from the house, you know the wife here would be more than happy to have her come over. She lost her mother about two months ago and would rather enjoy, I think, having somebody who can relate to talk with."

"Thank you, Norman. I'll tell her that." Harold poured himself another drink.

"And tell her," Norman said, "that I plan to go the distance for you, Old Man—whatever you need, anything in this world. It's just too bad it took something like lung cancer to get us in the same room again." With the flat of his hand he tapped himself on the top of his head, disturbing the exact placement of his hairpiece. "I take the blame, though. It's all my fault."

"We both were kind of young and kind of wrong," Harold said. "Just promise you and the others'll let me keep the job."

Without a word of warning Norman reached behind his head as if to scratch an itch at the back of his neck, but when his hand came forward it held the hairpiece. He was smiling with the conviction of one suddenly rid of an old, imperfect life and born to another, and now the tears ran clear to the edge of his jaw. Harold extended his glass to toast him but could think of nothing to say.

They clinked their drinks together and, after a moment in which neither spoke or seemed to breathe, Norman passed his hands over his scalp. "Why don't I leave this little strip of fur here," he said, "and let's go outside for a walk. Turns out the air in this house wasn't so good after all." The top of his head was crisscrossed with purple spider veins the thickness of sewing thread, and his face was pasty and dripping with sweat. "It doesn't bother you, does it, Old Man—me going around looking like this?"

"No," Harold said. "Leave it."

"After what you came here to tell me tonight I feel kind of stupid having it on. I don't know. . . ." He pointed at the wig. "This doesn't seem at all important right now."

Norman finished his drink and left his hair on the bar. As he reached to pull the door closed behind him, he looked back at his prosthesis as if it were the family dog he'd decided to abandon; then he averted his eyes and stepped outside. The night was cool, and a smattering of stars flashed in the sky; what sliver of a moon there was burned a rare honey yellow.

Harold noticed that Norman kept his gaze on the windows of the matching houses across the street. Every few seconds he shook his head and scratched the top of his scalp with his hands—as if, Harold thought, he were stroking invisible curls.

"This is the day you learned you're going to die," Norman said, "and here I am primping for the neighbors. It's just that they've never seen me like this. Thirty-some years."

"Don't worry about it," Harold said.

"My god you're brave." He put his arm on Harold's shoulder as he had years before. "Anybody ever tell you that?"

"Some girl I used to know," Harold said, looking off at all the things that filled the winter sky. "She was two weeks shy of nineteen when I first heard it. I was brave and I was going to protect her and make her happy."

Norman spun away: it was as if he had opened the wrong hotel door and glanced at something practiced by married couples far less inhibited than he and his wife. "This is Miss Rena you're talking about, isn't it, Old Man?"

"That's right," Harold said, starting up the street. "But like a lot of other things, that was half a lifetime ago and it don't look like it wants to come back anymore."

| **27** |

They headed in the direction of the state capitol building, about a mile away. Norman, who was barefoot, walked on either the balls of his feet or on his heels, careful not to cut himself on anything in the street. After less than a hundred yards Harold had some difficulty breathing, and he asked Norman, who at his fastest had been creeping along, to please slow down. Harold put his hands on his knees, leaned over and sucked at the breeze. His throat burned pulling in the cool, dry air. When he came up his head was light, and there was the taste of pennies on his tongue. "It's been a long day," he said.

"Take your time. Nobody's waiting for us."

"Not counting my wife," Harold said, coughing up a wad of phlegm. "You were the first I told. I tried to reach Champs LaRoux, I admit, because him and me are pals from way back, but he wasn't home. Poor bastard's lucky he wasn't."

"I'm glad he's away," Norman said.

Harold chuckled but didn't say anything.

"And I'm glad it was me you thought to call," Norman said. Embarrassed by the confession, he threw a fistful of rocks high into the trees, then another. The way he moved around, shifting his weight from leg to leg, Harold wondered if Norman might have to go somewhere and relieve himself. But then he said, "It's as if after what happened with those two recruits I could no more believe in heroes than the man in the moon. Something good and innocent had been washed out of me."

"Well," Harold said, "at Alabama they didn't turn out to be so great. We didn't lose much. So let's stop beating ourselves on the head about it."

"What I mean—" Norman was insistent—"is that you were someone set apart from all the others. It'd always seemed to me that there was a star up there in the heavens and it shone only for you. After the party, though, I didn't know what to think anymore. I doubted all you'd once stood for."

"There you go again," Harold said. "How come we keep beating ourselves on the head about it?"

Norman had lifted his eyes toward the sky, and now Harold lifted his. "Which one is yours?" Norman said, then pointed to a star shining alone in the east. "There it is. That's your star."

Harold found the one Norman meant. "It's sort of small," he said. "But damn if it ain't way out there."

They walked on in silence. At the capitol Harold stood near a clump of redtop hedges skirting the front parking lot and Norman sat on the ground and picked the pea gravel stuck on the bottoms of his feet. The names of the fifty states of the union were carved into the tiers of granite steps that led to the bronze portals of the rotunda. Back when Harold was a player, his coach, Bernard Toefield, often bused the squad here and ran it up and down these same steps. Sometimes, after everyone was exhausted and could barely complete the climb, Toefield ran along with them. As he crossed each step he shouted the name of the state carved on it. One night Toefield waited at the top of the steps while his boys returned to the bottom. Pulling his head back on his shoulders, he gazed up at the night and opened and closed his mouth, biting at the chill air. On his face were reflected points of colored light from the huge, Beaux-Arts building. When at last he descended, he once again read off the names of the states, his breath shallow from fatigue. In the parking lot the boys were crowded together, cheering him on. Harold was somewhere in the middle, repeating whatever the coach said: "Nebraska, Oklahoma, Kansas . . ." Toefield didn't stop at the final step but ran straight into their arms and collapsed. The boys lifted his limp body high over their heads as if he'd won a race, and they moved around the parking lot as one.

That was more than forty years ago. And tonight, standing at the foot of the steps with Norman, Harold struggled to remember what coach Toe looked like. His voice, though, came back to him now as clearly as if it were Norman's. Harold had always hoped Toefield's voice would ease him when his mind was troubled, but it never had. Nice as it was to hear, it was never specific enough in addressing any particular matter to guide him, and it often seemed to be headed in the opposite direction of where Harold wanted to go: toward detailing the beauty of a well-trained hunting dog when Harold needed suggestions on how to satisfy his wife, or toward the importance of doing his schoolwork when Harold had hoped for advice on how to keep his job. As he listened now, Bernard Toefield's voice was saying something Harold hadn't heard in years: "He might not be as big or strong or fast as most of the players he comes up against. But he's got one hard head." Harold always figured this was as important an asset as a ballplayer could have. Hardhead Harold everybody called him in those days. Whether Coach Toe ever said anything about lung cancer he couldn't remember, and even if he could it no doubt would've returned in memory as a political opinion or an observation on how to peel an onion.

| 28 |

"I used to run them steps," Harold said. But Norman, looking in the opposite direction, didn't respond. Instead he pointed and laughed.

"What's so funny," Harold asked, turning to see.

At the far center of the capitol lawn, the statue of the state's most famous politician, now deceased, was standing on a pedestal in a circle of storm lights. Pug-nosed and cleft-chinned, the former governor was wearing a double-breasted coat and church shoes that curled miserably at the toes. The statue didn't seem to have any idea what to do with its hands, whether to stash them in his pockets or build a picture with them; stupidly they filled the space at the ends of its arms.

"I just noticed the poor fellow," Norman muttered. "All

dressed up and no place to go. Standing forty feet tall on a soapbox with no one to hear him."

"Well," Harold said, "at least he's still around."

Norman stood and turned his face to meet Harold's. "That's a pretty nice statue, Old Man," he said. "But no matter how handsome it is, it still isn't the governor."

"Well, it's something, ain't it? At least he left something." Harold looked back at the monument, a gorgeous burning blur in the night. The figure of the governor seemed almost real enough to climb down from its perch and walk right on up the street, cross the river bridge and stride out of the city no less suspiciously than any other long, tall specter dressed all in bronze, although Harold guessed that it couldn't get very far in those old, beat-up shoes.

Norman nudged Harold's shoulder with his elbow. "You know what his last words were?"

Harold shook his head.

"God, don't let me die. I got so much to do."

As before on the street, Harold bent over and gasped for breath, felt the blood drain out of his head, tasted dirty copper. It wasn't an act, but he worried that Norman would think so. It really had been a long day, and the cool, dry air was like sandpaper on his lungs. He coughed and spat, then ground the bulb of mucus into the cement with the heel of his shoe.

"I thought I'd at least have a street by now," Harold confessed, talking straight into the ground. "Not that I really wanted one, but they took it away from me. Maybe too much came when I was too young for them to recognize me. Maybe they thought everybody recognized me already, which might of been so."

"Probably," Norman said. "But everybody recognized the governor and look what he got: fifty-nine bullets."

"What I wonder," Harold said, "is what he did for the people of this state that I didn't do more of."

It was true that they'd promised to name a street after Harold. After the Tenpenny game, the mayor told him he hoped to commemorate his triumph by changing the name of Florida Boulevard to Harold Gravely Road. But before he could pitch the idea to the city council, the mayor died suddenly of a mysterious viral infection and the man who replaced him was an alumnus of a rival school that Harold had beaten by forty-seven points. A few weeks after the special election, Harold paid a visit to the new mayor's office and brought up the Harold Gravely Road project; he was told to stop dreaming and asked to leave.

It was small consolation, then, when the next fall a farming community some fifty miles to the north named its high school football jamboree in Harold's honor. The Old Man Gravely Kickoff Classic was such a small, insignificant event that Harold was ashamed to have his name associated with it. Four schools, each with barely enough boys to outfit a team, competed in a round-robin tournament on what the day before had been a cow pasture; their parents and friends crowded the sidelines in tractors, flatbed trailers and pickup trucks. For days afterward everything smelled and tasted like cow manure to Harold, who declined an invitation to be on hand when the tournament was held the following year. Deeply wounded, the jamboree sponsors changed its name to Benny Fontenot's Kickoff Classic, after the owner of a local nursery who had donated hundreds of eggplant seedlings to the 4-H Clubs of the four participating schools.

"But a street, you know, is only some dirt under shell or pea gravel or asphalt," Norman was telling Harold, who was still slumped over. "Maybe what you need, Old Man, is a statue, like what the governor has here. A statue is a far step up on a street. And it's what a man like you deserves."

In an instant Harold's breath returned and the metallic taste left his mouth. Once again he could inhale without feeling that open blisters were lining his throat; in fact, his lungs now felt fine. When he straightened back up, he saw Norman's big wet stupid smile, and he offered one just as big and wet and stupid. Their faces were only inches apart.

"What'd you say, Norman?"

"What you need is a statue," Norman said, pronouncing each word as clearly as he could. "Like what the governor has here."

"Is that what you think, Norman?"

"It's what I said, all right."

Harold grabbed the collar of Norman's pajama top. "But is that what you think? I know it's what you said. Tell me what you think. And don't you dare lie to me."

Norman hadn't been completely serious, but something in Harold's expression convinced him that of course he had been. Harold released his grip and turned around again to stare at the lighted figure across the capitol lawn. Norman noticed that Harold's eyelids had narrowed to a point where you couldn't have gotten a straight pin through to poke the pupil: all Norman could see of them were two shimmering yellow dots holding the reflection of the statue. Even Harold's nostrils flared heroically. Norman started to say something, but Harold's arm went up and stopped him.

"Like the governor?" Harold said again, pointing.

"That's how I see it," Norman said, frantically twirling the invisible curls on his scalp. "Because a statue is a far step up on a street. And a street is nothing but dirt under gravel or asphalt or whatnot."

Harold put both arms around Norman and held him close. The sides of their heads touched, and Harold whispered into Norman's ear. "God, don't let me die. I got too much to do."

| 29 |

They took the same route home, but Norman, stepping lightly for his lack of shoes, dragged some distance behind Harold, who now seemed in a hurry to get back. At one point Harold stood in the middle of the road and spiked an imaginary football into the pale center line, then performed a victory dance as primal as those performed by some of his hardheads after scoring a touchdown. Norman begged him to slow down, but Harold skipped along as he had in the hospital parking lot earlier in the day.

"Please, Harold," Norman called. "These little twigs and bottle caps are eating up the bottoms of my feet."

Harold was so excited he had to struggle to restrain himself from taking off in a furious sprint. As he'd told John Ford Cage in the car, something wonderful was coming, he could feel it. But how was he to have guessed it would arrive this soon and come from someone like Norman Pepper—someone who for twenty years had wished all things bad for him, and who, it often seemed, would have preferred to see Harold dead and buried in a paupers' field than living forever in a suit of immortal, shining bronze?

"Old Man," Norman shouted. "Wait up. Wait for me."

"I'll wait," Harold said, but he didn't. He kept going. "I'll wait up at the house. Take your time."

He would make a beautiful statue because once he had been a beautiful man. Harold envisioned his likeness standing on a marble pedestal. Unlike the governor, he would know what to do with his hands: he would point with one and hide the other in his coat pocket, or he would hold them both above his head as if in victory, two tight knots strong enough to punch their way through the clouds. Like the governor's, the statue Harold imagined for himself was surrounded by a dazzling storm of lights, gleaming brightly enough to be seen for miles around. Its face and body looked the way Harold's had thirty years ago, when he was the game's top coach, the youngest ever to win the national championship, and it was welcoming everybody to Tiger Stadium, the playground he'd helped make famous. By now Harold was about a hundred yards in front of Norman.

"You sure don't move like a dead man," Norman shouted with the flat of his right hand pressed against his mouth. "You move more like Little Shorty and Pogo used to when they took it around end on the student-body sweep."

When Harold reached the house he stood on the top of the wrought-iron steps, posing like a statue. The only things on his body he let move were his eyes, and they fixed on Norman as he hobbled along under the lamplight. Harold's nose started to run, but he didn't wipe it. The wind blew and ruffled his jacket, but he didn't budge. Norman stopped to see what Harold was pointing at across the street, but the little houses were as still as ever. Nothing stirred.

"Who's there?" Norman called. "Somebody outside, Old Man?"

Harold remained quiet. He was picturing his statue wearing a double-breasted dress suit, the brim of a fedora cleverly angled over his brow. His lips, pursed in amusement, seemed on the verge of saying something extremely important: the quotation on the plaque bolted to the pedestal.

"When it comes time to run through those goalposts," Harold said, trying not to move his lips, "I want your butthole so wide damn open you'll need a pair of tenpenny nails stuck up it to keep your foul business from spilling out."

He sounded like someone who'd been gagged with rags and a strip of rubber tape, but keeping still this way made it easier for him to imagine the army of fans that would make spring pilgrimages to the city to see his immortal pose. He could see them placing bouquets of flowers on the marble pedestal.

"What are you pointing at?" Norman said as he sat down on the bottom step and started rubbing his feet. "And why are you pointing?"

Once again, when Harold spoke, he tried not to move his lips. "Just feel like it," he said, much like a mummy would talk.

Norman turned and looked over his shoulder at Harold, whose eyes had now frozen along with the rest of his body. "I'm sorry, Old Man. I didn't hear you."

Harold repeated himself but sounded even more muffled.

Norman stood up and shook his head in frustration. "Last time," he said, "I promise."

Harold lowered his arm and his whole body slackened. Yellow light filled his face. He wasn't pretending to be a statue anymore. "Just feel like it," he said, then wiped the snot off his upper lip with the sleeve of his coat.

| **Spies** |

| **30** |

Rena once happened to attend a movie that played to an empty theater. From where she sat in the back row, in the aisle seat near the tall wooden doors, she studied the colored light from the screen as it bounced off the plastic tops of the chairs. The movie itself was uninteresting, but the light on the chairs held her entranced, bouncing and swirling as it did, falling on no one but herself. Had the room been crowded, the moviegoers would have absorbed this light, each claiming his own small part of it, but now it belonged to her alone. Whenever she returned to the cinema she hoped to find it empty, to rediscover the feeling that being by herself in the great wash of colored light had given her. Several times she shared the theater with only a few people, but this, she discovered, couldn't satisfy her. They sat near her in the upper middle of the theater, not ten feet away, only a row or two over. She wanted to ask them why, with all this room, with all these chairs to choose from, they would pick seats so close to hers.

Did they retreat here from lonely, impoverished lives in search of the comfort of strangers? Did they care about what was playing, or did they come simply to be near others? She has no answers for these questions, only theories. And she knows that none is worth articulating as long as she can't explain why she herself so often spends her afternoons here, or what it is about a bath of light falling on empty theater seats that she finds so memorable.

Today's movie, a Disney animation produced more than forty years ago and redistributed earlier this summer, has attracted a full house, mostly children freed from school by the stormy weather. Of the eight films playing in the cinema, she has chosen the one that promises only mindless entertainment.

Although the cartoon characters are deftly anthropomorphized, their kisses are unconvincing, their struggles seem forced and contrived, their fates as predictable as the emotions they are designed to elicit from the young viewers.

She begins with Hawaiian Punch, Milk Duds and licorice spaghetti, but midway into the show graduates to a tub of buttered popcorn and Coke. Next to her is a child of five or six who, after complaining to her teenaged sister that she can't see over the person in front of her, leans her quiet, golden head against Rena's arm and surrenders to sleep. Before returning to the concession stand for a third round of refreshments, Rena builds the child a pillow with her purse and raincoat and wedges it between the chairs as a temporary substitute for her arm.

During much of the movie, which she saw as a child and didn't especially like even then, Rena studies the rows of faces lighted by the screen, the beautiful children bathed in swirling colors, the few older folks blinking off sleep, and battles the pain that has seized her lower intestines. Every few minutes her insides cramp and roll, sending feverish pangs to the base of her skull. Even with the crowd the room is cool, yet she sweats profusely. Salty beads of perspiration reach from her hairline to the fine, invisible mustache above her lip. Alternately she wishes she hadn't eaten so much and had never left the house, but not once does she consider getting up and walking to the bathroom. Although she would hate to get sick here, what with the sleeping child on her arm, she chooses to risk the possibility and ride it out. Can labor pains be worse? she wonders, daubing her wet brow with a napkin. The spasms come in waves about four minutes apart and last no more than thirty seconds. If not for her wristwatch, she would have thought the pain lasted three times as long.

As she sits waiting for the next cramp to overtake her, a power failure strikes the theater. The last image to fill the screen is that of a black forest being hammered by jagged streaks of lightning and lashed by yellow rain, an irony that does not escape Rena, who even in her pain giggles and stomps her feet disapprovingly, joining scores of others.

The darkness in the room is sudden and total until emergency lights come on above the exits. Then ushers carrying flashlights run down the aisles to the front of the theater and start leading frightened children to the lobby. They move them one aisle at a time, with one usher posted at the front of each group and another at the rear. Before more than fifty have been removed, however, the whistles and catcalls that erupted when the power failed have elevated to howls and shrieks of terror. Even the child next to Rena has joined the mad chorus, screaming frantically enough to curdle the blood. Rena tells her not to worry, but her advice is drowned out by more hysterical cries. She must shout to be heard, and this time the girl turns her bright, dancing eyes on Rena's. "It's fun," she says. "Aren't you having fun?"

Rena responds with a shout of her own and tosses what remains of her popcorn into the air, delighting the child, who flings a fistful of red-hots. Never in her life has Rena screamed so loudly, and when she yells a second time an electric ripple surges through her flesh. It suddenly makes sense to her why such primal howling has been used in treating psychological disorders. She tingles all over; tears of happiness fill her eyes. Her intestinal pain has subsided, and she is rid of other, more serious torments as well.

"Harold!" she screams. "I don't love you anymore! I don't . . . I don't love you, Harold Gravely!"

"Harold," the girl beside her is shouting. "I don't love you, either, Harold! I don't love you, too!"

At their present rate the ushers are several minutes away from reaching Rena's row. When one of the emergency lights malfunctions and blinks off, a general panic sweeps the room. Now some of the children in the middle of the theater fight to climb over others nearer the aisles, and some of those in the aisle seats push through the rows of children being led to the doors by the ushers. Several in Rena's vicinity are shouting about Harold, including the teenaged sister of the child next to Rena. "Harold," they are saying, "I don't love you! I don't love you!" With the panic these cries fill the hall, and in minutes it seems everyone but the ushers and adults are declaring their feelings about Harold Gravely. The shouting becomes a chant, and the chant rustles the red velvet curtains covering the walls.

When the ushers reach Rena's row she chooses to remain seated and let everyone step over her. The children take their cries against her husband into the lobby, where the noise fades to a low drone and eventually stops altogether. Fifteen minutes later Rena is alone in the theater. Everything is dark save one small circle of light splashing across the plastic tops of the chairs, and though she tries to study it as she did the colored light from the screen however many years ago, its harshness burns her pupils and rouses the pain in her lower belly. The spasm that now grips her intestines nearly takes her breath away and she hurts too much to speak, much less scream.

The ushers arrive and wave their flashlights at her, and she shields her face with her hands. "Come on, lady," one of them says. "Show's over."

"I don't love you," she mutters.

"Lady, it's over. Time to close up now." One of the young men reaches to grab her by the arm, but she swats his hand away.

"Everyone's gone home," the other says.

When they reach to help her up, this time she doesn't resist. They escort her to the lobby, one on each arm, their flashlights cutting a path in the darkness ahead. At the door someone hands her a receipt. "This is for any show in the future you might want to see," he explains, staring at her suspiciously. "We're sorry for the inconvenience."

In the parking lot the pain dissipates, and she turns her face to the rain and empties her lungs. "I don't love you anymore!" she is shouting. "I don't . . . I don't love you anymore!"

By the time she reaches the intersection where the Committee to Recognize Harold Gravely is soliciting donations, her throat is so raw and inflamed that the words come from her lips in a dry, hoarse whisper. At the red light the collectors surround the cars, rattling their give cups. The joyous feeling she knew in the theater has been replaced by one of despair, and her tears now aren't of happiness but of regret.

The man with the puttylike skin and mechanical eyes—the one who approached her earlier in the day—is tapping her window and shaking his cup.

"Your tires really sprayed me good that last time," he says through the glass. "I don't suppose you've changed your mind about that fifty dollars, have you, Mrs. Gravely?"

"I don't love you," Rena says, resting her forehead on the steering wheel and tapping her fists against the dashboard.

The man says nothing and walks over to the next car.

"I don't," she says. "I don't, I don't, I don't."

| 31 |

"What about those messages?" Mrs. Nancy Claude is saying now, sitting on the couch next to Harold and pulling up her stockings. "You want me to read them? Or you want me to wait?"

It is midafternoon. Outside, the storm Gabriel squats and broods, pouring rain. This is a day for sleepers and suicides, Harold tells himself: the living have no place in it. He reaches to touch her ankle, smooth and slender as a ballerina's, then runs his hand up the ribbed vein on the back of her leg. On the web of black nylon covering her narrow strip of pubic hair he draws triangles and figure eights. When, puckering his dry lips, he leans over to kiss the humped point of her crotch, she grabs him by the ears and jerks him away.

"How drunk do you want me?" she protests.

He sprawls on the floor with his hands still clutching her legs and quacks and babbles and stamps his feet.

"You can hold a woman like a six-pack of beer," he tells her now, sitting up and demonstrating. "Put your thumb here, your middle finger here"—she screeches when he presses against her bottom—"and walk right out of the room with her, pop the damn top wherever you please."

"You make me dizzy for nothing," she says, leaning back against the warm cushions.

She doesn't resist when he starts drawing pictures again.

"I should of known I wouldn't be able to do anything," he says. "All that happened downtown, the spy nearly running me over in his car, the pressure of inventing a quotation for the statue—it took my desire." Glaring at the limp, defeated object between his legs, he suppresses an urge to slap it. "How do you explain yourself, hard-head," he asks it and waits for a response.

"For one," she remembers, gazing off as if reading the stack of notes in her mind, "Mrs. Watts called. Some board matter, I presume. She didn't sound too pleased. Then your wife called . . . oh, about half an hour ago. 'This is Rena Gravely,' she tells me as if I haven't a clue, as if I'm so stupid I can't tell who it is. 'It's nothing important, Nancy. I just wanted to tell him I don't love him anymore.' She actually said that, and I actually wrote it down. 'Anything else?' I say. 'No, nothing,' she answers. 'Make sure to tell him, though.' "

"When they say they don't love you," Harold says, "that's when you don't have anything to worry about. It's when they say they love you all the time that you'd better look out."

"I wanted to ask her how she was coming along with all her house chores, but that wouldn't of been too smart coming from a secretary. I'd end up back where I was before you hired me—sitting in a trailer for a house, waiting for the sight of Jake Claude to remind me how it was I got around to wasting my life."

With a linen handkerchief she scrubs off a smudge of lip gloss from her teeth. "So I'm very polite to the woman," she says. "I even thanked her."

"You thanked her?"

"I did."

Mrs. Claude swats Harold's hand away, then walks across the room to his desk and picks up the telephone receiver. "Hello, Mrs. Gravely?" she says to the dial tone. "How are you, Mrs. Gravely? Pleasure doing business with you, Mrs. Gravely."

Harold shakes his head. "You should of known her when she was young. That girl would of done anything for me. She had ambition. She was always making plans for herself. Now all she cares to do is fold rags and keep footprints off the carpet."

The list of messages stands in a pile next to the telephone; Mrs. Claude picks up the top one. "And Norman Pepper, he called just to say hello. What a sweet person, that Norman. Who else?" With painted fingernails she drums her lower lip, a contemplative gesture that, for some reason, awakens Harold's slumbering desire. "Oh, and the police," she says, waving the yellow slip over her head. "Something about the statue."

"The police?"

"Lieutenant Cousins asked you to call."

As suddenly as the inspiration to possess her returns, it departs. This last message reminds Harold of the stolen coffers and the thief who got good and drunk at his expense. He buttons and zips his chinos, sits up and stares disconcertedly at the chalk- and inkboards across the room, the scribbles and diagrams that now seem to him as incomprehensible as Sanskrit.

"Ever wonder," he says, "doing what we do in here, if I might not give you a malignant knot on your lung?" This comes out like a confession, as if he's already done it.

"I'm not the cancer type," she replies, standing in front of the mirror on the closet door to stroke her hair with a bone-handle comb. "Some people, though, got the disposition. They got the word stamped across their forehead: *cancer.* Pale skin you can see their veins through. Tired all the time, always wanting a nap. Funny breath like they been eating soup meat. Me, if not for Jake I'd probably never catch anything. And that's the truth."

He swaggers over to her, puts his mouth on her shoulder and sucks, leaving a dusty pink mark that vanishes in seconds. As a cautionary measure against bruising, he gently rubs the spot, trying to erase something that isn't even there.

"I got a husband at home, remember?" Mrs. Claude objects. She too checks her shoulder in the mirror and seems satisfied that no harm's been done. "Good thing he won't be there when I get back tonight, but bad that he will be in about five more days." She confirms the date on the calendar in the acrylic holder on Harold's desk. "It's five, all right. I only wish they'd make it three hundred and sixty-four on the rig and one off. That would be the day I went to visit Mama. Life would be such a dream. No complaints here. Not a peep."

"Jake Claude may own the Ferrari," Harold declares, hoping to prompt a certain gratuitous response from Mrs. Claude. "But I got the gas that makes it run." When she reaches back and pats his rear, winking lasciviously at his image in the mirror, he has earned his reward. "All women, no matter how crude their men, deserve a fate better than what you got with Jake," he adds heroically. "The man's a pig."

"It's really Gerald, by the way. He read about some Jake character in a book when he was fourteen years old and changed his own name. He thought it fit his manly appetites."

Harold's eyes light on hers in the glass. "Does my breath really smell like soup meat, daughter?" he whispers.

"Oh, but you're not the type, either. You know that. I'm telling you, this cancer doctor you got's all screwy."

She holds the plastic clips in front of her breasts, fastens the back of her brassiere then slides the cups around and works her arms through the elastic shoulder straps. When she's fitted comfortably, he thrusts his arms under her armpits and places his palms where her nipples show through the lace, then tweaks them playfully. Under her conventional work attire Harold can always count on finding the boudoir dress of a tragically self-conscious whore. Rena, on the other hand, would never wear such provocative undergarments. A few years ago he bought her an ivory-colored satin chemise and a matching kimono from a London mail-order house, but with his permission she exchanged them for a conservative English breakfast gown and robe, neither of which she ever wore in his presence. When he asked why she didn't like them, she claimed they were too fine for housework but that she did put them on each morning for a few precious moments before and after her bath.

He discovered them a short time later under some empty shoe boxes at the bottom of her closet; both the gown and robe were still in their paper wrappers and appeared to never have been worn. He said nothing, but secretly held it against her: it was one more sign of how little she respected his needs, how she wouldn't go the distance for him.

Unlike his wife, Mrs. Claude played to win, and he expressed his appreciation by outfitting her with the most elegant undergarments he could find. At a boutique in a mall on the outskirts of the city, he bought her silk teddies with floral lace detailing, oversized crew shirts that reached her ankles, excruciatingly tight bodybriefs, fluted tap pants, high-cut French panties, assorted hosiery and see-through bustiers. All came in colors less enduring than Rena's requisite white and thus encouraged spontaneity: cranberry and fuchsia and sapphire and lemon and emerald and black. Black was his favorite. Her husband, he'd been able to determine, was partial to sapphire, for that was what she most often wore when he wasn't working offshore.

Today, he needn't remind himself, the color of her underthings is black, as black, he notices, as any he's ever seen. Without thinking of the terrifying list of possible consequences, he once again presses his mouth against the back of her shoulder and sucks, harder now, pulling her skin away from the bone.

"Don't play dangerous," she warns, pushing him away. "It's the count they took on my white blood cells."

"The count?"

"I bruise easy."

"Sorry."

She stares at him in the mirror, not batting an eye. He turns toward the lecture boards again, wondering how to redeem himself. "It's true what you said about my lung," he finally mutters. "Though I ain't lying about having cancer, sometimes I feel like I am. I've got a chest that makes me cough and all the other symptoms, but it ain't so bad. It feels more like a bug—the flu, you know."

"That doctor of yours is a fool," she says.

"After the Tenpenny game I stayed drunk for weeks, hardly sleeping, smoking cigars—remember, this was back before Rena introduced me to the wonders of Juicy Fruit—and my lungs felt like a pair of balloons that'd been pinched."

"It'll cure of itself," she says with an air of supreme confidence. "Sometimes you can think your unpleasantries away."

To be sure he didn't mark her, she checks the spot on her shoulder and seems mildly disappointed it didn't bruise. "No love blossom for Jake to slap me around for," she says. "You sucked any harder I'd have a huge pack of lies to tell."

"I knew what I was doing."

"You were right about him being a pig," she says, shaking her head. "Once he came home sporting a nest of pubic lice. I ever tell you that?"

In the mirror she points to the place, and the tip of her finger leaves a tiny round shadow no bigger than the head of a thumbtack. "Now there was a problem wouldn't for the sake of God cure of itself. All night they danced across my sheets like some kind of marching band on parade, only they were practically invisible. First I'd slap at 'em with a towel, then I'd try sucking them into the vacuum. Finally I went to the Motel 6 and called my gynecologist. He says to calm myself and prescribes something. That turns out to be the beginning of our end, but when I tell Jake that it makes him crazy. He cries and says he'll kill himself. He's hit me before, right here." She points to her eye. "You remember that nasty purple beamer I had? And still he wants me to believe he got his lice while out on the rig—from some tool pusher who shared the same stool."

Harold groans.

"I ain't stupid," she says. "I may be younger than him—this is what I tell him—but I wasn't born yesterday."

"You can cure lice. You're cured now, aren't you?"

She claps her hands, jangling the delicate ribbons of gold on her wrist, then points to the pile of messages. "The artist, too, Harold. Somewhere in there—I just remembered. He sounded depressed. He's another wanted you to call."

"Oni Welby-White." Harold nods; he was expecting him. "Tell me if I'm wrong: he's here for tomorrow's board meeting on the statue quote and wants to talk about doing some sketches."

"You already knew, then. Somebody told you."

"A little bird told me," he says. Actually, it was Rena; she reminded him as he was leaving for the office this morning.

"He's at the Prince Seurat. He wants to talk sometime today, swap some ideas about your pose if you have any. But, lord, he sounded depressed. I asked him if it was nothing Mrs. Claude couldn't fix, trying to be sweet—sexy, you know—but he hung right up. I ain't got nothing against an uppity artist queer, long as he knows I won't have nothing to do with him."

| **32** |

Harold returns to the couch and flops on the side nearest the window. In the corner of his eye he sees someone—or thinks he does—crouched in the windblown thicket of bamboo and palms, looking into the office. Rather than confront the man and risk frightening him away, Harold stands now and pretends to take a sudden and intense interest in one of the many framed photographs hanging on the wall. He watches the window peripherally, confirming his suspicion. Someone is definitely there, shielding the glass with flattened hands to give him a better view. Only the man's head is visible in the short space between the blinds and the sill, which, on Harold's side, is lined with potted primrose and dieffenbachias. Although it occurs to Harold that the rain might be responsible for distorting the appearance of someone who would otherwise be entirely familiar, this is no one Harold seems to know. The glass is wet and cloudy, making a positive identification all the more difficult.

From what Harold has allowed himself to see, the man's hair is both light and dark from the swirling shadows and fluttering gold bars of streetlight cutting through the plants, and it clings in thick, wet clumps to his forehead and partially covers his ears. He appears to be less bearded than unshaven, a current grooming trend made popular by a television actor. One thing Harold is certain of, the man is wearing a pair of tight-fitting aviator sunglasses, an odd accessory in such weather.

Separated only by glass, the man and Harold are less than ten feet from each other. What a fool this spy must be to expose himself, Harold thinks, but then he remembers the incidents this morning near the levee and downtown and decides the man has no intention of hiding. Clearly he wants to be seen.

To Mrs. Claude, who continues to prep herself before the mirror and chatter indefatigably about her husband's abuse, Harold says nothing. Were he to tell her to come have a look, she'd probably do something to spook the man, who, Harold has decided, is here to gather such information as the offensive and defensive formations scribbled on the lecture boards, and not to observe his and Mrs. Claude's carnal doings, however interesting they may be.

"Then there was the time," Mrs. Claude is saying, teasing her feathery crown of hair with the comb, "Jake comes home with lipstick on his shirt collar and strands of long red hair sticking to his blue-jean coat. He wants me to believe he got it from his cousin Holly who he happened to run into at Boone Sweeney's market. I tell him, 'Jake Claude, what kind of fool do you take me for? Holly Claude's a brunette.'"

In a giant brass spittoon near Harold's desk are several brightly colored umbrellas and the walking stick with which, years ago, he battered the papier-mâché head of the team mascot. Momentarily he considers driving the point of the cane through the window and impaling the head of the spy, but he knows his curiosity will be sated only by running outside and directly facing the man. Thrusting a pointed stick in the man's eyeball seems hardly an option anyway. In his present condition, Harold would be lucky to find the window and luckier still to summon the strength to force the wood through the thick pane of glass.

"He comes home with pizza on his breath," Mrs. Claude jabbers on, "and guess who's the one got to put on the fat . . ."

The year after the Tenpenny game, it became Harold's custom to walk around campus with the aid of the cane, chewing the stem of a pipe with a carved rendering of an Indian warrior's head on the cherry-wood bowl. He neither suffered any physical ailment that required the use of the cane nor much cared for the flavor of pipe tobacco, but he did think such attention to detail, no matter how superfluous, lent him a refined and worldly air. It was also true that he had no real business on the campus proper except to expand his already inflated opinion of himself with rounds of polite applause from the many students and fans he encountered. As props the cane and pipe boosted his confidence, especially so in the company of those tweedy university intellectuals who invited him to join them at their table at the prestigious Faculty Club. These were professors of philosophy, history and literature who spent long noontime hours smoking their own pipes and fingering the grain of their own fine wooden canes. Although they seemed too distinguished a lot to do such a thing, they allowed Harold Gravely into their circle only to bait him into discussions about the important issues of the day and watch him flounder. He might have been the best football coach of his generation, but he struggled terribly to make sense of the world at large. Ignorant of their game for weeks, Harold learned of it one afternoon from a student waiter who was trying out for a spot on the team. The boy managed to inform Harold that he was being made for a stooge without sounding altogether condescending and further humiliating him, but in so doing he forfeited his dream of becoming one of Harold's own. That same day Harold dropped his pipe and an unopened pouch of tobacco into the trash, then propped the walking stick in the corner of his closet and slammed and locked the door.

Rather than confront the pompous academicians and admonish them for their insensitivity, Harold had his coaches put the waiter through extra drills after practice. For starters, the boy was asked to endure a special session of gassers in the room with the blue cork floor. Then he was ordered to run the stadium ramps while wearing a weighted vest and ten-pound irons on his ankles and wrists. When after about an hour he fainted on the cement steps and smashed his mouth, sending a dribble of blood down his chin and neck and opening a wound that would require thirty stitches and leave him slightly but permanently disfigured, Harold directed the managers to clean out the boy's locker. He himself scratched the boy's name from the list of tryouts, citing "a dearth of intestinal fortitude." It was a phrase he'd learned from the PhDs with whom he'd so often dined.

| 33 |

"He's a person who thinks because he has handsome good looks and drives a classic automobile the world owes him something," Mrs. Claude is saying. "I hate a man with an attitude."

Harold horns himself into his rain-soaked Italian loafers and removes the walking stick from the spittoon. Shaped like a Bengal tiger at full stride, with its rear legs and tail curved back into the wood, the brass handle of the cane is warm, smooth and solid in his hand. Employing a full, baseball-style swing, Harold thinks, he could probably put a serious dent in the spy's skull, perhaps—were he better rested—even decapitate the sonofabitch. Harold edges toward the door, mulling over Mrs. Claude's account of yet another illness she was made to suffer as the wife of Jake Claude: yeast infection.

"It's like, far back as the honeymoon, I was allergic to him," she is saying. "I couldn't stand him in me, knowing what was certain to come next. . . ."

Prepared to watch him run, Harold turns quickly and stares at the face in the window with eyes that shiver and bulge with malice.

"You don't get it from eating bread or drinking beer," Mrs. Claude says. "This yeast's got nothing to do with that. . . ."

The man smiles and waves. "What the goddamn hell do you

want from me?" Harold mutters, slapping the brass handle against his desk.

The noise frightens Mrs. Claude into dropping her comb. "Did you hear me say I wanted something?" She wheels around now and stares at Harold. Again he waggles the cane at the man, but in return gets another cheap smile and backhanded wave.

"Anyway," Mrs. Claude says, "weren't you the one who set all the ground rules for this arrangement?"

Harold motions toward the window, but by now Mrs. Claude has spotted the man and is trying to cover herself. Although she is wearing a brassiere, she juggles her breasts like too many slippery pieces of fruit. As she leaps into the closet and pulls the mirrored door behind her, she leaves only enough space to frame her lovely, painted mouth, which produces a stream of blather. From what Harold can make of it, Mrs. Claude seems to be encouraging him to take some action while simultaneously vituperating their visitor.

"Just a spy," Harold says, trying to calm her down. "Just a spy looking to steal some plays. This time of year we get his kind snooping around here all the time."

Brandishing the cane, Harold bolts out of the room, sprints through the outer office, scurries down the hallway reeking of sweat and pine solvent, shoulders open the Players' Gate and runs screaming to where the man is crouched at the window.

Harold's manner rivals that of a deranged person beating back the ghosts of a lost life, a worthless past. He swings at the air, swings back, swings again. The noise he makes is similar to that of his hardheads in the throes of gassers; it is an animal racket that a human would hardly seem capable of making. Through the crush of bamboo and palms the spy emerges, but he doesn't look at all frightened. If anything, he seems highly entertained.

Setting his sunglasses on the tip of his nose, he watches Harold with eyes as round and full of wonder as those of a child at a petting zoo. His crew sweater and frontier pants are soaking wet; his smile seems genuine. "Old Man Harold Gravely," he says, extending a hand to shake. "It's good to finally meet you." Harold's hands remain in the pockets of his chinos. "Hope I didn't scare you there, looking through the window, but I checked several times, I banged on the door—no one. I could see the light in your office from the street. I thought I'd check."

Holding the walking stick in both hands, Harold drops to the sidewalk, plants himself on all fours and starts barking like a dog. It is a much deeper and more belligerent bark than any he's ever raised from his hardheads, and it fills the stormy afternoon. Plainly confused, the spy laughs and rubs his hands together nervously. "Coach," he says. "Hey, look, if I caught you at a bad time . . . I only wanted to meet you and introduce myself."

This peculiar introduction has attracted the attention of a group of students who, huddled together across the street, stand and watch under colorful umbrellas. Some of them are laughing, but others are too amazed to make a sound.

"Why don't we get out of the rain and go inside?" the man says, leaning over Harold with a curious expression. He rests his hands on his knees, and thus positioned, is unable to defend himself when Harold suddenly hops to his feet, rears back and throws the full, stunning force of the cane across his chest.

With a gasp, the man crashes backward into the bamboo and lands, sitting straight up, on his rear. Across the street the students disperse, shouting for somebody to do something. They're running in every direction.

"A spy," Harold calls after them. "Save your breath!"

When he swings again and slaps the man across the forehead, he half expects the top of the man's skull to burst open and reveal a cauliflowerlike jumble of brains and veins. The blow, however, isn't hard enough to knock him unconscious.

Harold has reared back and prepared to unleash a third home-run swing when Mrs. Claude appears, hastily dressed and shoeless but shielded from the weather by a purple-and-gold poncho, which she holds over her head.

"Oh, Harold," she says, grabbing the cane and trying to pull it from him. "You'll kill him!"

A slow trickle of blood, originating at the man's hairline, eases down his cheek and courses in a crooked branch through his stubble. A rosy gash blooms above his temple. The lenses of his glasses, which now dangle by a single stem, are chipped and cracked, the wire frame bent nearly in half at the bridge. Mrs. Claude holds the man's head in her lap and brushes back his hair.

She is sobbing with a peculiar feminine violence that gives Harold an urge to crown her too.

"Only what he deserved," he mumbles. "The spy had it coming to him. Save your pity, daughter."

"Your wife sent him," she says. "I could tell on the phone this morning. She knows. She's onto us, Harold."

"Don't fool yourself," Harold says. He takes another aimless swing at the air, missing Mrs. Claude by inches. "This is the first one I've seen in ages not stuck on the color red."

"It don't bother me for a second she knows, by the way. I just ain't into being sexy for some private eye at the window."

Harold reaches over and pulls the man's wallet out of his side pocket. The calfskin billfold holds less than twenty dollars cash, a few gasoline and department store charge cards, a religious tract proclaiming the virgin birth, an assortment of dog-eared business cards and an accordion of transparent pockets holding photographs. Most of the pictures are of people Harold doesn't recognize, but one, a small black and white, depicts a child standing before a Ferris wheel, his arms hugging the waist of a youthful-looking Mrs. Mary Elaine Watts, who in turn hugs the waist of a man wearing a homburg and a rumpled coat. The photo on the man's license, issued last year to Perry J. Watts, Jr., is identical to the face of the man in the bamboo.

"Didn't you say Mrs. Watts called?" Harold says. "Sometime this morning, was it?"

"Pretty early . . . not long after I got here."

"This is her son, Perry."

One by one Harold flips the picture, credit cards and license at the man; they bounce off his chest and fall to the muddy ground. "I seem to recall—this was at last week's board meeting when Champs LaRoux pounded his goddamn wooden hammer at me for not having my sentence—I seem to remember Mrs. Watts telling me her son wanted to come by and express his regrets."

He rifles through the compartments of the wallet once more before stuffing it back in the man's pocket.

Mrs. Claude looks up at Harold, terror forcing the gleam from her eyes. "I remember now," she says, her voice and her long, delicate chin trembling. "Those messages I told you about—I got them mixed up, Harold. Norman Pepper was the one calling about the board matter and didn't sound too pleased. Mrs. Watts was the sweet one—something about how you inspired her P.J." She pats the bleeding head resting on her lap. "But I never imagined him being this grown—why, he's a man. Look at them whiskers, Mr. Gravely. I pictured a child in sneakers."

"He must be another one of them people with some incurable disease searching for the strength to go on. Then he hears about the Old Man, what he's been through, and he's got to come out and have himself a look." Harold gazes across the street to where the students were standing, but no one's there.

"The near-dead or the undead," he grumbles, spitting a gob at his feet. "I don't know who recognizes me most."

The man mumbles something neither Harold nor Mrs. Claude understands and makes a spastic attempt to rise to his feet. Mrs. Claude restrains him and tells him to take it easy—"Please, just relax, baby"—then she coos like a bird.

"Being friendly is one thing," Harold says, "but you don't have to breast-feed the sonofabitch."

"There, now," she says, holding the man close and rocking against the bamboo. "Let's all be nice and quiet. Nancy's gonna look after you." He stops trying to stand and rolls over on his side, then drools a bit as she takes off his glasses. "That feel better, baby?" Mrs. Claude massages the sides of his head. When his eyes finally open, the lids are beating too rapidly—in rhythm, Harold thinks, with his own racing heart. The man coughs violently against her blouse, then snorts and coughs again.

"Mr. Watts is coming around," Harold says. "He'll be all right. He'll be just fine."

"Him maybe, but my shirt's ruint." She indicates the spot of blood and mucus the man spit on her clothes.

"Good thing I didn't catch him flush." Harold winces watching Mrs. Claude clean the gummy ring of blood around the man's nose with a white linen handkerchief. "That third time would of done it. I was swinging for the fences."

Harold thinks he hears the distant wail of sirens, but he can't be sure; the rain's still falling too hard. "Why don't we haul him inside," he says, reaching to help. "The hardheads'll be reporting for afternoon gassers before you know it, and I got important business at the Princess Rat with Oni Welby-White."

Harold and Mrs. Claude take the man's arms and wrap them over their shoulders, and together they hoist him to his feet. Trying to support himself on legs that can't manage more than a wobble, Perry Watts continues to mumble unintelligibly and chew his tongue. By the time they reach the Players' Gate neither Harold nor Mrs. Claude has the strength to support him any longer, so he collapses and drops to the cement floor.

"Not to worry," Mrs. Claude says, detecting a strong, thumping vein on the man's wrists. "He only looks dead."

Through the aluminum door Harold hears the approaching sirens of the campus police, much closer now. He and Mrs. Claude struggle to lift the man onto a bench, then situate him comfortably on his back. The man's arms hang limp at his sides, the knuckles of his hands resting on the chipped cement floor. Mrs. Claude bunches up her poncho and sticks it under his head.

"Tell the peace officers what happened," Harold says. "Just don't be too honest, and hold back on the details. Hard as I hit him, when Mr. P. J. Watts comes around he may not be able to remember what he eyeballed through that window."

With the tail of her blouse she wipes the rain and blood off the man's face. "Me tell them? Why don't you tell them?"

"They know the kind I been attracting, all the sick and infirm, the lame and dim-witted, the lonely. Tell them he's just another—I dunno, daughter, somebody hoping my strength'll rub off." Harold strides down the hall, heading for the door to the playing field. He stops before reaching Mrs. Claude's workstation. "And call Doc Hardhead and have him come look this boy over. I'm gonna put on some dry clothes, get my wallet and the car keys and go on about my business." He pauses. "This is supposed to be my big day." He takes a few more steps toward his office and stops once again. "And in case they ask, Mrs. Claude, a sentence is what I went looking for."

"You want me to tell the police you went out looking for a sentence—some words, Harold?"

"That's exactly," he says, "what I want you to tell them."

| **34** |

In his office Harold sheds his wet clothes, creating a second pile next to the first; then he puts on coaching pants and a sweatshirt and washes down some bourbon. Outside the sirens have stopped wailing, but the blue lights of the black and whites flicker and swirl on his window. He can hear doors slam and a police radio going. To escape he need only hobble down to the gate that opens onto the playing field, jump the fence and hedges at the bottom of the bleachers and find an unlocked turnstile leading to the parking lot, then double back out of view of the campus cops and steal away in his Cadillac.

As he enters the grassy floor of the arena, Harold wonders if he's ever seen it rain this hard in Tiger Stadium, and with the mind of one whose days are ruled by such signs, he wonders what that might mean. Should he go back inside and deal with Mrs. Claude, Perry Watts and the police; should he go home and try to reclaim the love of his wife; should he march forward?

Searching every corner of the bowl, he can find no open turnstile leading to the parking lot, and the concessions clerk, who has the only universal key, has left a note taped to the reinforced glass of his door saying he had errands to run but will return shortly. Through cupped hands Harold shouts an obscenity that bounces back in off the stadium bowl, multiplying in echo. When, after about thirty seconds, the word fades into oblivion, he shouts "How long is shortly?" and winces when the question flies reverberating back at him.

Harold is walking the length of the playing field, trying to figure a way out, when he spots a block of fluorescent light in the south end of the press box. Through the towering wall of glass someone is wiping the Formica tops of the desks where the news hacks file their game stories: it is Camille Jones, the head groundskeeper. For years now rumors have floated among the athletic department staff that

Camille dined each night on corn chips, pickled eggs and Pepsi-Cola stolen from the concession stands; they also claimed he made a home of the men's lounge in the press box. Harold, studying his friend closely, dismissed the stories as fantasy and noted that Camille's khaki work uniform and baseball cap were always as spotless and well pressed at the end of the day as they were at the beginning, strongly suggesting the presence of a woman at home with a handy iron and board and little tolerance for slovenliness.

Harold starts up the stairs, stepping carefully on the slick cement steps painted with purple tiger stripes and yellow numbers. Less than halfway up, pain wracks his chest; he stops, wraps his arms around his upper body and squeezes. The hurt, he once told Rena, was like an indolent old dog: it moved on its own accord, when and if it felt like it.

From above Camille Jones has spotted him. Standing on the desk top, he removes his cap and bows as if before royalty. Cursing the pain, Harold manages a wave, but his expression remains fixed in anguish. As he leans back on an aluminum seat, it occurs to him that except for those times when he and his hardheads sat in these same seats and posed for the annual preseason team portrait, he hasn't sat on the bleachers of Tiger Stadium in more than fifty years, the last time being with his mother and father. When he came here as a boy the seats were wooden and, for the most part, dry-rotted; he remembers how his mother worried that splinters from the boards would ruin her pretty new top coat. The end zone sections and upper deck had not yet been constructed, and the stadium could accommodate no more than twenty thousand spectators unless temporary stands were put up behind the goalposts. The year before, light standards had been erected along the east and west sides, and when a bulb blew during the halftime show, it sounded like a shotgun blast and sent several fans, including Harold's father, a reformed bootlegger, running for the exits. Because he was under twelve, Harold ate unshelled peanuts for free. They came in brown paper bags that he blew up with lungfuls of air and popped whenever the home team scored. A cup of lemonade cost two cents, a penny more with chips of ice in it. That was the only game he ever attended with his parents, and the purple and gold beat a heavily favored squad from West Point. Someone—his father's boss at the general mercantile, it comes to him now—gave them the fifty-yard-line tickets, a Thanksgiving gift. They took the bus up and back, his mother remarking every half-mile about the extravagance of such a journey. On the way home Harold dozed with his face pressed against her carpetbag, and he woke with sleep lines on his cheek. It was around midnight, and hand in hand he and his parents walked home from the station. The night was cold and windy and smelled of boiling peppers and vinegar from the cannery. "Doesn't that make you hungry for gumbo?" his mother said, her voice calm and lovely. On the red-bricked streets their shoes clopped as loudly as those of horses. Clearly he remembers the crisp tattoo, can hear it now above the rain drumming against the aluminum bleachers. At home in the morning his mother served café au lait in a dented tin pitcher and beignets powdered with confectioner's sugar, a rare treat in their home. He was so hungry he choked on his food trying to get it down and his father had to clap his back. While his mother cleaned the kitchen, he and his father read the paper, fighting over the sports page. The account of the game was exactly as it had happened, and their night at Tiger Stadium came alive for him all over again. At school come Monday, his father told him, he could tell his friends he'd witnessed history in the making. "When you grow up," his father said, "maybe you can play for State."

Had they lived, he calculates now, his parents would be in their nineties. But both were dead before he enrolled at the university and tried out for the football team.

As always when he allows himself the memory, this strikes him with a terrible sadness: neither his mother nor father lived to see his heroics as a player and coach, to read about him in the morning paper, to tell their friends at work come Monday that Harold Gravely was their son.

They were dust in the grave before he was ever recognized.

| 35 |

"What're you doing sitting in the pouring damn rain, Old Man?" Camille Jones is calling to him from the top of the steps, sheltered by the press box. "Come get on up here and talk to me. Or am I going to have to go down there and drag you up?"

"I'm coming," Harold says, coughing. "It's my lungs."

"Ain't it always something," Camille says. "Just be glad it ain't your liver, which is what I got."

Harold stares at him with flat, empty eyes. "Are you kidding me?" he says.

"Nope."

"You should of told me earlier."

"I dunno," Camille says, grunting. "You seemed so happy with yours, I didn't want to go and spoil it for you."

At the top of the stairs Harold doesn't stop to chat. He shakes Camille's hand then pushes by him, climbs the stairs that lead to the press box and heads straight for the elevator. With authority he punches the down button, rather like someone poking the eye of an enemy he'd like to blind. "It wouldn't work for Jesus Christ if he tried," Camille says behind him. "Something about the wires. The school electricians are all tied up on account of Gabriel. It won't be ready probably for two, three more days. Maybe a week if the power decides to fail."

"So I'm supposed to wait that long?"

Camille smiles, revealing yellow teeth. "I got some hooch."

Harold drops to his haunches and waits for the fast burn in his chest to subside. Eyes on the floor, he lifts his hand and in moments a cool glass flask fills it. On Harold's tongue the rye tastes like rancid cooking oil, but the old dog pain gets up and moves, and the steady throbbing in his head dissipates into a million odd beats that finally break and crumble and turn light as air. He expels what remains with one hard cough, then spits to make sure everything has cleared.

"When'd you find out about the liver?" he says. "Before or after I heard about the lung?"

Camille takes his bottle back and sips it. "Since when," he says, "was this a race?" For a drunk he shows little appreciation of the whiskey. The way his face squinches into a fleshy copper square and a shiver lifts him to his toes, it's as if some cruel nurse had just forced a spoon of castor oil down his pipes. "It ain't really cancer that plagues me. It's what them rummies get."

"Psoriasis?"

"No," Camille says. "Cirrhosis. Psoriasis is some kind of shit you get on the skin."

"Then why'd you lie and tell me it was cancer?"

"It'll kill me all the same, won't it?"

"Cancer's worse. Cancer's the worst there is."

"It's only the worst because you got it."

"Come on, Jonesie. Dying of cancer's worse than dying with what you got. I wouldn't mind dying with what you got on account of there's but one way to get it, and I like that way."

"You speak with the tongue of the sadly misinformed." Camille removes his cap and wags his head.

"Perhaps," Harold says. "But while I've got one foot in the grave, you're up here throwing a cocktail party."

"You always was superior," Camille says, forcing down the rest of the rye. "Even dying you got to go out with something better than everybody else."

"Not better," Harold gloats. "But worse, maybe."

"A funeral's a funeral," says the old groundskeeper, " 'least last time I checked."

Gripping his chest, Harold takes the stairs down to the parking lot and walks around the bend of the stadium. There's not a single police cruiser parked on the street that runs in front of the football offices, and this disappoints him. Students with bright umbrellas walk under the vast oaks and broad pines, dodging puddles; none seems to notice him. Harold wrestles with the sordid vision of Mrs. Claude and the Watts fellow tied up together on his Naugahyde couch, warming the cushions. She had, after all, cooed for him, blown on his face, nursed his wounds. No, he told her once, he didn't care if she turned white trash and went with someone else, for what they had was founded on mutual desperation anyway. He had no expectations beyond an occasional romp on the couch, he said; trust was the least of his concerns. When she pouted, feigning devotion, he told her it was on account of his Rena and her Jake that they were doing this. It really had nothing to do with either of them. And what's funny was that she seemed to believe him.

Now outside his window, Harold pushes through the crush of bamboo and palms and tries to see through the glass, but all the lights are out and he can discern only a smoldering incandescence from the clock hanging between the lecture boards. Pressing his ear to the pane reveals a humming torrent of ocean waves but nothing of a man and a woman enjoying each other. He taps a single knuckle against the glass, but no one responds.

At his reserved parking spot on the street, Harold finds a note wrapped in cellophane folded under the windshield wiper. "Who do you think you are?" it says. "Just who the hell do you think you are?" The penmanship is chicken scratch, worse than a doctor's, and the rain, swishing through the canopy of trees, makes the red ink bleed down the page.

| **36** |

Harold is no more than half a mile off campus, driving toward the Prince Seurat to see Oni Welby-White, when he spots the red car with the distressed convertible top in his rearview mirror. The face of the driver, distorted by the frenetic action of his windshield wipers, is an ambiguous dark smear encircled by shards of street light bouncing off the glass. When Harold slows, the spy slows; when he speeds up, the spy speeds up; he changes lanes and the spy changes lanes. Near an intersection choked with traffic Harold decides to make a U-turn and does so with the precision of a professional driver, squealing on the wet pavement but managing to keep all four tires on the road. The spy is not so fortunate. His car spins out of control, a dizzy red blur, and slams into a family van parked against the curb. Upon impact the car's engine dies, but in seconds the spy has it roaring again and pushing up the street.

Now the unknown driver sits on Harold's back bumper and prods him every few hundred feet. Harold despairs that his 10PENNY vanity plate will be smashed, but he's enjoying the ride. Past convenience and sporting goods stores and pizza parlors and Laundromats and hamburger emporia they fly. Across from the stadium Harold brakes to negotiate the turn onto the unnamed street that runs perpendicular to the levee, and the spy's unable to react quickly enough to make the corner. Harold speeds up the strip, and by the time the red car can recover, Harold has extended his lead to about a quarter of a mile. Without slowing he blasts over the humped railroad crossing that borders the Ponderosa and goes airborne for a few seconds before slamming onto the road and skidding forward. He figures the cushion he's built is no more than the long, unexcellent beat of a heart, but it affords him safe passage at the cattle guard at the foot of the levee.

Climbing to the crest, his tires churn ribbons of mud that rain upon his back glass, clouding it chocolate brown; he remembers those innocent summer evenings spent in his golf cart, cutting donuts and dreaming of a demolition run such as this. The cattle grazing on the rise watch him stupidly, the lone bull toeing the soft ground and snorting with his head down as if prepared to charge. To top the levee Harold floors the accelerator and shifts the automatic into low, but once there the air seems lighter, the weather less torrential. The weight of his Cadillac, greater than that of the spy's car, will be to his advantage on the treacherous mud road, and if he holds his course he will be uncatchable.

Heading with the flow of the river, he has advanced a mile or more down the levee before he realizes the spy is no longer behind him. Slowing and checking in every direction, Harold can see nothing of the convertible; it seems to have quit the chase. To his left, River Road is a vacant strip washed by rain; to his right, the Mississippi boils beneath a solitary tug and tanker pushing toward the refineries and petrochemical plants on the east bank.

Certain now of victory, Harold crows and pounds the dash with a tight fist.

He has driven another mile down the road when up ahead he spots the red car approaching, a muddy contusion churning in its wake, its headlights flickering from dim to bright in a manic appeal for Harold to surrender the road. As suddenly as the car vanished, it has returned. Harold steers straight on, pushing the Cadillac even faster now. His breath quickens; blood beats loudly in his ears. The cars are only fifty yards apart before Harold starts to brake; the more he commands the Cadillac to stop, the more its rear swivels from side to side. He shuts his eyes and braces for the collision. But it is the spy who finally cuts his wheel and turns off the road.

"Chicken!" Harold shouts as the red car glides down the embankment, cutting tracks a foot deep. "Come back here!"

By the time Harold can stop the Cadillac, the spy and his car have blown through the flimsy aluminum gate at the head of a feed ground studded with salt licks and bales of green hay. The gate clatters to the ground a few feet from a huddle of frightened cattle who buck and run in single file along the fence. Harold gets out of his car and screams for the spy—the chicken!—to come back. Down below the cows can't even hear him. By now the red convertible is too far up the road anyway, once again rounding the bend and moving toward the city's business district, once again vanishing as quickly as it arrived.

Most
People
Ain't
Harold

| **37** |

Rena was waiting on the back porch swing when Harold returned from Norman Pepper's. The gas lamp in the side yard was casting a shallow pool of light across the bricked sidewalk that lay between the garage and the house. Harold didn't realize he wasn't alone until he'd almost reached the porch steps. The warm, metallic smell of perfume tipped him off, and he stopped to lift his nose to the wind.

"Who is it?" he said. "Who's there?"

The sight of him made her gasp: she thought he looked like some pathetic old animal trying to catch a scent of supper on the breeze. For his sake she moved her legs and the swing creaked and groaned. "Is that my pie?" he mumbled, staring through the shadows, "or some escaped convict come to rape my home and pillage my wife?"

She felt a hard knot in her throat, as if she'd swallowed something wrong. "It's me, Harold," she answered.

The darkness revealed little, but she'd brushed her hair and touched up her face; instead of the baggy and stained housedress she'd worn earlier she now had on blue jeans and an angora sweater. To make them look used, she had rubbed the tops of her aerobic dance shoes with clumps of manure from the rose patch, leaving the bottoms white and clean. They were comfortable as sneakers went but cost as much as some of her dresses. Harold had bought the shoes a few months earlier, thinking they would help motivate her to shed a few pounds and get into shape. But after failing to endure the first fifteen minutes of a television exercise show she had buried them at the bottom of her closet, swearing never to put them on again. "Bunch of skinny minnies," she had shouted at the TV instructors. "Better hope the wind doesn't blow." When Harold asked why she never wore the shoes, Rena said they were rough on her feet. "I blister easy, remember?" The lie had made her skin blanch.

"I smell a pretty girl's perfume," he was saying now, stepping timidly across the sidewalk.

"It's mine," she said.

"Nah," he muttered. "Can't be my pie's."

"It is. It is your pie's."

A pair of floppy red leg warmers, the kind often worn by dancers to accent their colored leotards and hose, covered her ankles and reached midway up her calves, a daring departure from her everyday wear. And for the first time in more than seven years she was wearing her wedding ring: two matching gold bands soldered together, each with alternating emeralds and diamonds.

"Look what I have on," she said, holding up her left hand, as Harold climbed the steps. A trellis covered with yellow jasmine blocked the light from the gas lamp, and the porch was dark. Harold stumbled around like someone who'd never been there before. "It's the ring," she said.

"The wedding ring?"

"Can you believe it still fits?"

He didn't answer.

"It's practically the only thing that does," she said.

He ignored her upraised hand. "Aren't you freezing?" he said, sitting next to her on the wicker swing. "It's so cold I might have to cough a couple times to get my testicles out of my throat." When he coughed a gob of gunk came up, and he leaned over the rails and spat on the hawthorn bushes down below.

"Cancer," he said, pointing to where he'd spit. "You think the shrubs'll get it?"

She sat up straight in the swing. "I like the weather," she said. "I think it's pretty nice for this time of year."

"Cold to me," he grumbled.

"Tonight I bathed for an hour and thirty-five minutes in perfumed oil," she said. "Soon as the water'd cool I'd let some out and add more hot. By the time I got out my hands and feet were all wrinkled. The walls were sweating."

"We should all be so rich," Harold said.

His own smell told her he'd been drinking, but this, she knew, was too rare and fragile a moment to speak of it.

"It's two o'clock in the morning," he said. "Why're you still up, anyway? And what're those funny socks doing on your legs? What good do they do?"

"I wanted to tell you I was sorry," she said, pausing to let it register. She was trying to hold his eyes with hers, but he kept staring at her legs. "I was wrong for the way I talked to you earlier. Oh, Harold, I'm so sorry about everything."

"It's okay," he said.

"I suppose because of all the bitterness my first reaction was to protect myself. I went on the defensive. I didn't mean to sound so hard and unfeeling." Her voice was soft but had a desperate edge to it. "I guess I thought it was another excuse of yours for not accepting responsibility—another attack of sore throat, Harold."

"Don't you worry about it," he said, staring at the socks on her legs. "I haven't had a sore throat in over two weeks." He put a hand on his neck and rubbed it.

"Do you think I want my husband to die?" There were tears in her eyes, but for the darkness he couldn't see them. "Harold, I love you. I want to see you get well. You yourself said the doctors could help you. Let them help you."

He was thinking about the statue Norman had proposed erecting in his honor. "Did I say you wanted me to die?" he said. "I was just sitting here wondering about the socks you're wearing." He reached down and gave them a tug.

"They're warmers," she said. "I thought they looked nice with the shoes." She leaned back in the swing and lifted her feet. "I got them at a store in the mall for when I work out."

"Then why not put some on your arms, too? Aren't your arms cold? Or is it only your legs get cold?"

The tears were falling now, cutting crooked paths in her makeup, beading at the corners of her wide, splendid mouth. "I'm wearing a sweater over my arms, Harold." She pinched the fabric as if to prove it. "And it's really not that cold out."

"You know I have cancer, don't you?" He was smiling.

"Yes," she said, pushing her face against the side of his neck. "I know you do, baby. I know." She was sobbing now and muttering something he couldn't understand. She tried to snuggle against him, to wrap her arms around him and hold him close, but he wanted none of it. With the balls of his feet he pushed off the pine floor and started them swinging. To keep her balance she had to grab the chain on her side of the swing; even then she lurched forward and nearly fell off. Finally she dragged her feet and that stopped them. "We're way too heavy," she said. "Please, Harold. Let me tell you . . . why can't we sit still a minute, baby?"

Harold started them swinging again.

"The chains—" she cried, "these chains can't hold us. They'll break and then we'll both get hurt."

"No, we won't," he said, rocking them higher. "I've gone so high before I almost flew out of it like a bird."

| 38 |

She did not try to stop him. Her obvious discomfort—she was clutching the arm of the swing so tightly that veins now stood on her forearms—seemed to inspire him to push them higher. Harold likened the noise of the chains grinding together to a pair of ferocious alley cats screwing, but because the sound was so loud and unpleasant, she couldn't hear what he was saying. When he laughed, forcing his head back on his shoulders, she saw his lips turn white and his whole body shake, but all she heard was the noise of the chains competing with the sound of her own beating heart.

Long ago she had been young and vulnerable and foolish enough to believe he was a normal sort of man. He had looked normal. He was already famous when he took her hand and said, "Look at me, Rena. I'm as normal as the next guy." She had studied his face and eyes for signs that he was lying, that there was some strangeness in him, some defect that would show itself if she watched him closely enough, but nothing had surfaced. "See," he had said. "I even walk normal." And in the middle of River Road he'd stopped the car and gotten out and proved it, walking up and back on the steaming plank of tar as if out on a Sunday stroll. "It's true I got a bit of a limp," he said when he returned to the driver's seat. "But that's normal for somebody with my medical history. And I handle the car normal," he said as he got back in. "Plus I turn the radio knobs normal." The way he said a sentence was not so normal, but a lot of people, herself included, had peculiar accents where they lived. "You may not believe it," he'd told her, making his eyelids dance. "But I even kiss normal." On the side of the road he parked and walked around and opened her door. "For somebody who grew up without the first thing, I got normal manners, too." He held her hand and they climbed the levee and lay in the tall brown grass watching the river run. "Hold my ankles," he'd told her. And she'd held them. "Now count," he'd said. And she'd counted as he did sit-ups, one after another. He was wearing khaki pants and a faded jean shirt and a leather flight jacket ripped at the shoulder seams. She'd felt the strength in his legs; she had to strain to hold him. He was trying to impress her, but at the time that had seemed normal. Boys were always trying to impress her. "Notice," he said, "how normal it is for me to breathe like an ox doing this." The top few buttons of her blouse were open and, leaning into him, she knew if he looked he could see her breasts or at least the cups of her brassiere. Her first instinct was to let go of him and cover herself, but she didn't. "Eighty," she'd counted. "Eighty-one."

When he reached ninety she started counting backward. His face reddened and he himself started to count. "Eighty-nine," she'd said. "Eighty-eight, eighty-seven." She laughed, but he was too tired to join her. "Ninety-one," he'd groaned. "Ninety-two, ninety-three." At one hundred he collapsed and stretched out with his arms spread on either side of him, his fingers clutching the high grass, his chest heaving for air. "Only eighty," she'd said, still holding his ankles. "Twenty to go. Come on, don't quit." When he waved his hands in front of him, she grabbed them in hers and allowed herself to be pulled down against him. Then, too, he'd smelled of whiskey, and when their mouths came together she tasted it mingled with tobacco. It was not a bad taste, she'd thought, though different from Pogo's, who'd always tasted of chewing gum. She and Harold kissed, lips clenched and bloodless at first, then relaxed and open, tongues exploring the warm pink softness. She was only eighteen; he was thirty-something, a man.

"This may not sound normal coming from someone you hardly know," he told her. "But it's my plan to make you love me." His shirt was damp with sweat. She felt him harden against her. "No," she said, pushing away from him. "Harold!" She stood some distance from where he lay and patted the dust and dry grass from her skirt and blouse. Suddenly she'd felt so tired her legs nearly buckled. "I already have someone," she told him. "What about Pogo? I can't just leave Pogo." As soon as he caught his breath he had started doing push-ups in the grass. The first twenty or so had come so easily he ordered her to sit on his shoulders. "I promise you the ride of your life," he told her, pushing up and down, not even straining. "I promise you things that ain't been invented yet." She weighed a hundred and ten pounds then, but that was like air to him. She'd counted until he couldn't do any more, to fifty-four. Then they'd rolled down the levee, through the high, windblown grass, and she'd begun to hurt all over and think of Pogo when once again Harold told her he would make her love him.

| 39 |

"Harold! Slow down! Slow down, baby! Please!"

On the back porch, Harold felt his butt punch through the seat, producing a tear that extended all the way to the side where Rena was sitting, her legs drawn up and folded beneath her. Instead of the arm of the swing she was now clutching his leg, trying to drive her chewed nails through his pants and into his flesh. She could've tried once again to stop the swing by dragging her feet, but a fierce curiosity had seized her. How far will he take this? she wondered. What pleasure can he possibly derive from destroying something he values so much? "I promise you the ride of your life," he'd told her all those years ago, and here it was, or here was yet another unexpected leg of it. Rena yelped when the swing's straw back blew out behind her and she crumpled in a rush to the pine floor. But even as she fell, landing on her side and twisting clear of the wreckage, Harold had managed to remain seated.

Ripped from its chains, the swing disintegrated with Harold in the center of it, sitting upright with his legs extended in front of him. He was too stunned to move.

"Are you okay?" Rena said. "Harold?"

He didn't say anything.

"Are you okay?" she said again, more urgently now. "Harold, talk to me."

As she sat leaning against the sliding glass doors, he began to scavenge through the mess in search of the brass plate commemorating his Tenpenny speech. "I'm here, Harold," Rena said. "Over here, baby."

He tossed a scrap of wood at her. "I know where you are," he said. "Where'd my thing go?"

"What thing?"

"My Tenpenny thing."

She crawled over to the mangled wicker and in seconds found the plate near the porch railings. Two corners had been chipped clean off and a deep fissure at its center had cut into the lettering. "Are you okay?" she said, handing it to him. "You don't look okay."

"I'm fine," he said, clutching the plate to his chest. "My butt's a little sore is all."

"Mine, too."

She waited until he'd left the porch to start cleaning up. She stuffed what she could into plastic garbage bags and put them out near the mailbox for the trash collector to pick up in the morning.

In the study Harold cleared a spot for the Tenpenny plate in his trophy case, but an iridescent blossom of light from the overhead lamp reflected off the glass doors and prevented him from seeing it clearly from the chair behind his desk. It wasn't as if he didn't know what the plate said, but he experimented, placing it in different spots in the case before setting it right on his desk, balanced between a bottle of aspirin and a framed snapshot of himself on the shoulders of Pogo Reese and Little Shorty Grieg.

By the time Rena finished outside, it was three in the morning. Her mascara had run blue streaks all the way down to her lips, and her leg warmers were flecked with white straw from the swing. She no longer smelled of perfumed bath oil, and though it might only have been her imagination, she suspected her shoes of smelling.

When she took them off she pressed them to her nose and detected the faint but lovely odor of manure from the rose patch. She was in the utility room now. She put the shoes and a half cup of powdered detergent in the washing machine and turned it on, then sat down on the dryer and started work on a laundry basket full of rags, folding them into clever triangles. She'd folded about a dozen when Harold walked into the hot little room and asked if she'd lost her mind.

"I always make busy when I can't sleep," she said. "And nothing's on TV."

Harold was rolling a rubber band between his fingers. "I come to you with a contrite heart," he said, nearly whispering. "I come wondering if you'll forgive me for blaming you for all the hard things that happened in my life."

"Oh, Harold," she said, placing one of the rags over her mouth. She almost broke down and started sobbing again, but managed to control herself. "How did you get like this, baby? I don't . . . I want so badly to understand it."

He shrugged his shoulders and dropped to his knees, his hands pressed together at his chest. "It's just that I'm dying and I temporarily forgot how to behave." He was smiling as if he'd made a joke. "The cancer has affected my brain. It's made me kind of crazy. I worry I'm going nuts."

She hopped off the dryer, pulled at his shirtsleeves and tried to get him to stand, but he said he wanted her forgiveness first and refused to budge. "We live in a house," she told him, "where if one person isn't apologizing, then it's the other. Yes, of course, I forgive you. But why can't you forgive me? What must I do?" Tears moved down her face, and she swiped at them with the rag. "I want you to hear what I'm saying." She held his face in her hands. "I love you, Harold. I love you more than anything and anyone. And I'm going to fight for you."

He made a gun of his hand, fitted the rubber band around his fingers and shot it at her, missing wide to the left. Then, erupting in laughter loud enough to shake the house, he got up off his knees and strode to the bedroom without her.

| **40** |

Half an hour passed before she realized what she was doing—folding rags, unfolding them, folding them again—and stopped herself. Rena's mother had been a folder of rags, the first and only one she'd ever known. Some people played solitaire and other such card games, others cut cities of paper dolls, still others crocheted doilies and coasters that would never be used. When Rena was growing up her mother folded rags. In fact, the first time Harold ever met Lottie Cummins she was sitting at the table in the kitchen, folding a heap of rags. Dressed as if ready for Sunday church, smelling of green soap, Harold and Rena walked into the room and waited near the icebox. Lottie, lost in her thoughts, didn't notice them. "Mother," Rena said, "don't you want to say hello to your son-in-law?"

Lottie nearly jumped out of her dress. "Oh, sweet," she said, holding her hands to her chest, "I was just folding rags." Her mother said it might look like an idle activity, but folding rags occupied her time and got her mind off her troubles. Now that her husband had passed away she did it more than ever, and on this day it had taken her to another, less difficult place. Just then she was remembering the sunny morning when she and Chuck had gone fishing out at Jobie Ippolito's pond and came home with nothing but sunburn and a bunch of ant bites. Some people go plumb cuckoo when their hands sit still, Lottie explained, then Harold confessed that his own mother had a way of easing her worried mind. "She'd count the dots in the tiles in the ceiling," he said. "Then she'd make herself forget the total and start counting them all over again."

It wasn't until later, driving home in the early evening, that Harold admitted he'd lied about his mother counting dots. He'd felt so sorry for Lottie, he said, seeing her sitting there all by herself at the kitchen table, that he'd said the very first thing to come to mind. "Did it sound real?" he wanted to know.

With a rag Rena now removed the mascara streaks, eye shadow

and rouge from her face. When the washing machine clicked off she took the shoes out and placed them on top of the hot water heater to dry. Then she took the rag, the one she'd just used, and threaded it through her wedding ring, knotting both ends. She set the wash cycle and started the rag and ring washing. Twenty minutes later, when they were done, she moved the rag and the ring to the dryer and watched through the glass window as they tumbled for about half an hour, the gold ring ticking and scratching against the metal tumbler. When the rag was dry she took it out, unknotted the corners and put the warm ring back on her finger. Then she folded the rag into its proper form and placed it on top of the stack of rags she'd already folded.

By now it was almost dawn, and on the balls of her feet she made her way to the bedroom, stepping quietly to keep from waking Harold. But when she reached the door she saw that he wasn't asleep at all. The room was ablaze with lights and the console color television, though muted, was filled with the image of a preacher waving a Bible over his head with one hand, pointing at his viewers with the other. Harold, dressed in black-and-white plaid pajamas, was standing at the center of the bed, pointing back at the man, or just pointing. "What are you doing?" Rena said softly, careful not to spook him. "Why are you doing that?"

Harold dropped his hand and fixed his stare on hers. A disappointed smile lifted his lips; his eyes watered but didn't blink. "What does it look like I'm doing?" he answered, then flopped on his back and pulled the covers over his head.

| **41** |

At work in the morning Harold told Mrs. Claude to notify the sports information office that he wanted to hold "an emergency press conference" at the end of the week. Although he'd gotten too few hours of sleep, he was feeling like a much younger man. She pulled the pins from her hair and went the wild, sweaty distance with him on the top of his desk, upsetting only a brass cup full of pens, pencils and paper clips, which fell clattering to the floor. When they were done, she called the public relations people from the phone at his desk. She was wearing a lemon-colored undergarment, not his favorite but extremely provocative nonetheless; the sight of her sitting in his dimple-backed chair, fulfilling his command, worked to excite him again. It was rare when he felt like making love more than a couple of times a week, but to desire it twice in one day and within the same hour certainly was unprecedented.

Naked except for the gum in his mouth, Harold walked over to the couch to wait for Mrs. Claude, but as soon as she got off the phone she started to cry. The powdered flesh of her shoulders goosed and tears cut ridges in her mask of makeup.

"They wondered if you were planning to announce your resignation," she uttered between sobs. "They think you're going to quit your job, Mr. Gravely."

"I'll die before I quit," he said with a laugh, and immediately she brightened and joined him on the couch.

For the next few days the newspaper, radio and TV reporters, reacting as Harold had hoped they would to word of the press conference, quoted "well-placed sources" who said the board had given Harold the option of sparing his professional integrity and resigning or losing it and being fired. Any way you looked at it, everyone was saying, Harold Gravely was finished as coach, and the formal gathering of the news media was scheduled simply to give him the opportunity to defend his career and say good-bye.

At the stadium one afternoon, Norman Pepper assured Harold that he'd informed most of the board members of what he called "our tragic dilemma" and that they were all sympathetic and more than willing to help him in any way possible. This included awarding him a lifetime contract and a pay hike that would make him the highest paid football coach in the country, college or professional. Harold could use the money, but he was disappointed when Norman failed to mention the statue. He himself had avoided the subject for fear of appearing pushy and overeager.

"Well," Norman said, pointing to the top of his bald head, "what do you think of the new me?"

"I think he's a fine-looking fellow," Harold said. He opened the door and led Norman into the outer office.

"If only you knew how much our time together the other night inspired me," Norman said, extending his arms and moving to hold Harold. They embraced and patted each other on the back. "My god, you're brave," Norman said, sniffling.

There was no telling where the reporters were getting their information. The negative attention was making Harold's staff jumpy, but he rather enjoyed it—especially now that he owned the support of those who would decide his fate. Since his night at the capitol with Norman, Harold had come to regard the media as a harmless swarm—"bees without stingers" he now was calling them—and he enjoyed being the object of their frenzy.

In fitting with his design, the days leading up to the press conference were frantic. The moment he stepped through the Players' Gate for whatever reason, a mob of reporters brandishing minicams, boom mikes, notebooks and tape recorders surrounded him. The more he told them to wait until he issued his statement, the more insistent and vociferous they became. Often he could escape only by running, and then, what with his age and poor health, they caught up to him in no time. Each morning his staff passed the latest newspaper clippings around the office. Unidentified sources reported that Harold Gravely was considering coaching high school or selling life insurance at a local agency.

Harold decided that in their quest for the last word, the news hacks had once again resorted to interviewing themselves, stacking fabrication upon fabrication; soon they would pay for attempting to bully him into admitting his coaching days were over. He had, in fact, seen it happen before, most memorably in the months after the Tenpenny game when many had tried to toss him into Pogo Reese's soup. As soon as Pogo took the stand and, under oath, cleared Harold's name, they printed editorials apologizing for their rough handling of the matter and praised him for his many contributions to the community. He had promise to be "one of the best there ever was." For their part, the radio people replayed the entire broadcast of the Sugar Bowl, dedicating it to Harold, whom they called "a real inspiration to our young people, a great American, a model of strength and decency." Had television been around, Harold was certain, they too would have declared him a model of some sort or another, for by then he'd employed a local attorney of enormous reputation who'd leaked word that, as Harold's legal representative, he had every intention of suing the pants off of anyone careless enough to defame his client by trying to connect him to Pogo Reese.

On the day before the press conference, Larry McDuff and Chester Tully asked Harold if there was any truth to what everyone was saying, and Harold, hoping to test the waters, said there might be. Later that afternoon, the two assistant coaches were so inspired leading the squad through a workout in the weight room that five hardheads collapsed under barbells and had to be trucked off to the infirmary. Larry boasted that he was responsible for three of the victims, but Chester challenged him by claiming at least four. Larry and Chester might have exchanged blows had Harold not ordered them into his office and confessed his illness and plans to remain at the helm.

"Even though you have cancer," Chester said, disappointment flooding his face, "you really aren't stepping down?"

"I'm the Old Man, remember? The Old Man doesn't quit anything—at least nothing he's still got a chance of winning."

"So the board'll let you keep the job indefinitely?" Larry said, trying to reason it out. "For however long you can?"

"In my condition," Harold said, "indefinitely might not be but a string of frightful months. But then it could be years. I think the board will keep me around as long as I can function. I've got some pretty powerful characters behind me now."

They both said they were sorry about the cancer, but congratulated him on finding a way to keep his job. They pledged to do everything in their power to make him a winner again, and they left his office affecting the appearance of best and inseparable pals, laughing as they wondered after the health of each other's wife and kids.

Harold's meeting with Trent Orlansky produced a similar round of questions, all of which Harold fielded with aplomb. Harold hoped to appear proud and heroic before Mr. Memory, for he was certain that in years to come his associate athletic director would be regularly interviewed by sports historians searching for every possible detail to explain his reign at the university. Harold felt like the unvanquished King Arthur who, at the end of his life, described his Camelot to a young and eager partisan, knowing his works and dreams would continue and perhaps never die.

"Here," Harold told Trent Orlansky, unbuttoning his shirt and patting the place over his heart and lungs, "remember what I am telling you, and let no one—not now, not ever—forget how it was in the time of the Tenpenny Eleven."

Orlansky was saddened by the news, but he still couldn't help but resent Harold for burdening him with the torch-bearing assignment. As a much younger man, new to the job of associate athletic director, he had relished the attention Harold paid him. Harold often sought him out in the crowd, pulled him aside and confessed whatever was on his mind. Harold was a great man, everybody said so. And what a privilege it seemed then to know the details of his rich and fabled story. As time passed, however, Orlansky could often recall more about Harold's life than his own, and the situation only got worse as he grew older.

Orlansky's father had been a New Orleans financier, respected and politically connected, the sire of ten children, a collector of rare books and coins. But it was a different father who sometimes came to him in memory, and to this person he had attached a sentiment and devotion that were entirely unearned.

Orlansky remembered times that never really existed for him but somehow seemed to. There were days spent helping his father at the whiskey still he operated in a swamp near Harold's town, and others trapping nutria rats for sport and profit. There were nights when his father drank too much and walked into town looking to pick fights with black people. Orlansky's real father had been a refined and liberal influence, a man who did not, as far as he knew, partake of alcohol and who often spoke of the black race as being more beautiful if not superior to his own.

When Orlansky expressed his memory problem to his wife, she said it was okay for him to be a little confused as long as he remembered that it was her bed he was supposed to return to each night and not Rena Gravely's.

"But of course I won't forget," he was saying now in Harold's office. "How could I forget something like this?"

"You'll remember how the weather was?"

"How it was when you found out you had the cancer—or today, when you told me about it?"

"Make it today," Harold said. "Because I don't recall exactly how it was when I found out."

"Consider it done." Orlansky made a note of it in the pocket memobook he carried for just such occasions.

"I remember now," Harold said. "It was cool . . . it was cold that day." He slapped the flat of his hand against the desk top. "Change whatever you wrote down there, hardhead. Put in cold."

"It was cold when Harold Gravely learned he was going to die," Trent Orlansky read from the pocket book.

"Yes," Harold said. "I like the sound of it. And you might want to put some snow in there."

"It hasn't snowed this year," Orlansky said, taking a pack of cigarettes out of his pocket. When he remembered Harold had cancer, he quickly put it back and apologized.

"Sorry for what?" Harold said. "For claiming it hasn't snowed yet this year, or for wanting to light up a Winston when you know my lungs can't take it?"

Plainly confused, Orlansky flipped through his notebook. At last he said, "It hasn't snowed here in almost five years."

"I know it hasn't," Harold replied, irritated. "But some snow would add something to what you writer types like to call the atmosphere. It might not of happened, but it should of."

"All alone after learning I was going to die," Harold continued, dictating, "I walked through a long field, bundled up in a lamb's wool coat, a fedora on top of my head, hands in pockets. After about a mile I came upon a fork in the road—"

"I thought you were walking through a field," Orlansky said.

"The snow had covered everything up," Harold said irritably. "I didn't know I was walking on a road but it turned out, sure enough, there was one right beneath me, cutting straight through the field, a little dirt one."

"There were no cars on this road?"

"I didn't see any. I suppose the snow kept everybody away. You know how people are about driving in the snow."

Orlansky scribbled away.

"So I had a decision to make: here I was a man marked for certain death, did I go east or did I go west?"

"But how'd you know one from the other?"

Harold clucked his tongue and rolled his eyes. "The sun sets in the west, hardhead. And this was late afternoon. I figured if one fork's heading for what's red and round and hanging in the sky, the other's moving east."

"But it was snowing. There were clouds, bound to be clouds."

"Okay!" Harold conceded with a shout of righteous anger, "the sun wasn't there. But the roads were."

Orlansky amended his text.

"I turned my face toward the drifting snowflakes," Harold said. "And filled with the unutterable meaninglessness of life, I eyed each way to go—"

"If you were facing the falling snow, how could you also eye the forked road?" Orlansky tried to do it himself, looking up at the tiled ceiling while simultaneously trying to take in what he could of Harold and his desk.

Harold ignored him. "And that's when I noticed one road was well traveled. It was covered with dog and coon and horse and, yes, human prints, but the other was clean and fresh—it was as pure as Rena Cummins on the night we met."

"And that's the way you went?" Orlansky said.

"No," Harold answered. "I turned around and walked on back. I'd left my car parked up on the highway, and damn it to hell if the engine wasn't still running."

| **42** |

The night before the press conference, as he and Rena were readying for bed, Harold received a call from one of the delinquents who'd phoned during the season. "So they finally dug their hole, did they?" the boy said. "How deep did they go?"

Harold, worried that word of his cancer and imminent death had gone public, said nothing.

"Come on," the boy said. "Your rooter, Harold. They buried it, didn't they? And tomorrow's the funeral."

"Is that what you heard?" Harold was sitting on the edge of the bed, twisting the cord around his finger. Relieved to learn the news hadn't leaked, he stood up and started pacing the floor. "Tomorrow's the day, is it?"

"They decide to use one of them crane jobs or just a shovel?" the boy said. "Maybe all they needed was a garden hoe."

Rena lowered her magazine, sat up in bed and leaned against the headboard. She saw Harold's face fill with color. "Tell them," she said, tugging on the sleeve of his pajamas. "Tell them what you told me. Tell them you're going to die."

"Not time yet," he said, pressing the receiver to his chest to keep the caller from hearing.

"You're always trying to be dramatic." She slapped him across the shoulders with the magazine. "I hate that."

"I'm a coach," he reminded her. "A teacher. And a lot of people have got one hard bitch of a lesson to learn."

"You're a coward," she said, then hit him again with the magazine. "You're more afraid to live than you are to die. That tells me something. I know all about you."

Into the phone he said, "To bury my rooter, son, and I'm not saying anyone's even thinking about trying such a thing—" But Rena wrested the phone away from him before he could finish the sentence. She put the receiver to her ear and heard a humming silence, shortened by a hacking cough.

"You talking to your big, fat wife," the caller said, "or you talking to me?" A moment passed and the voice said, "Tell her she looks like a giant porker, Harold."

Rena wanted to respond but didn't. She told herself to be strong and that she could do it, then she hung up and unhooked the phone. "Go to bed," she told Harold. "You need your sleep. Tomorrow you'll want to look nice and fresh for the cameras."

In defiance, he shuffled around the room for several minutes before finally sitting in his favorite chair and opening the morning's paper to the sports page. She'd watched him read this same section earlier in the day and knew that he had turned to it now only to provoke her. The lead story speculated on what would happen at the press conference, and it included the famous black-and-white picture of Harold riding the shoulders of Pogo Reese and Little Shorty Grieg as well as a smaller, less dated studio portrait. But Harold was more interested in a story about a basketball game, or pretended to be. He read the first few paragraphs aloud, planting "goddamn" between every few words and sometimes sticking it between syllables of adjectives and adverbs. "The hard-nosed Tiger defense yielded only five goddamn points in the second goddamn period," he read. Rena went back to her magazine, and as she knew he would, Harold quickly tired of his little exercise and fell asleep, the gooseneck lamp burning a terrible white light into his face.

As she removed the paper from his lap, Rena studied Harold with equal parts alarm and sadness. The heavy stubble of his beard was gray, his lips were chapped and white and there was a crusty ring of snot around his nostrils. When it happened, she told herself, and he was gone, she would make them put some rouge on his cheeks and perhaps touch up his mouth, and she herself would comb his hair. She didn't want people to remember him like this.

"Harold," she said, shaking him now. "Come on, get up. Time for bed." She helped him to his feet. He leaned his full weight against her and staggered to the bed, murmuring about who was man enough to dare attempt to bury his rooter in the dirt. He had no idea what he was saying, and she knew this. Years ago it might have made her laugh and think him a wild, tempestuous sort of man, but tonight it only deepened her sorrow and regret. She fluffed his pillow and pulled the comforter to his neck.

After she turned off the bedside lamp and covered herself, she kissed his raw, scratchy cheek. It wasn't until after he started to snore that she let herself cry, and then it was only for a minute or two. That really was all it took to rid herself of the feeling that she was somehow partly responsible for allowing him to fall so low and destroy all that he'd worked so hard to build with his life.

| **43** |

Driving to work the next morning, Harold spotted new banners hanging from the facades of the fraternity houses. SO LONG, OLD SPORT said one. ENJOY YOUR EXTENDED VACATION, HAROLD said another. COACH GRAVELY: DOWN THE TOILET AT LAST said a third, the most offensive of the lot. Harold considered putting McAllen Friend back to work ridding the world of their puerile ugliness, but under the circumstances the signs seemed less harmful than before and he decided to let them remain. When he reached the stadium, a black funeral wreath the size of a tractor-trailer tire was hanging on the Players' Gate. The note accompanying it said, "Thanks for nothing, Old Man: L. S. Grieg."

Harold told Larry McDuff to get in touch with Little Shorty right away, but Larry said he already had and that Little Shorty vehemently denied sending anything. In the background Larry had heard Frances laughing like a drugged horse, so he'd figured Little Shorty was lying again.

"One day soon," Harold said, "the butthole of Little Shorty Grieg will be mine and I plan to grow some sweet potatoes in it."

"That's a good idea," Chester Tully said. "I'll hold him down while Larry crams in the seeds."

"You mean I'll hold him down," Larry said, "while you cram in the seeds. I'm not cramming no seeds in Little Shorty."

"You two fight over this and you're both fired," Harold said, ending what promised to be another argument.

The men slumped their shoulders and stared at the floor.

Less than an hour before Harold's meeting with the press, Mrs. Claude put a plastic dustcover over her typewriter, sat at the desk in Harold's office and watched him dress, remarking as he horned his stockinged right foot into a black leather shoe that his style was incomparable.

Harold was wearing a dark pinstripe suit with a silk handkerchief in the breast pocket. It was the outfit he often wore to funerals, and he was afraid it smelled of chrysanthemums.

"Did you say impeccable or incomparable?" he gloated, rubbing a splash of cologne onto his jaw.

"I could compare you to Gerald," she said, referring to her husband, "but to my knowledge he doesn't own a suit. He's kind of got a rough neck, if you know what I mean."

"Now don't speak unkindly of your beloved," Harold said, smelling the sleeve of his coat to make sure the cologne had served him well and overpowered the scent of flowers. "You wouldn't want him speaking poorly of you."

"I don't mind," she said. She stood on her toes and smacked the air in front of his lips. "I don't love him anymore anyway. I love you." Harold could smell the faint odor of antiseptic on her breath, and he found it intoxicating.

"Tippytoe and kiss at my mouth again," he said. This time when she did it he turned and watched the ball of her calf tighten under the exquisite casing of her hose. "Stay that way," he said. "Stay standing. Don't move."

As she struggled for balance, supporting herself with a bridge of fingers on his lower back, Harold reached down and felt the soft knot of muscle grow against his palm. "It's so nice here," he said, squeezing the calf. "It's like a tender hunk of something I could carve out and grill on the barbecue."

She whooped, slapped his hand away and bolted from the office, slamming the door behind her.

| 44 |

Because so little time remained before the news conference, Harold ruled out trying to get Mrs. Claude to join him on the couch. He wanted to look his best for the television cameras and feared that sexual activity would drain his face of color and slur his speech. His suit was crisp and he worried, too, that a round with Mrs. Claude might rumple it. He had intended to jot down a few notes for the meeting but decided now that a spontaneous presentation would serve him best. As he often did when there was time to burn, Harold flipped through some of the scrapbooks lining the shelves of the wall behind his desk. Arranged in chronological order, the books covered every year he'd worked as head coach of the Tigers—thirty-four in all, including the new volume for this, what promised to be his last season. Now he focused on the collection of clippings from the Tenpenny year, stopping at the pages that featured his heroic win over Clemson. His image on the shoulders of Pogo Reese and Little Shorty Grieg mesmerized him and left him a little winded. Had he ever really been that young and beautiful? he wondered, touching the face on the faded black-and-white picture.

Exactly what had he thought about when the game ended and he was suddenly swept aloft and carried to the midfield crest, the eyes of the whole country upon him? Being so inexperienced, could he possibly have understood that the desire to be recognized was like a carnal addiction he would never be able to shake, much less control or make sense of?

His former secretary, Mrs. Glenys Presley, had assembled most of the memory books, clipping the stories and pictures from the city newspaper each morning and saving them in the scrapbook for the current season. Until about eight years ago, Harold had kept them all in his living room at home, but when he'd begun to spend more and more time perusing the old stories and studying the photographs, Rena had asked him to take them to his office and leave them there. "If you're going to live in the distant past," she'd told him, "make sure you keep your past distant from mine." By then Mrs. Presley was retired and the chore of keeping up the scrapbooks had gone to the new girl, Nancy Claude, whose first year on the job had coincided with Harold's first losing season as coach. Mrs. Presley had labeled the front cover of each collection with this title: "One More Glorious Chapter in the Life of Harold Gravely." Harold forbade Mrs. Claude to mark the newer books this way, and chose instead to put only the year on the cover label. "I don't want my name associated with what's been happening around here lately," he told her.

Mrs. Claude had quickly grown discouraged and clipped only those stories and pictures she found particularly interesting. Once she overlooked a front-page game account in favor of a sidebar that quoted several longtime season ticket holders who were disgruntled about suddenly losing after winning for nearly half a century. With each new year Mrs. Claude's books became thinner, but Harold never complained because he never bothered to open them. Mrs. Presley may have been more competent managing the office than was Mrs. Claude, but she never was as supportive. On her lunch breaks she had not once warmed the couch cushions or put her mouth on his, and except for an occasional glimpse of the frilly hemline of her slip, Harold saw nothing of her underthings.

At Mrs. Presley's retirement party Rena had presented her with a scrapbook of her own, complete with pictures of everyone she'd worked with, their autographs and sweetheart notes wishing her well. "One More Inglorious Chapter in the Life of Glenys Presley," Harold had labeled it, an insensitive attempt at a joke that had made the woman storm out of the room.

Mrs. Presley's last job as Harold's secretary was to help find someone to take her place. She and Harold had interviewed more than forty applicants, and each had whittled the group down to five. Nancy Claude hadn't appeared anywhere on Mrs. Presley's list, but she'd topped Harold's. "Something in her eyes," he'd explained when Mrs. Presley asked what on earth he'd seen in her. "Or maybe it was the way her skirt fit." With Mrs. Presley, a born-again Christian and mother of five, he had rarely been so honest, but he laughed as if he were teasing. Then he'd said, "No, really now, Glenys. The reason I like her is she seems eager, almost hungry. She seems to need this place a whole lot more than any of the others, and that's what I'm looking for."

| 45 |

Back at his desk Harold buzzed Mrs. Claude and, over the sputtering intercom, asked her to please track down Camille Jones and have him report to the stadium at once. "And tell him to bring a shovel," he said. "I got some work for him to do."

"A shovel in the office?" she said.

"We're going to have a funeral," Harold said. "You're more than welcome to attend."

By the time Camille arrived Harold had already stacked the scrapbooks of the last seven seasons on a wheelbarrow. Camille's khaki work uniform was as neatly pressed as Harold's suit, and he wore a baseball cap with a collection of Boy Scout medals on the crown. One of his responsibilities as head groundskeeper was to supervise the scouts who served as ushers at all the home games, and over the years they had given him the brightly colored pins as tokens of their friendship. The blade of the shovel he carried into the office gleamed with oil, and Mrs. Claude said that if it dripped on her carpet she'd have him dragged outside by the lobe of an ear.

"Who's gonna do the draggin'?" Camille said, thrusting the blade of the shovel at her.

"I will," Mrs. Claude proclaimed. She was standing with a pair of balled fists resting on her hips, her chest sticking forward as if braced for combat.

"Then I won't spill," Camille said, lifting his free hand in surrender. "But if it was the fellow you work for doing the draggin' I wouldn't pay you no mind. I'd put my shovel wherever I damn well pleased."

With Camille's help Harold rolled the wheelbarrow loaded with scrapbooks onto the grassy field of Tiger Stadium. Mrs. Claude carried the shovel, but it was clear to both men that she didn't want to. Under both hands she'd placed some facial tissue to keep from touching the smooth, sweat-stained handle, and an expression of disgust gripped her face. Harold made sure he and Camille passed through the goalposts. Bernard Toefield, his old coach, was the first to preach that it was bad luck to enter the playing field without walking between the goalposts; Harold not only preached it, he also believed it. "Under the crossbar, hardheads," Harold said. "And as close to the middle as you can get."

By the time they reached the midfield crest—it was decorated with the eye of a tiger, extending to both forty-yard lines—both Harold and Camille were so tired of pushing the wheelbarrow that they let it go at the same time, spilling the pile of books onto the turf.

Mrs. Claude threw the shovel down and patted her hands together. "Are you thinking about doing what I think you're thinking about doing?" she said.

Harold pointed at the tiger's eye. "Start digging out the iris, Camille. Go three feet down, however wide and long you need. Just give me a hole."

"But I worked hard on them books," Mrs. Claude said.

"Say your prayers, daughter. And please don't hang your lip. No point in weeping for the dead."

Camille started shoveling up large squares of the purple-and-gold sod, neatly stacking the sections so he could replace them later. He didn't say anything, but both Harold and Mrs. Claude knew what he was thinking, which was that the Old Man once and for all had lost his mind and here was proof. For a winter day the weather wasn't too bad: the sun was directly overhead and seemed to be heating things up. What wind there was billowed Mrs. Claude's dress out in front of her, and her hair whipped in her face and annoyed her no end. It was times like this when she was tempted to cut it all off, or at least that's what she said. "I should have been a boy," was how she put it now, clutching a handful of hair. "Look at this!"

"And I shouldn't of been a coach," Harold said. "If I'd of been smart enough to be anything else, I wouldn't be burying the last seven years of my life right now."

Camille's hole was no deeper than a puddle, but presently he stopped to say, "You burying it? I'm the one with the broad back and the shovel. I think it's me who's burying it."

He leaned back on his haunches and swigged from the pint flask he always kept in his hip pocket. The whiskey trickled down his chin and dribbled onto the grass.

"The most selfish man I ever knew," Harold said of his friend. "If it was my bottle I'd share."

Camille returned Harold's gaze with burning defiance. "It's your hole," he said. "Why ain't you digging it?"

"Because I wanted to share this moment with you, Camille. And because I ain't fit for it." He coughed a couple of times into his fist, but neither Camille nor Mrs. Claude knew this suggested anything more than a red throat.

After a few more hits Camille offered the bottle to Harold, but there wasn't enough left to numb his tongue. When Harold waved it away, Camille threw the flask into the shallow grave. "I bet this'll be the only football stadium in the whole country with an empty jug of Early Times buried in its center," he said.

Mrs. Claude had quit fighting the hair in her face, and now it covered everything but her mouth, which Harold watched with immeasurable curiosity. Her lips were full and red, far too perfect for the crooked, gray teeth that were evidence of an impoverished childhood that passed without benefit of a dentist. "This bottle in the ground where you coached," she was saying, turning away, aware of what he was staring at. "Are you trying to tell us something?"

Her question, Harold believed, was rhetorical, but he probably wouldn't have answered even if it wasn't. Her unrefined manner, like her teeth, excited him, and he warmed over with the bright memory of their last intimacy.

"Too bad most men can't be like the Old Man and just every now and then start burying those things about theirselves they don't like," Camille said, continuing to dig. His breathing was troubled and sweat glistened and ran on his coppery face and neck. "We'd have dug up this whole country by now and put most everything we own in a hole. Think of all the things we'd of buried before we gave them the chance to change and right theirselves. Cars would be in the holes and dogs in the holes. TVs and radios and electric can openers and air-conditioning units and antique grandfather clocks. There'd be plenty of women in the holes. And men, too. There'd even be men digging their own holes. Most people would carry their shovels wherever they went. Somebody needed the bathroom, they carried the shovel into the toilet with them. They don't care for the way the toilet paper spun off the roll, they dig a hole and bury it."

Mrs. Claude rolled her thin shoulders and looked off to the heavens as if for an explanation.

"Camille only got as far as third grade," Harold told her.

"I imagine we'd dig ourselves right out of existence," Camille continued. "If all we had on the earth is people digging holes, I suspect we'd dig up everything before too long." He was so impressed with himself that he let go of the shovel, reached over and patted himself on the back.

"You're forgetting something," Harold said.

"What's that?"

"That most people ain't me."

"And thank the Lord they ain't," Camille said, returning to his labor. "I just thank the Lord they ain't."

Near the lip of the hole Mrs. Claude opened a scrapbook from four years ago and read the first paragraph. "A local legend at the crossroads, stranded in the dusk of his coaching career—"

"Whenever the hacks say you're at the crossroads," Harold said, "it means your job's in jeopardy if you don't act fast. And whenever you're in the dusk, it means you're too old to change. This person makes me sound like I got no future."

"Makes you sound like you'd better start wearing a metal hat on your head," Camille said, "because the buzzards are starting to circle and drop their certain loads of shit."

Harold tore the page out of the scrapbook and threw it in the hole next to the empty whiskey bottle. "Good-bye," he said, "and good riddance." The next page included a column poking fun at the archaic fashion in which Harold dressed on game days and a photograph of his quarterback that year getting hammered while trying to recover his own fumble: it too went into the hole where it belonged. The next few pages, personal favorites of Mrs. Claude's, concerned traffic control at the stadium; colored maps showed how to get there and where to park. Harold Gravely wasn't mentioned, and this alone was reason enough for him to rip them out and throw them at Camille's feet.

"I think you're deep enough now," Harold said.

"I'm only halfway," Camille said. "You said three feet and that's how far down I'm going."

"Get out of my hole this second or I'll bury you too."

"If I don't go deeper this trash'll come up with the first hard rain and I'll be out here digging again. Let me finish my job, Old Man. I know what I'm doing."

The city was just above sea level, and every few years a storm flushed some of the dead out of their cemeteries and sent them floating like canoes down the flooded streets. Harold remembered when the coffin of a great-aunt of Rena's was punched out of its tomb and washed with several others down a residential street covered with five feet of water. To ensure that the body was properly reinterred, Harold and Rena paid a thousand dollars for the burial of a woman who'd died nearly twenty-five years earlier. Her second time around had been in a perpetual care cemetery that guaranteed against such washouts, even during hurricane season. The one time he'd ever seen the woman had been at their wedding, and she'd cried and cursed God for burdening her favorite niece with "Harold Smarold Cracker Barrel," as she referred to him. Everyone had said she was a mental case, in and out of asylums all the time, and that Harold shouldn't take it personally. He really hadn't until her body was found floating down Government Street, leading a parade of others toward a pornographic bookstore. Then he figured that putting her away forever was worth double, even triple what he'd been billed, and now he thought of the scrapbooks as he did the old woman. He wanted to make sure that the memory of the last seven years wouldn't suddenly reappear a quarter of a century from now to float across the field at Tiger Stadium like coffins in a storm, asking to be remembered, waiting, once again, to be put to rest. "Dig your hole, Mr. Jones," he told his compatriot. "Dig until you need a ladder to get up out of that place."

Camille finished less than five minutes before Harold's press conference was scheduled to begin. When he stepped out of the hole he smelled like something that'd been found dead in the woods. Spots of dirt clouded his slacks and perspiration bloomed under his arms and lined his collar. Harold told him to take a breather, but Camille didn't listen and started throwing the books into the hole. "If that was your life," Harold said quickly, "I wouldn't be so rough."

"It don't feel nothing," Camille said. "I can promise you that. You could shoot it and it wouldn't feel nothing."

"Well, *I* feel it," Harold remarked. "So take it easy."

Mrs. Claude yanked last year's book out of Camille's hand and, leaning way over, dropped it softly into the grave. It didn't make as much noise as the others going down, but once on the bottom it looked no different.

"Why do I feel like we should offer a prayer?" Harold said.

"Because you think too highly of yourself, Old Man," Camille said after a moment. "You're sixty-some-odd years of age and you don't even know who you are."

"I'm boss hardhead," Harold said. "Coach of the Tenpenny Eleven, the Old Man. My name is Gravely; it's Harold Gravely. So don't go and tell me I don't know who I am. It's you who doesn't know who he is, talking to me that way."

"See," Camille said. "I was right. You think you're different from her and me."

"Why'd you have to drag me into this?" Mrs. Claude said, looking at the sky.

Harold wanted to watch the old man fill the hole back up—to know for certain the books were buried for good—but he was running late. "This stays with us," he said in a voice deeper than normal. "If it ever comes back to me that this happened here today, you'll both be out of work."

On their way back across the field, Harold and Mrs. Claude made sure to walk between the goalposts. Neither bothered to look back and see Camille sitting near the grave, reading a clipping about the time Texas A&M beat Harold's boys by fifty-two points.

**The
Perfect
Jesus**

| **46** |

At home now in the early evening Rena finds herself sitting on the dryer in the utility room, folding rags. If the power hadn't failed, she'd either be scrubbing the baseboards or buffing the kitchen linoleum. With her famous system so out of whack, she's jumpy and short of breath. Although the weather continues to rage, she has a mind to mow the lawn. It is, she needn't remind herself, her day of the week to work in the yard. Earlier, when she returned from the movie, she noticed unsightly weeds flourishing around the trees on the front lawn; it took more than a little forebearance to keep from firing up the Weed Eater. She was also tempted to start her gasoline-powered blower to clear the sticks and leaves off the driveway, but at the last moment common sense prevailed.

Through the window next to the hot water heater she spots her neighbor, Xavier Monroe, standing on the roof of his house and working on the television antenna, which has been ripped from its mooring by the storm. He is naked from the waist up, and it appears his shorts are either bikini briefs or the skimpy bathing kind most often worn by young boys. As Rena watches, a gust of wind lifts Xavier's firehouse ladder and tosses it out into the yard as though it were no heavier than a toothpick. The ladder lands about ten yards from the house, as do a couple of other items swept from the Monroes' patio, most notably an empty plastic flower pot and the lid to their Smokey Joe barbecue pit.

After Xavier anchors the bent pole to the eave of the house, he paces the length of the roof looking for a way down. Rena finds herself so captivated that she abandons her idle labor and walks out onto the back porch, where her view of the scene is better. Here, though, she is in plain sight of the Monroe house, and less than a minute passes before Xavier spots her and calls for help. Because of the weather, his cries are batted down and he's reduced to wild hand signals.

Rena leans against the porch railing and shouts, "You want your ladder back? You want me to stand it up for you?"

He shrugs and lifts his arms in exasperation, then cups both ears. He points at the heavens as if to remind her of the storm.

"You should know better than to try such a thing!" she hollers; but as before, he indicates he can't hear. "It's raining, you fool! Raining!"

She is wearing baggy plaid Bermudas, a yellow T-shirt and plastic sandals that don't want to stay on. Her safari hat, hanging on a peg on one of the columns, is the only item on the porch that could pass as rough-weather gear; she puts it on and starts across the lawn, the warm rain drenching her before she's covered half the distance. She tries to run but the sandals keep slipping off. By the time she reaches the Monroe house, Xavier has taken a seat on the slanted roof, his arms wrapped around his knees, his chin resting on his forearms. He doesn't stand to greet her. His are the look and posture of the unjustly vanquished, and he's assumed them for her sake.

"If my life were a movie," he calls bitterly, "this is where everybody but the sleepers would get up and go to the bathroom."

"Don't get testy with me," she says. "I go and get soaking wet trying to help you down and you come on like Mr. Attitude." She lifts the ladder and places it against the house. "You should be grateful I happened to be looking out the window."

As he descends she supports the ladder with both hands on the double spine and a foot on the bottom rung.

"You were watching for me, weren't you, my darling?"

"I was folding rags," she answers sharply, releasing her grip when she figures he's gotten close enough to the ground. "And don't get fresh, Xavier. It bores me. It really does."

He steps off the ladder and checks to make sure the television antenna is secure. "Days like this are good for only one thing," he says, teasing her with an arched eyebrow. "Too bad Beth isn't here to participate."

"Sometimes you remind me of a dog," Rena says. "If self-abuse doesn't satisfy, I suggest you join all the other canines in the neighborhood and take it to the streets."

He covers his mouth and points a hand at her. "You thought I was talking about sex, didn't you, doll? You thought it was only sex that rainy old days like this are good for."

She pales beneath the wide-brimmed hat, and he detects her discomfort. The blush of victory inflames his cheeks.

"For me," she says, "a day of stormy weather is no different from a pretty one. I'm an amphibious sort. I can work in the rain as well as I can the sun."

He leads her to the Florida room at the rear of the house. They stand side by side at the threshold, just out of the rain.

"What I was getting at before you mentioned sex," he says with a grin, "was that I like to watch TV when it rains. I like anything with a plot to it and with—"

"Look," she says, "I really do have a heap of rags to fold. And how is it you're watching television when there's no electricity to make it run?" When he doesn't answer she says, "The only reason you're out here is because you're an exhibitionist and your day isn't complete until someone in the neighborhood has gotten a look at your gross naked body."

He picks at one of no more than a dozen curly gray hairs on his chest and stares at it with bright, curious eyes. "How long do you think it'd take to finish this rag-folding enterprise?" he says. "Another five minutes? Ten, maybe? You can't have that many rags, can you, doll?"

"After the rags I've got my yard to cut," she says.

Although he's developed an impressive pair of love handles, and his hair's grown out to the extreme, and he's most often seen wearing severe casual attire that makes his penis protrude like a doorknob, Xavier Monroe still possesses the rigid, mathematical bearing of a soldier. Even at ease, as he should be now, an exceptional hardness dictates his carriage. To appear otherwise, as he did when he was sitting on the roof, requires work on his part. Now as he slumps, the bones in his shoulders and hips jut out. He strains so hard that his eyes bulge and his lips peel back.

"There may be a few rags to fold," he says, "but I happen to know you have no intention of cutting the grass." His voice is as hot and shrill as a drill sergeant's. "Gabriel is a major storm, my darling—it's no bowl of cherry-flavored Jell-O, I'll tell you that." He brightens. "What say we sit out in the sun room, sip some spritzers and watch the branches fall?"

He reeks of an uncommon odor—of sassafras, she thinks.

"Grass to cut," she says, starting back toward the house. "Sorry, Xavier. Maybe some other time."

"It's a hurricane!" he calls after her. "You think I'm a fool, doll? You're not cutting any grass in this weather! Nobody cuts grass in this weather!"

To prove him wrong, Rena marches into the garden shed behind the garage and gasses up the riding mower. Periodically she checks to see if he's still watching, and each time finds him standing at the open door of his Florida room, sipping from a gooseneck straw sticking out of the mouth of a wine cooler. In his left hand he's holding another bottle, no doubt intended for her.

Traditionally Rena's system of mowing has called for her to begin with the side yard, but because he's there watching she decides to start with the back. The storm has littered the ground with sticks and branches and knocked the fruit off the persimmon, fig and kumquat trees at the rear of the property, but rather than pick them up and build a pile for the trash collector, Rena decides to mow right over them.

The cut grass snakes out from beneath the mower in wet clumps; it strains her eleven-horsepower engine and forces her to reduce the speed to a virtual crawl. If she holds her head up too high the rain blinds her. The safari hat, which keeps her neither dry nor cool, feels like a stainless-steel pot, and she's tempted to yank it off and throw it toward the house. But Xavier Monroe might interpret this as a kind of surrender, and she's unwilling to allow him the satisfaction.

Now he's moved over to the property line, near a clump of hawthorn bushes, and when she completes her line and heads back toward the front of the yard, he holds up one of the wine coolers. She pretends not to see him and continues forward, the mower straining against the weight of the grass.

Presently he walks into her yard and points at a spot under her favorite oak. This is her pet cemetery, where she's laid to rest at least half a dozen house animals who didn't survive the challenge of life with the Harold Gravelys.

She puts the machine in neutral and walks over to where he's standing. Blades of grass cling to her shoes and ankles.

"You missed a spot," he says, squatting to show her. "Looks like a garden hose from a distance, but it's not. It's grass."

"So I missed a spot," she says. "Big deal."

"I'm a meticulous man," he says, sipping on the straw. "When I'm cutting, if I miss a spot I've got to get it right away or it drives me nuts. I'm like one of those obsessive-compulsives you might've heard about who's got to have everything just so." Again he offers one of the bottles, but she refuses it. "You don't want me to be neighborly, do you, doll?"

"I want you to walk right off of my property the way you walked on. I've got work to do."

"The grass can wait."

A blast of wind lifts her hat, nearly blowing it off her head, and when she reaches to hold it down she sees his eyes land on her underarms.

His mouth falls open and he takes a step back. "Very European," he says.

"Oh, yeah. You think so?"

"At certain moments, I understand, it can be quite erotic."

"You can leave now," she says.

"It's only hair, doll. I was stationed in Germany and used to see it all the time. You'd meet some big blonde at a bar and take her home, and there you'd find it. They didn't shave their legs, either, those German gals. But I see you do." He pulls the straw out of the bottle and takes a long swallow, his lips pressed to the glass, as Rena looks at her legs. "You wonder why in this country it's got to be such an issue," he says. "If it grows there naturally . . . I mean, if the Lord made woman with full armpits, why then does society insist she cut it off? Same with a man. Why don't they let their beards grow instead of shaving every morning?" He hesitates. "Personally, I'm at a loss."

"May I leave now?" she says, pointing to the Snapper.

"Grass, though," he says, "it grows naturally and still we cut it. If as a society we chose not to—"

"Society doesn't interest me," she says, then walks back to the mower and puts it in gear. As she moves forward he walks beside her, the cut grass flying against his legs. "Snakes," he shouts above the engine, jogging now to keep up with her. "Think of them. Think of all the snakes there'd be in the grass if we didn't cut it."

"Go home," she says. "You're boring me. Really."

She loses him momentarily by swinging the mower around and heading toward the other side of the house. When he catches up to her, she cuts another loop in the grass and heads in the opposite direction. Then, when he intercepts her again, she scoots away by shifting into a higher gear and pushing as hard as she can. By now she's carved a queer design onto the lawn, and to her eyes it looks like a note of music. His pursuit is dogged, and he won't stop yammering about what would happen if people didn't mow their lawns. "And rabbits," he's saying. "Think of the rabbits—all those bunnies copulating in the tall, green grass."

Heading toward the orchard, she drives over several fallen persimmons, spraying him with juice and bits of orange meat. She wheels around the trees, as close to the branches as she can get without being knocked off her seat, then rounds the corner and starts straight toward him.

At first he backpedals, unafraid. But suddenly he turns and runs, pink wine splashing from the bottles, the rolls of fat around his waist growing dimples an inch deep. She chases him to the property line before braking and turning back; smoke now flows in a cloud from the mower. She notices that the grass is no longer spewing from the mouth of the mower and figures she must have broken a belt. She drives the Snapper back to the garden shed and parks on the cement landing.

"That's what you get for trying to do harm." Xavier Monroe has sneaked up behind her. "There's this theory I picked up some years ago: if a person tries to do good, or if deep down he thinks of himself as being good, then good will come to him and mark his way, but if he looks to do bad, or if he thinks he's bad at the core and unworthy, then bad will haunt him all the days of his life."

"Wow," she says, knocking the side of her head with a fist. "That's really profound, Xavier."

"We dictate our wins and our losses," he declares.

This time she uses both hands to fist her skull. "Golly gee," she says. "You might not look it, but you sure are one smart somebody." There are a couple of straw brooms hanging from nails on the wall of the shed, and she takes one and brushes the grass and mud from her shoes and ankles, then begins sweeping the mower, which is still smoking. "How come you know so much?"

"I'm only telling you what somebody told me," he says. "Early on, something happens that makes us what we are—something to lean us toward the good or toward the bad. A mama who sleeps around, a daddy with too great an affection for alcohol, a general dislike for music or pretty words."

"Words, huh?"

He nods. "It's possible we blame ourselves for something and think it's our turn to be punished. Or there might be a secret we've decided to hide." He stares at her with knowing eyes.

"These things taint, do they?"

He leans against the handlebars of the Snapper. "On a person there is nothing worse than taint," he says.

She lifts her head. "I suppose taint is worse even than a smelly bunch of armpit hair."

"The good, though—which is the path I like to think I'm headed on—you can get turned away while trying to be neighborly and it stings no more than a skeeter bite."

She decides to keep quiet and sweep. If she ignores him entirely, she thinks, maybe he'll go away.

"A person who's good at heart," he's saying, "he can comment kindly on the neglect a certain woman shows her personal hygiene. He can try to make her feel like she's still clean and wholesome, and when she bites him like a skeeter he won't even feel it." His face has reddened; the doorknob at the middle of his shorts has shrunk to the size of a button. "And you know why it won't hurt him?"

"The skeeter bite?"

"Because of the good in him," he says.

"Tell me if I got this right," she says. "Good people don't feel mosquito bites, but bad people do. Is that what you're trying to tell me?"

He grabs the handle of her broom and yanks, but she doesn't let go. She can tell he's surprised by her strength and stubbornness. "Tell me the truth," he says, his voice gone all soft and wet. "You were watching for me out of your window today. You were waiting for me to come out into the yard."

She pulls the broom out of his hands and holds it so tightly that her knuckles whiten.

"You were hoping I'd come outside and invite you over for something neighborly. I don't mean a drink, either."

Somehow, she notices, his skin seems to have tightened on his skull, particularly around the temples. A couple of knots throb at the corners of his jaw. Through his wet hair she can see his scalp, and it's as sun-ruined as the rest of his body.

"You want me, doll?" she says. "How 'bout here in the rain?"

He steps back and crosses his arms.

"I said, Do you want me?"

A ball of spit rests on his lower lip. His chin quivers as if he were about to cry.

"It's true. I was watching for you from the window. I was hoping you'd come." She starts to pull her shirt up, to breathe heavily and gaze at him with wild longing. "Make love to me, my darling. Come here and have me." Swooning, she falls back against the wall of the shed, her shirt wrapped around her neck. She covers the cups of her brassiere with her hands. "Do you want me?" She is screaming now. "Come to me, doll!"

Without a word Xavier Monroe turns and starts running toward his house. Rena notices that the seat of his nylon briefs has crept into the crack of his butt and remembers that back when she was a schoolgirl everybody called this a melvin. That's what she hollers at him now. "Melvin!" she yells. "You've got a melvin, my darling."

He slams the door to the Florida room. The louvered windows fold shut, then curtains darken the space behind them.

Once she maneuvers the riding mower back into the shed and returns to the house, she doesn't feel much in the mood for rags. What she'd really like to do is call Harold and tell him she doesn't love him anymore, but the phone lines are jammed. She dials and dials but the best she gets is an erratic beeping. After hanging up she goes into the bedroom, changes clothes and starts packing her bags.

| **47** |

Harold drives to the Prince Seurat, once the finest hotel in the city, now a place where even the least self-respecting of prostitutes are reluctant to practice their trade.

Flanked by an abandoned industrial park and an all-night bingo tent, the old hotel was the site of many of Harold's greatest triumphs, most memorably his deflowering of Rena Cummins in a room with a king-size bed. For most of his adult life Harold regarded the grounds as sacred, but no longer. The new river bridge and highway—or what everyone refers to as the "new river bridge and highway"—were built some twenty years ago on the east end of the city, precipitating the construction of huge economy hotels, shopping centers and residential sections now crowded with simple brick homes, churches and schools. As a result, the west entry to the city has been left to perish, its ancient suspension bridge and blacktop road so neglected that stray tourists, lost on their way to New Orleans, are practically the only domestic travelers whose presence here is law-abiding. Others come looking for trouble—for illegal sexual liaisons and drugs and poker games and cars to steal. Truckers like taking the old highway because state troopers rarely police it; when they do show up with their blue lights flashing and sirens wailing, it's generally to assist local cops in investigating a holdup at a strip joint or a stabbing at a gambling hall.

The Prince Seurat has faded no less rapidly than the rest of the district, and only to those victims of a certain nostalgic preoccupation does its former splendor endure: the grand ballroom with chandeliers dripping crystal like rain, the polished oak floors dressed with exquisite Oriental rugs, the strong, masculine furniture, the bidets in the wedding suites, the cranky jazz bands in the bars, the fresh-cut flowers arranged in elegant vases up and down the hallways. Harold is friendly with the manager, and on a whim he once borrowed the key to the room in which he and Rena first slept together. Upon entering he discovered the stench of mildew, an unmade bed, a spent condom poking out from under the dresser, two cockroaches with swollen bellies lying on a scrap of something in the bathroom. A filthy shag carpet covered the floor. He very nearly wept at the sight of all that had been lost. "The Princess Rat" he began to call it.

Harold parks and crosses the parking lot to the hotel entrance. When he pauses momentarily to glance back at the road, the feeling that he is being watched strikes him with the force of a tightened fist. A few pickup trucks and a tractor-trailer rig blow by, spraying rolling arcs of rainwater, but the red convertible is nowhere in sight. Except for two men cloaked in yellow slickers working under the hood of a vehicle set on cement blocks, Harold is alone in the lot. Through the Rat's picture window he can see the manager, Les Lejeune, scribbling at his ledger, his reading glasses poised at the tip of his nose. But Lejeune's, he is certain, are not the eyes that follow him. He scans the battered front of the hotel property and sees no one. It's pouring rain, after all, and who but a fool would be out on such a day? An umbrella lies on the front seat of Harold's car, but it has not occurred to him to use it.

At last Harold spots who's been watching him. Standing on the second-floor balcony of the building's west wing, partially obscured by the dry gold leaves of an enormous banana plant, is the artist, Oni Welby-White. "Hello there," Harold mutters, barely loud enough to hear it himself. Not surprisingly, the man doesn't answer. He is dressed all in black, a black beard covering most of his face, his eyes hooded by black brows, the top of his head hidden beneath a black stocking cap. Binoculars hang by a strap wrapped around his wrist and they, too, are black. Harold has seen his picture—an affected artistic pose—in the city paper and has spoken with him briefly on the telephone, but they have never met.

Harold waves and the man waves back with a black-gloved hand, then turns and disappears into his room.

The Doric columns standing along the front of the Rat are shedding their ancient coatings of white paint, revealing the dry rot beneath. Chips and peelings rest on hedges that once were sculpted in the manner of Versailles but now have grown together in an unruly swarm. Outdated flyers and posters advertising performances by R&B groups and soul singers cover the hotel's front door, eliciting Harold's scorn. He was never one to pause long for music, particularly the more contemporary kind. Rena once told him that she often imagined her life put to song, that as she went about her days a soundtrack was playing that only she could hear. Her youth, she said, was lively and hopeful, like Mozart; her adolescence and young womanhood were at once fun and meaningful, like the best of the Beatles' old stuff; but her adult years with Harold were lugubrious, often depressing, like Ravel or Debussy.

In the lobby a young woman is arguing about her bill with Les Lejeune. "But the air conditioner didn't work," she complains. "And when I called the desk, they said you'd give me a discount." She could be a party girl, Harold can't tell. Almost every prostitute he's ever met wore something to signal her line of work, but this woman is wearing a button-down dress shirt, tight-fitting jeans and cherry-colored Sperry Topsiders, a moccasin worn in these parts mainly by fashion-conscious sorority girls.

"I worked the desk last night," Lejeune tells her, his voice as warm and patient as a good father's, "but I don't remember us talking on the phone." He has spotted Harold but doesn't acknowledge him. Over his smudged spectacles Lejeune is gazing into the woman's eyes. "In the last fifty years I've given discounts to relatives only, Miss Pauley, and once when a toilet backed up and spoiled a second honeymoon." Lejeune laughs.

"Today you will," the woman says. "You assured me last night that you personally would take care of it." She smacks her hands together then holds them out in front of her, palms facing the ceiling, grabbing at invisible change. There aren't any rings on her hands and, Harold notices, no makeup on her face either. Her hair is long and brown, apparently untouched by dyes.

Lejeune trades stares with the woman but is easily outmatched. "Okay," he says, opening the cash drawer. "But like I said, this just isn't done. Not in the Prince Seurat."

The woman settles her debt, paying in cash. She stretches and pops each bill to make sure no two have stuck together, then she folds and stuffs the wad into the back pocket of her jeans. Lejeune hands her some change, which she counts aloud to let him know she doesn't trust him. "I'm sorry for the inconvenience," he says politely. "We're a little short-staffed, you know."

She doesn't respond. On her way outside she stops suddenly,

taps her chin with a finger and says to Harold, "Don't I know you? Where do I know you from?"

Harold brightens. "I'm the one with the cancer they're building a statue for."

"Ah, yes. You're the one at the school they're collecting money for. The one with the lung." She points to Harold's chest.

"The one who coached the Tenpenny Eleven," he explains.

"But it seems like I know you. Have we met somewhere before—here one night, perhaps? Have we ever done business?"

Harold places his left hand on an invisible Bible and raises the right. "It wasn't me, I promise it wasn't. Maybe you're thinking of someone who only looked like me. There're still some of them around—impostors, you know. You get a little famous and they all want to look like you."

The woman and Lejeune look at each other, then away, then back at each other again. Incredulity fills her face, loathing and pity his. Finally Lejeune says, "This man wouldn't be here on business, Miss Pauley. This is Harold Gravely. He used to come with his wife back . . . oh, what, twenty, thirty years ago? They danced to the big bands that came through town."

"Everybody knew us," Harold adds.

Lejeune peers over his spectacles. "Well," he says. "Almost everybody. They were regulars."

The woman covers herself with a hooded raincoat. As she pushes through the heavy wood door, she flips a coin back at Harold. "Catch," she says. The quarter hits the marble floor and rolls toward the front desk, cutting a perfect bead in the dust. "For the statue," she says, polishing her lips with the moist, pink tip of her tongue. "Or for an umbrella. Whichever you need most." The coin comes to rest in front of his feet; it actually nips his shoe.

As soon as she's outside Lejeune walks around the desk and pockets the coin. "Finders keepers," he says.

Harold feigns disgust. "You don't know who's handled that damn thing," he says. "Put it back on the floor."

"When you go for a quart of milk at the 7-Eleven, do they ask where the money came from?" Lejeune doesn't wait for an answer. "This young woman—Miss Pauley, that is—she's got three small children ages seven through twelve, all attending parochial schools. If she's a tad testy and sullen it's not without reason. I admire her spunk. Nothing these days is more dangerous or misunderstood than her line of work."

"She's a hooker, then." Harold turns his face toward the darkened lobby. "I can't believe what you've let happen to this place. If thirty years ago someone would of said this was going to happen to the Seurat, I would of laughed in their face."

"It's not me who lies on his back. I just rent the rooms."

Harold spits on the floor and grinds it to paste with the heel of his shoe. "You don't let them in my room, do you, Lester? I mean this woman and the others you keep."

"Which room is that?"

"Mine and Rena's. Where we came that time."

Lejeune spends a moment studying the guest register. "Not since last week," he says. "Seven whole days."

Through the picture window behind the desk they watch Miss Pauley step into a compact car, start it up and drive away. Above the entrance the Rat's unlit sign is holding up against the tempestuous southern wind, but up and down the road cable-television and electrical lines bounce and sway between rain-blackened poles. When Lejeune tires of the view he takes Harold's hand in his and they shake and look each other over. It is a perfunctory act, but it seems to soothe them both.

Lejeune is wearing a dirty green cardigan sweater that's missing buttons and has holes in the side pockets. His navy sock tie reaches only halfway to his belt. If someone were to run into him on the street, Harold thinks to himself, surely he would cross over to the other side. Lejeune smells like near-empty beer bottles left too long in a hot car. He stares into Harold's eyes as if to make sure the color hasn't changed since the last time he saw them.

"You're here to see Mr. Welby-White, aren't you?" he says after a moment. "Here to talk about your statue."

Harold nods and stamps his feet, trying to shake off some of the rainwater that's slipped under his slicker and soaked into his clothes. "What's the room number?"

"It's a suite. The Tara, overlooking the garden."

"What used to be the garden."

"Of course," Lejeune says, chuckling. "What used to be."

Harold knows the way. Before the place started to die, he often rented rooms in the Prince Seurat for prized recruits, hoping to impress them with its glitter and grandeur. The Tara's overstated elegance worked to numb the boys into believing their days on the university football team would be filled with pomp and finery: baskets of fruit when they checked in, fancy towels in the bathroom, a kitchenette with a refrigerator filled with wine and cheese, beautiful maids who enjoyed seeing to it that certain hotel guests did not sleep alone unless they wanted to. More than a few of the recruits who eventually signed with the school complained that what they were shown and promised during their recruiting visits was not delivered when they reported to campus for August two-a-days. Harold warned that they were green as grass and had yet to prove themselves. Then he directed his assistant coaches to take the "ungrateful plain-tiffs" into the stadium exercise room with the blue cork floor for a quick but unforgettable lesson in humility.

| **48** |

As Harold crosses the lobby, he sees defeat where once there was greatness, decay where once there was life. Antique pieces of furni-ture stand covered by sheets and padded blankets. Persian and Oriental rugs have been rolled up and stacked atop one another. Scores of cardboard boxes hold a million forgotten details.

"You should learn not to get too attached to a piece of prop-erty," says Lejeune, trailing him. "The things of this life are tempo-rary. They can be replaced. What's eternal never fades."

"You're dead wrong." Harold steps up the pace, trying to distance himself from Lejeune.

"No, Old Man, I'm right. The only reason this hotel is open now is because the group that owns it needs a tax break and we're it. We shelter them is all. They don't care if we turn a profit. Truth is, they seem to prefer that we don't."

Harold stops near the foot of the stairs leading to the west wing and spins around on his heels, inspecting the ceiling. "You've let spiders make webs all over the chandeliers," he says, "and now it's so dark you can't hardly see in here."

Lejeune pats his lower belly and smiles, but he doesn't speak. Behind his glasses, his eyes are closed.

"The floors are all scarred and caked with dirt and gum and grease," Harold continues. "The wallpaper's peeling off where it isn't already stained with water drippings, and rat turds are everywhere. Your air conditioners don't work. And you're telling me nobody cares, even the people who own it don't care."

"Neither do the guests, it seems," Lejeune says, in the same patient voice he used with Miss Pauley. "You yourself spit on the floor. Would you do that in your home? No, of course you wouldn't. Would you do it in the home of your worst enemy? I doubt it." Harold stares at his hands as if they were to blame. "Two years ago we had to close the entire east wing because it failed the fire code," Lejeune explains. "And the owners weren't willing to pay for the changes. A hundred rooms gone. Our restaurant and bar didn't meet the health code either, so now they're part of the past. Eventually the west wing will be shut down." Lejeune shrugs his thin shoulders, then removes his glasses and sticks them in a sweater pocket. "The Prince Seurat wasn't meant to last. It's all temporary. If it were eternal none of this would have changed. It would be as it was thirty years ago when you first came to me with your child bride and asked for a room."

Harold leans against the wall and breathes deeply. He reaches for gum in his pockets but finds only wrappers and a few pennies. "I seem to remember the bellhops wore forest green suits trimmed in red," he says. "There were epaulets on their shoulders like the kind a soldier would wear. They carried big gold whistles with THE PRINCE engraved on the bellies."

"Yes," Lejeune says. "Temporary, though—all of it. I can show you those whistles. I saved them. They're all a mess now. They're not worth keeping. I don't know why I haven't thrown them out yet. Maybe I'll do that tonight, as soon as I get a break." Lejeune looks up at the high ceiling and seems to calculate the distance. "Life should not be so important," he says, "that everything we do carries the burden of remembrance."

He shuffles back down the hall, chuckling to himself, and wisps of dust rise in his wake. It has been five years since Harold last visited the Rat. When the Tenpenny Eleven gathered here for the silver anniversary of their championship, Harold wore the same suit he'd worn during the game. Lejeune met his limousine at the door, proclaiming, "All hail the king and queen! The Gravelys, ladies and gentlemen! The Gravelys!" Harold and Rena were early and no news hacks disguised as paparazzi waited to greet them, no fans, no idle hotel guests or workers or bellhops, no one but Les Lejeune in his tattered sweater and sock tie. Harold's hair, gleaming with Wildroot tonic, was combed straight back from his forehead, the thin part in the middle showing as many gray roots as dark. In his hands he carried a fedora cut along the same lines as the Tenpenny original, which had been trampled underfoot during the celebration after the game and lost forever. That night he was closing in on sixty but Les Lejeune, escorting him into the empty ballroom, said he looked not a day over forty. The hotel looked younger then, too, only five years ago. It had not yet become a ruin and the whores hadn't claimed it, or if they had, at least they were still discreet.

Lejeune is rounding the corner. "There was magic here," Harold shouts after him. "I remember it."

"Ha!" Lejeune shouts back. "Magic! There was magic, of all things. There was magic here!"

| 49 |

When poking the Tara's doorbell a dozen times fails to bring Oni Welby-White to the door, Harold pounds the brass knocker, drawing people from the rooms on either side of the suite. To his left stands a young woman of about twenty, clothed in underthings too transparent even for Mrs. Claude to wear. Bruises bloom on her pendulous, milk-white breasts; a butterfly tattoo lights on the soft point of her shoulder. Long razor bangs nearly hide her eyes and tight curls float over the nape of her neck. She smiles as if she's been expecting him, as if she, too, knows him. His nod and embarrassed wave prompt her to cover her mouth with a bejeweled hand and giggle. "Hi," she says. "How are you?" He doesn't speak. To his right stands an older woman wearing a flimsy tank top with the words NICE CHEST emblazoned across her deep bosom, a khaki skirt and high-heel shoes. Pockmarks corrupt her face, and a smear of strawberry-red pimples rise on her shoulders and upper arms.

"You come for Oni?" the girl says.

Harold turns back to the door and raps the knocker again.

"We ain't planning on biting," the woman to his right says. "You could be nice. You could open your big trap and see what comes out. It's not that hard, you know."

Mute, Harold stares at the knocker: a lion's head with a ring in its nose and a brass hammer for a mouth. It's not that he's never shown interest in ladies of this sort—in fact, he once got extremely friendly with one while at a national coaches' convention in Las Vegas—but he now regards them as he did the cockroaches and the condom and the filth he encountered in his and Rena's honeymoon room, as a sign of the end times.

"You're Harold, aren't you?" the girl says.

He doesn't answer.

"This woman asked you a question," the older one says. "Are you Harold? Somebody wants to know."

"I'm the Old Man. Yes."

"I knew it was you," the girl says. "I seen your pictures plastered all over Oni's walls."

Harold knocks again.

"Don't plan on him opening it," the older woman says. "He's a bore, a real loner, always keeps to himself. He's the kind you wake up one morning and read about in the paper shooting a bunch of innocent people from a tower he climbed somewhere."

To the door Harold calls urgently, "It's me, Mr. White!"

"It's Welby-White," the young woman says. "Two names for the price of one, a person so wonderful they named him twice."

"He won't open it on account of he's probably locked in his room, concentrating," the one on the right says. "All the man does is concentrate, back in the dark. Let me go call him from my room. He needs to know it's you knocking and not me and Trish."

Harold presses his ear to the door and in seconds hears the telephone ringing. When it goes unanswered, he tries rapping the knocker again. "Have you looked to see if maybe the door wasn't locked?" the girl says.

"No," he replies. He honestly hadn't thought of it.

"Try it, then. You might surprise yourself."

Harold turns the knob, gives it a nudge with the heel of his hand, and the door swings open.

"Go on in now," the girl says. "Don't y'all both be bashful. If it wasn't locked it means he was expecting you. Either that or he wasn't concentrating as hard as he should." She cocks her head to the side, thrusts her tongue out a few inches and licks the bright yellow wings of the butterfly tattooed on her shoulder.

| 50 |

The phone is still ringing when Harold, entering the Tara, steps into air as thick as cardboard. Everything about the unlit foyer smells old—old newspapers, old cigarette smoke, old socks and shoes—and he can almost feel its weight pushing against him. The living room is dark except for a narrow shard of light breaking through a crack in the curtains. As Harold stumbles across the room, mumbling the artist's name and bumping into furniture, he is struck again by the feeling that he's being watched.

"Mr. White," he calls. "It's the Old Man here. It's Harold." No one answers. To make sure he doesn't trip over anything, he thrusts an arm out in front of him like a blind man's stick. "You here, Mr. White?"

The telephone is on a breakfast table in the far corner of the room. "At last," says the woman next door when Harold lifts the receiver. "Oni, that creepy coach is outside and he looks like somebody just fished him out the river."

Harold hangs up and turns back to the darkness. "I came to talk about my statue, Mr. White." Then: "Hello?"

Still nothing.

Harold shambles across the room to a floor lamp, switches it on and sees what has been watching him, or what gave him the feeling he was being watched.

Tacked to the walls are pictures of himself in various poses. In the dark he assumed it was some kind of modern wallpaper, jazzy, metallic and dumb, but now he sees it's a montage of glossy black-and-white and color photographs, all of himself. Pinned to the lampshade is an eight-by-ten photograph of Harold on the sideline at Tiger Stadium, shouting at one of his players, a headset wrapped around his neck. In the photo next to it he's standing behind a microphone, some of the board members seated in tall leather chairs behind him. Harold remembers the event: the press conference several months ago at which he announced his illness and intention to coach until he died. There are pictures taped to the television screen, some on the seats of chairs, others lining the frazzled back of a sleeper sofa; pictures cover the wainscoting and molding. On the radiator there's an ancient image of Harold and Bernard Toefield standing arm in arm on the steps of the state capitol, the great building looming behind them. And on the marble-top coffee table, it so happens, he's pictured with five former university players handling Toefield's coffin, leading it to a cemetery tent on a cold autumn day nearly thirty-five years ago.

The effect is dizzying, almost terrifying: hundreds of eyes are falling upon him, and nearly every one is his.

There are even a couple of photographs dangling from the twelve-foot ceiling. One shows Harold riding the shoulders of Pogo Reese and Little Shorty Grieg as the crowd, swarming around them on the field, roars its satisfaction and reaches to touch his upraised hands. The other has captured him with his lips planted on the mouth of a referee. It is a picture, a moment Harold would rather forget, and he climbs onto the coffee table and reaches to pull it down.

| **51** |

Suddenly, the artist is poised in the doorway to the bedroom. "Be careful," he says. "Please. I couldn't forgive myself if you fell and hurt yourself."

Oni Welby-White has removed his gloves and stocking cap, revealing thick, blunt hands with scabs on the knuckles and hair cut in a bristly flattop about an inch high.

"You left a few things on your ceiling," Harold says, stepping down from the chair. "I thought I'd help you take them down."

"I hope it doesn't offend you. I've not done it without reason." Oni's voice is choked with emotion, small and frail. He strides from the shadows and into the dusty yellow light of the room, his hand extended in greeting. "Everyone has his own way of getting close to his subject," he says. "This may seem a bit eccentric, but it works for me."

His baggy turtleneck sweater is so thin at the elbows Harold can see his creased flesh, and his pants, several inches too short, are corduroys covered with lint. Hairy shinbones show above his floppy black socks. His clothes could belong to someone else, Harold thinks, they fit him so poorly.

"Is this how you got so good at making statues of Jesus?" Harold swings an arm at all the photographs on the walls. "You put pictures of him all over the place, kind of see him looking back at you wherever you go?"

"If it helps . . ." The man either can't or doesn't want to finish the thought; self-consciously he runs an ink-stained finger between the neck of his sweater and his beard.

"I don't know if I could stand it," Harold admits. "When I was a boy my mother had a picture of the Christ child hanging near the kitchen sink. It was the kind with eyes that followed you all over the room. That thing used to give me the creeps so bad sometimes I couldn't eat. Other times I'd get a feeling like I wanted to throw up and I'd have to leave the table and go lean into the bushes on the side of the house."

"As statues go," the artist says, carefully choosing his words, "Jesus would seem easy. No one's ever seen him to say I got his mouth or his ears wrong. And there's not a word in the Bible that tells us how he looks. Some churches with predominantly black congregations have murals and stained-glass windows depicting him with a dark complexion and frizzy hair. Churches with white memberships have him blond and blue-eyed and as aesthetically appealing as a Hollywood movie star." Oni moves his eyes over the pictures on the walls. "For years I tried to build the perfect Jesus. Then one day it dawned on me that I was wasting my time. If Jesus was perfect it wasn't because of how he looked, but rather how he didn't. For nearly two thousand years, in spite of his anonymity, he'd managed to live in the hearts of millions."

"I go and meet my first artist," Harold says, cracking a smile, "and he gives me a goddamn Bible lesson."

The flesh above Oni's whiskers burns a wintry scarlet, and once again he runs a dirty finger under his collar. Harold regrets his remark but can think of no way to make up for it.

"If we work together," Oni says, "you should be an easier piece than Jesus. People know you. They've lived with your image for as long as most of them can remember. If your head is too square I'll hear about it. 'He had a little birthmark here near his mouth,' they'll tell me. Or, 'His ears were more cauliflowerlike.' And they'll torment me until I get it right. That's why these pictures are here. If I work hard enough I can make you perfect."

"These pictures remind me of something," Harold says. "In the old days when it seemed I never lost, you wouldn't believe how people behaved on account of me." There's so much heat and pride in his voice that it would seem he's talking about someone other than himself. "Married women put my picture on their walls. I doubt, however, that anybody ever went this far. What husband would stand for it? I'd of ended up a dead man."

"I tried to divide the rooms as I thought your life was divided," the artist says. "This is the football room. It includes pictures taken during your years at the university—from your days as a player to the present. The bedroom is for your life outside the game—with your wife and friends, most showing you engaged in social activities.

Talks at banquets, charity balls, ribbon cuttings with the mayor, pedestrian stuff. The bathroom is for your youth."

"My youth?"

Oni nods. "But those photos were so hard to come by I could round up only a couple. You receiving some Boy Scout medal and you on the back of a horse. Newspapers, the sports information department, the library archives in your hometown, the one at the university—these are the places that helped me most, though there were others."

Harold taps the arm of a battered wing chair, stirring a cloud of dust into the air. "Mind if I sit?" he says. He peels a couple of photographs from its weathered back and seat and drops them to the floor. "You don't mind, do you?"

"Please," the artist says. "Make yourself comfortable."

Harold scans the room, still wondering how to feel about the pictures. "You don't happen to drive a red car with a convertible top, do you?" His eyes meet the artist's, but only for a moment. It isn't Harold who looks away.

"I don't leave home very often," the man says. "I work there, in a studio behind the house. I'm here only to do a job and do it as well as I can."

"You didn't answer my question."

The man lifts his black eyebrows. Fleshy bags encircle his liquid gray eyes. "No," he replies in his windy, poetic voice. "I don't have a car with a convertible top. I took a Greyhound bus to the Government Street depot, then a taxicab to the hotel. I've been hitching rides with the girls next door or borrowing Mr. Lejeune's van whenever I need to get out."

With the pictures on its walls and furniture, the Tara is a far sight nicer than Harold imagined it would be. The stained paper and the holes in the chairs are covered; at least there's something to divert his attention from the rot and mildew. "Why'd you want to stay here?" he says. "Why not stay in one of the new hotels on the other side of the city?"

"Because of the history of the place," the man says, apparently surprised that Harold would ask. "This is where, at the height of your career, you came to celebrate. In many of the pictures in the bedroom you are here at the hotel, on ground I'm sure you regard as hallowed—ground I had to get close to. I thought the atmosphere would help me concentrate. The better I concentrate, the better I work." The man chuckles, still staring at his socks. "And also—if I may be honest, Coach Gravely—the rate was good, twelve dollars a night. When's the last time you stayed in a suite in a grand hotel for twelve dollars a night?"

"I saw you with binoculars, standing out on the balcony. Don't tell me I didn't. You were spying on me."

"I was watching for you. Your secretary called—Mrs. Cloud, is it? She was worried about you being out in the storm. I phoned her back as soon as I saw you in the lot."

The artist sits on the edge of the couch, upsetting some of the pictures. He looks up at the photographs hanging from the ceiling. "I love those two."

"The one on the right's all right. If you tore the other into a handful of pieces and tossed them to the wind I'd be happy as worms in corn."

"You mean the one of you kissing that man?"

"I wish they wouldn't of given that one to you." Harold squinches his face as if he's just tasted something rotten.

"I like it. I find it curious." The artist waits a moment before continuing. "But I wonder—"

"I had my reasons for doing it," Harold says.

"Tell me, then. I mean, if you don't mind."

Harold walks to the window and pulls back the curtains. The high wall of glass, braced for the storm, has crossing strips of masking tape at its center. In the courtyard pinecones and splintered branches line the flagstone walkways. The pool is nearly empty; bottles and cans and other debris float on the few feet of brackish water at the deep end. The rusty steel frames of diving platforms rise to meet the tops of the stunted pine trees and banana plants, but none holds a board. The tropical wind bucks the torn and frazzled awnings that dress the entryways to what used to be the patio lounge and oyster bar, and rain flattens the high yellow grass that surrounds the outbuilding. Some windows on the opposite wing have been weatherproofed with strips of tape, but most are covered with sheets of plywood and pieces of old board.

Turning back to the artist, Harold says, "Before I start telling stories about why one man would want to kiss another, we need to discuss some important business."

"Yes," Oni says, pressing his hard, square hands between his thighs. "The statue."

Harold plants himself in the middle of the room and points straight ahead, his feet about shoulder width apart, his face fixed hard as stone. His hair is a mess and wet spots darken his pants and sweatshirt, but the message is clear: this is how he'd like to see his statue stand.

"I figure it covers what we're trying to get at," Harold remarks, doing his best to restrict the movement of his lips. "You should make me about thirty-three, though. Nobody in his right mind wants an old face on their statue."

The artist strides around him, inspecting the pose. His nostrils flutter and disappointment fires the watery gray ash in his eyes. "It doesn't work for me," he says, tugging at the whiskers on his neck. "It fails . . . absolutely."

Harold lowers his arm. "It works for me and most everybody else. They seem to like it."

"But does it . . ." The artist, pinching his lower lip, struggles to find a response. "Does it define who you are and who you were? Does it speak to the future? If you can tell me yes, then we'll proceed with it. I could make some sketches now. If not, I hope you'll consider something more spontaneous."

"Spontaneous?" Harold mutters.

Oni looks at the pictures on the ceiling. "I've made a clay miniature, a model—you on their shoulders. It's in the bedroom. I think it works."

Harold chides himself for thinking that a statue of a man pointing at nothing in particular could say anything but what's plain: for all the birds in the neighborhood to feel free to come roost on its outstretched arm. "I wanted something that would give people an idea of how I used to look," he says, suddenly bashful, "and I remembered I used to point a lot."

| **52** |

It was about four years ago when Harold kissed the referee. Down by two points in a game he figured he had to win to keep from being fired, he pressed his mouth to the lips of a man who, moments before, had flagged the opponent for roughing the kicker. Harold tasted wintermint on the official's mouth and immediately felt like spitting. This was late in the fourth quarter, and with the penalty, a fifteen-yarder, Harold's kicker found himself within range to boot the field goal; as time ran out, the ball curled through the uprights. Harold got his victory, but on the front of the next morning's newspaper there he was with his arms around the referee, a nice-looking, middle-aged man whose eyes were filled with horror. He appeared to be trying to free himself from Harold's stubborn embrace. Their mouths were enjoined, their heads angled just so. It looked as if they'd danced this waltz before, and at least one of them was enjoying it. "I been punched once after a questionable call," the official was quoted as saying, "but never kissed. I believe I enjoyed the punch more. For the record, remember, it was him that kissed me."

Despite his disclaimer, the lead to the story was that the embattled Harold Gravely received not only the win he needed to spare his career but also a congratulatory kiss from a most unlikely source: the referee.

"There are dozens of pictures that have intrigued me," the artist is saying, "but few as much as that one."

"It's weird, all right," Harold says, staring at the photograph. He feels himself growing weak with worry but doesn't want to reveal as much. "It made all the papers for a while. But like everything else, it blew over." As an afterthought, he says, "They couldn't make it stick."

"I suppose I put it up there because of the way the light is shining on your face. And also the strength of your expression. Look at how alive you are! Look at the sparkling clarity of your eyes! No picture but the one next to it—the famous one taken at the Sugar Bowl—depicts you in such a state of bliss. I couldn't *not* use it, if you know what I mean. It's what I'd like to capture and bring to the monument."

"One thing," Harold says, holding up a finger: "No one makes a statue of Harold Gravely kissing no man."

"Of course not." The artist waves off the suggestion. "Perhaps I misspoke. It's the *look* I want to bring to the piece—the look of a champion enjoying his finest hour. It deserves to survive you."

"But I was kissing the sonofabitch!"

Oni's face fills with frustration. Fingering his shabby beard, he paces rapidly across the room. "In the piece," he says, "you'll be kissing no one. This is how I see it: you on the shoulders of two of your ballplayers, it really doesn't matter which two. But your face will be *that* face—the face of the older Harold Gravely forever bound to the body of the younger, the two of you marching triumphantly into the future."

"I'd rather see myself sitting on the stool taking a dump," Harold says. He steps up on the coffee table and reaches to tear down the picture. "At thirty-three there were no liver spots on my cheeks. No spider lines under my nose, no wrinkles around the corners of my mouth. When I wanted a woman—" Harold stops; even he's beginning to tire of hearing himself talk on his own behalf.

At the window the artist is silent, contemplating the weather, wondering at his own insouciance. Through the southern wall comes muffled laughter: first a woman's, then a man's.

"Your girlfriend next door has herself a fella," Harold says, then hurries across the room and places his ear against the wall. Sure enough: they're in there, giggling and wrestling, exercising the bedsprings, pleased to have made each other's acquaintance. "It's a rumbling sound," Harold says, "like the ocean shore and two people splashing around in the water."

Oni casts a troubled glance at Harold. "Our opinions on art may differ, Coach Gravely, but will you at least look at what I've come up with and tell me what you think?"

"You already know what I think." His ear is still pressed to the wall, but suddenly everything has gone deathly quiet.

"Will you at least look and tell me?"

"Sure, I'll look," Harold says. "No harm in looking. But if it's that abstract crap you're wasting both our time."

The artist retreats into the bedroom and returns balancing a small brown statue on a square wooden board, carrying it as carefully as one would an enormous birthday cake ablaze with candles. The model, about three feet tall, is exactly as he'd described it: an elder-faced Harold, dressed in famous clothes, occupies a youthful, vigorous body; he's riding the shoulders of two football players, neither of whom resembles the originals. That the faces of Pogo Reese and Little Shorty Grieg have been replaced with one that is plainly Caucasian and another that is plainly black delights Harold. He blows on their miniature clay likenesses, both truncated at the waist, as if to cool them off. Oni places the statue on top of the coffee table. "Well . . . ?" he says.

"This is it," Harold asks.

"This is it," the artist answers.

When Harold first learned that a naive artist named Oni Welby-White had been given the assignment of building his monument, he was certain the man would misrepresent him. "Is that his real name," he asked Claire Peel, "or is it the name of some new law firm in town?" He imagined a statue that resembled a cartoon stick man more than it did a real person. He saw a crude, cheaply constructed figure that looked less like him than a child's idea of a coach. It was a potbellied old thing with skinny arms and legs and an oval-shaped face with buttons for the eyes and nose and a slimy, frowning string bean for a mouth. But the model, to Harold's satisfaction, is a perfectly realistic piece of work, though of course, studying it now, he sees some problems. Something about the nose is off, and the mouth is a little screwy.

Also, unlike his memory of the moment or the way the stills and newsreels captured it, Harold is shown resting both hands on the heads of his players, when in fact he raised both arms to the heavens, fists clenched in victory.

"You got a few details wrong," he says to the artist, indicating the statue's arms, "but I guess you know that."

Oni stoops to study the figure. "If you mean I changed the pose a bit, yes, I know. Artistic license."

Harold holds his arms over his head and knots his hands. "It was just like this," he says, punching the air. "Why'd you want to go and change it?"

"In my studio at home I instructed some of my friends—assistants, actually, they work with me—to carry me on their shoulders, and I found it impossible to do without shoring myself up as presented here. I felt I had to hold onto something."

"But you ain't the Old Man," Harold reminds him. "If that's how the Old Man did it, then that's how it was."

The artist pinches his lip again. "But the feel, the overall look of it—do you like it?" He pauses to take it all in himself. "That's what's most important at this stage in the project. And please be honest. We must collaborate on this."

"Do I like it?" Harold repeats, leaning closer to the figure. "You want to know if I like it?"

It is the wealth of nostril on the model that frankly bewilders him. The tip of the statue's nose is as lumpy as a fat man's fist, and on either side of it are craters deep and dark enough to house worms. It seems to Harold his nose was always big, all right, but his nostrils looked as normal as the next guy's—no different, truth be told, from the artist's.

"Are my nostrils really like that?" Harold says.

"Perhaps not," the artist replies. "But noses are hard, particularly when you're working from pictures. I can change the nostrils. I see now they misrepresent you. On my statues of Jesus and the Virgin I simply use the noses of my wife and brother. It's not accurate, no, but neither of the subjects has been around yet to complain."

Another thing Harold's noticed is that several teeth in the statue's mouth are crooked, and this, he believes, is an injustice even worse than the nostrils. Harold was always proud of his teeth. As a boy his mother said they were as straight and perfect as the false set of ivories his paternal grandfather wore, but here they are in miniature, bending into and over one another like a spilled rack of bowling pins.

"Are my teeth really that bad?" Harold pulls back his lips to expose his gums. As a set his teeth truly are impressive, a dentist's dream, and he knows it. "Are they crooked like you have them?" he says. "Or are they straight up and down?"

Oni admits they look better in person than he's depicted them here.

"What about your Jesus and your Mary teeth?" Harold asks. "You get your wife and brother to pose for them too?"

The artist pats his hands together, then bows in unqualified shame. "Please accept my heartfelt apology," he says, his voice even smaller and frailer than before. "All I need do to correct the situation will take five minutes."

"But you misrepresented me again." Harold is shaking his head disgustedly. Angry blue veins throb in his forehead. "Tomorrow morning I meet with the board of supervisors. I give them a quote for the pedestal, and I answer one question: Do I approve of your plan for my statue? If that meeting were held now I'd have to say no."

"But the changes . . . they're so minor. Nothing really." The wind, the poetry, has disappeared from the artist's voice. "I can reconstruct the face and make you young again, as young as you'd like, younger even than thirty-three. I can put your arms up in the air. I can reshape the nose and straighten the teeth."

"It's how I was," Harold confesses.

"I'll even change the faces of the two men supporting you."

"No," Harold says quickly. "No real need to go that far. Keep them a black and a white. Some of my best friends are black and I see it's your favorite color."

The artist looks down at his clothes as if noticing them for the first time.

"I always wondered why it was Little Shorty and Pogo had to carry me to the middle of that field," Harold is saying. "Why not McDuff and Tully, who love me like a father, or why not Bobby Peel all by his lonesome. Bobby Peel was big and strong enough to do it on his own. Why couldn't he have just thrown me up on his back and walked me into history?" With the tips of his fingers he touches the face of the statue. "But we can't return, can we? Nobody can make it like he wants it the way you can a lump of clay."

"All I seek," Oni half whispers, "is your approval. I'm not as inflexible as some who practice this line of work. The truth is, I've never done a living person before, so I'm willing to make concessions. This is very important to me." He points to the wing chair. "Go on and have a seat, Coach Gravely. Make yourself comfortable."

Harold coughs into his fist, forcing up some hock, then spits into a glass ashtray full of cigarette butts. "A statue is more for what almost was than for what really was," he declares. "That's the reason I need to have one."

It's a confession the artist only halfway hears, and one that Harold would be ashamed to have uttered were he in better spirits. While Harold walks around the room studying the many photographs, Oni lights a cigarette, positions himself in front of the clay model and begins picking at its teeth with the skinny blade of his pocket knife. Within seconds the teeth are as straight as those of a model in a toothpaste ad. A careful pinch reduces the width of the statue's nostrils to the size of a pinprick.

After consulting the Tenpenny picture, he smooths out the age lines on the mini-Harold's face, delicately lifts the setting of the eyeballs, presses the ears closer to the skull and removes some of their puffiness.

He slices off the double chin, strengthens the jaw and adds some prominence to the cheeks. He flattens the pea-round knot in the bridge of the nose and smooths the bumpy ridge of cartilage. He sharpens the angle of the statue's hat, then lifts its arms over its head and closes its tiny brown hands.

Because each fist is almost as big around as the model's head, he makes the necessary adjustment, wiping the superfluous clay on the seat of his corduroys. Once the hands are blunt and square, he carves the proper number of fingers and builds knuckles that swell with a fighter's arrogance.

"Almost done," he calls, but gets no answer.

| **53** |

In the bedroom Harold is peeling pictures off the wall near the door frame, trying to find the switch to the overhead light. By the time he discovers there isn't one, he's removed several months of his life from the wallpaper.

He switches on the nearer of two ceramic bedside lamps and

illuminates countless pictures of his days and nights outside the game. There seem to be fewer photographs in this room than the other, but that might be because it's smaller. Sketches of Harold cover the four-poster bed, all done on huge sheets of scratch paper, all initialed OW-W. On the wall opposite the bed, pictures of Harold blanket a collection of gilt-framed watercolors depicting the Prince Seurat in its prime. In these glossy black and whites Harold is a university student, and one shows him in a rumpled seersucker suit and bow tie dancing with young Rena Cummins on the hotel's ballroom floor. That the most interesting of the photographs emerged from the same era as the painting it covers is a mere coincidence, Harold decides, because the rest of the pictures seem to be a mad scramble, arranged in no particular order. Too few, he frets, show the sublime moments he's committed to memory, and too many contain the trivial and insignificant.

Here he's captured standing with Trent Orlansky under a candy-striped umbrella; here shaking hands with someone he doesn't recognize. Here he's eating a bacon sandwich at the Frostop Diner; here getting a shoeshine at his favorite barbershop; here walking around campus with a pipe and walking stick. Here he's swimming in the pool at the field house; here playing croquet on the lawn of an antebellum mansion.

"Was I really that ordinary?" he says aloud, loud enough for the artist to hear in the next room.

"Extraordinary, yes," Oni answers. "But ordinary? No, never ordinary."

The pictures range from youth to middle age, from as early as his freshman year at the university to some taken a few weeks ago. There's even one of Harold on the witness stand at Pogo Reese's murder trial. Wrapped around a footpost of the bed, it shows him leaning into a pineapple microphone, sweat glistening on his cheeks and forehead and clouding his starched white collar.

With one easy motion he peels off the ten by twelve, then folds, quarters and eighths it and stuffs it in his shirt pocket. "I'm taking one of these, Mr. White. Do you mind?"

"I've got to return them to the libraries," the artist calls back. "They're only prints, but they don't belong to me."

"I'll return it. Don't worry."

On the other footpost, curling back in under itself, is a picture of Jimmy Brandt being forced into the rear seat of a police cruiser, Harold hovering behind the strong-armed arresting officers. This picture, taken about twenty years ago, depicts a moment that had completely slipped from Harold's memory. Jimmy Brandt, he remembers now, got drunk after throwing four interceptions in a game and vandalized several rooms in the athletic dormitory. The last room Brandt ransacked belonged to Marcus Watson, a running back who'd amassed a record collection that included several dozen big-band titles. When the campus police arrived, Jimmy Brandt was throwing the albums out of Watson's third-floor window. One by one the platters sailed high into the night, then crashed and splintered on the asphalt parking lot. The cops tried to catch them, but in the dark they could save only a few. An onlooker was shouting, "More Benny Goodman, Jimmy. Throw some more Benny Goodman." And out more came.

By the time Harold, the dormitory proctor and the police could break down the door, Brandt had run out of records and was throwing clothes and books and threatening to throw himself.

"Mr. White?" Harold says.

"Give me one more minute," the artist answers. "Please."

"I'm taking another picture. You don't mind, do you?"

"Not as long as you return it."

"I'll return it," Harold says.

Now that it all comes back to him, the picture of Jimmy Brandt seems almost a lie. In it Harold's expression might lead one to believe he was upset by what happened in the dormitory that night, when in truth he was glad to finally have a reason to boot Jimmy Brandt off the team. The negative press attention might have concerned him, but dismissing a loser, as Jimmy most certainly was, couldn't have pleased him more.

As he did with the picture showing him at Pogo's trial, Harold folds this one into an accordionlike wad and makes room for it in his shirt pocket. "And where do I return them?" Harold says.

"It's stamped on the back," Oni shouts from the other room. "See it? In the middle of the back."

"On the back, you say?"

Harold walks to the window, forces it open and throws both pictures outside—right into the middle of a banana plant.

"Most of the copies in that room belong to the university library. See the word *print* on it?"

"Okay," Harold calls. "I see it."

While the window's open, he discards a few more pictures he doesn't like, including the one of him with Rena and the other showing him playing croquet.

"What about three?" Harold says. "Can I borrow three?"

"No problem," the artist answers.

"I'll handle them with care."

"Just make sure to return them."

"Will do."

Careful not to leave too many bald spots on the wall, Harold selects a few more pictures to toss out the window. Polishing the front fender of an Oldsmobile—a nice pose, but whose car was it? Kneeling in a pew at church—phony baloney—and pouring cane syrup onto a stack of buckwheat pancakes, which always gave him the worst kind of heartburn. And embracing Rena on the diving platform at the Rat's swimming pool—were they really ever that happy together? Because he doesn't remember these moments, it feels as if he never lived them. And staring out the window Harold now thinks of all the pictures that almost amount to lies, and of all the moments that seem to explain something but really don't.

"Mr. White?"

"Take them. Take all you want."

Harold decides to skip the bathroom and the pictures of his youth. He hardly remembers his days as a Boy Scout, much less receiving any medals, and what could he possibly expect to gain from seeing himself on the back end of a horse?

| 54 |

When Harold returns to the bedroom, the artist is crushing the stub of one cigarette into the glass ashtray and sucking on a fresh one. "What do you think?" he says.

"Better," Harold says, bending over to get a good look at the model. "Much better."

"You're young again." Oni turns his face to the picture on the ceiling. "Younger, even, than you were on the night of the Tenpenny Eleven. You could pass for nineteen."

"At least you got the teeth right."

"Thank you," the man says.

"But aren't the nostrils a little small?"

"No one really looks at a person's nostrils, Coach Gravely. Take my word for it."

Harold shrugs. "In the bedroom I was thinking that since it's my statue, maybe it should be only me in it. No one else."

"But then who will support you in this position?"

"Make them barstools, the two players. . . . I really don't care how you do it. But it should be only me. I don't want the slightest suggestion of anyone else."

The man resumes fingering his beard. "So you're telling me you don't want a black and a white?"

"Just rub out their faces. Make them a couple of lumps."

"It would hurt the piece," the artist says, whispering again. "One would question its integrity."

"Then make me pointing." Harold stands erect and assumes the pose. "Like I showed you earlier."

The artist laughs as if he doesn't believe it, then rubs out his cigarette, new as it is, and lights another. With his hands folded on top of his head he paces across the room and almost reaches the foyer before turning back. "I won't make you pointing," he says with conviction. "It's not what either of us wants."

Harold snorts and coughs. He could take the miniature in his own two hands and squeeze it until the smart brown head popped off. He could throw it against the filthy shag floor and pound it flat, then open the window and throw it outside with the pictures he didn't like. "You're wrong," he says. "It may not be what you want—I know it's not your perfect Jesus—but it is what I want." He spits on the floor and grinds it in with the heel of his shoe. "And just so you know, it's a tribute to my memory you're making." He pats his chest. "My memory . . . mine. Not yours."

The artist exhales a lungful of blue smoke and the words: "I won't do it."

Harold sees the smoke, but he's making so much noise of his own that he doesn't hear the response. He's barking like a dog, as he did earlier in the day with Perry Watts, as his hardheads had barked at practice this morning. In his hands the clay miniature comes apart like a hunk of raw biscuit dough. The chunks he throws at the window bounce off the pane and plop on the floor. Some he throws at the artist, who ducks as he runs screaming toward Harold, his arms flailing as if in a wild attempt to produce flight.

With the frenzied Oni Welby-White on top of him, throwing his huge, scabbed hands into his chest and face, it occurs to Harold that the woman in the room next door was right: this was exactly the sort of person who would climb a tower somewhere and start shooting.

| **55** |

Over his thirty years Harold has coached hardheads who went on to star in the professional football ranks, some who made fortunes wildcatting in the oil fields, dozens who worked for banks, real estate agencies and life insurance companies, one who designed skyscrapers in New York City, a pair who became politicians, scores who went on to coach and teach in state schools and hundreds who, having either flunked out or not made good enough grades to graduate, ended up riding on the backs of garbage trucks, maintaining roads for the highway department or working behind the counters of all-night liquor and convenience stores.

Never, as far as he can recall, did he produce an artist.

In fact, he cannot say with any certainty that he'd ever met an artist until this Oni Welby-White. Harold always figured an artist to be like those effete cowards who used to run from the rough-and-tumble games of his youth. As men, he believed, they carried their hands on bent wrists, wore earrings, expensive designer clothes and fruity cologne; in one another's company, they cackled like hens. This man, however, in the short time it's taken him to throw a battery of punches into Harold's face and shoulders, has dispelled these notions.

By drawing blood, and by nearly knocking Harold senseless, Oni has proven himself to be a credit to what Harold has long regarded as a less than manly profession.

The whores, pulled from their sweaty labor, finally stop the ruckus. The commotion has drawn them from their rooms and into the Tara suite. "Come on, you two!" they scream. "Break it up! Break it up now!" It is the older of the women who wrestles the artist away from Harold. With one of her spiked shoes she kicks him in the lower back, inches below the kidney, and drives him to the floor. He scrambles to a darkened corner of the room and thrashes in pain, his hands flattened against the spot where she nailed him. The younger woman, in the meantime, has covered Harold as if to shield him from further harm. Her strength and agility astonish him. She has pinned him to the floor no less convincingly than the artist did, and he can't free himself no matter how hard he tries. "I'm all right," he grouses, giving up, "if only you'd get your damn butt off my stomach."

She sits up a little, transferring the weight to her arms. As best as he can Harold points to the artist, who is now crouching with his back to the wall, anxiously running his hands through his bristly hair.

"This man attacked me for no reason."

"He destroyed my work," Oni replies.

"Did you?" The older whore stands over Harold, her fists balled at her hips. "Did you destroy this man's work?" She has a voice, he thinks, like fingernails dragged across a chalkboard. Harold can smell her cheap talcum powder; in the lamplight it appears to cover the pimply rash on her shoulders like sheer strips of gauze. "If you destroyed his statue," she is saying, "who can blame him for wanting to beat you up the way he did? I'd have done the same."

"I've got a mind to call the cops," Harold says, bluffing. "This man was unprovoked. And look at what he's done to my face. I bet I'm bleeding here." Harold pats his chin, smearing blood on his fingertips.

The artist straightens himself and walks across the room to the telephone. "I'll dial 911 for you," he says to Harold. "I'm doing it. Everybody see me doing it?" They watch him place the call. "Operator," he says after a moment. "Yes . . . operator, please have someone—will you please have a police officer report to the Prince Seurat right away. This is Oni Welby-White speaking. They'll find me registered in the Tara suite."

"Let them come out," Harold says from the floor. "I don't care."

"I care," the younger woman says.

"I care, too," her compatriot adds, sitting on the wing chair and checking to make sure she didn't break her heel. "Oni," she says, "you'd better hang that phone up. I'm not playing with you, either, child. You'd better hang it up this minute."

Into the receiver the artist is spelling his name. "I'm a guest at this hotel," he says. "My room has been vandalized. My property has been destroyed."

"I coached half the cops on the force," Harold says, relieved now that the girl has gotten off him. Although his lower lip is throbbing, when at last he does stand it is with a supremely confident air, as if he himself is the victor. "The chief before this one was a player on one of my first teams," he says. "We didn't win more than five or six games each of the years he was there, and he didn't get off the bench except to cover punts and kickoffs. But he was still a former hardhead of mine." He pats the dust and grime off his clothes. "Poor bastard was a suicide, though," he says. "They found him in his Ford Ranger in the garage at home."

The artist hangs up. "They're on their way," he says. "The

operator said she'd dispatch the car nearest to the area." At the window he picks up a ball of clay, the remains of the head of one of the men who carried the miniature Harold on his shoulders. "See what I'm saying? Look at this. Look at what this man has done to my work."

Oni hands the head and other mangled parts of the model to the women. They inspect each fragment with the care members of a jury might show a piece of incriminating evidence, then make a pile on the coffee table.

"I suspect they'll arrest you," the older woman tells Harold. "And since we witnessed the tail end of your little escapade they might want to get us involved. Only thing, Trish and me ain't inclined to get involved. We got our jobs to protect."

Weary of the commotion, Harold steps into the bathroom. He runs a sink of warm water and with a bar of yellow soap and a face towel cleans off the blood that has caked on his chin and neck. For the first time since the fight he feels the nicks and cuts that each seem to beat with a heart of its own. Two black-and-white images depicting him as a young boy hang from the mirror, but he avoids looking at them directly. They show a fat, scowling child whose thin, untamed patches of hair suggest an animal with mange. They show someone he would like to believe he never was, someone plain and common, unmemorable.

Harold pulls the pictures off the mirror, strips them into pieces and drops them into the toilet.

"Now he's destroying public property," the artist says from the open door. The two women stand behind him in the dark. "What you've just done is a criminal act, Coach Gravely. And there are three witnesses to it."

"Old Man," the girl says kindly, "I think you're in for a lot of disappointments. I almost feel sorry for you."

"We should go now," the older whore says, leaving the bedroom. "Trish, dear?"

"Yes," she says, already headed out the door.

Harold returns to the task at hand, washing the blood off his face. In the mirror his eyes find the artist's, but when he scoops more handfuls of water and looks up again he's gone.

Through the tiled walls he hears the muffled chatter of the women, growing fainter then disappearing altogether. Afraid of being alone with the artist, Harold hurries into the bedroom and locks the door behind him.

"They should be here any minute now," Oni calls from the other room. "I think I hear the sirens now." Harold hears his footsteps cross from one end of the room to the other. "Yes, that's them all right. The police are here."

"I own them," Harold says. "I coached half the force. Let them come all they want, it don't matter." Harold laughs to let the man know he isn't afraid, then retreats into the bathroom. There is a small gas heater, and Harold lights it and turns the flames all the way up. The small room was already warm, but now it's as unbearably hot as a sauna crowded with too many overweight men and their large, aromatic cigars.

As Harold sits on the toilet watching the glowing stove, sweat drips down his face and burns his open wounds. Though the pain makes his insides tremble, he resists cursing for fear the artist will hear and think him either seriously injured or troubled by the arrival of the police.

Harold has not started the fire without reason. He has decided to continue what he began earlier—getting rid of the offensive pictures. He begins with some of the sketches on the bed. After igniting the large sheets of scratch paper he drops them into the tub and lets them burn down to ash. He then graduates to the pictures on the wall that show him with people he doesn't like or remember, and those he finds generally unflattering. None of the photographs that reveal him in triumphant poses finds its way to the heater and tub. And he also spares the few that depict him pointing.

Because the bathroom is without a vent or a window, Harold opens the bedroom windows, but the smoke that hugs the bathroom ceiling doesn't stir until he swats at it repeatedly with a towel.

Suddenly someone pounds on the bedroom door.

"Go away," Harold says. "Leave me alone."

"They're here," the artist replies.

Harold laughs. "Okay. Fine."

"What are you burning?" Oni's voice is wild with alarm. "My god, what are you burning in there?"

"Just a cigarette. I'm smoking a Pall Mall."

"I'm telling you they're here!"

Through the wall comes the sound of a knock on the front door, followed closely by footsteps and voices. Harold sits on the toilet and watches the pictures smolder in the tub.

There's another knock on the bedroom door. "Mr. Gravely," the artist says. "Let us in."

Harold turns off the wall heater and starts the cold water running into the tub, flowing over the burning pictures and the delicate drifts of ash. The smoke makes him cough and sneeze so hard it feels as if he might accidently blow his brains through his nostrils. "Let me finish my cigarette," he says, straining to produce the words. "Give me a few minutes."

"Mr. Gravely—" it is the policeman now— "if you don't open this door I'm afraid we'll have to break it down. I am ordering you to let us in."

Harold wags his head. "Hello there, hardhead."

"Old Man—" Harold recognizes this voice as Les Lejeune's— "why don't you let us in? We'd like to talk to you . . . let's sit down and have a chat."

"We can chat with the door closed," Harold answers. "That man you're with is dangerous. He attacked me for no reason. He cut my face. And all because he couldn't take a little constructive criticism."

"I'll count to five," the policeman says. "If you don't open the door by then I'm coming in."

"One," Harold begins, determined not to be bullied.

"One," says the policeman.

"Two," adds Harold. "Two and a half."

"I don't want another broken door," Lejeune pleads. "Come on now. We've already got too many broken doors."

"Two," says the cop. Then, without pause, "Three."

"Why so fast?" Harold calls. "What's the hurry?"

"Four."

Harold gets up from the toilet and opens the door.

"Five," Lejeune says as the policeman and Oni brush by Harold into the bedroom.

The cop is a small man with a neatly trimmed mustache and a cleft chin. Moving on the balls of his feet, he carries himself with an imperious air. Harold has never seen him before, but he knows the type. What food is to Larry McDuff and Chester Tully, and what housework is to Rena, a service revolver is to this man. As he walks into the bathroom, he holds his shoulders square and drapes his strong, pale hands over the front of his belt, tapping his crotch at a musical clip.

"My god," the artist says, "he's burning pictures!"

Harold offers the cop a hand to shake, but he disregards the gesture and turns off the bathwater. "Go sit on the bed," he tells Harold. "And don't make a sound."

"I suppose you'd like an explanation," Harold says.

"Go sit on the bed," the cop says again, more forceful now. He's wearing a raincoat over his uniform, rubber galoshes over his shoes and a plastic covering over his blue hat. Harold sees his badge through the transparent slicker but can't make out the name. "I'm Harold Gravely. I'm the one who coaches out at the university, the one they're building a statue for." When the policeman shows no interest in the information, Harold adds, "Your ex-chief, Garland Duplantis, was once a player of mine."

The cop sits down on the lip of the tub. "You knew Duplantis?"

"Knew him? Why, I was like a father to him. I campaigned for the man, helped him get into office. I used to give him a pair of forty-yard-line season tickets every year."

"The Dupe was before my time," the cop says, "but they still talk about him down at the station." He clears his throat. "Killed himself."

Harold is quiet; he stares at the floor.

"Near the end," the cop continues, "all he wanted to do was work funerals." From the tub he's collected several unburned bits of photographs, the least damaged of which he places in a clear plastic bag he extracts from his breast pocket. "And what's funny, he'd cry even when he had no idea who it was they were burying."

Oni hands the policeman several pictures with the names of libraries stamped on the back. "They were like these until he got to them," he says. "This is public property he destroyed. He threw some outside, too. You can see them from the window." The artist points to the open doorway. "And that mound of clay over on the coffee table was a work of art until he tore it to pieces."

Harold moves over to the edge of the bed. "Garland had a nickname," he says. "But in the old days they all had nicknames: Tomahawk, Buttercup, Rolls-Royce, Fig, Jelly Belly—"

"You caught him in the act," the artist is saying, waving more pictures in the policeman's face. "You caught him destroying some of these things. And if that's not enough I can produce two other witnesses who—"

"—Garlic Clove, Apricot, Tin Can, Meatloaf. I remember we called Duplantis 'Swing Set' for the way he kind of danced whenever he went running down the field. It was his hips that made him sway— something about the negligent use of forceps on him comin' out of the womb."

Once again the cop covers his belt buckle with his strong, pale hands, but now his fingers are still. He steps into the bedroom. "Mr. Gravely," he says, "what you've done here—it's arson, sir, but I'm sure you're well aware of that. You look like a person who should know better than to go around burning things that don't belong to you."

"He's going to arrest you," Lejeune mumbles, a smile spreading slowly over his lips. "He's going to cuff you and read you your rights and take you downtown."

"It's funny," Harold remarks, "how when the wieners get to burning on the barbecue, all the dogs come scrambling out of the bushes."

"You're going to have to come with me, Mr. Gravely," the cop says. "Let's get a move on."

"Somebody get me a pencil," Harold commands, certain he's finally found a sentence for the statue.

"Temporary," Lejeune says, laughing. "It's only temporary."

"I want you to listen to me very carefully, Mr. Gravely," the cop says. "I want you to hear what I'm saying. You have the right to remain silent. Are you hearing me, Mr. Gravely?"

Harold is trying to memorize the sentence about burnt wieners and scrambling dogs, but for whatever reason the words are nowhere to be found.

**"Go
down,
death."**

| **56** |

In the Falcon, Rena started on her way to the mall and the huge department store that sold, among other things, Scandinavian furniture. But about halfway there a small red light on her dash panel began to flash and she smelled something burning. Steam poured from the hood and heat warmed the soles of her shoes. Of all the streets on which to get stranded she'd chosen Florida Boulevard, the city's busiest. She parked on the blacktop shoulder, turned off the engine and locked the doors. In the rearview mirror she watched a steady stream of midmorning traffic float by. The force of wind from the big trucks nearly lifted the car off its wheels, and some of the smaller cars came so close that she was afraid they'd hit her.

She waited with the radio tuned to an easy-listening station: Sarah Vaughan was singing Brazilian love songs. Rena found the music so stirring that she got a mild case of the shakes and her flesh tingled. She didn't know the songs but wanted so badly to sing along that she found herself inventing lyrics of her own. "Lonely, middle-aged woman," she sang, "why are you parked on the side of the road? . . ."

She waited nearly an hour and didn't find the courage to step outside and flag down help until an advertisement for an automobile repair shop came on the radio.

"Help," she mouthed to the traffic. "I need help."

In minutes a nice-looking man in a station wagon stopped and gave her a lift to the nearest station, where an attendant listened halfheartedly to her problems while filling in a credit form for another customer.

The attendant then drove her back in his tow truck and spent less than five minutes under the hood. He uncapped the radiator, which by now was no longer steaming, and refilled it. "You won't want to go too far," he said, then advised her to take the car in as soon as possible and let someone look at it. He lowered the hood and stuck out an oil-smudged hand. "Twenty-five dollars exactly." After paying she ignored his instructions and drove to the mall.

As Rena pushed through the revolving doors of the department store, it struck her that she might not make it home this afternoon. And in a way she regarded as cowardly, she hoped she wouldn't; her troubles on Florida Boulevard seemed like an adventure rarely visited upon someone who lived by a system such as hers. The experience had temporarily relieved her of her memory of Harold, but here she was an hour later walking around as if she wasn't the most miserable person in the whole world. She told herself to be strong—to try to get through the rest of the morning without succumbing to another crying jag—and then started through the store humming one of the Sarah Vaughan songs. She might've sung about a lonely, middle-aged woman shopping for a porch swing but was afraid she'd lapse into something about a lonely, middle-aged woman whose husband hated his life and marriage so much he wanted to die.

Rena found what she was looking for near the barbecue grills and bird feeders. There were three different swings to choose from, but even the least expensive of the teakwood sets was fifty dollars more than she'd hoped to spend. "Aren't these a little pricey?" she asked the clerk.

The swings were hanging from a metal stand, and the clerk nudged the middle one with her hip. "It's not like my boss has empowered me to mark them down," she said. "I only started last week."

"I wasn't blaming you, miss. I was just stating a fact. Your swings are a little pricey."

"For you, maybe," the girl said. "But others tell me the merchandise here is pretty reasonable."

Anger brightened Rena's face and neck. "My we're sassy today, aren't we?" she said.

The girl was tall enough to rest her misshapen chin on the top of Rena's head. Her yellow-streaked hair tumbled and curled all the way down to the middle of her back. She had a light mustache that grew darker and heavier as it tapered toward the corners of her mouth. "When I started here," she explained, "I told the floor manager I wasn't going to take nothing from nobody. He said I shouldn't have to." The girl flicked the price tag on one of the swings. "If you think it's too pricey—if you can't afford it, lady—then no one's stopping you from going somewhere else."

The world doesn't let you feel sorry for yourself, Rena thought; it hasn't the patience. "You must not want my business," she snapped. "Otherwise—"

"Otherwise I'd bend over backward to help you?" the girl said. "Hah! What a joke!"

Rena felt her jaw slacken involuntarily.

"My father used to tell me what it was like in this country before the filling stations went to self-serve," the girl said. "He said self-serve was a sign of our demise as a friendly nation. 'No one wants to show the first kindness to strangers,' he used to say. 'Not no more they don't.' "

Rena clutched her purse tightly to her breast.

"Daddy predicted restaurants were next, and sure enough when you go to one now you got to stand in line at a salad bar and make your own. 'Then comes your department stores,' he'd say. 'People'll walk in, take what they come for and charge it themselves on their credit cards.' What I've discovered is they leave the cards out of it. We're so spoiled we take what we want, we think we're owed it. And you know why?"

Too stunned to say anything, Rena shrugged.

"It's because no one wants to show the first kindness. We can't get past being strangers to one another."

Rena pointed to the least expensive swing.

"You want that one?" The clerk seemed prepared to challenge her choice. "You *sure* you want that one?"

"Yes," Rena said. "But I didn't want to spend more than a hundred dollars. That seemed . . ." She couldn't find the word.

"What did it seem?" the girl sneered.

"Reasonable."

"Reasonable is relative," the girl answered with a snort. "To me, reasonable is for people who've got all the time in the world to sit on porch swings and watch the cows graze." She flicked the price tag again. "If you want this thing, just say so. If not—"

"I'll take it," Rena said.

| **57** |

At the sales counter, fumbling in her purse for a credit card, Rena started crying. The clerk was saying, "A person has to be a computer whiz to figure out how to operate one of these registers," when Rena fell to the floor in an unquiet heap, knocking over a stand of Valentine's Day cards. As she lay there, covered with pink paper Cupids and cartoon hearts, a peculiar whiteness clouded her vision and a burning sensation raced through her limbs. Her eyes were open but she couldn't see anything; when someone asked if she was okay, it struck her that she couldn't speak. All that came from her lips were tiny bubbles of spit.

Over the store's intercom the clerk was reading instructions from a card, and now people in noisy but sensible shoes were encircling her, warning one another not to touch her. Were they afraid she'd injured her spine, she wondered. Why didn't they help her up? Hours went by, it seemed, then someone put a wet rag on her forehead and a sharp, terrifying explosion filled the space behind her eyes. As she rocked back and forth a peppery trickle ran from her nose and wet her lips. She sneezed, then a second blast erupted.

When Rena's vision returned a woman was leaning over her, holding a cracked capsule of smelling salts. Her name tag identified her as Mrs. Russell, a licensed practical nurse.

"Lord, I thought we had us a dead one," the clerk was saying. She stood at Rena's feet, directly behind the nurse. "You know how scared you had me, lady? I nearly had a coronary."

Rena sneezed again and yanked the towel off her forehead. She tried to sit up but Mrs. Russell grabbed her shoulders and held her down. There was someone kneeling behind her, holding the back of her head to keep it from hitting the floor, but Rena couldn't lean far enough back to see who it was. "Relax," the nurse said. "Stay still. Think of something pretty, and when you feel better we'll take you to the employees' lounge." Mrs. Russell turned to a man standing at

240

the front of the crowd. "Mr. Angelle, would you mind fixing a Coke for this young lady? No ice, please."

In a throaty whisper Rena instructed him to make it diet, and everybody laughed.

"We got us a regular joker here!" the clerk said.

"Anything hurt on you, ma'am?" the nurse said. "How's your head feel? I bet you got a nice little knot up there."

"Woozy," Rena said, suddenly cold and tired. "All I feel is woozy."

"It was over that swing," the clerk was telling Mrs. Russell. "I told her if it was more than she wanted to spend, she should take it on down the road."

"Get me away from that person," Rena said to the nurse.

Mrs. Russell nodded and helped her to her feet. Some of the people in the crowd applauded, and the clerk bowed and started to dance. "Never had nobody crash on me before," she told the onlookers. "Put the fear of God in me, I tell you that!"

In the employees' lounge a couple of women in blue work clothes were sitting at a dinette table smoking cigarettes and drinking coffee from paper cups. They were watching television and didn't even glance at Mrs. Russell, Mr. Angelle and Rena, who shuffled along as if in a somnambulistic trance. The nurse led her to a vinyl couch and Mr. Angelle gave her the glass of Coke. "It's diet," he said, smiling. "I know all about those calories." He patted his distended belly.

The liquid was bitter on Rena's tongue but the carbonation helped clear some of the cotton balls from her head. "Thank you," she said, handing the glass back to him. "I think I'll be all right now."

Mr. Angelle leaned over and whispered to the women at the table; without saying anything they gathered their things and left the room, their lipstick-stained cigarette butts still smoldering in the bottoms of the coffee cups.

"Why don't you lie down and catch your breath?" Mrs. Russell said. "No one'll bother you here and I'll pass by periodically to make sure you're okay." She joined Mr. Angelle at the door. "Shall I turn off the lights and the TV?"

"Doesn't matter," Rena said.

She didn't feel well enough to be embarrassed. Ten years ago she might have hidden her face in shame, but now she wanted to close her eyes and sleep and wake in the body of another person. If she could choose, it would be the Rena Cummins she knew before she married Harold Gravely. She had passed out only once before—while watering the plants on the back porch—and then, too, Harold had been partly to blame. When she came to hours later in bed, Doc Cage was in the room, clutching the handle of a leather medicine bag with one hand and massaging the back of Harold's neck with the other. You'd have thought it was Harold who'd collapsed. He was sobbing, sitting in a chair with his chin set hard against his chest. It was the first time she'd ever seen him cry, and she pitied him as she never had before or ever would again. A few hours earlier he had learned that he was the reason she couldn't conceive. "Fault!" he'd shouted at her. "You think it's intentional! You think I want this!"

At first she was unable to explain to Doc Cage why she'd fainted. They were finally alone in the bedroom, and she feared Harold was listening at the door. Her hands were shaking as she reached for the switch to the bedside lamp, which she wanted off. Had she eaten anything that day, Doc Cage asked. She said she had. Was she on any medication? She wasn't, but come to think of it she'd taken a few extra-strength Tylenol that afternoon when Harold came home with the news. Had she been getting enough sleep at night? Eight, sometimes nine hours; last night around ten. Had anything happened, anything out of the ordinary? His brow tightened and she knew he wanted her to say it. When she didn't he put his mouth against her ear and whispered, "Harold will be fine, my love. It might not seem at all possible now, but in the long run this will make him a stronger person." She shook her head as if she didn't believe him; her tears bled into the pillow. "You have to stop blaming yourself," the doctor said, pulling at his beard. "You did nothing wrong. This is Harold's cross to bear, not yours. And you shouldn't let him make it yours."

| 58 |

When she woke, she was no longer alone. The ceiling lights were on, and several well-dressed men and women, their backs turned to Rena, were seated at the dinette table watching television. With all you bozos here, Rena felt like asking, who possibly could be minding the store? Sitting up, she felt a stiffness in her hip that penetrated deep into her right buttock. The back of her head was sore and tender, and when she reached up she found the knot that Mrs. Russell had predicted. She checked her watch and discovered she'd been asleep for more than an hour. It now was one o'clock in the afternoon.

She was careful taking her first steps, then spotted the young clerk across the room. "Lady! Hey, lady!" the girl called, but the people watching TV shushed her.

"Leave me alone," Rena said.

The clerk was standing next to her now, sucking on a bottle of strawberry soda. "I can get you another Diet Coke if you want."

"No, thank you."

"You forgot your purse," she said, handing it to Rena. "Guess what?"

"I fainted and hit my head," Rena said. "Big deal."

"Mr. Angelle said to give you a discount on that swing. Those fifty dollars you didn't want to spend, he said to go ahead and take it off the regular price." The girl offered a gentle whistle. "Now talk about showing the first kindness to strangers! Wait till Daddy hears about this."

Rena heard Harold's voice in the room, and for a moment she wondered if perhaps Mrs. Russell had located her driver's license and called him over from the stadium. But then she realized it was coming from the television set, and when she looked over Harold's image was on the color screen. He was standing before a crowd of reporters, pointing. To his left stood John Ford Cage and Trent Orlansky, and to his right his secretary, who was crying hysterically as she yanked at the sleeve of his jacket. In the upper right-hand corner of the picture Norman Pepper, Champs LaRoux and Mary Elaine Watts sat in high-back leather chairs, their faces hidden in their hands. In the lower left-hand corner were the words LIVE EYE 9: SPECIAL REPORT.

"That's that old fellow," the clerk said. "That coach."

Once again Rena felt light-headed.

"Everybody counted on him calling it quits, but turns out he's dying with something or other."

Rena's first few strides to the door resembled those of a newborn colt attempting to run from its mother, but she soon established a comfortable gait. It occurred to her that she hadn't run in at least eight years and she marveled that she could still do it. The shoppers didn't seem to notice her, but some of the clerks cast startled glances her way. She moved from luggage to sports, from pet supplies to toys to kitchen appliances. At recreational furniture she blew by the swing she'd wanted and noticed that a red label marked SOLD had been pasted on the price tag. She was breathless and sweat ran beneath her clothes, yet she was so cold her teeth ached. If she stopped, Rena told herself, she would fall and never be able to get up. She would die. At electronics the voice of her husband spoke to her again. A group of people were standing in the middle of the showroom, staring at the banks of television monitors that lined the walls. In each of dozens of sets Harold was standing and pointing, talking about "the enemy death" as if it were a team on next year's schedule. "Down," he was saying. "Go down, death."

As she pushed through the crowd that watched in stunned silence, Harold's rumblings sounded as fraudulent as distant thunder on a luminous winter night, but to everyone else it rang of a truth that made their hearts swell and soar. Several women lifted handkerchiefs to their eyes; some of the men rocked from foot to foot and played with the change in their pockets.

In the parking lot her car wouldn't start. She tried pumping the accelerator, but not until she pounded her elbows against the dash did the engine turn over, expelling bursts of black smoke from its rusty exhaust. She reversed slowly, careful not to hit anything, but halfway out of her parking slot Rena glanced in the rearview mirror and saw the clerk. Walking from car to car, peering through the windshields, the young woman was about fifty yards away and closing fast. Rena considered ducking under the steering column, but then what? Instead, she floored the gas pedal, lurching backward, then switched into drive and roared away. Before long she was speeding back down Florida Boulevard, heading home. "Slow pokes," she yelled at the cars in the right lane, raising a fist in triumph.

She didn't dare turn on the radio for fear Harold would be on it, lying with every breath he took, threatening death as if it were a wife or assistant or player who wouldn't acquiesce to his demands. Eventually she passed the gas station where she had gone for help, and then the spot where her car had overheated. For whatever reason she blew the horn and waved, but she attracted no one's attention.

At the head of her street Rena braked and pulled over, not quite ready to be home yet. Her heart seemed to be beating in every part of her body except her chest. And as before, when the car broke down on Florida Boulevard, Harold Gravely was the last thing on her mind. She was remembering how Pogo Reese used to drive on those autumn nights after ballgames. He'd push his car well above the limit, never letting on that he was doing anything wrong or that he might get them into trouble. He drove with only one hand, the left, and kept the other on her right shoulder. On quiet residential streets they'd raced, on River Road and on the bumpy dirt strip at the crest of the levee. Back in her dormitory room, sleeping in her little cot, she'd always felt as if the night wind was still blowing in her face, the earth rushing beneath her at speeds as high and danger-ous as her dreams.

She felt that way now, or close to it. But being forty-seven years old and childless, few of Rena's dreams were ever high and danger-ous.

When she couldn't restart the car, she walked the rest of the way home.

| 59 |

Almost everyone was standing as Harold left the crowded board-room. Little Shorty Grieg had come hoping to see Harold announce his retirement, and even he was on his feet, tears dribbling down his swollen red face. Harold extended a kind greeting, but Little Shorty was too upset to speak. He nodded and bit his lower lip, cutting his eyes to the floor. To a couple of the newsmen who'd had fun at his expense, Harold waved and mouthed a friendly hello, but neither could look at him. They turned back to their notebooks and wrote with unsteady hands.

Harold couldn't recall the last time a press conference had been this quiet and well behaved. No one shouted questions or thrust microphones in his face. No one looked at him with anything but awe and respect, even love. The only sounds he heard came from whirling tape and minicam recorders and from Mrs. Claude, who, in her excited emotional condition, was being led kicking and screaming by Chester Tully and Larry McDuff through a side door.

Doc Cage walked in front of Harold, forging a path, and Trent Orlansky trailed behind. Harold felt like a victorious prize-fighter being led out of the ring and into his dressing room, though he made sure to keep his face from betraying any such feelings. Having delivered the speech, he now wanted to look the part of a man with no tomorrow.

Outside, a considerably larger crowd had gathered on either side of the macadam path that crossed the grassy lawn. Even the traffic on nearby streets seemed eerily silent. Harold saw a young boy positioned in a tree.

"Where to?" Doc Cage said, frantically twirling his long white hair. "Where're we going, son?"

"Just keep walking," Harold told him.

"Where on earth did all these people come from?" Trent Orlansky wondered. "And how did they get here so fast?"

Harold didn't answer. He'd noticed a cluster of men in wheel-chairs, many of whom were saluting as he passed by. "Thanks for coming out," he told them. "I appreciate your support."

They finally cleared the crowd at the memorial clock tower, and Harold pointed at the Faculty Club across the parade grounds. "You hardheads hungry?" he asked.

"Sure could use a club sandwich and some potato chips," Cage answered. "Maybe a dish of their famous bread pudding."

"Me, too," Harold said. "But first I could use a drink."

At the restaurant they had a difficult time enjoying their cocktails and food. They were seated near the center of the large banquet room, and all around them the diners stared at Harold and whispered. Few seemed hungry, and those who did eat were careful not to clink their silverware and china. The waiters, too, were solemn. Harold knew they'd feed him by hand if he asked them to, one morsel at a time. "Quiet as the time in church when the old padre's about to hand out Holy Communion," he told the waiter.

After his third bourbon Harold started to relax. He told Cage and Orlansky about Bernard Toefield retiring and giving him the job, but both already knew the story. Cage had lived through it and Orlansky had read about and memorized it. Neither stopped him because both were relieved to think about something other than how everyone was watching them.

"Coach Toe had been head coach forty years when he announced his retirement," Harold said. "I was twenty-nine years of age, his offensive coordinator. When they called me up to say a few words my voice wouldn't work—I mean, hardly any words wanted to come out. One of the news hacks wrote that I looked like a frightened little boy afraid to leave the diddie."

Now the diners at the nearby tables were leaning back in their chairs, pretending to stretch their limbs as they strained to hear what Harold was saying. He obliged them by raising his tone a notch. " 'Into thy hands I commend my spirit,' Coach Toe told me, but I was so scared and flustered I couldn't think straight. 'However you want to do it, Coach,' I replied, and the place cracked up."

Everyone but Harold laughed and whispered their approval.

"I remember it well," Cage said. "Your suit looked like something a Chicago gangster would wear. Wide lapels, pinstripes. Your tie was orange polka dots."

"First suit Champs LaRoux ever sold me," Harold said. "I emptied out my bank account and paid thirty dollars cash. I had to take the tie and the socks on credit."

Once again the neighboring tables rang with laughter, encouraging Harold to continue. "After me and Coach Toe answered some questions and mugged for a few pictures, we went out for drinks at the Prince Seurat, and he told me something I never forgot. 'This morning,' he says—we were sitting in the courtyard on a day not unlike this one, under a beach-style umbrella. 'This morning,' he says, 'I did something I'm almost ashamed to admit. I went to the public library and looked up the newspaper clipping that announced my birth, my entry into this world. It was the first time my name ever appeared in print.' He kept wringing his napkin in his hands— this being such a big moment for him. I didn't say a word. 'You see,' he went on, 'after being public property for almost three quarters of my life, it'd suddenly become important to me to go back to when I was the exclusive property of just two people, that being my mother and father. Libraries always seemed a stale kind of place to me, but this experience made me weak. I shall never forget it.' "

Harold screeched and pounded the marble-top table, but everyone around him was quiet, including the waiter who had arrived with a pot of coffee. One woman at a neighboring table stood up and ran sniffling to the rest room; another followed.

"Heard a lot of Bernard Toefield stories," Doc Cage mumbled. "But never that one."

"Me neither," said Trent Orlansky. He took a notebook from his coat pocket and wrote in it with the stub of a pencil.

They returned to their sandwiches, Harold to his memory. "Coach Toe was dead the following spring," he said. "He's buried up in the northern part of the state, in the town he grew up in. When I got back from the funeral service I stuck the pallbearer's flower they'd pinned to my lapel in the dictionary on the page listing the word *rose*. The flower happened to be a rose and I didn't want to forget where I put it. But Rena was cleaning up—you two hardheads know how that woman likes to clean—and she found it and threw it away. When I asked her why she said she didn't want it attracting bugs."

Again Harold slammed his knotted hands against the table top. Cage and Orlansky stirred cream and sugar in their coffee, but neither ordered the famous bread pudding. Gradually everyone at the surrounding tables returned to their own conversations, speaking louder than they had since Harold and his two friends entered the room.

"I'll take care of the bill," Cage said. "You boys feel free to run along. I'll see you later at the stadium."

Harold got some applause on his way to the door, and like an actor at a curtain call he bowed three times, pointed to the crowd and offered it a generous hand himself. He felt genuinely heroic until he noticed Doc Cage leaning back in his chair, running the tip of an unlit cigar over his lips. His frown was small and terrible, and his eyes were filled with some unspeakable injury.

"Poor Doc Hardhead," Harold said. "If looks could kill he'd have already shot himself."

Orlansky said he had to be getting back to the office and wondered if Harold might like to walk with him. As far as he could tell, no crowds were waiting outside; he thought he and the Old Man could use "some quality time together." To keep from telling Mr. Memory that no time spent in his company was ever quality took a lot of effort, but Harold managed. He looked back through the French doors of the Faculty Club and saw one waiter refilling Cage's coffee cup while another rolled a tray of desserts by the table. Cage told the first waiter something and the second hurried the cart out of sight. Although it meant he'd have to reenter the stage after the curtain had fallen, Harold told Orlansky there were a few "cancer-related matters" he and Doc Hardhead needed to talk about and returned to the dining room.

"If I'd known those ham sandwiches were going to put you in financial straits," he told Cage, sidling up to him, "I'd have paid for them myself." He reached into his pocket and pulled out a pack of gum. "Is it some Juicy Fruit you want, hardhead?"

Cage looked directly into Harold's eyes. "You want to own up to something, son?" he said, pushing the gum away. "You want to own up to this little girl you got for a secretary? Her name's Nancy, isn't it?"

Harold folded a stick of gum into his mouth. "Mrs. Claude," he mumbled.

"Because it wasn't your wife there by your side a while ago in that boardroom," Cage said. "It was this girl you hired to open your mail and answer your telephone. And from what I could see with these old yellow eyes of mine, she had herself one helluva time showing off in front of all those cameras and newspaper people." Cage bit off the end of his cigar and spit it on the table. "With you up there pointing and whatnot and her bellyaching you went and turned a tragedy into a regular carnival. All we needed was some elephants."

"I don't have to listen to this," Harold said, getting up from the table. "And I won't. Not today, anyway."

"Go on, then," Cage replied. "You don't have to listen to anything anybody who loves you ever tells you again. But for your own sake you ought to, son. You really ought to."

| 60 |

When Harold left the dining room this time, the applause was less enthusiastic and he didn't stop to show his gratitude. He pushed through the French doors and strode rapidly across the street onto the breezy expanse of the parade grounds. Under his breath he cursed Mr. Memory, for there were plenty of onlookers. The first one to reach him was a woman with gray teeth, sunken eyes and hair that looked to be falling out of her head even as Harold watched. Over her plain cotton sweatsuit she wore a fancy top coat that might have fit her once but now covered her shoulders like a sheet thrown over a clothesline. Her hands were encased in rubber ski gloves and her feet in fur-lined snow boots.

A handsome, dark-skinned man joined her. "My wife," he announced with a strong Latin inflection, "Gloria Benitez."

The woman removed her gloves and placed her hands in Harold's. She was flesh and bones, and Harold could feel the veins pulsating in her knuckles.

"We were watching TV," the man said humbly, "and my Gloria tells me, 'Ramos, I must meet this Old Man.' So we get in the car and come."

Harold said, "Thank you for your support," and walked on.

Next he encountered a young couple holding a child swathed in a pink blanket. The baby was no more than a few months old, but even Harold could see it wasn't well. "This is Jacob," the father said, "our firstborn." He held out the child at arm's length.

"I've touched a couple of sick persons since I started across this field," Harold said, wiping his hands on his pants. "I wouldn't want to get your boy no sicker." He turned his head, covered his mouth and sneezed. "Myself," he added, "I never had children."

The child rolled his almond-sized eyes around in their sockets.

"One of the great disappointments of my life," Harold said. Then he chuckled. "It's not like I didn't try, though. In a way I'm still trying, if you know what I mean."

"We saw you on the news," the mother said. "We saw your wife, too. So young and pretty. We're real sorry, Mr. Gravely."

Harold didn't correct her. He looked over at the steps leading up to the student union, but no one sat staring at him. Those who'd stood under the mimosas had also disappeared. "I thank you for coming by," Harold said. "I thank you for your support." He placed a hand on the baby's feverish forehead and that—Harold's touch alone—seemed to please the parents. Smiling, they walked off in the direction of the law building. Harold took a few steps forward when a feeling of déjà vu crowded his senses. Although he couldn't say where or when, it seemed he'd seen the couple and their baby before. The smell of the ryegrass, flattened now by the wind that blew across the field, was also familiar.

But when he turned around, they were nowhere to be seen. Like Ramos and Gloria Benitez, they seemed to have vanished as quickly as they'd come.

Harold had made up Bernard Toefield's library story, and also the part about placing his flower in the dictionary. Toefield had been orphaned as a child, and his name wouldn't have appeared in any newspaper until he enlisted in the army. And after his funeral, Harold had thrown the rose in the kitchen trash can, but Rena had plucked it out from a mess of coffee grounds and eggshells and put it in the Bible, in the Book of Genesis. Doing so showed respect for the dead, she said. Genesis meant birth, and a new life in a glorified body, free of all earthly torments, was what she hoped for Coach Toe.

It was Harold who wanted to find the clipping that announced his birth. Having appeared so often in the press, he yearned to see how his name looked its first time in cold type. And he meant to find out today. There was nothing at all mystical about this desire: it had come to him while he was warming the cushions with Mrs. Claude, and he hadn't been able to shake it from his head since.

Harold walked over to the library, introduced himself to the reference librarian and explained what he was looking for. The young woman didn't recognize him, and when she wrote his name down on a scratch pad Harold noticed that she misspelled Gravely. He didn't mention it because he figured that she would learn of her mistake soon enough and recall their meeting with astonishment. Now, however, she was looking at Harold as if this were the oddest request she had ever received. She drummed the pad with the eraser end of her pen.

"Please," he said. "All of a sudden it seems important."

He gave her the name of his hometown and the year of his birth, but she only shook her head.

"In our microfilm room," she explained, "we include several papers from the area, though none for the place and year you've requested."

"I thank you for your support," he said as he left.

Near the stadium, he saw a crowd gathered in front of the football offices. Most were TV or radio crews holding electronic gadgets, but a few looked as sickly and feeble as those he'd met earlier on the parade grounds. Although he had letters to draft and several calls to make to high school recruits, Harold decided that he would accomplish nothing by returning to work. Each reporter would want half an hour alone with him—to get "up close and personal," as they liked to describe their more sensitive interviews—and each would ask him to repeat the same details of his so-called bout with cancer.

In minutes he was on the road, driving toward the southeast with wide cracks in all four windows. To keep from getting sleepy he periodically stuck his head out the window and screamed whatever obscenities came to mind; the force of his dirty language slapping back in his face worked to keep his eyes from closing shut. It was an hour-long drive, keeping to the speed limit, but Harold made it in under fifty minutes, arriving in the middle of the afternoon. By outward appearances the town seemed to have changed little from when he lived here as a boy. On the outskirts a number of massive aluminum buildings housing oil-field equipment hugged the road, but nothing else looked any newer than it had on the day he left. Downtown, especially, was exactly as he remembered it. Built at the turn of the century, the rows of wooden stores and law offices needed paint and a visit from termite control. Old men sat scratching themselves on the benches in front of the luncheonette, and across the street a drunk leaned against the obelisk memorializing the Confederate dead.

Harold parked in front of the library, the lone Cadillac on the street, the lone car in front of the two-story building.

At the desk he was greeted by an elderly woman who acted as if she'd been expecting him. "Welcome home," she said with an air of formality. "Though sad to learn of your declining health, we're honored to have you back." He told her what he'd come for, and she escorted him to a basement room crowded with book stacks and study cubicles; green-shaded lamps hung from the tin-plated ceiling.

"Some libraries are equipped with microfilm," the woman told him, "but not us. We're still operating in the Dark Ages." She found the clipping in a manila envelope sealed with a red string. "Here we are," she said, handing him the slip of newspaper.

He handled the brittle clipping with such care that the librarian thought to say, "You're holding it as gently as one would the newborn it describes." The story, under the heading IT's A . . ., was no longer than two column inches. Harold Gravely, it said, was the only child born in the town that day. He weighed eight pounds three ounces and was delivered by Dr. Maximillian Land at the patient's address, 42 Parish Road.

"Anything else," the librarian asked. "I can look up your first-grade class picture if you like. We been saving those for seems like a hundred years."

His hands were shaking and he was glad to give the piece of paper back to her. Suddenly he felt bloated. "No ma'am," he replied. "That's all I come for."

Outside it was still cool and sunny: trucks were coughing up on the highway but nothing else made a sound. All along the street people were standing with hands up to their faces, shielding the sun that hung just above the rooftops of the buildings behind him.

Though he didn't recognize any of them, it didn't surprise him that they all were staring at him. He lifted a hand and waved. "Thank you for your support," he hollered.

He considered driving by the house where he lived as a boy but decided against it. He hadn't been back since his mother's funeral, just a few months past his eighteenth birthday. The bank had sold the house and property to a chicken farmer who had turned it into a feed depository, and with the few hundred dollars Harold had gotten for it he paid off his parents' debts, bought some new clothes and put a down payment on his first car, a used Cadillac. All these years he'd left the chore of recruiting this area to his assistants, and he'd made a vow to himself never to return. But here he was, standing in the middle of town for everyone to see, proving himself to be as big a liar as Rena always said he was. He had given the place up to guard against nostalgia, but now it suddenly felt like it belonged to him again, or him to it. And that, it occurred to him, was the beauty of being recognized: distances shortened and strangers knew your name. You could even go back to where it was you came from and not feel as if you'd wasted the last forty-some years of your life.

| 61 |

At dusk Harold turned into his street and drove by Rena's car without stopping. He saw the Falcon as clearly as he did the road in front of him, but nothing registered; all he could think about was his statue. It loomed before him everywhere he looked, huge and magnificent. When they were first married, Rena used to occupy him this same way. He could look at a park bench and see her combing her hair or rubbing perfume on her neck. There was something she'd always said whenever he fell into one of his trances: "It's a good thing I'm no Indian cobra, Harold Gravely, 'cause you'd be snakebit and dead of the poison."

He found her in the study trying to make room for all the flower bouquets and telegrams that had arrived since the press conference.

In particular she was occupied with a bunch of gladiolas that didn't want to stand up straight.

"Doesn't it smell like the worst kind of funeral home in here?" she said as Harold walked from the antique secretary to the bookshelves, smelling the flowers.

"More like the baby floor of a hospital, if you ask me," he said, realizing immediately that he'd set himself up. He took his nose out of some pink carnations to see how she'd respond. He felt his smile relax and braced himself as if for a physical assault.

"I really wouldn't know one," she said, busy with her arranging, "as I haven't been lucky enough to spend much time on the baby floor."

Under different circumstances he probably would've left the study, retreated to the bedroom and locked the door. But tonight he was of a mind to keep peace in the house. He had no reason, he reminded himself, to keep feeling guilt over a simple quirk of nature, though he was convinced she'd like to see him tarred and feathered daily for it. "Wasn't nothing I asked for," he mumbled, but she didn't hear him. "Not like I ordered it from the wish book," he added.

With a pair of scissors she was manicuring another bouquet, this one crowded with lilies. "Norman Pepper came by while you were gone," she said. "He brought those." She pointed at some yellow roses.

"Norman, huh?" If there was a hint of disbelief in his voice, it was merely to disguise his satisfaction.

"He told me to tell you the board met to start work forming a recognition committee. I explained I had no idea what he was talking about, and he kindly informed me of the statue."

"Something I meant to tell you about, pie. But I forgot." To testify to his good intentions he snapped his fingers and slapped his knee. "They want to build a statue of me, pie—to stand outside the Players' Gate at the stadium. It was Norman who came up with the idea."

She pretended to be surprised. Her mouth made an exaggerated "oh" and her eyes glistened with excitement. Clearly she was mocking him.

"You're not normal," Harold said. "You used to think it was me who wasn't normal when all along it was you."

She placed her hands over her heart, turned her rapturous expression toward the ceiling and started swaying across the room. She was holding the hem of an invisible dress, a long pretty one with skirts that dragged on the floor.

"A normal wife would be proud," he said. "She would want all the good that comes to her husband."

He could make a list of the things that stood as conclusive proof of how abnormal she truly was. One was her system of keeping house. Two was her abundance of telephone friends and lack of real ones who paid regular visits. Three was her sexual cowardice. Four was the way she recited children's poems to her plants. Five was her passion for dancing alone. Six was the Grade-A jumbo egg he found that time in a robin's nest. Six alone, he figured, was all the evidence he really needed, for it was a chicken egg, still cold from the refrigerator, that she'd stuck up in the tree. He had carried the egg back into the house and put it where it belonged. But later that night he caught her returning it to the nest. Standing on a wooden stepladder and shining a flashlight, she was so witch-eyed that he was halfway afraid she'd finally gone mad. Only after he pressed her did she offer an explanation: it was an experiment. Would a robin or a cardinal or some other sweet, colorful bird lay on it until it hatched? He told her things didn't work that way; it ran against the natural order. But she had insisted they leave the egg in the nest anyway, and every day she had watched from the green room, waiting for her miracle.

Presently she swept by him, pirouetted and spun away. "That egg you stuck up in the Japanese magnolia," he was saying, "now that should of told me right off you were anything but normal. 'By god, my pie ain't a normal woman,' I should of told myself. A normal wife would be so proud of her husband she'd have baked a cake and a casserole and bought him a new necktie. She'd have turned over the bedcovers and changed into some pretty pajamas."

Rena was dancing as she had in the ballroom of the Prince Seurat thirty years ago, and he was surprised at how smooth she still was on her feet. "This is how normal you are," Harold added. "You're so normal you stick branches in the ground thinking they'll grow. Out in public you see a young man and his girlfriend holding hands and showing their affection, you get so you want to kill them or scream, I can't say which. That's how normal you are, Rena." He chuckled to himself. "You're so normal," he concluded, "I'm almost afraid for your mental health."

Some of it, he was willing to admit, maybe even a lot of it, had to do with them not having a family. With envy she used to tell him about her friend Polly Andrus who bore seven children, one after another, and all before she was thirty-two years old. But then, a few months after Polly delivered the last child, her husband Tommy was driving home from work and spotted her walking down the side of the road. She was barefoot and wearing a nightgown splotched with baby formula; if it looked like she hadn't slept in a week, it was because she hadn't. Tommy pulled his car over and asked where she was going. She told him to follow her and see. She was headed toward the Mississippi River bridge less than a mile up the road, going to jump off. Tommy wrestled her into the car and drove her home.

Harold often wondered if what Rena was feeling these last ten years or so involved the same kind of unfathomable female emotions, only over the exact opposite situation. As he often reminded her, she was old enough for menopause, but her behavior seemed far more complicated than anything he had ever heard or read about "the change," as he called it. Did her cherished magazines, he wondered, explain why someone would want to put a chicken egg in a bird's nest or a dried-up old stick in the ground? Did they explain why a woman married most of her life would become enraged at the sight of two young lovers? If there were women like Polly getting severely depressed over having babies, Harold had convinced himself, then there were bound to be women feeling the same way over not having them at all.

"I may die without issue," he said now, pointing at her as she danced around the room. "But at least they won't forget."

| **62** |

When Rena stopped twirling around the study, she flopped on Harold's desk chair and leaned so far back that she almost lost her balance and fell to the floor. She was at a loss to explain why she felt like dancing after the day she'd had, and luckily the doorbell rang as she was beginning to make up a story. Harold thundered out of the room, headed for the sliding glass doors that opened onto the back porch. He figured, as she did, that it was a neighbor or a friend paying an informal visit, here to offer their condolences, but no one was there. "In the front, Harold," Rena called from the study. "It must be the delivery boy again." As he crossed the house he padded over her raked carpets and clicked his heels on the parquet as hard as he could. She felt like locking him outside and not letting him back in until he promised to vacuum and clean up the marks himself, but with visitors in the house she couldn't well threaten him, much less make a scene. That he would purposely bully her at a time like this made her resent him even more.

From the desk Rena could look in a mirror down at the end of the hall and see Harold at the front door. Whatever he saw through the peephole didn't please him, because he opened the door only as far as the chain lock allowed, a couple of inches. Rena was so winded and light-headed as she walked over to the living room that she had to support herself with a hand on the wall. She whispered for him to be polite, and to her surprise he was. "Sure you got the right place?" he said, sounding friendly. "It's the Harold Gravelys who reside in this house."

Somebody answered, but Rena couldn't quite place the voice. It belonged to a man, that was certain; but it belonged to a man who wanted to cry, thus making it sound like an elderly woman with smoke clouding her lungs. Rena sat down on the love seat and waited with her hands resting in her lap.

"Get up off your knees," Harold commanded through the crack in the door. "That isn't necessary. It isn't necessary at all."

Now a woman spoke. "Come on, L.S.," she said. "You're gonna crush those poor petunias."

"Rena," Harold said, turning to face her, "make some room in my study. Little Shorty's got one more item to add to all them pretty flowers."

Harold flipped on the outside light, unlocked the door and flung it open. On the front steps leading up to the landing, Little Shorty Grieg and a woman Rena had never seen before were standing and studying the dirty wet spots on his knees. In one hand Little Shorty held some wildflowers, and in the other the Heisman Trophy he was awarded after his senior year. By the way he slumped to his left side it seemed the flowers were far heavier than the trophy, and not until he reached out and handed them to Harold did he stand up straight. Even so, he was still several inches shorter than the woman, whom he now introduced as Frances, his next-door neighbor. Frances had frosted hair and a dry, wrinkled complexion. Her lips gleamed with a fleshy, high-gloss polish, and her eyes were spaced too far apart, making them seem closer to her ears than the bridge of her nose. Rena thought she resembled the kind of person who didn't wash but once a week, that being on Saturdays and in a metal tub in the kitchen; then she admonished herself for being so quick to judge. Frances wasn't wearing a wedding band, but Rena knew that didn't mean anything. Little Shorty, married for most of his life, wasn't wearing one either.

"My wife's visiting her mother at the old folks' home," Little Shorty said once he noticed Rena staring at his left hand. "Been up there pretty damn long now, waiting for something to happen."

"Sorry to hear it," Harold said. "But I can't say I don't know what it's like."

"She weighs sixty-four pounds last I heard," Little Shorty said, "my mother-in-law does. She's so skinny she's like a pup tent you got to assemble yourself."

Rena had always been a bit afraid of Little Shorty. In college, she remembered, there had been a question on the final examination of her freshman philosophy course: if the world were destroyed by a series of atomic explosions, and all of human life with it but you and one other person, with whom would you most like to spend the rest of your days? For extra points the professor had asked with whom would you least like to spend them. The first part of the question had been obvious. Pogo Reese, she wrote, because together we could begin to repopulate the planet with happy blue-eyed children. To the latter she had answered Little Shorty Grieg. He was so muscular he scared her, she wrote, and he always smelled like a dog that'd been tracking rabbits. Also, she said, his neck resembled an elephant foot one of her great-uncles brought home from Africa and now used as an umbrella holder. She had flunked the test. In the margin the teacher had written, "What about A. Lincoln? K. Marx? Madame Curie? W. Shakespeare? After a nuclear holocaust no one will care about your football heroes."

Harold handed her the flowers. "You remember my wife Rena?" he said to Little Shorty, who nodded and bowed his head. Then to Frances: "She's been in charge of me nearly as long as your neighbor here has been in charge of that trophy."

Frances entered the room first, and Little Shorty, fast on her heels, apologized for letting all the cold air in. He was unshaven and little white nuggets of sleep hung in the corners of his eyes. Rena had a mind to tell him to take his shoes off, but instead she said, "How about a drink?" then started moving toward the kitchen with the flowers. "Soft or hard, we got them both."

"No thanks," Frances said. "My bladder's full as a tick."

"The bathroom's just down the hall," Harold said.

"We won't be long," Little Shorty said. "She can hold it."

Everyone was still standing when Rena returned from the kitchen. She had placed the flowers in a crystal vase, which she set among some brass conversation pieces on the coffee table. Harold was holding the trophy, studying it as if it had just been presented to him at an awards banquet. "I suppose I should say something," he said, inspecting the inscription on the pedestal. "A few words of appreciation."

"That's all right," Little Shorty said. "Time in this house waits for no one, and me and Frances wouldn't want you to have to waste too much of it on the likes of us."

There was a long, uncomfortable silence during which everyone stared at the muddy set of footprints that Little Shorty had tracked across Rena's floor. Finally Frances spoke: "Me and L.S. here have got a pair of confessions to make."

"Please," Rena said, "let me fix you something to drink first. How about a glass of burgundy. Aren't you thirsty?"

"We've been drinking malt liquor," said Little Shorty, who would've been staring straight down at his toes had his chest and belly not blocked his view.

"The kind with the charging bull on the can," Frances said. With her index fingers she made horns at the front of her head and wiggled them. "But, lord, they go right through me."

"Them letters you and the board were getting back a few months ago," Little Shorty said with a stutter. "The ones from Helen Dumars and the unsigned ones trying to make people think you had something to do with what happened to Pogo—"

"Those were from us," Frances announced, plainly pleased to have said it. "I was at school a semester and knew her, then this goddamn railroad brakeman left me for pregnant. Helen was in my sorority. Best as I could recall, I pieced together some silly-ass story I'd heard."

Harold nodded. Rena sat on the edge of the love seat again and stared demurely at her folded hands.

"It's always perturbed me how with some people," Frances continued, "you put them in front of a crowd and they think their you-know-what smells like cotton candy."

Harold finished admiring the trophy and handed it back to Little Shorty. "It was a nice gesture," he said, "bringing that here. But now that I'm sick with cancer I won't be needing it."

"Hell," Frances said, "L.S. don't need it neither."

"No, I sure don't," he said. "I got no real use for it."

"When I moved next door—this was about a dozen years ago— I went by with a sweet potato pie as a kind of hello present, and there was this big trophy standing by the sink with some dishrags on it. I told him he should use the rags to mop off the dust, then see if somebody'd want to pay him to melt it down. My second husband was a melter—cans, silver, gold, anything. I really had no idea that this thing meant he'd been the best football player in the whole country until L.S. explained it to me."

Harold cleared his throat. "In case you two haven't heard," he said, "they'll be turning me into a kind of Heisman Trophy before too long. The board's planning on putting up a statue of me outside the football stadium."

"Congratulations," Little Shorty said. "We heard."

"Ditto," remarked Frances, digging in the pocket of her tight white jeans for a cigarette. She pulled out one already three-quarters smoked and an eddy of ash drifted to the floor. "You mind if I indulge," she asked Rena. "Like nothing else it gets my mind off my bladder and onto more positive situations."

"Better not," Harold said. "My wife's allergic."

The cigarette was dangling from the woman's mouth. "Well," she said, "can I hold it here on my lips as a reminder?"

"Best put it away altogether," Harold said. "Poor darling used to swell up when we first married—finally she figured out what was causing it and quit buying me cigars and chewing tobacco whenever she went to Sweeney's. Instead she'd come home with Juicy Fruit, which had a taste that pleased her. Now I'm hooked on yellow gum; all those expensive brass spittoons I invested in, she went and converted them into plant pots."

Frances stuffed the cigarette back in her pocket, then turned to Little Shorty and pointed at Harold. "If you don't tell this man you're sorry right this minute, L.S., I'm gonna wet all over his wife's pretty floor."

"Back of all them good looks and charm," Little Shorty said to his shoes, "Pogo must of had a kind of wildness in him."

Everyone was looking at Rena, perhaps hoping she'd expand on this observation, but she remained quiet. The wildness in Pogo belonged to most boys she knew back then, and also to some fully grown men, Harold included. It was more glandular than anything, and Pogo's tended to show itself whenever they were parked under the willows by the campus lakes or those times when she gave him permission to drive fast. The wildness came and went, but it had never seemed powerful enough to kill a person.

Little Shorty started for the door, making a second set of tracks next to the original. When he stopped and wheeled around, Rena thought it was to apologize for muddying the room, but instead he threw an arm around Harold and drew him close. The trophy poked Harold in the abdomen and nearly knocked the wind out of him. "For heaven's sake, don't kill the man," Frances said, then she pushed Little Shorty through the door and onto the porch.

From the window in the living room Rena watched Little Shorty back his Chrysler down the drive. He drove all the way to the corner with his feet on both the accelerator and brake pedals, the taillights flaring brightly even as the car advanced. They got only as far as the head of the street, near Rena's little Falcon, before stopping. Rena saw the car's ceiling light come on and Frances step outside, then she saw Frances unbutton her pants and pull them down to her ankles. Little Shorty sat unmoving at the wheel, his face turned away from the woman, who now was squatting between the doors and making a puddle of water. At the window Rena ground her teeth and squealed. After a minute Frances got back in the car and Little Shorty negotiated the corner, driving as if he suddenly had remembered an important meeting he and the woman had on the other end of town.

Rena fetched a bucket of warm soapy water and a sponge and was cleaning up the footprints when the telephone rang. Harold picked it up in the study, and she could hear his voice, gentler and more cheerful than it had been all day. She hurried across the hall and pressed her ear to the door.

"I knew all along you wouldn't try to bury my rooter in the dirt," he was saying. "But let me say here and now, hardhead, how very much I thank you for your support."

"What was there about me you didn't like?"

| **63** |

A power failure strikes the downtown business district as Officer Andrew Washburn is en route with Harold to the police station. In an instant everything blinks to darkness: traffic signals, street lamps, store signs. Cars line up at major intersections, waiting their turn at what suddenly have become four-way stops.

In the backseat of the squad car Harold has spotted the red automobile with the convertible top. It keeps a distance of about fifty yards, always three or four cars back. At one point, frustrated by the snarled traffic, Washburn puts on his revolving blue lights and speeds by on the shoulder of the road. The red car follows fast on his bumper, and behind it, several others. "They're breaking the law," Harold says, finding the policeman's eyes in the rearview mirror and motioning to the cars behind them. "You plan to ignore that?"

When the cop laughs his muscular shoulders bounce up and down. Harold, his hands cuffed, lifts his legs and pounds the back of the front seat with his feet. "You should ticket the sonofabitches."

"Think so?" Washburn says, still smiling. "If I started writing tickets I'd never stop." He turns down the volume on his police radio. "They'll all end up using the shoulders before too long, anyway. It's like feeding time in the shark tank when the lights go out."

Harold keeps watch on the red car. Whenever he looks forward, trying to ignore it, a strange sensation seizes his gut and the back of his head suddenly feels vulnerable to attack. He has the urge to wrap his arms around his head, to protect himself, but because of the cuffs he can't.

"We've been followed since we left the hotel," he says, looking through the rear window. "He's back there now."

"Everybody on this road's being followed," the cop says.

"Yeah, I know. But we're really being followed. Somebody's been trailing me since about eight o'clock this morning."

The cop's well-shaped shoulders bounce up and down again. "Maybe it's some undercover deputy with the FBI. They pegged you as a Mafia boss and now they got you under surveillance."

Harold shakes his head.

"Or somebody with the CIA, all the way down here from headquarters at Langley, Virginia." Washburn slaps the top of the steering wheel. "No . . . no, that's not who it is. It's one of them KGB agents—one of them Russkies with nothing better to do than follow you and me around in a hurricane."

"It's a spy," Harold says.

"Yeah," the cop answers, laughing even harder, slapping the steering wheel. "It's a spy!"

A few blocks before they reach the police station, the red car turns into a side street and disappears. "Well," Harold says, "looks like our friend is gone. I guess he was afraid of getting caught."

Washburn's heavy scowl thickens; he checks the sideview mirrors. "The spy's gone, you say?"

"He took a right on Clairborne. I saw him go."

"Yeah," the cop says. "He knew better than to get too close. All them Russian spies are afraid of us police."

| 64 |

Inside they photograph, fingerprint and book Harold. The whole process takes about half an hour, though under normal conditions it probably would have taken less than half that. A generator provides some of the offices with power, and in others the cops and office staff use kerosene lamps and battery-operated storm lamps. To Harold's dismay, no one recognizes him: not the female desk sergeants working the switchboard, not the cops scurrying around with flashlights, not any of the people waiting their turn to complain at the desk. Of course, it's easy to conclude that panic over the electrical failure is the reason no one pays him any notice—easy for Harold, that is. Because this is what he keeps telling himself, over and over.

Although Harold doesn't bother to ask, Washburn informs him that he's been charged with simple arson for burning photographs in the bathroom of Oni Welby-White's hotel suite. "But we're letting you slide for what you did to the model," he adds. "The artist was contracted and given a down payment to do it. So as best as I can figure, that makes it your property to do with as you please." Washburn's expression belongs to a man fully impressed with himself. "Still," he adds, "Mr. Welby-White might want to sue. That'd make it a civil dispute. What we have here with the pictures is criminal."

They are in a cluttered office down the hall from the main lobby, sitting on brightly colored plastic chairs identical to those found in the cafeteria of the athletic dormitory. A state map hangs on the wood-paneled wall, a yellow arrow with the words YOU ARE HERE indicating the city.

Two other officers are in the room, both with prisoners of their own, both filling out forms with ballpoint pens. "I miss my electric typewriter," one of them says.

"I never thought I'd hear you say that," says the other.

"Me neither," Washburn chimes in. He's flipping through a paperbound volume listing the revised criminal statutes. "You'll want to use the phone," he says to Harold. "Feel free to make as many calls as you like."

"In the movies they give you only one," Harold says. "That seems like the standard procedure."

"Okay, then," Washburn replies. "You're allowed only one call."

"Considering the circumstances, there's nobody in particular I care to talk to."

"You'd better call your lawyer." Washburn doesn't look up from the pages of the book. "That's who most people call."

"I don't have a lawyer."

"Do you have a wife?"

Harold runs his fingers over the cut on his face. "Sometimes I have a wife," he confesses. "But the last ten years she's been more like a housekeeper."

"Then your housekeeper can call her lawyer. You'll want to post bond. I don't think you'd much enjoy getting stuck in the bullpen. There are some real unsavory types back there."

Washburn offers him the telephone, but Harold holds his hands in his lap, moving them like a pair of birds cleaning themselves—not small birds, either, for Harold has been known to wrap his fingers around the thickest of cocktail glasses and meet the tips with the nail of his thumb. His wrists are chafed and sore from the cuffs.

"Simple arson," Washburn reads aloud, "carries either a twenty-five-hundred-dollar fine or maximum five years in prison, with or without hard labor."

"You're new at this, aren't you?" Harold says. "You're newer at it than a baby at its mama's tit. You're so new you think you're a prosecutor and not a cop, reading to me from a book."

"Not so new that I don't know a crime when I see it." Washburn, as composed as ever, writes something on the arrest form. "And speaking for all of us here, Mr. Gravely, I'd appreciate it if you refrained from using profanities."

Harold has to think for a moment before coming up with what might be considered a curse word. "Since when did the word *tit* become a profanity?"

Washburn drops his pen and turns in his chair. "You said it once already," he says, waggling a bony finger. "I asked you not to say it again and then you went ahead and said it anyway. Say it a third time and see where it gets you."

"Where's the shift commander?" Harold mutters, starting for the door. "The poor, sad bastard calls me at work all morning long, leaves message after message with my secretary and now that I'm here he's nowhere to be found."

"Generally, at this time of day Lieutenant Cousins would be out having a cup of coffee with the chief," Washburn replies. "They go to a place down the street. But with the power outage and the weather like it is he's probably out working." With the pen he points to Harold's chair. "So sit down, please, and don't speak unless spoken to."

"Who usually minds the store while the boys are out playing good citizen? Don't tell me it's you, hardhead."

Washburn closes the book and throws his pen on the desk top. "You call me a dickhead again," he says flatly, "and I'll make you wish you were never born."

"I called you a hardhead," Harold says.

Washburn shouts, "Any of you fellows hear this person call me a dickhead?"

Neither of the police officers looks up from his paperwork, but both answer in the affirmative.

"Any of you fellows see me offer this man the use of a telephone and get told there's no one in particular he cares to talk to?" Washburn is leaning back in his plastic colored chair, straining to glimpse how they respond.

Again the men keep their eyes on their work and answer in the affirmative. The prisoners, both handcuffed, concur.

"I'll have to take your personal effects now, Mr. Gravely," Washburn says. "Your rings, wallet, change, keys. I'll take your belt, too, and your shoelaces. You may not want to hang yourself, but some of the men back in the bullpen might."

Without objection Harold gives him what he's asked for and looks over the policeman's shoulder as he records the items on a form. "How much cash you have on you, Mr. Gravely?"

When Harold doesn't answer, Washburn rifles through his billfold. "Thirty-seven dollars," he says, writing it down. "Now, how much change?" He counts that too. "Eighty-nine cents."

"On top of the cancer," Harold remarks, "I think I'm getting a sore throat. I can feel everything starting to tingle."

Washburn points at his mouth. "Open up and say ah."

"I'll have your badge," Harold tells him. "And when I do you'll never get it back."

"I don't mean to be presumptuous," Washburn says, standing up, "but sometimes a man like you needs to be humbled in ways he can't begin to imagine. He doesn't know, for instance, how equal he is to everyone else until he has to share a commode with seven criminals who care only that you don't cut into their share of the toilet paper. I'd give you one of them orange jumpsuits to wear, but I've got a feeling that within the hour you'll be banging on the cage door, asking to call your wife to bail you out and take you home." The cop laughs to himself. "Or maybe that spy of yours will come and get you—right, Mr. Gravely?"

| **65** |

At the door leading to the jail area, Washburn hands his pistol and billy club to a cop who apparently recognizes Harold. In the cone of light from his lantern, the man's eyes widen in disbelief and a generous smile exposes his collection of gold-capped teeth. He's standing behind a metal desk and can't seem to decide where to put his hands.

"Giving him the nickel tour, Andrew?" the man says to Washburn, as he flips through his roster of inmates. "I don't recall seeing any of his boys back in there."

"I'm putting him in the bullpen," Washburn says, flicking on his flashlight. "Gravely here got careless with some matches."

"My god, Andrew."

"It was simple arson. I caught him burning certain items that didn't belong to him in a room at the Prince Seurat. If I hadn't got there right away it might've been aggravated arson. He might've burned the whole place down."

"That would of been no great loss," Harold says. "The way Lejeune's let it go, the Rat deserves to be torched."

Reluctantly the man gives Washburn a key. "Cousins'll howl over this," he says. "I don't want no part of it." Then he turns to Harold. "It ain't me involved in this, Old Man."

Harold nods. "What's your name, hardhead?"

"Leonard Wilson, sir." He points to the name on his badge.

"You're exonerated of any wrongdoing, Mr. Wilson."

"Thank you, sir," he replies. "Thank you kindly."

Washburn pushes the door open and Harold follows him through. "The thing you'll notice," Washburn says, shining his flashlight on the bars of the cells, "is that everyone here is innocent. No one really did what they're in here for."

"They're innocent," Harold says.

"That's what they'll tell you. They're all innocent."

Although there are empty two-man cells in the general lockup, Washburn leads Harold to one of several community cells, unlocks the door and shows him to his bunk. If not for the splashes of dusty, gray-colored light breaking through the bars and layers of wire mesh fronting the thick, bottle-glass windows at either end of the cell, the jail would be as dark as a tomb. As it is, Harold needs a few moments to adjust his eyes to the steely gloom, and even then he can't discern much of anything beyond the narrow beam of Washburn's flashlight.

Primitive clotheslines, made of garbage pail liners rolled up and tied together at each end, cross the room diagonally, and from them hang magazines, underwear and sweat-stiffened T-shirts. Sheets of yellowed newspaper have been woven into some of the bars at the front of the cell, blocking the view of the toilet from anyone standing in the hallway. The heavy odor of perspiration overpowers the ammonia fumes steaming off the concrete floor.

"Hello, incorrigibles," Washburn says in a chipper voice. "This here's your new roommate."

The introduction draws no response. All of the men, wrapped in dingy sheets, appear to be sleeping. Only one has his face exposed, and it's a face like those too often painted by tormented artists leaning toward brutal self-destruction. It belongs to someone who deserves no place on this earth, Harold thinks, to one whose role in the hereafter will be to stoke the flames of the furnace and fry the meat. A rubbery scar, similar in texture to the keloid on Harold's hip, begins at the man's chin and runs across the middle of his mouth, snakes along the left side of his nose, straddles the knotted bridge, scuttles between his shrunken eyes and climbs his forehead before disappearing into an unruly mass of hair.

"The boys must've stayed up all night playing cards," Washburn says. "Otherwise, I'm sure they would've had party hats and some curly snake whistles and a giant cake with candles on it to greet you."

"You're a real wit," Harold says, turning away from the ravaged inmate. "You're a man who missed his calling. You could be packing them in at all the New York comedy clubs."

The scarred man rolls over in his bunk when Washburn shines his light on him. With his tattered sheet and the square of yellow sponge that serves as a pillow, he covers his face.

"Dat's DeGeorge," Washburn says in an unconvincing Italian

accent. "He's de one dey tried to slice, dice and circumsize in de pen up at Angola." The cop laughs at his own callow humor but frowns when Harold reveals no appreciation for it. "DeGeorge was de ladies' man until de knife got him. Now he's de big bad wolf. He's de scary boogey monster."

Harold's bunk is under one occupied by the only snorer of the group. The man's right arm, paralyzed with sleep, hangs down and nearly touches the undressed rubber mattress on Harold's cot.

"I'll be leaving now," Washburn says, closing the door behind him. "When you're ready for your phone call just holler. Wilson up front'll be more than happy to accommodate you."

| **66** |

Harold hasn't yet figured how to turn his arrest and incarceration to his advantage, but he's certain he'll find a way. His big worry is the statue project; the threat of jeopardizing it brings a pain to his chest, and not the kind he commonly associates with his lung condition. How will his arrest affect donations? Coupled with the Perry Watts incident, will this sink everything he's been counting on?

The inmate in the bunk above Harold's has stopped snoring. In the place of his arm, the man's bare feet hang inches from where Harold is sitting. "We get a new roommate?" the man says, hopping down to see for himself. "Or did the zookeeper come back here just to rattle our cage?"

Harold walks over to a small plastic table near the cell door, pushes off some of the scraps of paper lying on top and takes a seat. "I won't be here long," he says. "I'm here only until someone discovers it's me—now that I think about it, until the shift commander gets off his coffee break."

"Me, too," the man says. "In fact, all of us here are. Don't you just hate it when a guy thinks his afternoon cup of java is more important than your walking papers."

In the greasy half dark the man stretches his arms and grabs at the air above the crowded clotheslines. As he yawns, he laughs at his and Harold's exchange, or at something else he suddenly finds funny, and a rope of spittle escapes from his mouth.

"Forgive me my slatternly display," he says after he's wiped his lips with his sleeve. "Last night the fellows and I stayed up playing dominoes until dawn, and then we had to scrub the floors. About an hour after lunch we all dropped down to nap, as is our custom, and here it is late afternoon already."

The man looks to be about Harold's age, though it's hard to tell in the dark. He's rolled the short sleeves of his orange jumpsuit up to the points of his shoulders, exposing a pair of extraordinarily powerful arms.

"How do I know you?" the man says after a moment. "I'm sure I know you from someplace."

Harold doesn't answer. The man strikes him as familiar, but he can't place him. It also occurs to him that it might not be wise to reveal his identity; he's not, after all, at a barbershop waiting his turn in the chair.

"I was going to ask you the same thing," Harold says timidly. "You look like somebody I used to know."

"Did you used to know a lot of people," the man asks, studying the spot on Harold's arm where he scratched himself.

"Pretty many," Harold says. "I still do."

"You must be famous, then."

Harold considers a number of responses, then says, "You might say I'm widely known."

"Then maybe I'm somebody you knew once but forgot about since you've met so many people over the years. Isn't that right?"

"That sounds reasonable."

"Why, thank you. Coming from you that means a lot." He sits next to Harold on the table and leans into him, his face no more than an inch away. "Recognize me now, Harold?"

Harold blinks and concentrates. "I can't say that I do."

"Then you don't," the man says.

"That's right," Harold replies. "I guess I don't."

The inmate with the scarred face tosses in his bunk and says, "Shut up." His head hangs over the side of the mattress, his thin, sinewy neck bent at a strange angle.

"Sorry," Harold says. "We'll keep it down." He and the man

look at each other and shrug. They are silent long enough for DeGeorge to fall asleep again.

"Ever spend any time in the state pen?" the man says.

"None," Harold answers.

"What about the podunk jails out there?"

"Out where," Harold asks.

"Out there in this great land of ours," the man replies sarcastically, making a sweeping gesture with his right arm.

"Except for a few times to spring people out of the drunk tank, I never been in a jail in all my life."

"So, technically, Harold, this is your first time?"

"This is it."

"Then we oughta celebrate." Although he seems to mean it, the man doesn't move. He sits for a while watching DeGeorge sleep and yawns again without covering his mouth.

Harold, remembering something, says, "By the way, how'd you know my name was Harold?"

"Is your name Harold?" The man looks surprised.

"Yes. Didn't you call me Harold?"

"Did I?' the man says, looking even more surprised.

"You did, you called me Harold."

"Well," the man says, moving his face so close that Harold can smell his breath, "I guess I must've known it then."

DeGeorge sits up in his bunk and drops his feet to the floor. In the bolt of ashen light from the window he's even easier to make out than the man next to Harold. He's unzipped his orange coveralls all the way down to his navel, baring rolls of fat that seem to tremble even as he rests. Sprays of hair stick out of both of his ears, and they're darker and more abundant than the hair spilling from his nostrils. If someone, at this moment, were to ask Harold to compile a list of the most hideous-looking human beings he ever laid eyes on, this person would top it.

"Mr. Paris DeGeorge," says the man next to Harold, "I'd like you to make the acquaintance of Mr. Harold Gravely."

DeGeorge moves only to run his hands over his face and to extract a fleck of wax from his ear.

"Hey," Harold says. "How'd you know my last name? You really do remember me from someplace, don't you?"

DeGeorge lies back down, this time on top of the sheet, his head on the square of yellow sponge.

"You yourself said you were widely known," the man answers.

"I know but—"

The man places a finger against Harold's mouth to shush him. "You ready for me to tell you a story, Harold?"

The man's breath is more pungent than all the other odors—the sour feet, the cleaning solvent, the sweaty clothes, the open toilet. "I'd rather know your name," Harold says, "than hear a story."

"Why's that?" the man says. "Something about me you don't like?"

Harold presses his hands together between his thighs. The cell is warm and humid, yet he feels a shiver cut through him. "No," he says. "Nothing about you bothers me. It just doesn't seem fair that you should know my name when I don't know yours."

The man reaches over and pats Harold on the back of the head, then gently strokes his hair. "You're right," he says. "It isn't fair. There's not one fair thing about it. But that's what you get for being famous."

"Who are you?" Harold feels powerless to push the man's hand away.

"Who am I? *Who am I?*" The man's voice rattles the aluminum light fixture hanging from the ceiling, but the men sleeping in the bullpen don't stir. "You've hit on the eternal question, Harold. Who am I?"

"Who are you?" Harold says again, barely loud enough to hear the words himself.

The man pulls his hand away, crosses his arms and leans forward, resting his elbows on his knees. "I'm a murderer," he says after a moment, gazing into Harold's eyes. "I'm a killer, Harold. That's who I am."

He and Harold share a hearty laugh together, then both fall grave and silent. It takes enormous effort for Harold to build the next sentence; to utter it requires an absolute force of will. "They wouldn't stick a murderer in here."

From his bunk DeGeorge erupts with laughter, then muffles it with the square of sponge.

"Oh," the man says, "I'm not in here for murder. I stole somebody's money and went and got drunk on it, me and Paris here.

But just because I'm a thief, too, doesn't stop me from being a murderer. Once you murder, Harold, you're a murderer."

DeGeorge unleashes another peal of laughter.

"Ask Paris how he got that scar on his face," the man says, nudging Harold. "Go ahead, ask him."

Harold keeps quiet, his eyes on the sweating floor. He is going through the alphabet, listing names that begin with each letter, trying to match one with the face of the man.

"Hey, Paris," the man says. "Tell Harold here how you got that scar on your face."

After a moment DeGeorge says, "I cut myself shaving." And his wild, animal laughter fills the cell.

"For me, Harold, it was unintentional. I didn't mean to do it. It was an accident."

"What are you talking about?" Harold says.

The man starts rubbing the back of Harold's head again, raking his hair with his fingers. It sends a rush of gooseflesh down Harold's back and onto his arms.

"Why aren't you following me, Harold?" he says. "Is what I'm saying that difficult? Because if it is I can slow down. It's not like we're not locked up in here. We can take all day."

Harold begins to shake uncontrollably. He's reached the letter D and still hasn't come up with the right name: Daniels, Davis, Davies, Darwin, Danton, Dejean . . .

Now the man is massaging Harold's shoulders. He squeezes and rubs, squeezes and rubs, then he slaps them with the rigid flats of his hands. "That feel good, Harold? You like it?"

Harold doesn't answer. His jaw slackens and his chin rests on his chest. He graduates to the letter G: Garr, Garfield, Garland, Garson, Garbo, Garby, Garreau . . .

"As far as what he meant to me—he really meant no more to me than I must mean to you. He had a name but I didn't know it." For a second the man looks off contemplatively, as if, like Harold, he's trying to bring something long forgotten back to mind. "He was lying there, Harold, blood running out of the back of his head, yet he was still able to speak."

"A talking corpse," DeGeorge calls from the bunk.

The man nods. "He sounded as if he was already dead, or knew that any second he would be. 'What was there about me you didn't like?' is what he told me. And it was real sincere, you know, like he meant it. There he was with his brains running all over the pavement and he couldn't understand what there was about him that had made me want to kill him. Was it his looks that made me do it, or his personality, or some wrong he'd done?" He laughs and shakes his head, perhaps at the unlikeliness of it all. "That's the last thing he ever said, and for years I kept hearing it and trying to find an answer."

"Don't look at me," Harold says.

"Me neither," pipes in DeGeorge.

The man leans over and presses his mouth against Harold's ear. "But I thought you might have the answer," he whispers. "I thought you of all people might be able to tell me."

"Tell you what?"

"What there was about him I didn't like," the man says, patting Harold on the arm. "But don't let it worry you, Harold; it isn't worth it. I worried about it for more than half my life, and then one day not too long ago I got my answer. It came to me like a slap across the face." He sighs heavily.

"Tell me," Harold says, swallowing hard.

The man holds both hands out in front of him. "I killed him with these," he says, opening and closing them. "Just your average pair. Nothing fancy about them, really. Ten fingers . . . well, make that eight fingers and two thumbs. Isn't that right, Harold?"

Harold nods and the man goes back to massaging his neck.

"They convicted me of manslaughter and sentenced me to twenty-one years, the maximum by law in this state. They intended to make an example of me, because I was what you might call a role model. You may remember the case; it was in all the papers."

Harold moves to the letter *J:* Jacobs, James, Janes, Janson, Jacobson, Jamison, Jarrell . . .

"Was it that he stunk or something?" DeGeorge says. "Was he ugly? Did he talk a lot of garbage?"

"Patience," the man tells him. "Please." Then he turns back to Harold. "Paris and I go back many, many years, Harold, to my earliest days as a ward of the state, in fact." The man stops rubbing Harold's neck and turns back to DeGeorge. "Hey, Paris. Tell Harold how you got that scar on your face."

DeGeorge rocks with laughter; he kicks at his sheet and drums the bed frame.

The man next to Harold laughs along with him and slaps his hands together. "Come on, Paris. How'd you get it?"

DeGeorge flips over on his back again. "Cut myself shaving," he says, and the two men wail and scream.

"What the hell's so funny?" the inmate in the bunk over DeGeorge grumbles, raising his head.

DeGeorge kicks the wood slats under his bunkmate's rubber mattress. "Shut up before I rip your goddamn throat out," he tells him.

"Go back to sleep," says the man next to Harold; the one over DeGeorge obediently turns onto his side and pulls the raggedy sheet over his head. "I got 'em all trained," he tells Harold. "I should've been a coach." After a pause he adds, "Just like you, Harold."

| **67** |

As Harold sits staring into the man's face, a wash of light steals in from behind him and fills the room. At the cage door, Leonard Wilson stands holding his lamp, a swarm of moths swirling in the bright yellow halo above his head. "Everything okay in here, Old Man?" he says. "These sleepy-headed monsters aren't giving you too hard a time, are they?"

Harold doesn't answer, still searching the alphabet for a name.

"Pretty warm in here, isn't it?" Wilson says, wiping his brow with a handkerchief. "Electric company says it won't be till tomorrow we get the power back. Sorry it's so uncomfortable."

"Since when did you care?" DeGeorge says, sitting up in his bed. "This ain't the Waldorf-Astoria."

"I started caring when he came aboard," Wilson says, pointing at Harold through the bars. "This here is my hero."

In the light of the lantern the man next to Harold radiates a rare, gentle beauty. Saddling his unmarked nose, and set deep in his exquisitely formed skull, are eyes that explode with color. His irises are as big around as shooter marbles and bluer than any Harold can recall ever having seen before. His hair, though dull and uncombed, is as full as a healthy teenager's; his teeth, framed by thin, almost feminine lips, are straight and pearly white. The absence of crow's-feet and wrinkles indicates fewer years on the man than Harold originally figured.

"Mr. Gravely," Leonard Wilson says, heading back to the lobby, "I want you to holler if you need me. You holler and I'll get you to a telephone." He rattles the tangle of keys on his hip. "I got the way, remember."

"Fine," Harold says. "Thank you."

The guard leaves, and with him the hot yellow light and the busy swarm of bugs.

"May I continue now?" the man next to Harold says.

"Please do," DeGeorge answers. "We're waiting."

Packard, Pagan, Paillet, Palmer, Pargas, Parks, Pastor . . .

"It was the question I couldn't forget," he begins, once again stroking Harold's hair. "At the state pen I'd spend hours writing it on blank sheets of paper, like a kid doing lines as punishment after school. This is what I'd write: 'What was there about me you didn't like?' And then I'd write my response. I'd write 'You keyed my car' or, when the guilt of what I'd done was too much to stand, 'I am deeply sorry. Please forgive me. But you ruined the paint job on my fabulous automobile.' I did this for the seven years I was at Angola— almost every night and first thing in the morning, and sometimes during meals—and after I was paroled I continued to do it. It was like having a song in your head you can't get rid of and you don't even remember its name."

Rabalais, Rachal, Ray, Raney, Ranson, Rawlings, Ravare . . .

Harold plunges his face into his hands. "I know who you are," he says. "I know you. . . . I know you now!"

"Relax," Pogo tells him. "Please, let me finish." He licks his mouth with his tongue then does the same to his perfect teeth. "After I cleared parole I left this part of the country," he says without emotion. "I was born into money, Harold, lots and lots of money, and during the time I was in prison my father died. Being the sole heir, I suddenly found myself an independently wealthy fellow, though I must say I didn't live like one. I told myself that I couldn't begin to enjoy my life until I found an answer to the question I'd been asking."

"What was there about me you didn't like?" DeGeorge says.

"I would deny myself everything until I got my answer—good meals and clean clothes, a sip of alcohol, an ice-cold Coca-Cola, a spin on the dance floor, the embrace of a lovely woman."

He walks across the room to the sink, turns on the faucet and takes a long, noisy drink of water. He rinses his face and the top of his head; then, with a plastic-bristle brush, he combs his hair straight back from the forehead. When he returns to the table, he sits down in the same spot.

"In Carson City, Nevada," he says, "I worked for a time cleaning ashtrays in a casino—to punish myself, Harold, to remind myself that I was imprisoned by the memory of what that man had told me. You know how many ashtrays there are in a casino? I was like an invisible person in there, moving from table to table. I rarely spoke except to apologize to someone I might've bothered at the roulette wheel or keno board. The words I said most often were: 'Sorry to have disturbed you. Let me move this out of your way.' Meaning their ashtray, Harold. I had no one, nothing but the voice in my head. . . ."

He covers his ears as if to shut out the sound of it. His eyes close.

"There were other cities," he begins again, his voice lower, more defeated now, "and other jobs. Until recently it was like I'd wiped out everything except for that one moment—the one when I killed, Harold—and I rarely lived beyond it." He laughs and rubs his perfect nose. "It obsessed me, all right, but I just couldn't figure it out."

"Didn't you hear me?" Harold says. "I know you. . . . I know who you are!"

"Memory can be the ruin of the best of us," Pogo says. "It demands too much. Take it from me, the voice of experience. It can make your heart a tiny, rocklike thing."

He puts his arm around Harold and pulls him close. Then he presses his mouth to Harold's ear and whispers, "What was there about me you didn't like?"

Harold is too weak to pull away. Pain tightens his chest and shoulders.

"It came to me, Harold, only recently—last week, to be precise.

I overheard these two men at a hamburger shack talking about a statue some school planned to build for its dying coach. Apparently they'd read about this in the newspaper or heard it on the radio. And they thought it was the smartest thing ever—a tribute is what they called it. They remembered your name and were even planning to send you a generous donation via the mail."

DeGeorge gets up from the bunk and waddles over to the table. "And what was it?" he says, sitting down next to Pogo. He bares his ruined teeth. "The man's name that they remembered. What'd he go by?"

"Harold," Pogo says. "He went by the name of Harold."

"This Harold?" DeGeorge says, placing his hand on Harold's neck and rubbing it. "Not *our* Harold?"

"Yes," Pogo answers. "That's the one."

| 68 |

So Harold has been recognized.

He bolts across the cell, dives into his bunk and scrambles to cover himself with the sheet and heavy wool blanket. The pain in his chest intensifies. He can't speak for the terrible thickness of his tongue, the searing lack of air in his lungs.

The two men follow and sit down in front of him on the hard floor.

"What I was going to tell you," Pogo Reese is saying, "was that I got my answer that night, after overhearing that conversation. On a blank sheet of paper I was writing 'What was there about me you didn't like?' when it came to me that the man I'd killed said what he said only because he'd done nothing wrong. His personality wasn't particularly off-putting, and his looks weren't the least offensive, and the only thing he'd said was 'Great game, old sport.' A compliment. He was innocent, and I was beating his brains out for no reason. All those years, Harold—right at thirty, counting this one—when I wrote 'You keyed my car,' I was writing a lie. Way deep down inside of me I may have known the truth going back to the night it happened, but not until then did I let it come forward and reveal itself. It was very cathartic, I must say."

Pogo yanks the sheet from Harold's head, and in a soft, mournful voice says, "It wasn't him who keyed my car. It was someone else. It was you, wasn't it, Harold?"

Harold shakes his head. Even more than Pogo's accusation, the pain in his chest has robbed him of the courage to speak.

"As I remember it," Pogo is saying, the words coming faster now, "we'd had a few shots of tequila at the bar, me and you, then you left, saying there was somewhere you had to go. When I got outside the decedent—the one I killed, Harold; in a court of law everybody calls dead people the decedent—was standing in front of my car, looking it over. . . . I mean really eyeballing it, Harold. This wasn't uncommon, though, because mine was a car like no other for five hundred miles in any direction. My old man had ordered it straight from the factory. A gift because he was proud of all I'd done."

"What color was it?" DeGeorge says.

"Red," Harold mutters. "It was red."

Pogo holds his hand up as if to block the interruption. "I walked up and saw the scratches all along the sides, on the hood and trunk. 'Great game, old sport,' he tells me, the decedent does. And what's amazing is how delighted he was to see me, to happen to meet me there in the parking lot. You remember how they used to get when they recognized you. It was like their day was made, nothing could've possibly pleased them more. I asked him what he had in his pockets. He reached in—" here Pogo reaches into the pockets of his overalls "—and pulled out some change and a bunch of keys. I was holding a beer bottle. I took one last swallow and threw it toward the trees on the side of the road."

Pogo presses his face against Harold's and kisses him with a wet, open mouth. "It was you, wasn't it? You were the one who did it."

Harold braces against the hard, stinging shudder that runs through him. "No," he says. "I swear it wasn't."

"Who was it, then?" Pogo whispers. "Who keyed my car? I want to ask him something."

"It wasn't me," Harold blurts out.

Pogo gets up from the floor and walks over to the table. From the breast pocket of his colorful overalls he extracts a pack of gum. "Juicy Fruit?" he says to DeGeorge, who gladly accepts a stick. "What about you, Harold? You want some gum?"

Harold doesn't answer.

"Good enough," Pogo Reese says, putting the gum back in his pocket. "It always worked wonders for me, though. Plus, if I remember correctly, the young girls used to like the taste of it when we got to kissing." With a snigger Pogo folds the foil and paper wrappers into a ball and tosses it at Harold. "I remember one girl in particular," he says. "She'd chew hers and I'd chew mine and when we parked and got to kissing we'd swap them one for the other."

DeGeorge removes a magazine from one of the clotheslines and opens it to the centerfold. "Not much different from this one here?" he says, glaring at the naked female form filling the glossy pages. His eyes widen. When he holds out the magazine spread for Pogo to see, Pogo shakes his head disgustedly and looks away.

"She had long, dark hair," Pogo whispers, "and the nicest, warmest skin."

When DeGeorge once again thrusts the magazine at him, Pogo throws a shoulder into his ribs and knocks him against the cage door. The force of the collision rattles the clotheslines and sends assorted undershirts and shorts fluttering to the floor. With trembling, fisted hands DeGeorge covers his face.

"You should know better," Pogo says. "She wasn't nothing like that. Hear me, Paris?"

DeGeorge wipes a smear of blood from his mouth with his shirtsleeve, then brushes by Pogo and returns to his bunk. He zips the front of his overalls all the way up to his collar, pulls the sheet to his neck and buries his face in the square of yellow sponge.

"You ain't hurt, are you, son?" Pogo says, touching him lightly. "I didn't hit you too hard, did I?"

DeGeorge grunts, nothing more.

"I didn't mean to cut you if I did," Pogo says. "I want you to know I'm sorry. I hope you'll accept my apology."

"I do," DeGeorge mumbles.

"Thank you," Pogo says. "Thank you for accepting my apology."

The scuffle has drawn some of the inmates out of their bunks.

Yawning noisily, they stand in the shadows, their eyes heavy with sleep.

"Back to bed, everybody," Pogo says, clapping his hands. "Come on now. Give me a few more minutes alone with Mr. Gravely here, then we'll pull out the dominoes and the matchsticks and take up where we left off."

The men comply, too tired to argue. One by one they drop into their beds.

"I hope you'll forgive Paris for what he said about your wife," Pogo Reese is saying, drawing a glass of tap water. "At Angola they damaged more than his face. He sometimes exhibits a woeful lack of tact, as was the case just a minute ago. But I like the man. He means no harm, really."

Although Pogo is speaking loudly enough for everyone in the bullpen to hear, DeGeorge doesn't stir or utter a sound.

"Here, Paris," he says, pulling the pillow from his face and holding a plastic glass of water to his lips. He helps him drink. "Feel better now?"

DeGeorge nods, though he's swallowed no more than a mouthful. Pogo places the glass on the floor and says, "I came back to town about a week ago. I'd hoped to find you, Harold, and Paris was the first person I looked up. Poor boy, he doesn't get out in public very often, on account of his face. People stare and call him names. You'd think he was some kind of beast and had no feelings. If only they knew him when he was beautiful and all the female guards at the prison drew straws each night to see which one of them would get to share his bed." As he did earlier with Harold, Pogo runs his fingers through DeGeorge's hair. "Him and me, Harold, we've kept in touch ever since, mainly because we have so much in common. We can identify with each other because we come from the same places. We're what everybody used to think me and Little Shorty were, only better."

Harold tries to move from the bunk, but doing so requires too much effort and he collapses back down onto the mattress.

"Would you prefer that I didn't finish my story, Harold? I'll stop if you like."

When he doesn't answer, Pogo says, "Tell me if I'm right, Harold. It was because of Rena that you scratched my car—just like it was jealousy over all the women he could get that they went and put their fucking knives to Paris's face."

"I didn't scratch your car."

Pogo moves over to Harold's bed and sits back down on the floor. "Did you do it because you wanted her? Were you angry with me because she was mine and you felt you deserved her?" He smacks his gum loudly. "She was something, wasn't she, Harold? Of all the girls to choose from, Rena Cummins was the best. And you end up with her."

"It wasn't me," Harold says.

Once again Pogo leans his face close to Harold's, his mouth on his ear. "Don't be afraid to tell me," he whispers. "I've come all this way . . . well, I guess to be honest it was to hear you admit what you'd done and to get my apology."

"But it wasn't me," Harold says. "You're talking to the wrong person. I never scratched your car."

Pogo ignores him. "I forgive you," he says, still whispering. "That's another thing I came all this way to tell you. I forgive you, Harold. Soon as you apologize, you'll be as free of it as I am. There'll be no memory of any of it to hold you back anymore. It'll all be over."

For some reason Pogo finds this funny, and he laughs so hard he starts to gag.

"But you've got the wrong person," Harold insists, shaking his head. "It wasn't me, I swear it wasn't."

"Say the words." Pogo closes his eyes.

"What words?"

"You know the ones I mean."

"I'm sorry? Is that what you want me to say?"

Pogo grabs Harold's shirt and almost pulls him out of the bed. Harold can hear him breathing. "Not a question. Say it like you mean it."

"I'm sorry," he says.

"Are you apologizing to me, Harold?"

"Yes," Harold says. "I'm sorry."

Pogo's lips peel open like a flower in bloom, then quickly close. Harold waits for Pogo to rip into him, the way he'd done with DeGeorge, but he doesn't.

Finally Pogo gets up from the floor and strides to the front of the cell, where he grabs and rattles the cage door. "Too many people go at life backward," he says. "They remember when they should be trying to forget. They search when there's nothing to find. And you know what else?"

Harold opens his mouth to speak but nothing comes out.

"They don't know what an apology can mean."

Harold gets up from his bunk and walks over to where Pogo's standing. "I'm sorry," he says, doing his best to sound sincere. "I'm sorry I scratched your car."

Pogo's face runs with tears, and his lips tremble. "For a murderer," he says, looking at Harold, "I sure am a crybaby."

"No," Harold says.

"No, I am?" Pogo says with a sniffle. "Or no, I'm not?"

"No, you're not," Harold guesses.

"That's what I thought."

Down the corridor there's no sign of Leonard Wilson, not even the glow of his lantern. Harold hears music playing on a cheap transistor radio, and farther off there's the tinny patter of rain on the roof. "Guard!" he shouts. "Guard!"

The lobby door swings open and Wilson appears, pulling at the keys on his hip. Instead of the lantern he carries a flashlight. He unlocks the door and lets Harold out.

"When I leave this place," Pogo says, so softly that Harold has to strain to hear, "I'll pay back what I stole from your statue fund and throw in some extra, and maybe a little for Paris, too." He sticks his hand through the bars and Harold grabs it and shakes. "After all," he says, "it's not like I needed your money. I'm a rich man, remember?"

Harold walks in front of the guard and doesn't say a word. He follows the circle of light Wilson shines on the floor, careful not to trip over anything.

At the door at the end of the corridor, Harold hears the voice of Paris DeGeorge and his wrecked laughter. "What was there about me you didn't like?" he's saying.

| **69** |

In his study at home Harold sits listening to the magnolias scratch against the side of the house. The digital clock on the desk shows the hour and minute the power went off that afternoon; he last checked the grandfather clock in the living room at midnight, moments after Rena retired to the master bedroom and locked the door. For what felt like a couple of hours, Harold repeatedly begged her to be let in.

Since giving up he's been trying to remember the names of the starting Tenpenny Eleven but keeps coming up with an incomplete lineup. In those days players went both ways, playing offense and defense; though it would seem simple enough to recall the most celebrated players he ever had, he can't do it. Moments ago he started to call Trent Orlansky, but then he remembered what Orlansky told him after he'd posted bond and was driving Harold home from the city jail. "Lately, Coach Gravely, it's as if you have this death wish. If you don't slow down . . . well, no amount of money will be able to bail you out of your funeral."

After ruling out Orlansky, Harold considered phoning the sports desk of the city paper to ask if anyone there could recall the names of the all-conference offensive lineman, the ne'er-do-well Cajun boy from Golden Meadow, and the flanker with the great sprinter's speed who died in a water-skiing accident one summer some fifteen or twenty years ago. But after beginning to dial the number at the paper he put the receiver down, imagining what would happen if his voice was recognized and something new was added to his list of troubles.

There were Bobby Peel, Chester Tully and Larry McDuff, of course, and the running backs Pogo Reese and Little Shorty Grieg, and the center Tyler Duhe; and there was Bubba Rubin. But Bubba Rubin, it occurs to him now, might've been the center, and Tyler Duhe one of the tackles. Then what positions did Red Johnson and

Flaubert Rich play? They were both big boys, big enough for the line, but were they on the Tenpenny Eleven or a few years off?

At the bedroom door now, his face pressed to the wood, Harold says, "I can't bring them back."

Rena takes her time before responding. "Bring who back?"

"If I can't bring them back something's wrong. Something's terribly wrong, pie."

That night in December nearly thirty years ago, they rode home from New Orleans on a chartered Greyhound bus. They shared bottles of pink champagne, ate ham and roast beef sandwiches and squares of homemade lemon cake. On the darkest stretch of the highway Harold instructed the driver to turn on the overhead lights, then he told the boys they could remove their nails now. "No need to wear them any longer," he said. "Just don't wipe them on the seats." They applauded and he bowed, one hand on his belly, the other on the small of his back.

It was the most exciting time of his life. How is it that he can't remember their names?

"If I can't remember, then I must be dying."

"You'll kill me first," she says. Her voice seems to be coming from far away. Perhaps, he thinks, the constant, drumming rain has created this illusion of distance. "You're not dying any more now than you were when you tried to kick in the door a few minutes ago. You're as healthy as I am. And you can stop pretending. I know you're not sick, but I won't tell anybody. You'll get your statue."

"I can't remember them," he says.

"You can't remember who?"

His face burns with shame. He is afraid to tell her.

"You can't remember who?" she says again.

"The Tenpenny Eleven. I've forgotten some of their names. I can't recall their positions."

There was a trooper escort, he remembers, two-tone Dodge cruisers in front and back. Their swimming emergency lights filled the cabin. Harold was drunk before they reached Laplace, and by Prairieville he could hardly stand. Cinder-block motels stood on either side of the highway that cut through the swamp. Filling stations burned a million neon lights. The bus rocked and swayed as he and the boys danced in the aisle. The windows were sweating. At

Tiger Stadium, parked near the Players' Gate, he was the first one out. The crowd surged and pressed to touch him.

"Don't be silly," Rena says. "That was thirty years ago. Why don't you worry about learning the names of the boys you have on this year's team, or don't you care about them? You missed the afternoon practice, you know. I'm sure Tully and McDuff had a fine time playing boss, but what are those kids supposed to think?"

Harold sits on the floor and leans back against the door. "In the jail Pogo thought I was the one who keyed his car."

"In the jail . . . *what*?"

He can hear the bedsprings squeak, the padding of her footsteps on the carpet. She's standing on the other side of the door, and he can hear her heavy breathing above the rain.

"Who thought what?" she says again. "Harold!"

"Pogo Reese," he answers. "He was in the jail this afternoon. He thought it was me who keyed his car in the parking lot at Tuesday's. He said he forgave me and I shouldn't think about it anymore. He thought he was doing me a favor."

"That was awfully nice of him," she says.

"Yeah," he mumbles, "especially since I didn't do it."

She's laughing now in a way he can't recall ever having heard before. Her delirium frightens him.

"You think that's funny?" he says.

She can hardly reply, and he needs a moment to piece her words together. "I scratched his car," she is saying. "It was me. I was the one who did it."

"Later tonight after I'm dead," he says, "you two can get together and talk about it. He'll want you to apologize, but frankly it's none of my business."

"He forgave you for scratching his car!" Her laughter builds into a hard, violent scream. He hears something crash against the floor, then glass shattering. Her footsteps beat across the room and back again.

"You can sleep with him in our very own bed for all I care. Have at it. You two deserve each other."

He wonders: what of the two boys whose names elude him now? Why do they seem no more familiar than a couple of strangers he met over drinks at a bar?

"Don't you want to know why I did it?" she says.

"It don't matter."

"He did something wrong, I guess. He wouldn't dance with me or he didn't want to take me home when I thought it was time to go." There is a helplessness in her voice. "I was . . . what, eighteen years old? Maybe I wasn't getting the attention I thought I deserved. But if he got some mud on his hubcaps, he was out cleaning it with a bucket and a brush. He'd devote an entire afternoon to it. He'd get it to shine like new, then he'd go racing down the streets just to dirty the car up again so he could get out his bucket and his brush and start cleaning again." She pauses. "But to do the same for me, to take me back to the dorm when I was ready . . . I suppose scratching it up seemed a better idea than taking off with some other guy."

"You wouldn't of left with anyone."

"I'd have left. The very same day they convicted him I sure let you take me home. Only we didn't go home first, did we, Harold? We went to the levee."

"That was different."

"It wasn't different. I told him I'd wait for him. I was supposed to be in love with him."

"Well," Harold says, "I'll be dead by morning. I can feel it coming. If you want him back, all you have to do is go to the city jail and bail him out. Takes about half an hour and he's back on the street." Now it's Harold's turn to laugh. "When you think about it, there's really nothing to show we were ever married, is there? There's not a voice in this house but our own."

Although he no longer hears her laughing, more glass breaks on the floor; the door shakes against his back.

"It wasn't even a key," she says. "It was the little metal snap on my compact mirror."

"You can give him my study and all my things. You might have to buy him a new wardrobe, though. He's bigger than I am. And he can have my car. Our choices in women and automobiles always seemed to run about the same, didn't they, Rena?"

It was a feeling like this was why he'd been born, he had told the newspeople gathered in his office. They'd grown so quiet he could hear their pens and pencils scratching on their notebooks. This was why he lived, he said. They scribbled furiously. Some people were bankers, lawyers, doctors—he listed a score of jobs. Druggists, butchers, railroad engineers . . . But he was a coach, he told them. He would always be a coach.

She cracks the door. "I want to show you something," she says, shining the beam from the flashlight on her face.

He stands, slowly, and stares at her. The veins in her neck show blue beneath the soft, pale flesh. Dark bruises encircle her eyes. "Show me," he says.

"See this?" She lifts one of her arms and shines the light on an unshaven armpit. "I've had them for weeks now and you never noticed." She rubs the strips of hair with the burning head of the flashlight. "All our life together, there were lots of things about me you didn't know."

"But this wasn't one of them," he says, pushing past her. "Sometimes the sleeves of your gown crawled up when you were sleeping."

"You never said anything."

He shrugs.

She returns to the bed and covers herself. In the darkness he can't see but a few feet in front of him.

"What was it you broke?"

"The lamps," she says, shining the flashlight on the corner of the room, revealing the mess. "I kept turning them on, waiting for something. Finally I just got so frustrated—"

"Whitley," he says with some exuberance. "Was there a Whitley on that team?"

"Tom Whitley played a few years ago. He made all-America."

"Was there an Adams?"

"There was one. . . . I dunno, that was twenty years ago now."

"Lane Adams. He had the piney woods in him. He'd even wear his flannel shirt and boots to church."

"That's him," she says.

"Adam Lane, was it?"

"No, Harold. Lane Adams. His name was Lane Adams."

In the dark he dresses into his favorite Flarico No. 110 jockstrap, khaki pants and a shirt that says TIGER FOOTBALL over the breast pocket. He sits on the chair in the corner and puts on white athletic socks and black coaching shoes. "When it happens," he says, "it should be at the stadium."

She turns the flashlight on him.

"Stop it," he says, blocking it with his hand.

"I want to see you when I tell you what I have to say," she says. "Look at me. Let me see your eyes."

He feels as if he owes her an explanation. "If I can't remember the all-time best there ever was," he says, staring at the floor, "then something's wrong."

One of the windows is open. He can smell the weather and feel the dampness pushing through the screen.

"I wanted more," she says. "I expected more than this."

"You mean children, don't you?" Angrily he tugs at his socks. "I know you did. But you weren't the only one."

She is wearing a white cotton gown. Her long distressed hair sits heavily on her shoulders and covers her breasts. "It has nothing to do with children. It has to do with you, Harold, with what you've become." The beam from her flashlight finds his face again. "You don't even look like yourself anymore."

At the dresser he digs into the top middle drawer and removes an open pack of gum. For a few blind moments he chews on a stick, remembering the incident with Pogo, then spits it against the wall. With the sleeve of his shirt he wipes the sugary taste off his tongue.

"I'm not happy," she says.

"Damn him!" he says. "Damn him and damn you, Rena. Damn the both of you."

In bed she folds her legs beneath her. "When was the last time you held me, Harold? When did you touch me last?" When he doesn't answer, she does. "You haven't touched me in months. And if you did it was by accident, like it was a fluke. You brushed your arm against mine on the way to get a bottle of whiskey from the cupboard."

From the dresser drawer Harold removes a cigar. It tastes of cellophane. At the window, his back to Rena, he moves it from one corner of his mouth to the other. His lungs and heart feel like the same organ rioting at the core of his chest. Suddenly he is filled with terror. "This storm," he mumbles. "This rain. I feel so old, Rena. I feel older than old."

"If you go to the stadium," she says, "I won't be here when you get back. If you go to that place, Harold, I'll leave. I've already packed some things. You can check the closet."

"It never rains at Tiger Stadium. Remember we used to say that?"

"We used to say a lot of things." She turns off the flashlight and lies back in bed, pulling the comforter over her legs. "Both of us, Harold—we promised more and delivered less than any two people I ever knew."

He tries to smile. "Put a robe over your nightgown. Comb your hair. And come with me, Rena. Maybe I'll say something."

"I won't."

"If I say something tonight and no one's there to hear it . . ." He's frantic now, shouting. "Oh, Rena! Please. Come with me. Bring a notebook. If I say something—"

"I won't," she says again.

| 70 |

Out in the garage Harold can't find the Cadillac. It takes a moment before he remembers that it's still at the Prince Seurat, that he hadn't thought to pick it up after Mr. Memory got him out of jail. With all the strength he can muster he drives a forearm into one of the huge electric doors, at once managing to relieve some of his anger and to hurt himself. Then he walks out into the side yard and kicks the trellis covered with yellow jasmine. He's now stuck having to choose between two fairly primitive means of escape: an ancient three-speed bicycle with a flat rear tire or his wife's dilapidated Falcon.

He finds the keys in the ignition and settles behind the wheel. "One day at Sweeney's or the mall somebody's going to steal that bomb," he once told Rena, after seeing she'd left the keys in the car. "They won't touch it," she said. "It's too much like me. It's too old and ugly." After a moment he said, "You're right. Who wants anything old and ugly?"

He shifts into neutral, pumps the gas pedal and turns the key. The car whines and shudders, so he tries again, careful not to ride the accelerator too hard and flood the engine. When it finally turns over and fires, he takes a few minutes to let it warm up. Static crackles on the radio; an occasional voice drifts in and then out again.

Hard as he tries, Harold can't remember the names of the last two members of his famous team. "The Tenpenny Nine," he says to himself. "Tomorrow it'll be the Tenpenny Eight, next day the Tenpenny Seven." By late next week, it occurs to him, it'll be as if they didn't exist at all. Everyone will be forgotten.

On the rain-swept drive to the university he encounters few cars. The darkness is immense, as thick as the deepest sleep, and his headlights hardly penetrate it. Along the city streets the stores are dark, too, all the gas stations and movie theaters. He creeps along miles below the speed limit, his left foot resting on the clutch. The storm winds buffet the car, threatening to push it off the road.

Less than a mile from campus, the top end of a telephone pole, splintered in half, blocks his lane. Several hundred yards of black and silver line lie on the ground. Orange flares outline the scene, and a policeman in a Day-Glo safety vest waves him over with the incandescent stock of his flashlight. He bends at the waist and signals for Harold to roll down the window.

"We're going to close the street in about ten minutes," he tells him. "We got some power lines down."

"Fine by me," Harold says.

"Drive careful, Coach Gravely. It's not a good time to be on the roads."

Harold waits a few seconds before saying anything. "You know me?" he says. "You recognized me, didn't you?"

"I did," the officer says.

At the stadium he parks near the football offices. The trees are swept furiously by the weather; pinecones and needles litter the macadam path. A couple of aluminum trash cans have blown against the bicycle racks. Chains slap against the flagpoles that stand near the Players' Gate. As Harold walks past the window of his office, he sees the glow of a lantern on the blinds. The light shines silver on the blades of the palm fronds and the shivering bamboo leaves; it spills in a fractured pool on the muddy ground. In the window the light brightens momentarily, then fades and finally disappears altogether.

Harold looks all around him for the red convertible, but the Falcon is the only car in sight. Once through the Players' Gate he moves quickly down the corridor to Mrs. Claude's station, confident of his step even in the gloom. But nearing his office door he bumps into Mrs. Claude's swivel chair and sends it crashing into her metal desk.

When the door flies open he sets his feet at a comfortable angle, squares his shoulders and tightens his fists in a posture of self-defense. But it's Camille Jones, the old groundskeeper, wearing nothing but his boxer shorts.

"What the damn hell are you doing here at this time of night?" Camille says, stepping back to let Harold enter.

He is holding a Coleman lantern with a soot-stained chimney, and in the bath of light his skin, glistening with sweat, is the color of mustard.

"I was about to ask you the same thing," Harold says. "It's a little late to be working, ain't it?"

On the couch there's a blanket and an eviscerated seat cushion of some kind, and at its foot a near-empty bottle of whiskey, several pickled eggs wrapped in paper napkins and two small bags of garlic-flavored potato chips.

"I live here," Camille says, "and I suspect I'll die here." He bends at the waist. "Welcome to my humble abode, Old Man. Or, as I like to call it, Chateau Jones."

Harold tempers his tone, hoping not to betray his sense of outrage. "So it's true, then . . . you do live in the stadium."

"Well," Camille says, "usually I stay up in the press box, which nobody seems to bother with except for the six or seven times each year you and your boys play here at home. The men's lounge is bigger and cleaner than any apartment I could rent, and there's some lockers in there where I keep my things. Only now with the elevator broke and the power out, I can't get up and down like I'm used to. The stairs make me pass blood."

Harold's confusion darkens his expression.

"You know," Camille says, gripping his crotch. "The cirrhosis, I guess. My liver can't take much jumping up and down. Instead of yellow water mine comes out pink like a rose."

Harold takes the lamp from his friend and puts it on his desk. From one of the shelves he removes the scrapbook Mrs. Presley compiled celebrating the triumphs of the Tenpenny Eleven, and he rubs his fingers over the title on the cover: "One More Glorious Chapter in the Life of Harold Gravely."

"When my wife threw me out," Camille says, "I had no place to go. So I came here." He opens his arms wide as if to embrace the whole of it. "Better than some cheap motel."

"No need to explain. It don't matter."

"It matters to me," he says, sitting on the couch and pulling the blanket over his bare legs. "Sometimes I feel like a rat—scavenging around in here when everyone's gone home and all the lights are out." He drinks from the whiskey bottle and bites one of the eggs. "The best peace I know, though, is being in the middle of the field late in the evening when it's clear out and the stars are shining. I lay on the grass and imagine all the fine, young men in their uniforms running over me like they were buffalo on the stampede, and all the people in the stands, and how the band plays. It gets to where all the shit I been feeling almost goes away."

Harold opens the scrapbook to the souvenir program stapled at its center pages. The team roster lists in the neighborhood of fifty hardheads, arranged from top to bottom by their jersey numbers. Starting with number eleven, Rusty deGravelles, a reserve safety, he traces his finger down the page.

"Some of them evenings on the field," Camille is saying, "I'm tempted to get up and run around myself, like somebody was chasing after me, but my health don't allow it. As a boy I could, though. Only as a boy I had somebody, there was always people around— brothers and sisters and Mama and my Aunt Raney and Uncle Roy— and you wouldn't catch me alone like a rat in a place this big and empty."

Roland Stanton, Harold reads, was a tackle, number seventy-nine. He was Cajun and could speak French better than he could English. His father ran a shrimp boat. And Billy Guillot, it turns out, was speedy as they come running pass routes but he couldn't swim to save his life.

"I'm going to read off some names," Harold says without looking up from the scrapbook. "And I want you to count them for me. Can you count them for me, Jonesie?"

"Yeah, I can count."

Harold closes his eyes and recites from memory: "Guillot, Peel, Stanton, Johnson, Rich, Rubin, Duhe, Reese, Grieg, McDuff and Tully." He leans back in the chair and tops his head with crossed hands. "What's that come to?"

"Eleven."

"You sure?"

"Eleven," Camille says again, "right on the nose."

Harold picks up the telephone and starts to call Rena but gets no dial tone: a lonely sputtering is all.

He remembers the downed lines he drove by earlier, the splintered pole, the police waving their colored lights, and puts the receiver back in the cradle.

"Rena," he would've told her, "the Old Man must of been overtired is all. He must of gone temporarily blank is all."

Camille lies back on the couch and covers himself up to his belly. He balances the bottle of booze on his chest with one hand and picks up an egg with the other. "One thing about an egg," he says, "it makes you feel full even when there's nothing else in your stomach."

Harold closes the book and returns it to the shelf. "Rain makes the corn green," he says, surprised himself to hear it. He'd planned to comment on the weather.

"That it does," Camille says. "And the sun turns it yellow. If the worms get to it the corn turns brown."

"Rain makes the fish swim."

"Their little flippers is what makes 'em swim. Rain keeps their lakes and streams moving."

"Rain makes the spiders shy," Harold says.

"I don't know nothing about no spiders being shy on account of no rain," Camille says, clearly irritated. "I know when I see one, though, I leave it alone or pop it dead with the swatter."

"Rain keeps the statues clean."

"I wouldn't argue with you on that. You know more than I do about statues. I bet you know more about statues than anybody else in this whole country. You're our resident expert."

Harold walks over to the couch and sits down next to the old man. He takes a drink from the bottle and returns it to Camille's chest. "Statues know nothing about pain or disease or disappointment," he says. When he reaches for the whiskey this time, Camille slips it under the blanket.

"Statues don't need no apologies," Harold says.

When Camille laughs Harold can smell the pickled egg on his breath. "When they're as no-good as you and me they do," he says.

"Only somebody's got to apologize for them, because a thing made of stone or whatever couldn't talk if it tried."

"Statues don't lie," Harold says. "They don't have to reinvent themselves every time they tell a little story."

"You're getting too deep for me."

"A statue lives forever."

Camille laughs again and Harold gets up and moves to the other side of the room. He can't stand the egg smell and the sight of the old man's bloodshot eyes.

"A statue never dies."

Camille drops the bottle to the floor and it rolls, whiskey spilling out of the mouth, and bumps to a stop against Harold's shoe. By the time he can reach down and pick it up, all but a swallow's gone.

"A strong man with a good back and a hammer could make a rubble of a statue," Camille says. "One blow in the right place would do the trick."

"You intending to wreck mine?" Harold says, more for the sake of conversation than anything else. The only real threat Camille has ever posed is to himself.

"Nope," the old man says, biting into another egg. "I ain't intending nothing of the kind. The way I been feeling I doubt seriously I'll even get the chance to see yours in the first place. I got a picture of it in my head, though." He taps his skull. "The only problem, it don't look nothing like you. It looks more like me."

Harold walks over to the desk, leans over the lantern and blows out the flame. "Take care of yourself," he says.

| 71 |

Outside in the rain, Harold stands about twenty feet in front of the Players' Gate, wondering how he could ever think it was possible to compose a sentence that made sense of all he knows.

At each end of the street, steam flows from the drains and twists in the rain. It floats in wisps at Harold's feet and climbs the length of his body. Spools of it bend around his arms and neck, then curl and dissipate in the wind.

Harold is pointing straight ahead, in the general direction of the assembly center. His legs are shoulder-width apart; his face set in a proud, artful grimace.

This is where, as soon as the Committee to Recognize Harold Gravely can appropriate enough money, his statue will stand, towering above banks of brilliant white lights shooting up from the neatly trimmed hedges at the foot of the pedestal.

"Rain makes my hair wet," he says now in a dim whisper, his voice lost in the storm. "Rain makes my skin itch."

Come dawn, he tells himself, his assistant coaches will find him here, standing and pointing.

McDuff and Tully, carrying their girth in front of them like overstuffed suitcases, will ask if he's okay. Does he want to go inside and change clothes and get something to eat? "Rain makes my stomach growl," he'll tell them; keeping with custom, they'll say the same. When his last team shows up for morning gassers they'll encircle him and stare, trying to decide whether he's real or not. They'll reach to touch him, to place the tips of their fingers on the tips of his. Then, a few minutes before nine, the Committee to Recognize Harold Gravely will arrive carrying coffee cans and give cups full of money. They too will find him here. Bobby and Claire Peel will tell him it's time for the board meeting; doesn't he want to comb his hair and shave and put on a tie? They're praying for him, they'll tell him. Finally Norman Pepper, Champs LaRoux and Mary Elaine Watts and the rest of the board will come. "Do you have it?" they'll say. But he won't reply. His face will reveal nothing. "Harold, what are your thirty words?"

He'll keep standing, pointing at the past before him, standing and pointing like a statue in the rain.

He'll remain there even after they've all gone inside. The rain will continue to fall. It'll fall through the trees, through the streamers of fog lighting on the pavement. It'll fall on Tiger Stadium, on the long rows of aluminum seats, on the red metal roof of the press box, on the lush green field.

"Rain makes me think too much," Harold says. His voice could belong to someone else, it sounds so weird. He strains against the weight of his arm. His elbow starts to bend even as he instructs it not to. "Rain makes my head hard," he says.

On the road in front of the stadium the yellow headlights of a car appear, the driver moving cautiously through the storm. Harold feels a new energy fire within him, and holding himself in position no longer requires as much work. His arm gains a rigidity he once thought reserved for people suffering from bursitis, and he reconsiders his expression, now letting it grow more relaxed.

The red convertible stops at the curb a few feet behind the Falcon, and the driver, a man of average height, steps out. To protect himself from the weather, he puts on a baseball cap and covers his shoulders with a camouflage parka, leaving his arms free. He leans against the trunk of the car and steps into some rubber pants, then spends a minute loading a pistol.

When he starts walking toward Harold, he takes long, easy strides but doesn't seem to be moving very fast. He could be out on a Sunday stroll. Harold feels his pointing finger curl in, making a fist of his hand. It takes some doing, but he manages to stick it back out again.

"Harold Gravely?" the man says, holding the gun by his side. It is a police revolver.

The rain beats against him, but Harold doesn't make a sound. Involuntarily he finds himself moving his arm and directing his pointing finger at the man's face, whom he recognizes from the pictures on Mrs. Claude's desk.

"Who you think you're pointing at?" Jake Claude says.

Harold has to bite his lower lip to keep it from trembling. The one thing he can't control is his blinking eyelids, and they're blinking so rapidly that it would seem bugs had settled on the lashes and decided not to leave.

"I come to tell you I don't appreciate you fucking my wife," Jake Claude says. He raises his arm and holds the pistol straight out in front of him, then he steps forward, just enough to let the end of the gun barrel touch Harold's fingernail. "And I come to punish you for it," he says flatly.

If Jake Claude were to shoot, Harold wouldn't mind losing the finger, figuring he's got plenty more of them. It's keeping the gun away from his face and upper torso that concerns him. He struggles to think of something to say. "I'm sorry, Gerald," he says, once it comes to him. "Please, accept my apology."

"Two things," the man says, cocking the gun. "I don't like the name of Gerald, and I never been of a real forgiving nature."

Having spoken, Harold knows his statue facade has been broken, but for some reason he doesn't alter his stance.

The man lowers the gun and with the handle taps the name tag over his breast pocket. "See what it says? It says Gerald. I told them Jake but they put Gerald anyway. This is a major oil company, and they had to go and get picky."

"With some people," Harold remarks, "you never know."

Jake Claude looks at Harold and through him. "Like with boots," he says now, one corner of his lip reaching up almost to his nostril. "On the rig you got to wear steel-toes. Wear a soft-toe and they stick you on a helicopter, send you to company headquarters and fine you on the spot. Fifty dollars just because your toes weren't right." He snaps the fingers of his left hand to show how fast the money can go. "Whiskers—now that's another thing. They're so picky you can't wear none." The man smiles, but not for long. "Whaddaya say, Mr. Gravely? Would I look good in whiskers?"

"I think you would," Harold answers, though uncertain whether Jake Claude's really interested.

"But they're way too picky for a mustache," the man says, shaking his head. "Another thing they're picky about is the weather." He turns his face to the sky, opens his mouth and traps a swallow of rain. "A little tropical depression wipes out a few Cubans and starts moving up the Gulf and all of a sudden they decide to shut down the rigs. They shuttle you to land and say to report back when the storm passes. So then whaddaya do? You get in your car and drive home. You intend to surprise your wife at the office and take her to lunch, but there she is in the window with her boss, trying to get reamed."

Jake Claude pulls the trigger and the hammer falls on an empty chamber. Harold feels the breath punched out of him. His knees buckle but he doesn't fall. His arm sways and bends and it takes all that's in him to straighten it out again.

"Tell me if I'm wrong," Jake Claude says, glaring at the gun. "Tell me I was only seeing things in that office window."

"You left your car running," Harold says.

"I did what?"

"You left your car running."

When Jake turns toward the street Harold swipes at the gun and misses. Before he can regain his statue pose the man has pressed the gun barrel against the end of Harold's nose, hard enough to force his head back on his shoulders.

"You'd better get back to pointing," the man says, more amused than angry.

"I'm dying of cancer," Harold says. "I got a tumor on my lung the size of a grapefruit."

"I know what you got."

"You wouldn't kill a dying person."

"No," he says. "But I'd kill a living one."

Jake Claude pulls the trigger, but again there's a hollow sound. "I guess I didn't load all the chambers," he says. "These bullets, by the way, are hollow-points. When they go into something they sort of work like a blender set on puree. Everything sort of gets mashed together."

Harold's finger is shaking so hard it looks as if he's trying to scratch something off a piece of glass. "I said I was sorry," he says, his teeth chattering. "I never should of touched your wife. I apologize."

"You already done that. But maybe if you got down on your knees . . ." With the gun he points to the ground. "I ain't never been of the nature to forgive, none of us Claudes has, but a growed man on his knees might excite what pity's left in me."

Harold drops to the pavement.

"Stick your arm back up," Jake Claude says. "I like the way you had it before."

When Harold does as he's told, the man turns to see what he's been pointing at, but there's nothing between here and the assembly center but grass and rain.

"What was there about me you didn't like?" Harold murmurs.

"I thought I told you already," the man replies. "It was you and my wife."

Harold is sobbing. "Forgive me! I'm asking you to forgive me!" He drops to his hands and starts to crawl, but Jake Claude kicks him under the chin with one of his steel-toe boots. Some of Harold's teeth shatter and he bites off a chunk of his tongue. The blood comes out of his mouth in spurts, and he tries to scoop it up with his hands.

It strikes him how odd he must look, a man with only half a tongue trying to put blood back in his mouth.

"What are you doing?" Jake Claude says. He grabs Harold by the front of his slicker and forces him back on his feet.

Without instruction, Harold begins to point again. His arm pops up automatically, almost magically, and it soothes him.

"Anything else you wanted to say?" Jake Claude says.

Harold thinks hard on the question. "Peaches and peas," he mutters. "Peas and peaches."

Jake Claude bares his teeth. "That it?"

"When it comes time to walk through those goalposts," Harold begins, having to spit the words for the blood, "I want your butthole so wide damn open you'll need a pair of tenpenny nails stuck up it to keep your foul business from spilling out."

Because of the tongue, it takes Harold a good minute to deliver the famous quotation.

Jake Claude's never heard it before.

"Nobody name of Harold," he says, choosing his words carefully as he lifts the gun, "is going to stick no nails of no kind up no butthole of mine."

Harold's reaching to catch more blood pouring out of his mouth when the man shoots him in the head. The first bullet enters the right eye, the second the humped bridge of his nose. It's pretty sloppy shooting, so the man waits until Harold has stopped bouncing and twitching on the ground to put a third bullet in his forehead and a fourth in the place right over his heart.

By the time Camille Jones can put on his khakis and get outside, Jake Claude has disappeared in his convertible and Harold's blood, diluted by the rain, has formed a pool that looks almost deep enough to wade in.

"Old Man!" Camille shouts as he shakes Harold. "Don't you die on me, Old Man! Don't you dare die on me!"

| **Pie** |

| **72** |

At half past noon Rena hears the thudding of feet on the wooden floor of the porch, followed closely by a knock on the sliding glass doors. In the living-room mirror she checks for sleep in the corners of her eyes, and with a long painted nail scrapes an errant fleck of something from her chin. She runs her hands over her red pleated skirt and pinches the padded shoulders of her silk blouse. "Okay, pie," she tells herself, inhaling deeply. "Be strong. You can do it."

When she exhales her breath fogs the silver glass.

Although for days now she has dreaded their visit, the sight of Bobby Peel and Norman Pepper fills her with joy. "Bobby," she says, extending a hand. "Good to see you again. And hello there, Norman. Come on in and get out of the cold. Make yourselves comfortable."

The two men stand in the green room, admiring her Christmas tree as the red and white lights flicker on and off.

"To get a good flocked one," she explains, "I thought I'd better go early. The Jaycees were the first to put some out, so there I was at seven o'clock in the morning with this silly truck I borrowed. . . ." She considers the tree, the beating lights. "Is Thanksgiving too early a time to put one up?"

Both men shake their heads.

"By the look of this one," Norman says, "I'd say November is the best time. It's really lovely, Rena."

"Thank you," she says. "Oh, gosh, your coats. Here, Bobby . . . Norman, let me help you."

She hangs their heavy black overcoats on the hall tree, one on top of the other. "I'll take your hat," she tells Norman.

He takes it off and immediately reaches to make sure the placement of his toupee hasn't been disturbed, an unconscious gesture. Finding both Rena and Bobby Peel staring at him, he lowers his hand in embarrassment. "Trying to get used to it again," he murmurs.

Their suits are black wool. Each wears a white button-down shirt and a dark club tie. Rena wonders if they discussed what to wear before dressing to come over. They're as colorless as the Mormon boys who often make rounds through the neighborhood, looking for sinners to convert.

"All told," Bobby Peel says, withdrawing a cashier's check from his shirt pocket, "it comes to right at thirty thousand dollars. The artist, being related to my wife Claire, and understandably feeling some responsibility about what happened, refused to accept any payment."

Rena feels the blood drain from her face. Why, she'd like to know, does she blanch when most people blush? Where does the color go? Her cheeks are cold and as pale as her hands.

"This is really awkward," Norman says, looking at the check in Bobby's hand. "May we sit down, Rena? Neither of us has any idea about how to do this."

"God, yes, you can sit," she says, leading them to the couch. "I'm sorry. I suppose I temporarily lost my head."

Bobby puts the check in a brass dish at the center of the butler's table. He and Norman take a seat.

"As I was saying—" Norman says. His voice cracks and he puts a fist to his mouth and clears his throat. "I was saying this is awkward for Bobby and me. We loved Harold."

"I know you did," she says.

"It was such a shock," Bobby says. He runs his hands through his yellow-gray hair. "I still can't believe it. It doesn't seem real."

"I don't want to sound cold," she says, "but it didn't shock me in the least. The affair was just a small part of it."

"I didn't know the husband." Norman crosses his legs and rubs his knee, then stares at the check in the plate.

"A Christian should forgive," Bobby says, rising in his seat, "but I hope they give Gerald Claude the chair."

"Would you boys like some coffee or something?" Rena says. She gets up and starts for the kitchen. "I can put some on . . . some decaf, too, if you like."

"Not for me," Bobby says.

Norman shakes his head.

"The thing about the statue," she says, swinging around and walking back into the room, "it doesn't hurt me at all that the board's decided against it. I never believed it would happen anyway. A man of Harold's limitations, you have to ask yourself, did he deserve such a memorial? Was what he did all that special?" She waits for an answer, but none comes. "I always knew that in time people would catch on to him, and I suspect he did, too. He kept seeing spies, you know. So don't go blaming yourselves or feeling bad about anything for my sake."

"I fought for the votes," Norman says.

"No need to explain," she says.

"If money were the only issue," Bobby says, "it would've gone through. After what happened at the stadium we got so much money in the mail we could've built the best statue you ever saw. One anonymous donor gave ten thousand dollars cash. But then with the papers and TV turning it into a scandal . . ." His voice trails off dismally.

"No need," she says again. "Please."

"I really did try," Norman says. "But I was in the minority. Even Champs and Mrs. Watts voted against it. They told me just last week they couldn't support it because they couldn't justify immortalizing someone who ended up the way Harold did. Dead is dead, I argued. But they didn't see it that way. All Mrs. Watts cared to talk about was how he beat up her son."

"I don't blame anybody," Rena says. "I told you that."

"Even without the statue," Bobby says, "he won't be forgotten. They'll be talking about Old Man Harold Gravely long after the three of us are dead and gone."

"He'll be forgotten soon enough," she says.

"The Tenpenny Eleven alone—" Bobby stammers.

"Dumb," she says, reaching for the check. "And a bit obscene, too, if you ask me. Not the team, but the whole mythology around it, this nail business. It's probably the only original thing Harold ever came up with, but to think he first said it to a bunch of boys, some of them teenagers. . . . Does that seem as weird to you as it does to me?" She stops to remember something. "When I was young," she says, "he'd say it as a sort of promise, letting the words come off his tongue one at a time. But the older he got, the more it sounded like a threat. The words all ran together." She covers her lips with a curled finger and laughs. "I could see him doing it. Isn't that terrible? I once had a dream about him and those nails, and all these young boys lined up in their Jockey shorts."

The men stir in their seats. Bobby coughs into his fist and Norman pats his perfect hair.

"Thank you for this," she says, holding up the check. "It'll help. I never finished school, you know."

The two men look at each other.

"I mean to say, I never got a degree, and I understand it's difficult to get a decent-paying job these days without one."

"Hard enough with one," Bobby says.

"It'll help, all right," she says, more sober now. "He had insurance, and there's his retirement, but that's all for getting by. I still owe the funeral home alone something like eight thousand." She waves the check. "I can't begin to tell you how much your gift will help ease the strain."

This seems to please them; it's what they came for. Norman Pepper clears his throat again. "Well," he says, uncrossing his legs. "Thanks for having us over."

She folds the check in half and drops it on the plate. "You fellows sure you don't want something to drink?"

"Not for me," Bobby says.

"Positive," Norman says.

All three of them stand watching the tree; they are like children before it. Splashes of color wash over their faces.

"I wanted to thank you, too," she says to Bobby, "for the invitation to the winter ball."

"Yours was the first we dropped in the mail," Bobby says, excitement lifting his voice. "Think you'll be able to make it?"

She hesitates before answering. "Yes. Yes, I think I might."

"Then you must promise me a dance." Bobby takes her hand in his and presses it against his mouth.

"A slow one," she agrees, patting him on the shoulder. "I warn you, though. After thirty years, I'm bound to be as rusty as an old tin can."

When they leave, each in his own car, she watches from the green room until they reach the stop sign and turn at the corner. For a moment it feels as if she is being watched, that Harold has returned to observe her system at work. She presses her forehead against the window and looks down in the shrubbery. "Checking for beetles?" she wants to say. "Lose something in the azaleas again, Harold?" After a few minutes she walks up to the head of the drive and finds herself waving at the long, empty street.

| **73** |

She begins these winter mornings by reading the want ads in the newspaper. Determined to live beyond the pages of her magazines, she has let the subscriptions run out. To keep from reaching for back issues was no less difficult than curbing her appetite for sweets and other junk at her daily movie, so she threw them away. The classifieds never interested her until now: in no less than four months, the section has become what she reaches for each dawn, often before starting the coffee.

In particular she would like to find an antique automobile—if not the kind Pogo Reese used to drive, one similar to it. The dream of riding again in such a car has come to obsess her. And now, with Harold's statue money, she has the means of buying one. She desires tail fins, heavy chrome fenders, enough sitting room for a family, a convertible roof and a paint job bright and busy enough to blind.

Under the heading CADILLAC she finds Fleetwood Broughams and coupes, Sedan DeVilles, Eldorados and Sevilles, but no mention of a Biarritz.

She calls Bailey Brothers, a dealership that promises the reader "ABSOLUTELY No Credit Check" and "The WIDEST SELECTION of IMMACULATE Used Cadillacs (NO, WE AIN'T AFRAID TO SAY IT: THEY'RE USED) IN THE SOUTH." Bailey Brothers is also "HONEST!"

"I'm looking for a Biarritz," she says on the telephone.

"I'll need details," the salesman says. "What year?"

When she tells him, listing some of the things she remembers about Pogo's car, he laughs. "Good luck," he says. "Last time we had one of them on the lot it stayed maybe two minutes."

"Two minutes, huh?"

"I said maybe two minutes. It might not of been that long."

She thanks him and hangs up.

That afternoon she drives to Bailey Brothers in Harold's car. Cadillacs crowd the white shell lot, some with prices and slogans painted in chalk on the windshields. BUY ME! one car says. NO MONEY DOWN! says another. ONE OF A KIND says a third. A small house trailer surrounded by cement statues of stable boys, donkeys and Mexican bandits serves as the office. Streamers of red, white and blue flags reach from post to pole; bare yellow bulbs blink in the cold sunlight.

A short, heavily built man in perma-press slacks and a baggy yellow sweater walks up to Rena with arms spread wide and asks if he can show her something. His grin is as phony as it is huge.

"I'm looking for an Eldorado Biarritz," she says. "An old one, about thirty years or so. It has to have fins."

"You call earlier?" The man crosses his arms as his face lights up with recognition.

"Yes. But I wanted to see for myself."

"I've got two hundred and fifteen Cadillacs on this lot, lady. But not the one you're looking for."

"Where can I find it?"

"An auto show, maybe." He lights a cigarette with a plastic lighter. "Sometimes at shopping malls they'll park antique cars where everybody walks. You might see one there. Or at a car museum." He looks at Harold's car, then swings his narrow eyes on her. "You rich, lady?"

She takes a moment to think about it. "Comfortable," she replies. "But not too—"

"One in mint condition," he says, blowing a smoke ring, "it'll probably run fifty, sixty grand. And I'm being conservative here."

"Sixty thousand dollars for a thirty-year-old car?"

He nods. "It's like any antique. The fewer there are to be found, the more people seem to want them. And the more they want them, the more they're willing to pay." He crams the cigarette into the fork of his fingers and points at her. "Lemme tell you something, lady. It's no real difference with people. When we opened this lot there

314

was four of us Bailey brothers. Now I'm the only one and I never been so appreciated in all my life." He blows another smoke ring.

Rena really isn't interested, but for whatever reason she asks what happened to his brothers.

"Nobody knows," the man says, looking off down the road. "But each took a car. Drove it right off the lot while their wives sat home changing baby diapers. In three years I lost three brothers, and there wasn't even a war on." He holds up the proper number of fingers and walks around to the front of the rose-colored Seville, his eyes growing narrower as he inspects the 10PENNY vanity plate. "Are you a carpenter?" he says, pointing his cigarette at the grille.

"I'm a widow," she says. "This was my husband's car."

"It ain't bad," he says. "Ain't bad at all." He takes a red rubber glove from his back pocket and fits it onto his right hand. "Mind?" he says. She shakes her head no, and he runs his gloved hand over the hood. "As a youngster I fooled with so many engines that I developed this problem with oil in my fingertips. I'm like an ink pot. My wife'll make me a sandwich, and if I'm not wearing gloves I leave smudge prints all over the bread." He opens the door on the driver's side, sits behind the wheel and moves the gloved hand over the dash. "Was he a railroad man?"

"Who?"

"Your husband."

"He was a football coach," Rena says, in a shallow whisper. "He coached a team called the Tenpenny Eleven."

"They any good?" he says.

"It was a long time ago. But yes, they were very good."

The man gets out of the car and shuts the door. He takes one more drag of the cigarette, then flicks it onto the white shell. "I never cared for the game myself."

"No need to apologize."

Suddenly he remembers something. "He wasn't the coach out at the school, was he?"

She hesitates. "His name was Harold Gravely."

"He wasn't the one they shot, was he?"

She looks away, twirling the car keys. "I'll be going now, Mr. Bailey. Thank you for your trouble."

"Because if he was the one they shot, that tells me something." With the gloved hand he motions for her to keep still. His eyes burn

with something that wasn't there a minute before. "Because if he was
. . ." He nearly gags trying to find the words. "If he was the one
they shot, that means your car might have some historical value to a
person like myself." This time when he spreads his arms wide, his
yellow sweater pulls up at the waist, exposing his hairy belly. "An
even swap," he says. "Any Bailey Brothers car for this one."

She laughs at the suggestion. "You said you didn't have a
Biarritz. That's all I really wanted."

She reaches to open the door, but he grabs her wrist with his
gloved hand. "At least give us a look. Walk around the place. See
what there is." He removes the glove and stuffs it back into his hip
pocket, then he lights another cigarette. "No obligation," he says.
"Just a free look."

She starts at the front of the lot, near a ditch flowing with
bubbly, sewer-colored water. Most of the cars are less than five years
old, though as she moves deeper into the lot they appear to age,
growing older with each step she takes. The salesman trails behind
her. "Have you noticed something?" he says, his voice swelling with
pride. "They're in chronological order, all my cars are. Bailey
Brothers is the only one in town with a lot like that. And that's a
fact."

"There's nothing here I want," she says.

"Not that purple d'Elegance?"

"Nope."

"It's mint. I could get twelve, maybe fifteen for it."

"Nope," she says.

The wind blows, swirling leaves dropped by a twisted run of
chicken trees, and she buttons her short fall jacket against the chill.
She can smell fried chicken from the restaurant next door, and it
makes her stomach growl. "I've seen enough," she says.

"Keep walking. Maybe you'll find something."

At the back corner of the lot, behind the office trailer, Bailey
Brothers has parked the oldest of the cars with their rear bumpers
pressed against a crippled chain-link fence. Most of them rest on flat
tires, some on cinder blocks and stacks of bricks, but the last of the
lot, a Series 62 convertible, looks as if it just rolled off the assembly
line. Its top is down, and in the sun the white paint and leather seats
reflect shimmering buds of light. Rena feels her muscles go lax and

shields her eyes against the glare. The hot light fills her head, erupting in brilliant explosions that leave her faint and a little winded.

"Does it have fins?" she murmurs.

"As big and white as those of an angel," the man says, the smoldering stub of his cigarette glued to the corner of his mouth. "A real classic, this baby. One year shy of thirty years of age. There's not another like it on the road. Low mileage, original roof, whitewall tires and not a spot of rust." He raps the hood with his hand. "I knew you'd want it when you saw it."

"Did I say I wanted it?"

"No," he says, "but everybody else does." He reaches into his back pocket for the rubber glove. "It ain't for sale, anyway. This one stays with me."

Her head has acquired a weight that strains her neck. Even in the bright winter cold, perspiration beads on her upper lip.

"You'd think at one time a rich banker owned this car," the man is saying, "and there'd be a safe in the trunk full of diamonds and gold. On Sunday afternoons he took his young wife on country drives. He'd let her ride in it, but he was the only one who drove." He runs his gloved hand over the top of the windshield, which, marked with chalk, says NADA. "But a decrepit old woman owned it, name of Winona Turner. I got it at an estate sale after forty-some minutes of vigorous bidding."

"What does *nada* mean, Mr. Bailey?"

"It means 'nothing,' " he says. "I got a dictionary in the office. You might want to look it up."

"Nothing?"

"I don't sell it for nothing."

Without asking permission, she swings the door open and sits behind the wheel. Before her the hood glides for what seems like forever. She punches the radio board, the cigarette lighter, the flippers for the power windows. She opens the glove compartment and peers inside. She turns every knob.

"In this car," the man says, handing her the glove, "everyone wears one of these."

"I'll take it," she says, surprised at the authority in her voice. She refuses to put on the glove. "You said an even swap."

"Nada," he says.

Slowly she pulls her eyes from the dash panel and fixes them on the used-car salesman. As before, his grin is huge and artificial and his eyes are skinny red slits. She sits up in the seat and throws her tangled hair back over the headrest. "They shot my husband four times," she says. "Here, here, here and here." Her hands move over her body, finally stopping at her chest. "The last one pierced his heart, went through his back and cut a chip out of the sidewalk. The fellow who found him—he was an old friend of Harold's—it took three cops to pull him off the body. He wouldn't let go."

The man spits what remains of the cigarette at his feet. "I'll want the plates," he says.

"Go get the damn keys," she tells him.

| **74** |

By New Year's Eve, the day of the winter ball celebrating the thirtieth anniversary of the Tenpenny game, the redwood fence Rena hired a crew of carpenters to construct still hasn't been completed. To her delight, however, the men were able to raise the section fronting the Monroe house within a week of winning the contract. For their efforts each of them earned a bonus of fifty dollars and a barbecue dinner, complete with thick wedges of hummingbird cake and what bottles of whiskey Rena could find in the cabinets. While drawing up the papers, she figured a few incentive clauses might speed their work, and she was right. This morning their hammers and electric saws rouse her at dawn, nearly an hour before the beeping digital alarm clock sounds. With something like cotton crowding her sinuses she lies in bed hoping to hear Louise, the maid, moving about the house.

"Dear one," she calls. "Are you here yet?"

Nothing.

Rena rolls over, stuffs a pillow between her belly and the mattress and drifts back to sleep. When she wakes some thirty minutes later it is to a dappled splash of sunlight on her face, more noise from the carpenters and the seductive aroma of coffee coming from the kitchen.

"Louise!" she now calls, more urgently. "Will you come back here, please! I need a minute!"

The maid enters wiping her hands on a rag. A dirty red bandanna covers her hair, and over it she's fitted an athletic sweat band. Her clothes are as faded as her espadrilles, which squeak on the floor. She is almost double Rena's size but moves like an accomplished athlete. Thick calluses pad her knees, reward for a lifetime of scrubbing floors. She is of Creole descent, and on the phone with her young children she often speaks with a dialect no longer common in the area. It is an exotic gumbo of languages that sounds almost otherworldly to the virgin ear. Rena once asked her to "talk, say anything that comes to mind" and sat down in her favorite chair in the green room, listening with her eyes closed.

"Guess what today is?" the woman is saying.

Rena groans and covers her face with the goose-down comforter. "I don't think I want to be reminded." She hugs the pillow at her side. "I've changed my mind. I'm not going."

"Fire me, then," the woman says. "Send me back home. I don't want any part of you."

Rena stretches, driving her toes into the mattress. "You don't know how you inspire me, Louise. And to think it's only our third week together."

The woman blows her nose into the rag and shakes her enormous head. "I should of met you a hundred years ago, Miss Rena. You'd be so inspired by now you wouldn't know what to do with yourself."

Rena pulls down the covers and they exchange smiles. "You've got a rag," she says, pointing. "Don't think I didn't notice. You promised me you'd gotten rid of them."

"This is mine," Louise says. "I brought it from home."

Rena makes a fist and beats the air with it. "Louise, you were supposed to help me."

"One little rag ain't gonna hurt nobody." She pivots and strides out of the room, her weight rocking the bed and shaking the pictures on the walls. "Now hop on out of there and go sit on the porch. It ain't too cold out."

Rena shoves her feet into her leather slippers, pulls on a robe and heads for the kitchen, where the Mr. Coffee spits and gurgles, slowly filling a glass pot. There's a sheet of buttered drop biscuits on the stove, Louise's recipe, and opened jars of apple butter and strawberry jam on the counter next to it.

Rena takes a cup of the hot chicory coffee out onto the porch and sits on a bath towel, her back against the railings. The carpenters, dressed all in white except for work boots and colorful baseball caps, are at the rear of the property cutting and nailing treated redwood planks onto the frame they've constructed. A cloud of spinning orange sawdust hovers over them, and after their saws stop singing they brush it off their sleeves.

Along with the coffee Rena can taste the fine wood shavings on her tongue. As she presses her lips to the cup, her nose begins to run; and even before she can call for Louise to hurry up and get some tissue the woman has pushed her arm through a crack in the sliding glass doors. "Looking for this?" she says, handing her a box of Kleenex. "I was reading your mind."

"Come talk to me," Rena says, patting a place on the floor. "Can't say why, exactly, but I'm in need of company this morning."

"What you need I could make a list of," the woman says, haughtier than ever. She remains standing, her muscular arms crossed on breasts that hang down to her waist. "And I'd start with a chair for the porch, or a swing. Something to set your butt on. Any old slop jar would do."

"We used to have a swing, a real nice one, but it broke. You should've seen the mess, Louise. It tore apart right out from under us." Rena laughs, mainly to keep from getting too close to the memory. Her hands start to shake and she's afraid she'll spill the coffee. "Me and Harold scrambling around in the dark . . ."

The story doesn't interest Louise. "Whoever heard of sitting on a towel to drink her coffee, and with all the money you got. Let me go find you a folding chair."

"No, none of that. Just tell me your list."

"A man. A big, ugly one. But I'd end it with that."

"My lord, it hasn't been half a year yet."

"Nobody but you's counting. Big, ugly men don't care about time anyway. I thought you knew that."

"At night when you leave," Rena says, "I keep thinking he's

coming home. I watch for his headlights from the green room. I stand at the window, looking past the trees."

"He'd of been mine," Louise says, "five minutes after he was dead I'd of had myself a new one."

"Well," Rena mutters, "I suppose your pain threshold is higher than mine. What else?"

"His clothes out of the bedroom closets, his shorts and socks and things out of the dresser. His toothbrush and shaving tools out of the bathroom. That's all your space now."

Rena doesn't say anything. She takes more tissue and blows her nose, then she warms her hands on the coffee cup.

"Don't you want to know what else?"

"Tell me," Rena mutters, watching the men work.

"One biscuit dripping with apple butter, another with strawberry jam. Let me go get you some on a dinner plate."

"Later, maybe. But not now." Rena clutches the sides of her thighs and squeezes. "I need to get rid of some of this, and you're supposed to help me. You promised."

"A new battery for that car you used to drive. That's another thing on the list. I tried it the other day while you was at the movies but it wouldn't start. And a brush with some detergent to clean it."

"I've retired the Falcon for now, maybe forever. Thanks, though, Louise. It was nice of you to offer."

"I wasn't offering," the woman says, stepping back into the house. "I was just listing."

Rena spends most of the morning on the back porch, watching the men at their sweaty labor and working on her houseplants. She's noticed that since the carpenters started work no birds peck at the ground under her trees, neither the ubiquitous blackbird nor the rare cardinal, neither swarm nor solitary traveler. Their absence saddens her, but the fence will be worth the expense and trouble if it succeeds in shielding her from Xavier Monroe. She sometimes finds herself battling pangs of guilt and gazing off in the direction of his house. With the high wall of wood, all she can see now is the roof, the antenna, the chimney stack and the pale green tops of his pecan trees. She considers writing him and his wife a note saying she hopes they don't take the fence as anything personal, and that her life alone at home now, without Harold to make her feel secure, seemed to require some protection. But she decides against it. He, at least, would know she's lying.

At noon she and Louise have lunch at the dining-room table. The biscuits, warmed in the microwave, break apart in her hands. She dips crusty pieces into a saucer brimming with cane syrup. "We'll diet next week," she tells the maid. With her mouth full, Louise moans in agreement.

After the kitchen has been cleaned, Rena gets the shampoo and conditioner out of the master bath and asks Louise to start running the water in the sink. "What sink?" the maid says.

"The kitchen. I need you to give me a hand."

"I never heard of nobody washing their hair in the kitchen sink. Now if it was dishes I wouldn't argue."

"It's the way I've always done it," Rena says. "There's a hose attachment and the basin's twice as big."

"You could take a shower and do it there."

"But I like a bath."

Louise turns on the water and lets it warm. "You're set in your ways like nobody I know."

"I'm almost fifty years old, so by now I guess I should be. I've earned the right." After a moment she says, "I suppose it really is a system. You think of it as a system, Louise?"

"Don't know to answer yes or no," the woman says. "But I do know tonight you're going to meet a big, ugly man. He'll turn the clock back. You'll be young again."

Rena lowers her head into the sink and Louise lathers shampoo into her hair and massages her scalp. When they're done, Rena wraps her hair in a long bath towel and Louise retreats to the bathroom to start the water pouring into the tub. "Make it really hot," Rena calls after her. "And put in some suds."

| 75 |

At her vanity table about half an hour later, Rena pats her face with a powder puff but doesn't know why. There's no powder on the puff and she hasn't bathed yet. Louise is vacuuming somewhere on the other side of the house, probably in the green room. The sound makes her think of Harold, not in a bad way. She starts to imitate it and wonders if Louise remembered to make the floors look as if they'd just been raked.

"Dear one!" she calls.

Nothing.

She opens the bedroom door and screams down the hall. "No footprints, okay? Can you remember, dear one?"

Still nothing.

In the bathroom Rena takes off her clothes before the wide, unadorned mirror. Her evening gown hangs on a brass peg at the center of the walk-in closet. She bought the dress about five years ago, thinking it was something she had to have, but she wore it only once, to a Saturday matinee of the musical *Cats* at the Saenger Performing Arts Center in New Orleans. Because Harold was in Las Vegas at a convention, she went with her mother. "Too bad he didn't get to see how nice you look in your new dress," Lottie told her. That was practically all she remembered of the afternoon, her mother's kind words; the show itself was like so many other things she lived through but is unable to recall.

In her hands the blue satin feels like something she'd like to sleep on, a bedsheet. It's not really a formal gown, but she couldn't see spending several hundred dollars on something new. The tea length, she has decided, will either charm or infuriate the wives and friends of the celebrants, as will the bare shoulders and the white fichu neckline, the long virgin gloves, the glass necklace. All the others will no doubt be wearing more formal attire. But let them.

In the tub she soaks for what feels like seconds but is more than half an hour. The smell of the milky bath is intoxicating; she could almost drink it. When preparing to shave, she recalls having once read in the health and hygiene section of her favorite magazine that you should make sure to let the hot water open the pores of the skin. Hydration, the story called it. Louise has placed a bar of rose-scented glycerin soap on the lip of the tub, and Rena removes it now from its fancy cardboard box. The soap is transparent pink; when exercised into a frothy lather it turns white, yet smells no less exquisite. With vigor she scrubs her armpits, thoroughly moistening the skin, flooding the hair follicles. A collection of disposable razors sits on the top shelf of the medicine cabinet, but Rena chooses Harold's straight razor to cut the hair. Her motion is fluid and assured, as steady, she would guess, as a practiced barber's. The hair drops into the sudsy bath and floats toward the edges of the pool, clinging to the porcelain shell. As Rena watches, tears trace down her cheeks and a smile finds her lips. "Of all the things to get sappy about," she mutters to herself, then folds the blade back into its sheath and throws it across the room. The razor clatters against the white tile floor and slaps against the baseboard. "Of all the goddamn things." Then she says, "Be strong. You can do it."

| 76 |

Pogo once asked her, after they'd been driving for an hour or more, to get out and press her cheek against the hood. In the night there was no one to see them. They were on a street near the river, and all the houses were dark. The sky was orange, burning with light from the flares of the refineries. "Scared it'll ruin your pretty makeup?" he said, rubbing a cloth damp with oil over the dash. "No," she replied. "Of course not." When she walked to the front of the car she could see him through the glass. He was as orange as everything else, and he was smiling as if he were about to present her with a gift. "Do it," he said. "Come on, Rena. It's not like I didn't have curfew half an hour ago." She put her face on the smooth metal and felt the warmth run through her. "Now take your feet off the ground. Stand on the bumper." She told him no. There was a trick he was up to; he was going to blow the horn or take off all of a sudden. "It's nothing to worry about," he said. "This is something I want you to experience." With her cheek flat against the hood, she could see him put the car in neutral, then the engine started to idle at an accelerated rate. He was pressing down on the gas pedal, revving the engine. A cool breeze lifted her skirt and she reached back to pat it down. Her hair fell into her eyes. The engine roared, but in her ear it was a sweet, melancholy sound. There were no ticks or knocks, just the warm, droning sound and vibrations pulsing to the bone. "How was it," he asked once she was back in the car. They were on River Road, driving toward the university, away from the orange, burning sky. Up ahead they could see the lights of the capitol and, to the side, ships on the dark Mississippi. "It was like this," she said. She leaned over the armrest and pushed her mouth against the side of his face. She could taste his aftershave. When he started to laugh, she threw her hair back and let the wind take it.

At a few minutes past eight, Rena leaves the house with the roof of her Series 62 Cadillac in place, the windows rolled up. Louise sees her off; they wave to each other and blow kisses. The heater is on, but still she can feel the cool night stealing in through the floor. She couldn't find a coat that matched her dress, so she doesn't wear one. On orders from Louise, there is a sweater on the seat, "just in case the north wind starts to blow," and a small handbag. It has taken some doing, but at last Rena has become accustomed to the scent of her perfume, and now it seems most pleasant. Periodically she presses her wrist to her nose, as a reminder, and because it makes her feel good.

On the highway she's tempted to pull over and put down the roof and take off her gloves and shoes. Driving in three-inch heels is no easier than walking in them, and she misses the feel of the wheel in her bare hands.

She can see, now, the hotel up ahead. Signs in the median direct the traffic. I'M GOING DANCING! one says. ARE YOU? Clearly this is the work of Bobby and Claire Peel. Poster-board cutouts of arrows point the way, and she follows as if she'd never been here before.

At the head of the lot, an old man in a forest green suit is conducting traffic. He stands before a wooden barricade, waving his arms, a whistle clenched between his teeth. "Are you here for the ball?" he says, and Rena shows him the invitation. "Why of course you are. Welcome."

It is Lester Lejeune. His epaulets make his shoulders seem too large for his head, and a few of the buttons near the collar are missing. His tie is red velvet trimmed in gold braid.

"We almost had a problem," he says, pacing the length of the car. "It was the fire marshal again. He came yesterday afternoon and threatened to close down the west wing, including the ballroom. When I told him about the Tenpenny Eleven dance, he said we'd talk about it Monday. A reprieve!"

"It's me," she says. "It's Rena, Les."

He takes a pair of reading glasses from his breast pocket and places them on his nose. "My lord," he says, "it is you. And aren't you lovely tonight."

His hand rests on the door frame, and she covers it with both of hers. "Wherever did you find that suit of clothes, Les?"

"Don't you like it?" He reels back and admires himself.

"Yes," she says, "I do. It's absolutely the most charming thing I've seen in ages."

"Don't fit, though, does it?"

"You can always get it altered."

"No need," he says. "It's only for tonight, just temporary. I found it the other day going through a closet. I guess a bellhop must've left it there a hundred years ago."

The car behind her flashes its lights from bright to dim. "These boys still think they're heroes," he says. "They all think they've got to get there first."

She pulls over and waits while he attends to those behind her, directing them to parking spots near the bingo tent next door. When he returns he's holding a bottle of liquor. "That was Flaubert Rich and Red somebody," Les says, "both looking older than me." He leans over to get a better look at her. "You don't want any of this, do you, Rena?"

"I don't think so," she says.

He rears back and tosses the bottle into the ditch, then he pats his hands together. "I didn't either," he says. "But these heroes— that's always been what they're best at."

She presses the brake and shifts into drive.

"They got Pogo this year," he says. "I saw him not five minutes ago. And he ain't changed a bit."

She leans over and slips the invitation into her handbag. "I don't think I believe you," she says.

"Okay, then," he says.

"They didn't get him?"

He shrugs his shoulders and shakes his head.

"I'm not surprised," she says, then punches the top of the wheel with the heel of her hand. "They meet every five years, always the same damn crowd."

He doesn't seem to hear her. "You know about the two fat boys, I guess."

"Who's that?"

"Larry and Chester."

"No," she says, "I guess I don't."

"They hadn't talked to anyone with the school since the board hired that outsider to coach. They didn't even RSVP the invite. Them and Pogo are the only ones who didn't." Another car pulls up, and Les waves it into the lot.

"Will you dance with me tonight?" she says, giving him her best smile. "We can talk more inside."

"Sure," he says, "I'll dance."

"A slow one?"

"If there ain't a line to you," he says, reaching over to kiss her on the cheek. "Have fun, Rena."

He blows his whistle and swings his arms, guiding her to a slot near the entrance. Parked next to her is a new Porsche 928, complete with a cellular telephone, compact disc player and twelve-speaker Blaupunkt stereo system. Intentionally or not, the owner has left the sales sticker on the window. Rena notes the itemized list of equipment, standard and extra, totaling nearly seventy thousand dollars. "My lord," she groans, running her gloved hands over the hood.

"I beg your pardon."

A man in a dark suit and hat steps from the shadows of the untamed shrubbery along the front of the building. In the pale green light Rena can see his face; a scar about an inch thick runs from one end of it to the other, twisting deliriously. She gasps and covers her mouth, letting her handbag drop to the pavement.

"Please, lady, don't touch the merchandise."

Except for a soft, fearful moan she doesn't reply. She leans over and gathers the hairbrush, house keys, compact mirror and chewing gum that spilled onto the ground. When she straightens up again, prepared to apologize, the man is nowhere in sight.

"Hello!" she shouts. "Sir?"

From behind her someone says, "You don't have to call me sir, Rena. You know that." It's Bobby Peel, accompanied by his wife, Claire.

"I think I saw someone." Rena points to the bushes. "He was dressed all in black."

"The Prince is haunted," Bobby says, "but we're the ones to blame, aren't we? We made it that way."

Flanked by the Peels, she walks through the lobby, waving and nodding at those who speak her name. Occasionally she turns and looks over her shoulder, afraid that the scarred man has followed her inside.

"If he comes after you," Claire says, "I don't think Bobby would have any problem squashing him like a bug."

"Look how big I am," he tells her.

At the ballroom entrance she pauses to admire the crush of partygoers: men in black tie, their shoes a high gloss, women in chiffon as light as air. They hold cigarettes and glasses of champagne. Above them the chandeliers burn amber shades, crinkled spools of purple and gold crepe paper crossing from one to another.

"No one's dancing," Rena says.

"Wait until the bubbly kicks in," Claire tells her. "You won't be able to drag them off the floor."

On a stand at the rear of the hall, a twelve-piece band is playing a song from thirty years ago, its leader, a celebrated New Orleans trumpeter and vocalist, singing in the guttural, eyeball-popping tradition of his musical forefathers.

"Mrs. Gravely promised me a spin on the floor," Bobby tells Claire, shouting to be heard, "but I'm hungry. Wouldn't you ladies rather eat first?"

Without waiting for a reply he leads them to the smorgasbord, where waiters in white dress uniforms stand behind banquet tables crowded with food and drink. There are gigantic roasts of beef and pork standing side by side on wooden carving blocks, finger sandwiches topped with slices of pimiento olives, mandarin orange and

Key lime punch, sugar and gingerbread cookies shaped like football players stiff-arming their way to glory, meatballs drowned in barbecue sauce, boudin chips and wedges of hogshead cheese, Chinese spareribs and, at the center of it all, a four-foot-high ice sculpture of Pogo Reese, Little Shorty Grieg and Harold Gravely frozen in their immortal Tenpenny pose, but now melted beyond the point of easy recognition.

"Suddenly I've lost my appetite," Rena says, considering the statue. Then she laughs. "Somebody run and get me a drink."

Neither Bobby nor Claire seems to have heard; their mouths stuffed with sweet pickles and chicken salad, they probably couldn't have answered anyway. "I think some Dom Perignon will serve me better," she says, more to herself than anyone. Eyes fixed on the wet, steaming sculpture, she backpedals to those waiting at the champagne bar.

"Rena, come up here," Norman Pepper is shouting at the front of the line. "Let her up here, folks."

It is less than an hour into the evening, and already Norman has the inflamed look of one bent on drinking until every last bottle has run dry. Tilted at a perilous angle, his bow tie is a Scotch plaid identical to his cummerbund. His toupee sits on the back of his head like a tired little bird's nest. "Make room for Rena Gravely," he is saying. "Come on, everybody, move it. Let the lady through."

"Thank you, Norman. But I'll wait my turn." The people, many of whom she recognizes, step back as ordered. "Really, now," she tells them. "I don't mind."

She watches as Norman makes a show of removing several bills from his wallet and dropping them in the waiter's tip jar. From an ice-choked steel tub he selects two unopened bottles of champagne, cradles them in his arms and begins slashing through the line. He is, Rena assumes, pretending to be a running back trying to squeeze through traffic and break into open field. The bottles, then, are his footballs, and at this moment nothing in Norman's world is as important as protecting them from the people who stand in his way, hoping to see him fumble.

"Norman," Rena asks once they're seated at a table near the bandstand, "were you ever an athlete?"

Perhaps her sarcasm escapes him, for he seems to take the question as a compliment. "I don't wish to disappoint you," he remarks, flushed with pride, "but no, I never really was—unless of course you call the more cerebral endeavors such as chess and cooking and—"

"No," she says, "I guess you weren't."

Rena drinks one glass of champagne after another, swallowing each mouthful without really tasting it, often turning to the bottle for a swig before refilling her crystal goblet. Drink, she tells herself, is nourishment: her body needs it, she deserves it and damn if it doesn't make her feel good. One by one the Tenpenny Eleven, their wives in tow, stop at her table to offer their condolences, in phrasing that sounds as rehearsed as the brassy numbers performed by the band.

Although most introduce themselves, as if to a dignitary or total stranger, Rena recognizes them all.

"Mrs. Gravely, I'm Little Shorty Grieg," the thickest and stubbiest of the lot tells her. "I want you to know how sorry I was to learn of your tragic loss."

"I know who you are, Little Shorty," Rena says, taking his hand. "You were in my home less than a year ago. You offered Harold your Heisman Trophy. You had a woman with you."

He nods, and she seems to hear his considerable bulk trying to break through the seams of his tuxedo. "That was my neighbor Frances," he says. "She's here tonight—I just saw her over by the buffet." He clears his throat and fastens his eyes on hers. "That mother-in-law of mine, she's down to a bag of bones, I understand, and still laid up in the old folks' home. Betty Anne called just the other night and said it should be any moment now."

"Well," Rena says, unable to find a suitable response.

"Anyway," he continues, "I'm sorry I missed the funeral. But I took sick that day with a sore throat."

Once he leaves, Rena leans into Norman. "This is turning into a bloody wake, Mr. Pepper." Then she smiles. "Shall we dance?"

Reluctant to join her, he gives a quick, ambiguous smile and knocks back the slippery dregs in his glass. "You're a single woman now, Rena. My wife . . . well, she decided not to come tonight, and as I was leaving she says, 'You will behave yourself, won't you, Norman?' I didn't have to ask what she meant."

"Widows and divorcées," Rena says, nodding with unqualified

wisdom. "Easy, sleezy and cheesy. But don't expect me to believe that's the real reason you're staying off the dance floor."

"Fine," he says. "Believe whatever you want." He sucks in a chest of air, lifts his chin and flutters his eyelids. "Being the only member of the board present here tonight, I do have my reputation to protect."

"That ain't it, either," she says. "You've never danced before, have you, Norman?"

"Never danced?" He chuckles and attempts to straighten his bow tie, managing only to tilt it more.

"That's right, Norman. I don't think you have."

With both hands he checks the status of his toupee and, as with the tie, does not seem to mind finding it out of place. "Please, Rena, don't tell anybody, okay?"

"Everybody!" she says, standing tall, her voice raised a notch. "I wasn't supposed to say anything about this—" He yanks the back of her dress and she plops back down. "Only teasing, Norman. I don't mind if we don't dance. It's not like something I can't do by myself."

"Alone, you mean?"

"Yes," she says. "Alone."

Of the celebrants, only Trent Orlansky has ventured onto the dance floor. Rena spots him standing at the foot of the bandstand, not twenty feet away. A cigarette hangs from his mouth, the ash falling onto the largest pair of feet ever to run across the field at Tiger Stadium.

"Have you been avoiding me, Mr. Memory?" Rena shouts through cupped hands. "Can't you say hello?"

He waddles over and dumps his cigarette into an abandoned champagne glass. "I'd appreciate it, Rena, if you didn't call me Mr. Memory anymore."

"From Mr. Memory to Mr. Touchy," Norman grumbles, "all in a matter of seconds."

"I meant to come by," he says to Rena, "I really did. But you looked busy with all those people standing around."

"Yes," she says. "Everyone seems to have decided this is the best time to apologize for not attending Harold's funeral. I've never had so much attention in all my life." She swallows and smacks her lips.

"When you Tenpenny Eleven people throw a party, Trent, you really know how."

"She wants to dance alone," Norman tells Orlansky, laughing as if this were the most preposterous thing he'd ever heard.

"I was sorry to learn," Orlansky says, lighting another cigarette, "of your recent loss."

"I'm sure you were," she says, rising from the table. "The day of the funeral, did you have a sore throat too?"

"Did I have a what?"

"You can leave now," she tells him, and he seems happy to go.

When Rena begins to dance, she is acutely aware of the eyes that follow her across the floor. The band members, delighted to see someone more interested in their music than the food and drink, pick up the tempo of their ballad. She holds one hand flat against her lower belly, the other, the right, high at her side and folded in on itself, almost like a fist. Emboldened by the champagne, she navigates the floor several times, then closes her eyes and lets the music guide her. Her steps are steady and true. To boost her confidence, she keeps telling herself that this is the green room at home and she's among her plants and furniture, leaving tracks in a place that otherwise would remain as clean and unmarked as a garden bed. Though she tries to ignore it, a frantic bustle of activity at the edge of the floor distracts her. Someone is calling her name over and over, and others are laughing.

She cracks her eyes wide enough to behold Bobby Peel standing at the center of a huddle of partygoers, most of whom wear wicked grins and appear fascinated.

"Didn't you want a partner, Rena?" he says, his mouth still stuffed with food. "Mind if I join you?"

She whirls away, faster now, headed for the bandstand. On the parquet his steps are dull and heavy; when he reaches to embrace her she spins away, and he stands, hands on hips, watching in both frustration and amusement.

Presently a commotion near the ballroom entrance attracts Bobby and the rest of his crowd and momentarily silences the band. Voices echo across the hall: one roaring in anger, another shouting in fear. Still dancing, Rena watches as several members of the Tenpenny Eleven force someone out into the lobby. Although she isn't certain, the person looks like the scarred man she saw earlier in the parking lot.

"Don't touch my face!" he's screaming, trying to break free. "Stop, don't touch it!"

The band kicks into a lively number that pulls everybody back into the room and several couples onto the floor. Bobby Peel, breathing obstreperously, grabs Rena in his arms and begins what feels like a fox-trot. She resists, but he squeezes her so hard she can hardly breathe. "Easy," she murmurs. "Take it easy, Bobby."

The ballroom doors slam shut, the lights dim to a dusky sienna and a new party seems to have commenced.

"Nothing like a little bloodshed to fire the old hormones!" Norman hollers from the table.

"Poor guy," Bobby whispers. "You should've seen his face."

As they dance, Rena keeps her eyes on the floor as Bobby drones on about what a shame it is Harold didn't "survive" to attend the ball. When the song ends, he steps back and thanks her with a nod.

"You move as pretty now as you did at eighteen," he says. "I'm much obliged, Mrs. Gravely."

"You're very unwelcome," she answers.

At the table Rena collects her handbag and has one last swallow of champagne. "I don't belong here anymore," she tells Norman, who looks to be on the verge of passing out, "and you don't either. Why don't you stop making an ass of yourself and go home?" She bends forward and speaks directly into his ear: "Hear me, Norman: go home."

"Leaving so soon?" he says. His head begins to bob. "What about that dance you promised? You promised me a dance, 'member?"

In the lobby Rena walks past Les Lejeune, who's arguing with a young woman. She must be getting the better of the debate, Rena decides, because Les keeps filling her open palm with money and because he's too preoccupied to say good-bye. "This just isn't done," Les is saying. "Not at the Prince Seurat it isn't." The woman snaps each bill, making certain no two have stuck together.

The night air is cool and smells of diesel fumes. Remembering the scarred man, his face set in terror as the Tenpenny sergeants at arms cuffed him on the back of the neck, Rena feels a rush of goose

pimples cover her flesh. To her relief, the Porsche he was guarding is
no longer parked in the slot next to hers; a dilapidated Volkswagen
van with Texas plates has replaced it. Except for two scantily dressed
women soliciting customers, the lot appears to be empty.

From her handbag she removes the compact mirror, flips it open
and studies herself in the small round glass, indifferent to what she
sees. She daubs her cheeks and nose with the powder puff, then
tosses it in the bushes behind her. Up ahead on the old highway, a
tractor-trailer rig blows by.

She begins by pressing the metal clasp of the makeup kit into
the hood of the Cadillac and moving from the grille to just below the
windshield wipers, drawing like a child with her first crayon. Clouds
bloom in the paint, some flat and angry, others as fluffy as cords of
fleece.

She is working on the passenger's side of the car when she spots
someone walking toward her from the bingo tent. His movement is
familiar: the smooth, unhurried stride, the exaggerated swing of his
arms, the rhythmic tattoo of his shoes on the pavement. He's wearing
a black tuxedo, a red carnation pinned to the lapel. Her first impulse
is to get rid of the compact, but then it strikes her that she has done
no one any harm here tonight.

"Why, Pogo," she murmurs when he's only a few feet away,
"what on earth are you doing here?"

"Wondering," he says without pause, "why you'd want to go
and scratch up this pretty car."

"It's mine," she says, holding up the keys. Her hands are
shaking and suddenly she's short of breath. "I own it."

She can tell he doesn't know how to react, whether to believe
her or not. He looks at the car and then at her, then at the car again.
"See what getting old does to you?" he says. "I'm confused."

"Do we really have to talk about it now?"

"No." He shakes his head. "We don't have to talk about it now.
And if it's okay with you I'd be happy if we never talked about it
again."

"Fine," she says, more than a little relieved. "But I really would
like to explain. There's a lot I'd like to tell you."

He waits a minute before speaking, and then it's with his eyes
on everything but Rena. "I was wondering if you'd be here tonight—

I admit that. I thought, if you liked, we could go for a spin in my new car. But I see my driver's already left in it."

"The Porsche? That Porsche was yours?"

"Very good," he says, drawing closer, close enough for her to smell gum on his breath. "You saw it then."

"Saw it—my god, how could I miss it?"

"The chauffeur," he says, pointing to the front of the building, "you saw him too?"

"The man with the scar on his face?"

Pogo nods and traces a crooked line from the middle of his scalp all the way down to his Adam's apple.

"They threw him out about a half-hour ago," she says.

"Bastards," he murmurs. "Who wants it anyway? As soon as I saw this dump of a hotel again I should've known it wasn't for me." He turns and stares toward the bingo tent. "I was sitting with a bunch of old church ladies, watching the little red balls spin around in the hopper, you know, and trying to get up the nerve—"

"Maybe we could dance," she says, cutting him off. "What do you think, Pogo? Maybe we could go inside and dance."

He runs his hands through his hair. "I don't know, Rena, I really don't. The last time I danced it was with you, and that was here, I think. Wasn't it here?"

"You wore a blue suit. And you were beautiful. You really were. Everyone said it, all the girls. I was so proud."

"I remember the suit," he says, laughing. "But the beautiful part . . . now that's something I seem to have forgotten."

Behind them a man and a woman push through the doors. Upon glimpsing Pogo the man stops and stares, but he doesn't say anything. Finally the woman grumbles for her husband to speed it up, and together they walk across the lot.

"Billy Guillot," Rena says. "You remember him?"

"Sure, I remember him. Only I could never pronounce his name. We used to call him Billy Goat for short."

"You should've told him something."

Pogo stuffs his hands in the pockets of his jacket. "Perhaps," he says, so softly she can hardly hear him. "I'm fifty-one years old, Rena. What am I supposed to do—call him Billy Goat?"

"You're right," she says. "You've outgrown it."

"It really wasn't him I came to see, anyway. And it wasn't all the others at that rinky-dink party in there." He stares at the old building as if he'd like to see it blow up. "That driver of mine may not look it, but he's a good person, one of the best. And besides, who can judge a person's heart? Will you tell me that, Rena?"

She tries to meet his eyes, but he won't allow it. "Did you want to see me, Pogo? Am I the one you came for?"

"What?" he says, pretending not to have heard.

She unlocks the door and gets in, then lowers the windows and folds back the roof. "I know it's a little cold out," she says, starting the engine and gunning it, "but are we going for a ride or not?"

"A ride?"

"That's right," she says, waving him over. "A ride."